IAN HAMILTON MYSTERIES

EDINBURGH TWILIGHT

· CAROLE LAWRENCE ·

THOMAS & MERCER

Published by Thomas & Mercer, Seattle

www.apub.com

Amazon, the Amazon logo, and Thomas & Mercer are trademarks of Amazon.com, Inc., or its affiliates.

ISBN-13: 9781477848814
ISBN-10: 1477848819

Cover design by Ed Bettison

Printed in the United States of America

For my cousin Carey Larsen, ever the truest of friends

Half a capital and half a country town, the whole city leads a double existence; it has long trances of the one and flashes of the other; like the king of the Black Isles, it is half alive and half a monumental marble.

—Robert Louis Stevenson, *Edinburgh: Picturesque Notes*

PROLOGUE

EDINBURGH, 1881

As he trudged up the steep incline to the top of Arthur's Seat, the moody volcanic ridge looming over the city of Edinburgh, Stephen Wycherly could not stop shivering. It was a wretched midwinter Wednesday afternoon; the sky was spitting rain, and a chill breeze blew in from the Firth of Forth, cutting through his already damp overcoat. But the fit of trembling that seized him as he reached the summit was more from dread than the biting February wind. Clutching the letter summoning him to this godforsaken spot, he shielded his eyes from the rain and looked around. He had not seen another soul on his lonely trek up the hill, which was hardly surprising—who in his right mind would venture out in this weather? And why did his tormentor insist they meet on this jagged outgrowth of rock on such a day?

Stephen fingered the money in his pocket. It was all he had— he hoped it was enough. He never imagined he would be a victim of blackmail; it was like a bad dream. He glanced at his watch—already ten minutes past the appointed meeting time. His heart leapt at the prospect of having arrived too late for the assignation. The ruin of his reputation suddenly seemed a small price to pay to escape the creeping terror overtaking him as he gazed down at the city of Edinburgh. He was just about to leave when he became aware of a figure approaching from the steeper trail that ascended the summit from the east. The man smiled when he saw Stephen, but there was no friendliness in his face, no warmth in those icy eyes.

"You came," the man said. "I did not think you would."

"Of course I came," Stephen said, projecting a confidence he did not have. "Let's get this over with."

"Very well," his companion agreed. "Wait—what's that?" His gaze was fixed on a point over Stephen's shoulder, and, his instinct for self-preservation overcome by curiosity, Wycherly turned around to look.

That was all the distraction the other man needed. Stephen felt the garrote around his neck before he could turn around again to face his opponent. Flailing, he staggered backward, hands clawing vainly at his throat as his attacker tightened the ligature. The last thing he heard before consciousness slipped away was a soft voice in his ear.

"There, there, now—it will all be over soon. Sweet dreams."

<hr />

Holyrood Park was deserted as Christopher Fallon began his long trek beneath a bleak February sky. His wife said he was a fool for taking exercise in such weather, but then, Bettina thought he was a fool for most things he did, so he didn't let it bother him. The lamb stew she was making would taste even better after a brisk walk. His job as a cobbler required long hours sitting bent over a last, but as it was midweek market day, he had taken off earlier than usual. He enjoyed stretching his legs as he roamed the windswept plain sandwiched between the majestic Salisbury Crags to the west and Arthur's Seat to the east.

The rain of the past few days had thinned to a light mist, and visibility was limited, but Christopher enjoyed this kind of weather—no use trying to explain that to Bettina, who would just roll her eyes and say he was daft. He was humming a little song to himself when he saw a dark shape on the ground to his right. Taking a few steps toward it, he peered through the mist to make out what it was. His first thought was that it was a crumpled heap of clothes lying in the damp soil. Just as he was wondering who would leave a bundle of rags in the middle of Holyrood Park, he got close enough for a proper look. He had been right about the clothes—but what was in the clothes made his limbs go cold. The body of a young man lay sprawled upon the rocky ground.

"Mary, Mother of God," he muttered, wiping his damp forehead, sweating in spite of the chill air. He looked up—the body lay beneath the summit of Arthur's Seat, the craggy ledge directly overhead. He had heard of people casting themselves to their death from its rocky heights, but had never given the stories much thought. The poor fellow was obviously dead—that much was clear from the vacant, staring eyes and unnatural stillness of the body. There were bruises and scratches on his face, and the odd angle of the limbs made Christopher's head go woozy. It was as if the fellow had been tossed like a rag doll from the rocks above, arms and legs all higgledy-piggledy, as his wife would say. Christopher's legs took off at a run before he was aware of having willed their flight.

High above, a pair of pale eyes gazed down upon the scene, and a smile came to the face of the one who watched as Christopher hurried back in the direction from which he had come.

CHAPTER ONE

A young man with unruly black hair stood upon the summit of Calton Hill in the wee hours of a Thursday in early February. He peered up at Arthur's Seat, looming moodily over the city of Edinburgh, as a thin dawn pushed through the wintry sky.

From his perch, Detective Inspector Hamilton was contemplating whether the young man who had plunged to his death the day before had taken his own life—or whether he had been pushed. Stephen Wycherly's body had been found less than twenty-four hours ago, and already the newsboys were crying the story from every corner of the town.

Ian Carmichael Hamilton was long and lean, solid as a caber, the wooden pole tossed by beefy Scots at the Highland games he had attended as a boy. Having joined the Edinburgh City Police barely out of his teens, he had risen through the ranks; now at the age of twenty-seven, he was the youngest member to earn the rank of detective inspector. It had never been his intention to follow his father into the police force. As a boy, he was forever scribbling stories, intent on becoming a great writer—the next Sir Walter Scott, according to his aunt Lillian (though he preferred Shakespeare and Poe). His dreams of literary immortality died in the same fire that took his parents, his home, and his childhood. He turned instead to the study of crime—though he still secretly wrote poems he shared with no one.

Firmly convinced the fire was set deliberately, Ian transferred his fierce ambition to pursuing criminals, his determination so dogged that some on the force found it extreme. Now he saw an opportunity to prove himself worthy of his new rank. He didn't just suspect Wycherly's death to be murder—he *willed* it so. As a writer, Ian believed he had a keen eye for the truth, the ability to see through the masks people wore. He believed writers and policemen shared the knack of seeing the darker side of their fellow man. It was not always a gift, he knew—and once you had it, you could not turn your back on it.

Eyes trained upon the ascending ridge of rock, he tried to imagine how a would-be murderer could drag someone up there against his will. It would be nearly impossible, especially if the victim was a muscular fellow in his twenties. No, Ian thought, it was more likely he knew his attacker. They had gone up together on some pretext; young Wycherly had been taken unawares and pushed to his death. Ian imagined his last moments, hands clawing the air as he fell, the face of his killer the last thing he saw before death.

He shivered and drew his cloak around his shoulders. Made of good Scottish wool, it had been sheared from shaggy Highland sheep, woven on Borders looms, and sold in the High Street shops lining Edinburgh's famed Royal Mile. A gift from his aunt Lillian, it bore the green-and-blue Hamilton clan hunting tartan. And now, standing upon these ancient hills as his ancestors had for centuries, he was wrapped in a cocoon of his aunt's love. The rest of his family gone, it was just the two of them now, alone in a tremulous and tumultuous city.

Ian turned to gaze at the skyline below as a lone crow wobbled across the horizon. Gaslights sprinkled throughout the town shone bleakly in the dim light as night surrendered reluctantly to a feeble gray sunrise. Edinburgh's heavy stone buildings loomed over narrow cobblestoned streets so tortuous and twisted, they seemed to double back on themselves. Ian did not like the city, longing for the wide sky and soaring hills of the Highlands he knew as a boy.

He squinted up at the dim outline of the craggy hilltop, often likened to a sleeping lion. Perhaps the crime hadn't even been planned—the killer might have acted on impulse. But what kind of man—or woman—pushed someone from a great height on impulse?

Ian yawned as he trudged toward the sleeping city below, past the Nelson Monument, its tipsy inverted-telescope design listing downhill like a drunken sailor. Several things bothered him about the suicide theory—not the least of which was the statement Wycherly's landlady gave Wednesday evening, declaring firmly that her tenant was neither depressed nor despondent. If this was a murder made to look like a suicide, Ian thought, he was just the man to get to the bottom of it.

CHAPTER TWO

Detective Chief Inspector Robert Lyle Crawford glanced up from the pile of papers on his desk at the young man standing before him, then down at the report he was reading, attempting to concentrate. Finally he gave up, leaned back in his chair, and glared at his subordinate.

"Must you stand there gaping like an idiot, Hamilton, when you can see I'm busy?"

"I'm afraid my face looks naturally idiotic in repose, sir."

"Very amusing," Crawford grunted. "Aren't you just the closet wit?"

"'Better a witty fool than a foolish wit,' sir."

Crawford narrowed his eyes. He disliked it when Hamilton quoted Shakespeare—it reeked of insubordination. "Well, what is it?"

"It's about the death of young Wycherly, sir. The one who fell from—"

"What about him?"

"I'd like to pursue an investigation into his death."

Crawford gazed dolefully at the already cold cup of tea at his elbow. He had much on his mind: his wife, Moira, had taken sick, and he was desperately worried about her. He found it hard to concentrate on his job. Outside, the slow clop of horses' hooves signaled the milkman making his Thursday morning rounds, the wheels of his cart creaking as they rattled over the uneven cobblestones. He twisted a piece of string between his thumb and forefinger, a nervous habit. "I suppose you have come up with a theory?"

"Not as yet, sir."

Crawford threw his meaty hands into the air. "Then why do you insist on wasting my time?"

He knew his reaction was overwrought, and not really about Hamilton, but he couldn't help himself. His voice rang off the high-ceilinged rafters, bouncing off the heavy oak beams of the High Street police station. A few of the uniformed constables on the other side of the glass that separated his office from the central room looked up from what they were doing. A couple of the younger policemen glanced at each other apprehensively. DCI Crawford was noted for his temper and booming voice, and it sounded as though DI Hamilton had stepped into a tongue-lashing.

"I respectfully request an autopsy, sir," Hamilton replied.

"On what grounds?"

"Suspicious death," he said, thrusting a form at his superior officer.

DCI Crawford studied it gloomily. Sighing, he slapped the paper down on his desk on top of the others and wiped a hand across his oily forehead. He was a tall, portly man with small blue eyes and a florid complexion. What little hair was left on the top of his head was made up for by an abundance of ginger muttonchop whiskers, so long they touched his shirt collar. As detective chief inspector, he oversaw the work of a dozen detectives, but none was as troublesome as Detective Hamilton. He was a Highlander, as were most of the others on the police force, and too much like his father before him.

The Hamiltons were a stubborn lot and didn't know when to leave well enough alone.

"How long have you been a detective inspector?"

"Going on six months now, sir. But I've studied every case in our files, past and present."

Crawford rubbed his eyes. "I'll just bet you have. And I s'pose you're eager to have a case of your very own, eh?"

"Well, sir, I—"

"What evidence do you have to prove your murder theory isn't a load of bosh and bunkum?"

"There was no suicide note, sir."

"I don't suppose every poor bugger who offs himself takes the time to write a note."

"The victim had recently brought home a puppy."

"A *puppy*, is it? And you know this because . . . ?"

"His landlady, sir, a Mrs."—Hamilton pulled a notepad from his pocket—"Sutherland. I spoke with her yesterday, after his body was found in the park. She rents rooms on Leith Walk, and Mr. Wycherly was her tenant. According to her, he had just acquired a puppy."

"Quite commendable of him, but I don't see what—"

"A man contemplating suicide is hardly likely to get a dog."

"And you've ruled out the possibility it might be an accident, have you?"

"My aunt used to climb Arthur's Seat regularly, sir."

"Good on your aunt for being so fit, but I don't see how that—"

"A well-coordinated young man doesn't just tumble from a trail tame enough for elderly women to stroll on—sir."

DCI Crawford crossed his arms. "A young man under the influence of whisky may do any number of unlikely things, Detective."

"There was no indication he had been drinking."

"I admire your initiative, but the coroner's office is overworked as it is, and we can't—"

"Can't afford to look into a potential murder? Is that what you were going to say, sir?"

Crawford sucked in a mighty lungful of air, ready to blast this irritating flea of a detective across the room. Then he exhaled, releasing all his rage in a single breath. The expression on Hamilton's face was so serious that Crawford had the unfortunate impulse to giggle. The urge to laugh often hit him at inappropriate times, especially when he was exhausted and anxious. He tried to suppress it, emitting a strange squeaking sound, like a frightened mouse.

"Sir?" said Hamilton, frowning.

Crawford gazed at his neglected mug of tea and sighed. "What precisely do you expect to find, Hamilton?"

"I don't know, sir. That's why I'm requesting an autopsy."

Crawford bent down to turn up the gas in the grate. Nothing seemed to ease this blasted chill in the air, which seeped into his bones. The chief inspector sniffed and wiped his nose. He hoped he wasn't getting a cold. "The morgue corridors are rather narrow. What about your . . . uh, problem with enclosed spaces?"

"I have never allowed it to interfere with my work."

"Surely you can see how a man in your situation could be . . . sensitive, shall we say, inclined to look for foul play everywhere."

Hamilton's hands tightened into fists at his side. "My suspicions about Stephen Wycherly have nothing to do with the fire that killed my parents."

"'Suspicion is a heavy armor—'"

"'And with its weight it impedes more than it protects.' I don't believe Robert Burns was talking about police work when he wrote those lines, sir."

Crawford's jaw went slack with amazement at Hamilton's audacity. It was well-known around the station house that the chief inspector was fond of quoting Burns, and no one had dared interrupt one of his recitations. It was even more irritating that Hamilton actually knew the blasted quote.

DCI Crawford rose from his chair, the movement rather like a whale breeching the surface of the waves.

"Sergeant Dickerson!" he bellowed.

A short, flame-haired young officer with chin whiskers and a burgeoning potbelly appeared at the door. He was like a fledgling version of Crawford himself, but with more hair.

"You called, sir?"

"Will you be kind enough to escort DI Hamilton to the morgue?"

Dickerson shuffled his feet and coughed. "What about th' matter of Mrs. McGinty's pig, sir?" His accent was decidedly North Yorkshire, the vowels twisted and wrung out before finally being released from servitude in his mouth.

"I suppose her pig can look after itself for a while, Sergeant."

"If you say so, sir."

Though the City of Glasgow Police had the distinction of being the first of its kind in Britain, the Edinburgh City Police had already produced several distinguished members, notably famed detective and author James McLevy. However, the constabulary duties included such things as "Regulation of the Keeping of Pigs, Asses, Dogs, and Other Inferior Animals." Mrs. McGinty's pig was a habitual offender, and the job of keeping the good lady and her porcine cohort in line had fallen to Sergeant Dickerson.

"Never mind the blasted pig," Crawford said. "DI Hamilton here wants to look at a body. I want you to go with him."

Hamilton looked at DCI Crawford. "Sir?"

"See here, Hamilton, I'll be damned if I'm going to waste the coroner's time. However, I will allow you to view the body in the company of Sergeant Dickerson here, if you promise to be quick about it."

"But—"

DCI Crawford narrowed his eyes, a scowl tugging the corners of his mouth. "Be grateful I'm in a generous mood," he said, doing his best to sound fierce.

Hamilton blinked and saluted. "Thank you, sir."

Crawford glared at him before casting his small blue eyes upon Sergeant Dickerson. "Mind you keep an eye on him in the morgue, Sergeant."

Dickerson looked puzzled. "Sir?"

Crawford sighed. "He's liable to go wonky. Doesn't like enclosed spaces." Hamilton stiffened at this, but they both knew he was in no position to deny it. "Tag along and keep him steady, eh?"

Dickerson's pudgy body snapped to attention. "Right you are, sir."

"Be gone, both of you, lest I change my mind."

They obeyed, and DCI Crawford turned his attention back to the stack of paperwork on his desk, sweat pricking his forehead. If only his subordinates knew how much of his famous irritability was an act, calculated to intimidate. The effort to project a cantankerous persona often had the effect of making him truly cranky. He gazed glumly at his cold tea, the cream condensing on top in a thin, unappealing swirl of white. He stretched his six-foot-four frame and lumbered over to the center window, its iron crosshatched panes splattered with rain.

Outside, an anemic drizzle speckled the cobblestones. People hurried along High Street, hunched against a cold, damp wind that managed to thread its way through the thickest cloak. Even the horses looked miserable, their hooves sending sprays of water in all directions as they landed in puddles. A lone ragpicker huddled over his heap of clothing, face hidden beneath the broad brim of his oilcloth hat.

February was a foul month, and Crawford was in a foul mood. He pulled the gold-plated watch from his breast pocket and flipped open the cover. The watch had belonged to his grandfather, his namesake and one of the founders of the Edinburgh City Police. Much as he tried, Robert Lyle Crawford never felt up to following in his august ancestor's footsteps. He tucked the watch back into his pocket as he returned to his desk. He wanted nothing more than to be at Moira's side, to stroke her hair, and hug her to him. It was a gloomy day, and the sooner it was over, he thought, the better.

CHAPTER THREE

The Edinburgh city morgue was dark and dank; it smelled of mildew and lost promise. Ian heard the scuttling of rats and the slow drip of water from an unseen source—a steady, hollow sound, like the slow knelling of a church bell. The more he tried to ignore it, the more the sound wormed its way into his brain. *Drip, drop, drip, drop.*

Sergeant Dickerson crept along behind him, noiseless as a cat—he didn't appear to like the place any more than Ian did. Leading the way through the stone corridor, lantern held high in front of him, was the attendant on duty, a short, bushy-haired Welshman by the name of Jack Cerridwen. Ian had crossed paths with him before, and though Cerridwen was an ill-tempered little man, a fifth of single malt did much to soften the rough edges of his personality. Ian had plied him with a bottle of Cardhu, which cost half a week's wages. He hoped it would be worth the investment.

Ian felt as if the walls were closing in as he followed the Welshman down the dank corridor. He forced himself to take deep breaths to stave off the dread simmering in his stomach. He did not care for anything that reminded him of the basement he had been trapped in all those years ago. The passage of time had done little to dim the terror of confinement. Cold sweat prickled on his forehead, his hands and feet tingled, and his heart thumped like a kettledrum in his chest. The slow drip of water continued relentlessly. *Drip, drop, drip, drop.* Taking a deep breath of musty air, he willed himself to put one foot in front of the other.

Cerridwen opened an imposing iron door that appeared to have been hewn in the Dark Ages. It clanged shut behind them with a hollow shudder reverberating through the cavernous building. He led them through to a large room with a tiled floor and stark brick walls, thick with decades of paint. Ian couldn't help thinking about what those layers of paint had covered up, what misery these walls had seen. Gaslight flickered from sconces hanging from the muddy-colored brick walls; a single bank of long, narrow windows let in what little light managed to struggle through the wet winter haze. Ian relaxed a little, more at ease in the spacious room with its high ceiling and tall windows.

A row of stone platforms on steel supports bolted to the floor lined the room's far wall. Each was just long and wide enough to support the body of a man. On the third platform lay a body covered by a dingy, stained sheet.

Cerridwen whipped off the sheet covering the body with a flourish, as if he were a magician unveiling a trick. "Here ye go. Poor bugger's just waitin' for someone to come claim him."

Ian stared at him. "No family, no fiancée—nobody?"

Cerridwen shook his head, the smell of stale alcohol wafting from his grizzled whiskers. "Nope. Could be someone came around on the night shift, but I don't think so."

Ian gazed down at the young man on the slab. He was still fully clothed, and his head lay at an odd angle—it was evident his neck and possibly several vertebrae had been broken in the fall. But in spite of considerable bruising, contusions, and other injuries, in life he appeared to have been fit and well-groomed, even rather handsome. Thick blond hair framed an oval face with regular, clean features. His clothes, though also damaged, were moderately expensive and of good quality. Ian thought it highly unlikely such a person would have no friends or family to mourn his passing.

"I see you have not yet removed his clothing. What was in his pockets?"

Cerridwen shifted his feet and cleared his throat. "Naught much—a soiled handkerchief, a set of keys, and—oh, yes, a single playing card. The three of clubs it were, sir."

"I'd like to see it."

"Hang on a minute—think I've still got it," he said, fishing around in his lab coat pockets. "Ah, here it is!"

Ian took the card and studied it. The design was unusual—it featured dancing skeletons, each wearing a jaunty red fez. Each of the three clubs was incorporated into the body of a skeleton, forming part of the torso.

"That's an odd-lookin' card, sir," Sergeant Dickerson remarked, peering over his shoulder.

"Indeed it is," Ian replied, sliding the card carefully into the breast pocket of his jacket. "You found no wallet or personal effects such as rings or watches?" he asked Cerridwen.

"I'm afraid not—p'haps it were already taken by those who found the body."

"No doubt," Ian remarked drily. Edinburgh morgue attendants were notorious for relieving the dead of unattended property, but they were difficult to prosecute, being adept at hiding evidence. The city's numerous pawnshop owners and "resetters" were always eager to fence stolen goods before they could be traced.

Cerridwen shuffled his feet again and coughed, no doubt impatient to get to the bottle waiting for him in his tiny office. "Will you be needin' me further, gentlemen?"

"Thank you, Mr. Cerridwen; I think we'll be fine on our own," Ian replied.

"Right, then, I'll leave you to it. Just give me a whistle when you're ready to leave." He turned and strode briskly from the room, his footsteps fading rapidly down the stone corridor.

Sergeant Dickerson scratched his chin. "Shouldn't he remain here while we examine th' body, sir?"

Ian looked after the rapidly retreating Cerridwen. "It won't be the first time a morgue attendant has skipped his duty for the lure of a bottle, Sergeant."

Dickerson snickered, the sound oddly out of place in the solemn surroundings. He quickly choked back his inappropriate response and looked down at the dead man before them.

A human corpse is a curious and somber sight. First, the observer feels an instinctive physical aversion to death and dead things. That is followed by a kind of sickened curiosity, wonderment—and finally, sadness. If the body is in good condition, there is sometimes the odd expectation that the person is not dead after all, but will, at any moment, sit up and open his eyes.

Ian was no stranger to dead bodies, yet every time he was in the presence of death, he went through all of these stages. Young Wycherly's body had already begun to bloat as the gases in his digestive system expanded. His skin had the mottled gray pallor of death, as the blood seeped from his tissues to collect on the underside of the body, in the process known as lividity. And yet in spite of that, his face in repose suggested some of the man's gentle, unassuming personality. Perhaps Ian was prejudiced in this opinion by what Wycherly's landlady had told him, but he thought it was a damn pity that such a boy should die so suddenly and violently. A stanza from one of his early poems popped into Ian's head.

> We meet again at death's dark door
> you have quit this world
> with its untidy yearnings and disappointments
> all joy and sorrow drained from your pale face

Dickerson shifted his weight uneasily from foot to foot. "Right, then, sir, what's next?"

"What do you make of young Wycherly, Sergeant?"

Dickerson wiped sweat from his forehead—in spite of the cold, damp room, his face was flushed. "He's—dead, sir."

"Well done, aye—but apart from that."

"I don't quite take your meaning."

"The dead can't speak for themselves, so we must speak for them."

"Right y'are, sir."

"So . . . ?"

"Uh, what exactly d'you mean, sir?"

"Every crime is a narrative, a story told backward. We know the ending, and it is our job to discover the beginning and middle."

"How d'we do that?"

"Look at him, Sergeant—describe what you see."

Dickerson peered down at Wycherly's body and swallowed hard. "Well, he's quite young, I s'pose."

"What else? What do you notice about his person—his grooming, his manner of dress?"

"His nails are well tended."

"Good. What else about his hands?"

Dickerson suppressed a shudder and lifted one of the dead man's arms, turning it over so he could study the hand. "Very smooth skin, I'd say, sir."

"What does that tell you about him?"

"He's definitely not laborer. I'd say he's spent most a' his life indoors."

"Excellent!" Ian said. "Well done."

"Thank you, sir," Dickerson replied with a little cough. Ian knew well enough that DCI Crawford's men anticipated little in the way of commendation, and they were rarely disappointed in their expectations.

"If you view his life as a narrative, the moment where it intersects the life of the criminal, a new story begins."

"And that's the story we're int'rested in?"

"Precisely! Now, what about his clothing?"

Dickerson straightened his spine and crossed his arms. "He's dressed like merchant, or per'aps business clerk. Pro'bly works in office."

"That's the stuff," Ian said. "Now you're thinking like a detective."

Dickerson frowned. "His landlady could ha' told us that, sir."

"Ah! But we must sharpen our minds to a fine point so we may glean clues wherever we find them."

Dickerson pursed his lips dubiously. "If you say so, sir."

"Now, please help me remove his clothes."

"Sir?" Dickerson looked positively green.

"We must examine the body."

Dickerson gulped and bit his lower lip, but soldiered on manfully in spite of his evident queasiness.

Rigor mortis was already beginning to fade, and as they tugged at the sleeve of Wycherly's jacket, his arm suddenly went limp. Dickerson nearly tumbled backward at the touch of the pliable flesh. His ruddy face turned an even darker shade of red. He took a deep breath and loosened the stiff collar of his uniform.

"Are you quite all right, Sergeant?" Ian asked. He recalled his first dead body, as a young constable—a poor old wretch who froze to death in an unheated tenement in Skinner's Close. His supervisor insisted he close the vacant, staring eyes, and Ian still remembered the marble coldness of the flesh under his fingers. The face haunted his sleep for weeks after; in his dreams, he was unable to close the eyes, no matter how many times he tried. They gazed up at him, pleading, accusing, horrible in their stillness. After that, he vowed never to be caught off guard by the presence of death again.

Dickerson cleared his throat and wiped the sweat from his upper lip. "Steady on," Ian said, laying a hand on the sergeant's shoulder.

"I'll manage, sir," Dickerson muttered, reapplying himself to the task.

There wasn't much blood. The worst injuries must have been internal, Ian surmised as he and Dickerson began removing the dead man's clothes, carefully peeling away the green tweed jacket. It bore a London label from a high-end tailor shop Ian recognized. Turning it over, he noticed the cuff on the right sleeve was missing a button.

"What do you make of this, Sergeant?" he asked, holding it out.

Dickerson squinted at the jacket sleeve. "Left arm has two leather buttons for decoration, but th' right sleeve is missing one, sir."

"What does that tell you?"

"Could be Mr. Wycherly was in need o' seamstress."

"But look at the rest of his clothes—except for the damage sustained by his fall, they are in perfect repair."

"So th' button were lost—"

"In a struggle, Sergeant—the one that took place on the top of Arthur's Seat."

Dickerson scratched his head. "Beggin' pardon, sir, but 'at's hardly conclusive evidence."

"True enough. I'm looking for something else to confirm my theory."

"What exactly are ye lookin' for, sir?" Dickerson asked, laying the jacket carefully on a nearby stool.

"I wish I could tell you, Sergeant," he said, unbuttoning the collar of the linen shirt beneath the jacket. "I am hoping I'll know it when I see it."

And there, on the corpse of young Stephen Wycherly, was precisely what he had been looking for.

CHAPTER FOUR

Lillian Grey stepped from the butcher shop, treading with care on the uneven, rain-slickened cobblestones. She could call a hansom cab—several had already splashed by—but even at her advanced age, Lillian valued the effect of exercise on one's complexion. Clutching a wicker basket containing a brown paper package, she threaded her way up the High Street in the direction of the High Kirk of St. Giles, to pay a wee visit before heading home. She tried to stop in for dear Alfie's sake once a week. Lillian didn't believe in any god of man's creation, but Alfred had been a lifelong Christian, bless him, and she did it to honor his memory. After forty years of marriage, she owed him that much. He had left her a tidy fortune, for which she was grateful, but she would much rather have his warm body still next to her in bed on cold Edinburgh nights.

She pulled her woolen cloak closer as a spray of water from the wheels of a passing carriage slapped against her cheek. The coach driver ignored her glare, snapping his whip smartly against the flanks of two matching dapple grays. Lillian wiped the rainwater from her face with her gloved hand, lifting her skirts to avoid a puddle. She had lived in this town half her life and knew the weather well enough, but it was one thing to know it and another to become accustomed to it.

Even the sun misbehaved in Edinburgh. At the height of summer, it refused to retire at a reasonable hour, shining bravely on well after nine o'clock. In winter, the land descended into perpetual twilight, the sun barely scraping the horizon as it slunk across the sky in search of rest, as if exhausted by its summer excess.

She climbed up the High Street, past the Tron Kirk, its sharply pointed steeple slate gray in the chill rain. She pushed on to St. Giles'—Alfie always admired its grandeur and pomp; after all, as he liked to remind her, it was *the* center of Scottish worship. Behind her lay the house of John Knox, founder of the Scottish Reformation, who survived nearly two years as a French galley slave to lead the Scots away from French Catholicism. Though Lillian had no place in her life for Christianity, she admired Knox as a Scottish hero. She preferred Spiritualism, attending Madame Flambeau's Friday night séances with regularity.

She shivered as she entered the great stone building, her footsteps echoing through its solemn walls. In the main nave, a group of schoolchildren spilled out of a pew, giggling and poking one another.

"Hush! Come along, children!" their teacher hissed, herding them like so many gray-and-blue-clad sheep. She was a sturdy matron in a thick woolen suit—sans corset, Lillian noted with disapproval. They followed her, whispering and stifling laughter, their leather soles clacking on the marble floor. A couple of the older the girls stared at Lillian in a way she found most impolite, and she glared back at them.

Lillian knew she was old, but she couldn't abide people dismissing her because of her age. She was still a lively woman with a keen mind and the energy of folks half her age, and it galled her when a young shopkeeper's assistant spoke more slowly to her, or raised his voice, assuming she was hard of hearing.

"Lower your voice," she would snap at him. "I'm not deaf!" She enjoyed the startled expression that came over his face, but it didn't make up for the indignity inflicted by the careless arrogance of the young. She remembered being that age, thinking the grace and ease of youth would last forever—getting old was something that happened to other people.

Lillian Grey was a curious combination—the spirit of a revolutionary affixed to the stern sensibility of a conservative Scottish matron. She was aware of her oddness, but proud of it, too, in the contrary way of a true Scot. She shuffled to the rear of the nave, with its soaring stone arches, her movements hampered by the large basket on her arm. She stared up at the crosshatched, stained glass window on the western end.

Lillian had studied art as a young woman—it was said among the family that she had "an artistic soul." After Alfie's death, she had taken up photography, rather by accident, having acquired a bulky wooden camera at a jumble sale. She gave her neck a cursory rub with her strong fingers as she stood beneath the depiction of the archangel Gabriel wielding his flaming sword. Lowering her head, she breathed a silent homage to her dear departed Alfred (she wouldn't use the word "prayer," because that would imply a faith in God she was proud not to have).

When she was finished, she drew a small gold watch from her skirt pocket and peered at its face. She was astonished to see it was nearly five. She had half an hour to get home and put the kettle on before her sister's son Ian, her favorite nephew, arrived at her flat. They had always gotten on, but now that dear Emily was gone, they had a special bond. The sausages in her basket were for him—she was making bubble and squeak for tea, one of his favorites. After Alfie's death, she insisted on giving Ian a yearly stipend—she had more than she could possibly spend—and though he could have lived on that alone, he continued working as a policeman, bless him.

She scurried from the church onto the High Street. As she passed the kirk's western entrance, a couple of boys in school uniforms loped past, pausing to spit energetically on the heart-shaped mosaic built into the cobblestones. Known as the Heart of Midlothian, after the nickname for the infamous Tolbooth prison, the mosaic marked the former entrance to the building, now demolished. The prison figured prominently in Sir Walter Scott's nationalist novel, *The Heart of Midlothian*, and was also the place of public executions. Spitting on the Heart was considered both good luck and a sign of Scottish patriotism—though Lillian considered it merely an excuse for boys to spit in public.

She charged uphill on her sturdy legs before turning south toward her home near the university, passing students and professors on their way to Thursday evening classes, long gowns flapping behind them in the wind like great black wings. Arriving at her spacious town house, she shoved the sausages into the icebox next to a nice bunch of cress she had bought from a street vendor near the Lawnmarket. The doorbell chimed as she was pouring the cream into the bone china pitcher her sister had given her. *Poor Emily*, she thought as she hurried down the long hallway to the front door. She could see the outline of her nephew's lean form behind the smoked-glass panels.

"Hello, Auntie," he said, kissing her on the cheek as she closed the door after him. He handed her a bunch of greenhouse carnations, and she inhaled their sharp cinnamon smell, reminiscent of spring breezes and hope.

"Ach, ye shouldn't have," she said, her Glaswegian accent thickening in his presence.

"You'd never forgive me if I didn't."

She swatted him affectionately and bustled him into the front parlor, where a steaming teapot perched upon a lace antimacassar on the round rosewood table. She arranged the flowers in a vase and put them on top of the upright piano that had belonged to Emily. Lillian didn't play, but she was determined to learn—the piano had been spared in the fire that killed her sister, which she took as a sign. Though she didn't believe in a Christian God, Lillian saw no contradiction in being heartily superstitious. After putting the sausages and potatoes in a skillet over a low fire, she joined her nephew in the parlor.

The gas lamps were turned low, and a fire blazed merrily in the hearth. A lump swelled in her throat as Lillian thought of all the tea she and Alfred had shared together at this table. Still, she had had forty years with him before the heart attack ripped him from her. Lillian was inclined to focus on the positive, a trait that ran in the Grey family—though not, alas, in the Hamilton clan.

"Shall I be mother?" she asked as she reached for the pot.

Ian inhaled the aroma of steaming tea. "Hot and strong, just the way I like it."

"You're on a case," she observed, handing him a cup.

"You never did miss much, Auntie," he said, reaching for a raisin scone.

"Mind you don't spoil your appetite for the sausages."

"No fear of that," he said, biting into the scone, sending crumbs tumbling onto the carpet.

"Who's the lead detective?"

"I hope I am."

"Oh, Ian—your first proper case!" she said, clapping her hands like a schoolgirl.

"It's not official yet—"

"This calls for a celebration!" she said, ignoring his protestation. "We'll have to break out something decent with supper." She stood and reached for the empty teapot, suppressing a groan as her aging joints protested. The damp weather cut through layers of woolen clothing, making her knees swell and creak, but she was not about to let her nephew see that. She picked up the pot and headed toward the kitchen, doing her best to straighten her stiffening spine. She turned the sausages and potatoes, and returned with a bottle of single malt and two brandy snifters. After pouring them each a generous amount, she settled back into her chair. "All right—I want all the details."

"Did you happen to read about the young man who was found in Holyrood Park yesterday?"

"One would have to be blind and deaf to avoid hearing about it—it was in all the papers." She leaned toward him. "So it *was* murder? I thought as much!"

"You never cease to amaze me. What made you think that?"

She smiled. "If I give away all my secrets, I won't surprise you anymore."

He took a sip of whisky. "Perhaps you should be a member of the constabulary instead of me."

"Well," she said, "we both know why you joined the force." She saw his lips tighten, and veered away from the subject. "Do you have any promising leads?"

"Not yet. That reminds me—are you still a member of the Amateur Photography Society?"

"I'm the treasurer!" she declared proudly.

"I wonder if you would be so kind as to lend me your expertise."

"I should be delighted."

"Are you free tomorrow?"

"I am."

"Can you meet me at the morgue first thing in the morning—is seven too early?"

"Ach, nae—I'm up with the sun. Have you cleared it with DCI Crawford?"

"No, but I will."

"How exciting. But let's eat. I'm famished, and I'll wager you are as well."

"Let me help you serve."

"Stay where you are."

"But—"

"You can clean up, if you insist," she said, bustling to the kitchen. Though utterly independent and self-sufficient, Lillian missed having a man around to wait on. She had enjoyed serving dear Alfie his tea, fussing and clucking over him, and now that Ian had taken his place, she was not about to let the opportunity slip by.

"Eat up, Skinny Malinky Longlegs," Lillian said, sliding a hot plate of sausages, potatoes, and cress salad in front of her nephew. She enjoyed trotting out archaic Scottish phrases.

Ian grimaced. "Auntie—"

"You'll never catch the eye of a young lady if ye don't put on a stone or two," she said, spreading some fresh butter on a scone.

"I'm not looking to catch anyone's eye."

"Your brother never had a problem with his appetite," she replied as she bit into the scone, savoring the flaky sweetness. "Have you heard from Donald lately?"

"No," he said flatly. "Last I heard, he was working his way through all the pubs in Glasgow."

His older brother, Donald, had been on his way to a promising medical career when the fire took their parents, reducing all of the family's possessions to ashes. Donald never recovered from the shock of returning in the middle of the night to find their home in flames, his younger brother trapped in the basement, their parents perished in the fire. He dropped out of the University of Edinburgh, and had spent the past seven years slouching around Scotland and the Continent, working odd jobs as a longshoreman, sheepherder, and bartender.

"Is he still gambling, then?" Lillian asked.

"And drinking."

"What a pity," she said, and silence settled over them. It was an uncomfortable subject, one she regretted bringing up.

"A leopard doesn't change its spots," Ian remarked, and she was sorry to hear the bitterness in his voice.

Outside, the rain beat hard upon the roofs of saints and sinners alike, hammering a steady, insistent tattoo upon the city's ancient dwellings. Anyone with the misfortune to be out on a night like this might peer through the parlor window at the two people huddled before the crackling fire with envy at the cozy, peaceful scene. Lillian knew that her nephew's mind was elsewhere, though—his long fingers fiddled with his napkin, and he gazed silently into the leaping flames.

"More sausages?" she offered hopefully.

"No, thank you."

"Go on with you, then."

He looked at her in surprise. "What?"

"I know well enough when you need to be alone. Get along—go play that damn pennywhistle or whatever it is you do when you need to think."

He rose from his chair without arguing. "I'm sorry I'm not very good company."

She dismissed him with a wave of her hand. "Ach, gae on wi'ye," she said in her thickest Glaswegian accent.

"Tomorrow, then? Bring your camera."

"Seven o'clock sharp."

He smiled. "I do adore you, Auntie."

"Now you're talking proper nonsense—get along, then!"

With a quick kiss on her cheek, he went.

CHAPTER FIVE

The lone figure standing on George IV Bridge looked out over the sleeping city and lit a cigarette. The match flickered briefly before dying out. He inhaled deeply, the ember of his cigarette a glowing red eye in the darkness. The night enfolded him in its arms like an old friend. He felt safe, invisible in the inky blackness.

But even darkness was no protection when he was a child. He would creep up to bed, hoping his father was passed out from drink. If he was lucky, he would fall asleep to the old man's snores shaking the roof rafters. The next morning, he would tiptoe past his father, who would still be sleeping it off, splayed out over the kitchen bench. Those were the good days. On the bad ones, the steps would creak with heavy footfalls as his father staggered upstairs, muttering curses. When he saw the dreaded crack of light at his bedroom door, he knew it was all over.

"Get up, you little faggot! Time to prove you're a piece of chicken sheit who couldn't hit the side of a barn."

The covers would be thrown off as his father dragged him from his bed, down the stairs, out to the yard behind the house—or if there was snow on the ground, to the cold, damp basement. The two boys would do their best to satisfy their father's commands, battling until they were slippery with sweat and exhausted, but even that failed to placate him.

The fights only stopped when the old man ran out of booze or cigarettes, or fell asleep perched on the rain barrel.

At first, he thought his brother was as much a victim as he was, but later resented him for not intervening—after all, he was older. Was it not his duty to protect his younger brother? He began to hate his brother, blaming him for not standing up to their tyrant father.

Stephen Wycherly reminded him of his brother, but that wasn't what sealed Wycherly's fate. Their friendship had begun well enough, over a pint at the local pub. Wycherly initiated the conversation, but the next day they were in his digs on Leith Walk, and Stephen made a play for him. That was when the poison began to seep in again. He had been trying to mend his ways—dear God, he had tried, even moving to Edinburgh from another continent in hopes of breaking the spell—but to no avail. He was attracted to Wycherly, and the idea of killing him held a thrill nothing else could touch.

He began to think about killing Stephen, until he could think of nothing else. It was easy enough to lure him up to Arthur's Seat by threatening to reveal his secret, which would ruin his law career. Wycherly took the bait, and agreed to pay his "blackmailer." After strangling him, he pushed the law clerk over the ledge for good measure—maybe the death would seem like a suicide. The familiar feeling of power was irresistible, and the lust for more victims returned, stronger than ever. He realized Wycherly was just the beginning of a new cycle. He needed more.

A faint moon struggled to break through the overcast sky, and for a moment the buildings in the eastern sky were sharply etched silhouettes in its pale light. The clouds soon won the struggle, vanquishing the pallid moon, and the streets lay once again in shadow. The man on the bridge finished his cigarette, shoved his hands into his pockets, and strode off into the darkness. He smiled a secret smile as he headed into the heart of the city. The thrill of the hunt tingled in his loins, and his blood quickened at the thought of new conquests. *Oh, there was so much evil in a man, one hardly knew where to begin* . . .

Somewhere deep in the Old Town, a hound howled mournfully. Another responded, and soon the air rang with the sound of dogs baying to the moon. The moon had already succumbed to the darkness, but still they howled, the sound plaintive and hollow in the empty air.

CHAPTER SIX

"Ligature strangulation, sir."

DCI Crawford looked up from his desk. The bell on Greyfriars Kirk had not yet struck nine on this Friday morning, he was still on his first cup of tea, and standing before him was his most irksome lieutenant. DI Hamilton looked triumphant—smug, even. A smile tugged at the corners of his mouth, and his eyes actually *sparkled*. By God, that was too much, Crawford thought glumly as he drained the dregs of his tea. He was exhausted, having been up half the night with Moira. He had sent the scullery maid's son to fetch the doctor, but the good man was out all night attending to the cases of cholera that had struck the city like a bolt of divine vengeance. Crawford had finally administered his wife a dose of laudanum before taking some himself and falling into a comatose state until shortly before dawn.

"Very well, Hamilton, let's hear what you have." He sighed, looping his fingers through the piece of string he kept in the drawer. Even that calming ritual sometimes failed him on days like this, he thought as he twisted it round his palm.

Ian pulled an envelope from his coat pocket and dropped it on the desk.

Crawford sniffed at it as though it were three-day-old fish. "What is this?"

"Open it, sir."

As the chief inspector lifted the envelope, three photographs fell onto the desk. They showed the corpse of a young man—Steven Wycherly, no doubt. Ringing the lad's neck were ugly purple bruises.

Hamilton cleared his throat. "Judging by the placement and shape, I'd say most likely ligature strangulation, sir."

Crawford looked up at the detective. Why were people so damn irritating, even when they were admirable? *Especially* when they were admirable, he thought as he tossed the photos back onto the desk.

"Where did you get these?"

"My aunt took them."

Crawford sat bolt upright in his chair. "And how did your *aunt* get into the morgue, I'd like to know?"

"I let her in."

"Where was the morgue attendant at the time?"

"Nursing a bottle of single malt."

"Which he procured . . . ?"

"The same place anyone would, I suppose."

"Do you find it strange that a morgue attendant could afford to drink single malt?"

"'The miserable have no other medicine.'"

"I am not in the mood for your quotes this morning," Crawford said icily, glaring at Hamilton with his most intimidating expression. Sergeant Dickerson nearly wet himself when Crawford looked at him like that. But it had no effect on the detective, who gazed back at him with a placid expression on his annoyingly good-looking face. Crawford didn't trust handsome men—and he trusted beautiful women even less.

Crawford rubbed his throbbing forehead and tossed the photos across the desk. "Very well—have your investigation. Sergeant Dickerson!" he called.

The sergeant appeared at the office door, and Crawford beckoned him in.

"Take Dickerson along with you. You deserve each other."

"Thank you, sir."

Crawford waved a hand at Hamilton, dismissing him, but the detective didn't move.

"I'll keep you informed on what I find, sir."

"No doubt," Crawford said. "On your way out, ask the desk sergeant to bring me more tea."

"Yes, sir."

"Oh, and, Hamilton . . . ?"

"Sir?"

"When are you next seeing your aunt?"

"We have tea every Sunday."

"Would you deliver a message from me?"

"Certainly, sir."

"Ask her if she would be interested in working as a staff photographer with the Edinburgh Police."

"I will—thank you, sir."

Crawford watched Hamilton leave, Sergeant Dickerson trailing in his wake, before sitting heavily at his desk. The chief inspector ran a hand through his sparse hair and looked at the ever-mounting pile of papers on his desk. It was going to be a long day.

CHAPTER SEVEN

According to Stephen Wycherly's landlady, he worked as a clerk in a solicitor's office on George Street, a part of the New Town boasting a goodly number of law offices. Ian found himself wandering past rows of handsome entrances with polished brass nameplates and matching door knockers—a far cry from the warrens of dilapidated buildings in the Old Town. Sometimes Edinburgh seemed like two cities, the inhabitants leading such different lives it was as if they were on separate continents.

Ian stopped in front of chambers with a polished brass plaque proclaiming "Harley, Wickham, and Clyde." He stepped up to the burnished wooden door and rapped sharply three times. He heard a man's voice from within—muffled, as though coming from a back room.

"Just a moment—I'm coming!"

There was a rustling sound, as though papers were being shuffled about, and the sound of a chair scraping against the floor.

"I'll be there straightaway!"

More rustling, then a thump, like something being dropped on the floor.

"Oh, blast!" the man inside muttered. The door burst open abruptly, and Ian was confronted with a singular-looking gentleman. He could not have been more than five feet tall, a gnomelike individual with a crooked spine and a tuft of stiff brown hair over a long, weathered face with a beak of a nose and watery blue eyes. His age was impossible to tell; he could have been forty or eighty. He wore an elegant frock coat, a crisply knotted cravat, and striped stovepipe trousers, all of the very best material. The incongruity of such fine clothing on such a misshapen form was striking. Ian could hardly imagine the man was vain; no doubt he dressed like that to impress clients.

He peered at Ian through gold pince-nez, his rheumy blue eyes sharp behind the thick spectacles. "Well?" he said in a cultivated Edinburgh accent. "Whom do I have the pleasure of addressing?"

Ian held out his badge. "Detective Inspector Ian Hamilton, Edinburgh Police." Normally he did not feel the need to prove his identity, but this gentleman exuded an air of authority, in spite of his diminutive and deformed figure.

"Ah, yes, of course," he said, extending his hand. "Eugene Harley, Esquire."

Ian shook the hand, which was thin and dry, the bones like a loose collection of sticks.

"Won't you come in, Inspector?" Harley said. His voice was pleasant and plummy, his manner refined and gracious.

He opened the door and led Ian into an office in dire need of a file clerk. Papers and folders were strewn everywhere. Briefs, motions, and other legal documents were stuffed into cubbyholes, stacked in piles upon the thick oak desk, or scattered on the floor like fallen leaves. Ian realized what he had heard from outside—Eugene Harley struggling through the forest of paper to get to the door.

This seemed to worry Eugene Harley not a bit. He flicked a few papers from a handsome oak office chair and gestured toward it.

"Do sit down, won't you?"

"Thank you," Ian said, settling into the chair, padded with green leather and quite comfortable.

His host perched upon the edge of the desk and crossed his thin arms. "Now then, I presume you are here about young Wycherly?"

"Yes, sir."

Eugene Harley shook his head sadly. "Unfortunate fellow—terrible business, that. Poor Catherine is so distraught, she failed to come to work today."

"Catherine . . . ?"

"My niece. She assists me in my practice and, when she has time, tidies the place up. As you can see," he said, waving a hand at the piles of paper, "we are much in need of her services."

"So your niece is also the housekeeper for your law firm?"

"I like to keep it in the family, so to speak, with all the legal documents lying about. You can never be too careful, eh?" he said, with a squeaky little giggle, like a rusty door hinge.

Ian made a note of the girl's name in his notebook. "I presume you can tell me how to contact her?"

"Most certainly," Mr. Harley replied. "She lives with me. My poor brother and his wife died of cholera some time ago, and I have cared for the girl since she was in bloomers. As I have no children myself, she has been the great joy of my life," he added, tears gathering at the corners of his pale blue eyes.

"And your partners?" Ian asked quickly. He was rather taken with the old gentleman and wished to spare him the indignity of crying in front of a stranger.

To his surprise, the solicitor's face crinkled into a wry smile. "Ah, yes, my—partners."

"Misters Wickham and Clyde?"

Eugene Harley Esq. cleared his throat. "They don't exist—or rather, not as human beings."

"I beg your pardon?"

"Those are the names of my cats." Mr. Harley chuckled and leaned forward, crackling sounds emanating from his twisted spine. Ian had an impulse to offer his chair, but there was something mesmerizing about the old gentleman, and he remained seated, caught up in his spell. "You see, Detective Inspector—Hamilton, was it?" the old man said. Ian nodded. "Well, you might be surprised to learn how comforting it is to potential clients to see more than one name upon the nameplate. It confers an aura of respectability—creates confidence, as it were."

"So your firm consists solely of you and your niece—and the unfortunate Mr. Wycherly?"

"Yes, indeed. You may find it odd that our clients seldom inquire about the whereabouts of Misters Wickham and Clyde, but such are the mysteries of human nature. Do you mind if I partake of some tobacco?"

"Not at all," Ian replied, expecting him to light a pipe or cigarette, but instead Mr. Harley slid a tin of snuff from the pocket of his frock coat and delicately placed a pinch in each nostril. Throwing his head back, he sneezed mightily, with such force Ian feared his fragile-looking form would crack. But Mr. Harley was made of sturdier stuff than his appearance suggested. Wiping his face with a voluminous silk kerchief, he beamed at his visitor.

"There now—that always puts some vinegar into my blood! Much better," he said, replacing the handkerchief in his pocket with a theatrical flourish. "Now, what was I saying?"

"You were speaking of your niece."

"Ah, yes—dear Catherine! I'm afraid poor Wycherly's death came as quite a shock. Between you and me, I think she quite fancied the lad. This morning she declined to emerge from her room, so I left her in the capable hands of my housekeeper and came to the office myself."

"Was there anything unusual in Mr. Wycherly's behavior in the days leading up to his death?"

"Not that I can think of; he seemed quite himself . . . Oh, wait, yes, there was one thing. Perhaps it's nothing, but—"

"What was it?"

"He received something in the afternoon post the day he died—a letter."

"Did you chance to see whom it was from?"

"Sadly, no—though I did see him open it, and he seemed disturbed by it. He folded it and placed it in his pocket, along with the envelope."

"And he never spoke of it?"

"I'm afraid not."

"Did anyone else see him receive the letter?"

"My niece, Catherine, was in the office at the time—she may have seen it."

"Did you see him leave the office that day?"

"No—I spent the rest of the afternoon going over a case with a barrister in his chambers. When I arrived back here, young Wycherly had already left."

"Thank you for your time, Mr. Harley."

Mr. Harley waved a thin hand in dismissal. "Anything I can do to help. Here is my address," he said, handing Ian a smartly embossed card. "If you wish to call upon my niece in the next few days, I will leave instructions with my housekeeper to admit you, in case of my absence."

"Your cooperation is much appreciated, Mr. Harley."

The old man shook his head. "I cannot imagine who should want to harm young Wycherly. He was such a harmless fellow, quiet and mild—one might even say retiring. Of course," he added with a sharp glance at Ian, "I am assuming his death was the result of foul play. Your presence here rather suggests that it was."

"Your assumption is correct. Stephen Wycherly was murdered."

They looked out the window; a smattering of rain was beginning to fall.

"I hope you catch the person or persons responsible," Harley remarked, "before anything sinister befalls my niece."

"Why do you say that?"

"'I am a very foolish fond old man, fourscore and upward'—fear has lodged itself in my head, an unwelcome visitor."

"That's from *Lear*, isn't it?"

"Ah, you like the Bard?"

"I do."

"The latter part was my own addition. In my case, at least, advanced age has brought with it increasing anxiety."

"Please do not concern yourself, Mr. Harley. I see no reason either you or your niece would be in danger."

Mr. Harley waved a gnarled hand. "Tut-tut—I'm old, and have not so many days left. But Catherine is another matter—you will look after her, won't you, Inspector?"

Ian cleared his throat. He was charmed by the old man and suppressed an impulse to tell a comforting lie. "I'm sorry that the Edinburgh Police can't guarantee the safety of an individual. We simply haven't enough manpower."

"I see," the old gentleman said, but his tone suggested that he didn't.

When Ian stepped into the street, he failed to notice the cloaked figure leaning against a lamppost. The man's posture was casual, but a pair of keen eyes watched as he made his way back toward the Old Town. As Ian rounded the corner onto Hanover Street, the man followed at a discreet distance.

CHAPTER EIGHT

George Frederick Pearson, chief reference librarian at the University of Edinburgh, was a collector. What he acquired was immaterial—books, bottles, bric-a-brac, beer coasters—but part of his brain seemed specifically designated for this task. It began at an early age, when he brought home bits of string, discarded tea tins, and broken pieces of pottery from rubbish bins. His mother initially regarded this eccentricity with fond indulgence, but after a couple of years during which he squirreled away items in various corners of his room, she began to grow concerned. One day after finding a stash of outdated market flyers underneath his bed, she marched out to the street where he was playing with his friends and demanded an explanation for his excessive acquisitions. He could give her none that satisfied her. He hardly understood it himself; it was something he felt compelled to do.

She marched right back into the house and promptly threw all of his treasures into the rubbish bin, which only cemented his compulsion. What was formerly a desire became a desperate need as objects assumed a role of absurd importance to him. That day haunted him for the rest of his life. Waking or dreaming, he could see his mother on her hands and knees, digging through his beloved possessions, stray strands of hair clinging to her sweaty forehead, the sleeves of her gingham frock rolled up to the elbows, her face flushed with determination and rage.

He wished never again to be the cause of such destructive fury. So he hid his compulsion, living alone in his cluttered flat on Princes Street, while employed at the university library. He never dreamed that his "hobby," as he called it, might be of use to anyone else.

Until a rainy Friday in February, when the only visitor in the reading room was a studious-looking young man with a pile of curly black hair and eyes that were slate gray in the dim glow of the gaslight. George approached him and coughed discreetly.

"May I be of service, sir?" They were roughly the same age, but George treated all visitors to the library with the same courteous formality.

The young man cocked his head to one side and studied George, which made him a bit uncomfortable. As it was seasonally raw weather, he was dressed in a thick blue jumper with shoulder patches, rather than his usual three-piece suit. Born and raised just outside London, he liked Edinburgh because the Scots were less formal than the British—though his English dialect was not always well received in some quarters.

"Detective Inspector Ian Hamilton," the man said. "Do you have any books on crime investigation?"

George extended his hand. "George Pearson, chief reference librarian. Pleased to make your acquaintance." Hamilton's handshake was firm, his hand strong. "May I ask if this relates to a particular case?"

"A potential case, perhaps."

Hamilton's speech was educated, and though it displayed hints of an early life in the Highlands, it was definitely Edinburgh, possibly Royal Terrace. George was very good with accents. His posh inflections made George relax a bit—well-heeled Scots tended to be less anti-English.

"Anything in particular?" said George.

"I'm interested specifically in strangulation."

George kept his expression neutral, but he was intrigued, being something of an amateur crime buff. "From a medical perspective or a forensic one?"

"Both, if possible."

"We'll begin with science, then. Right this way."

George led his visitor to the stacks. "Here's something you may find helpful," he said, sliding a book from the shelf. "*Uses of Science in Examining Crime Scene Evidence.* Translated from the French. The author was an associate of François Vidocq, the great French criminologist."

"That alone is a recommendation," Hamilton said, taking the book.

"I see you have heard of him."

The detective smiled. "I have copies of everything he wrote."

"I see," George said, envy forming a knot in his stomach. To have a complete set of anything was the collector's ultimate dream. "Perhaps I can be of further assistance? I have a rather interesting collection of crime books myself. At my flat, I mean," he added. Panic swept over him, leaving his knees weak—he had not invited anyone to his residence for a decade. "I can perhaps bring you some tomorrow," he said, "if that is convenient."

"That is very kind of you. In the meantime, I will take this one, please."

"Certainly," he said, leading the way to the lending desk. On the way, they passed the rack of newspapers with all the daily broadsheets, and the detective's eyes lingered on the front-page headline of the *Scotsman*:

TRAGEDY ON ARTHUR'S SEAT—YOUNG MAN TUMBLES TO HIS DEATH. SUICIDE OR MURDER? WILL EDINBURGH'S OVERWORKED POLICE FORCE INVESTIGATE?

49

George coughed again discreetly. "Right this way, sir." Hamilton followed silently, apparently lost in thought. He said nothing as George entered the title of the book in his ledger, in his careful, spidery script. He wrapped the book in brown paper and held it out to the detective. Just before letting go of the book, George said softly, "Is this regarding the death of that young man found in the park?"

"I'm afraid I'm not at liberty to talk about an ongoing investigation," Hamilton replied, a little too quickly.

George nodded. "Of course," he said, finally releasing his hold on the tome. "Still, it did seem an odd incident," he added, pretending to busy himself arranging papers. "Very curious, if you ask me."

"I suppose so," the detective said, tucking the book underneath his arm.

"Well-dressed young men are not given to tumbling from well-trodden paths in the middle of the afternoon."

Hamilton regarded him suspiciously. "How did you know he was well dressed?"

"Why, it's in all the papers, sir—you could hardly avoid reading about the story if you tried. He appeared to be wearing office attire, if I'm not mistaken. Curious thing, that."

Hamilton stared at him. "How do you know that?"

"His photograph was in all the papers."

The detective frowned. "I should have known. If a Welshman can be bribed by a policeman, I suppose he can be bribed by a newsman."

"*I'm* part Welsh," George said, frowning.

"I didn't mean anything by it. It's just—"

A couple of other patrons seated at the long oaken tables looked up from their reading with disapproval. A sharp-faced woman in an absurd hat resembling a parrot gave a loud, "Shush!"

"The person who murdered him has all the answers," George remarked casually, though he felt anything but casual. His stomach churned with excitement—he hadn't felt this alive in years.

50

"Perhaps," Hamilton murmured, standing motionless, the book still tucked under his arm. The sharp-faced woman gave another loud, "Shush!" He regarded her with surprise, as if only just realizing where he was. "Thank you for your help, Mr. Pearson."

"My pleasure to be of assistance," George said, lowering his voice so as not to aggravate the woman.

"I must be off now."

"Shall I bring you the books tomorrow? The ones I spoke of earlier?"

"But tomorrow is Saturday," Hamilton replied. "Surely you're not open?"

"Quite right—I had forgotten. I can meet you somewhere at your convenience."

"Well, I . . ."

"What about the White Hart Inn? They do a fair steak and kidney pie."

Hamilton studied him for a moment as though sizing him up, and then nodded. "Very well—shall we say around seven?"

"Capital. I shall bring the books."

"Thank you, Mr. Pearson. I am in your debt."

"Think nothing of it. Until tomorrow, then."

He watched the detective walk away, lost in thought—no doubt thinking about the case. A regular chap, George thought, and a damn fine-looking fellow, if a bit absentminded. Oh, well, perhaps he, too, would be preoccupied if he were trying to solve a murder case. A thrill of adventure shot through his spine as he turned to shelve a pile of books in the stacks. His life had never been particularly exciting, but he saw his future unfolding before him like a beautiful pink blossom—sweet, soft, and inviting.

He hummed a little tune as he slid the books into their proper places. The sharp-faced woman glared at him, and George had an impulse to stick his tongue out at her. Instead, he smiled sweetly and gave a little nod. He could afford to be gracious—after all, he was about to aid in the capture of a murderer. For the first time in his life, George Pearson felt truly important.

As he stood lost in dreams of an exciting future, a clean-cut young man with pale eyes slipped into the room and slid into a chair at one of the long tables, across from the sharp-faced woman. Looking up from her copy of *Shield*, the Anti-Contagious Diseases Acts Association's weekly circular, she couldn't help gazing at his arresting face and elegant clothes. The look he gave back cut through her like a blade. She shivered and drew her wool cardigan close, returning to her magazine. When she looked up again, he was gone.

CHAPTER NINE

"Why bother t'strangle someone if you're gonnae push 'em off a cliff anyway?" Sergeant Dickerson panted, struggling to catch up as they clambered up the hardscrabble path to the top of Arthur's Seat late Friday afternoon.

"Excellent question, Sergeant," Ian replied, leaning into the sharp wind blowing in from the Firth of Forth. The sky was threatening, the clouds glowering darkly overhead, but the rain had retreated, at least for the time being.

"The fall alone would kill a bloke," Dickerson continued, breathing heavily.

"It is curious," Ian said, slowing his stride. For every one of his steps, Dickerson took two, and Ian took pity on him—the sergeant was panting heavily as he trundled behind. "Perhaps this killer had a *need* to strangle his victim."

"An' maybe he thought th' fall would disguise the cause of death," Dickerson said, squinting against a gust of wind that nearly blew his cap off his head, "makin' it look like suicide."

"Or the place had some symbolic significance for the killer, beyond providing a convenient way to dispose of the body."

"Pity there were no witnesses," the sergeant called out over the increasingly stiff wind. "I s'pose that's because it were nasty day for a walk."

Ignoring the barb—this was hardly an ideal day, either—Ian contemplated Dickerson's remark. Did the killer bank on that fact, knowing that on a rainy day, few people were likely to scale this trail for the love of it? Or was he simply lucky? Ian still wasn't sure if it was a premeditated crime or one of opportunity, though he leaned toward the former.

"Sir," said Dickerson, "what d'you s'pose DCI Crawford meant when he said we 'deserved each other'?"

"He was just having his fun," Ian said, picking his way around a stone cairn someone had placed in the trail. He shivered a little—cairns always reminded him of tombstones, used since prehistoric times as grave markers.

"I don' s'pose it were a compliment, then?"

"The chief inspector has a lot on his mind, and that makes him irritable."

"Aye," said Dickerson. "D'you think he planned this all owt, sir? The murderer, I mean?"

"I don't know, Sergeant."

"But why strangulation, sir? Why not just push the poor blighter and be done wi' it? He'd be right dead enough either way."

"Perhaps the answer will help lead us to the motive," Ian suggested, "and if we're lucky, maybe even the killer."

Dickerson paused beside a windblown gorse bush, hands resting on his knees. He removed his hat and wiped sweat from his forehead.

"You might want to step up your fitness regimen, Sergeant," Ian said, pulling a canteen of water from his rucksack and handing it to him.

Dickerson drank deeply before returning it. "Right you are, sir," he said gamely, settling his cap back on his head. "You seem quite well prepared—d'ye hike often?"

"I've been known to roam a glen or two." Ian's longing for the mossy green hills and deep valleys of his native Highlands had only grown stronger with time. The landscape of Lothian had its appeal, but nothing could compare with the stark grandeur of Invernesshire. His desk was full of fevered, passionate poems scribbled late at night when he was seized by fits of longing—odes to the romance and beauty of the Highlands. His nostalgia was deepened by the memory of those early days as a time when all was right between his parents. The trouble came later; in his mind, it was synonymous with the move to Edinburgh.

"What do you s'pose he used—the killer, I mean?" said Dickerson.

"Any number of weapons might be used in strangulation: a cravat, a belt, a scarf. Your hands might do the trick, provided you were strong enough, but he preferred to use a ligature."

"So does it mean he were weak—or jes prepared?" said Dickerson.

"Another excellent question. Stephen Wycherly's attire suggests he wasn't expecting a vigorous climb. He was dressed for the office."

"I wonder what lured 'im up 'ere?" Dickerson mused.

"Another key question," said Ian. "We'll make a detective out of you yet, Sergeant."

Glancing at the rapidly darkening sky, Ian quickened his pace. Night would soon be upon them, the February sun barely pulling itself from its slumber before slouching back to bed. Pushing onward, they climbed the final stretch to the summit, the wind whipping their shins like an angry dog. The only vegetation up here was ground cover like gorse and heather, brittle and brown in the wintry air.

To the northeast, the Firth of Forth glimmered dimly in the fading light; below them lay the sweeping rise of the Salisbury Crags. Beyond their rocky slopes, the spires of the city reached skyward into the dim twilight as the gaslights went on, one by one. Pockets of yellow light glimmered in the gathering darkness as Edinburgh's "leeries," or lamplighters, tended to their evening duty.

"Where d'you s'pose he were standin' when he were pushed?" said Dickerson, coming to stand beside Ian on the windswept hillside.

"The body was found directly below here. Look around and see if you spot something. Look sharp, Sergeant—anything at all."

"Right you are, sir," Dickerson replied, and began dutifully scouring the area, bent over, nose close to the ground, like a ginger-haired bird dog on a scent.

Ian did the same, peering at the ground for anything unusual or out of place. A sense of stillness descended upon him, as it often did around dusk, a feeling at odds with the knowledge that a murder had taken place upon this spot. Just when he was beginning to think the entire expedition was foolish, Dickerson called out to him.

"Sir! Over here!"

Ian hurried over to where he stood, on the other side of the stony promontory. "What is it, Sergeant?"

"There." He pointed to the ground.

Ian peered at the spot indicated. Something in the muddy ground caught his eye. Plucking it out of the dirt, he held it up so Dickerson could see it.

"The missing button, sir?"

It was indeed the matching leather button missing from Stephen Wycherly's jacket.

"Well done! We've been rewarded more than I hoped for," Ian said, tucking the button into his rucksack as a few drops of rain leaked from the sky. "We'd better be off—I have a feeling the heavens are going to open up again."

His prediction was accurate. They had hardly gone a hundred yards when a clap of thunder shook the skies and a deluge of biblical proportions loosed itself upon the citizens of Edinburgh. By the time they reached the foot of Arthur's Seat, both men were drenched to the skin. Ian sent Dickerson home in a hansom cab, though it was a bit like closing the barn door after the horse has escaped.

When Hamilton reached his own flat on Victoria Terrace, the first thing he did was draw a deep, hot bath. He dragged himself out of it, too tired to eat, and threw himself into bed, where he dreamed of a dusky hillside populated by two faceless men locked in mortal combat at the edge of a precipice. The harder he tried to make out their faces, the more inscrutable they became. He tried to call to them, but no sound came from his throat.

He awoke to a great clap of thunder, jolting him into sudden alertness. Dragging himself from bed, he padded to the kitchen and brewed a cup of tea. He sat with it in front of the cold grate in the parlor, inhaling its warmth, while the storm raged outside his windows. As jagged streaks of lightning surged across the sky, his hands found paper and pencil. Still lost halfway between the world of dreaming and waking, he scribbled a few lines of poetry.

Crossing the Canongate

Ancient footsteps echo through corners of a town
accustomed to bloodshed
Suffering carved into paving stones
The cries of victims seep from its fortressed walls
falling like rain upon sleeping inhabitants
unwary and snug in their deep unknowing

His breathing relaxed as he wrote—committing his darkest thoughts to paper always seemed to ease his mind. Ian sat with his tea until the thunder and lightning subsided, slowly giving way to the steady thrumming of rain upon the rooftops. Returning to bed, he fell asleep to the rhythmic pounding of rain, sliding into a deep, dreamless slumber.

CHAPTER TEN

Bobby Tierney was ready for a fight. Stepping into the early winter twilight from his tiny flat on the London Road, he took a deep breath of fetid air and swaggered down the street, his head ringing with a thirst for violence. He was twenty-three, a member of Edinburgh's vast underclass of the underpaid, underfed, and overworked, and his limited brain contained but one desire on this fetid Friday: to pound someone. Anyone would do—Bobby held no particular personal grudges, only overriding malice toward all. His body surged with the kinetic energy of a young man in his fighting prime, in the most dangerous of circumstances—he had nowhere to go, no money to spend, and no one to check his wilder impulses. He had only his fists for entertainment, and tonight was not the first on which he had sauntered forth looking for trouble. He usually found it—in Edinburgh, trouble was not hard to find.

Robert James Tierney was an Irishman, part of the vast, desperate diaspora that dumped citizens of the Emerald Isle on the shores of any country that would take them during the devastating potato blight of the 1840s. In Ireland, it was referred to as simply the Great Famine, and those too poor to afford transatlantic passage to America tumbled onto boats headed for neighboring Scotland—only to find that country suffering its own crisis from a similar disaster in the Highlands. Proud sons of farmers whose families had tended the same land for generations streamed into the cities, inspiring anti-Irish sentiments from resentful Scots who feared their livelihood would be snatched by invading hordes of Hibernians.

Bobby was just about fed up with the attitude of the citizens of Edinburgh, as well as the squalor of life in "Little Ireland," the warren of crumbling and crowded tenements along the Cowgate. A good fight would clear the air, and clear his head, he thought as he strode into the center of the Old Town, headed for the Hound and Hare, where the ceilings were low, the conversation loud, and the beer flowed freely. He was sure to find some kindred souls there—angry young men spoiling for a brawl.

He threw open the door to the sound of alcohol-fueled conversation, laughter, and the clinking of glassware. The voices were loud and coarse, overwhelmingly male, the beer mugs thick and sturdy, made to survive long nights of heavy drinking. He looked around for his mate Mickey, a bullet-headed Irishman from Dublin with a foul mouth and a talent for head butting. Spotting him at the other side of the room, Bobby began shouldering his way through the press of bodies. The air was thick with cigarette smoke and beery breath, and Bobby's eyes burned as he pushed his way toward his friend.

He felt his foot tread upon another person's, and before he could see who owned the offended appendage, a hand clamped hard upon his shoulder. He turned and looked into the coldest pair of eyes he had ever seen. Anger Bobby could understand—rage smoldered in his own gut, an unquenchable flame born of injustice and social inequality. But these eyes did not burn with anger; they seemed to be of pure blue ice, immoveable as a frozen lake.

Before Bobby could murmur an apology, the man leaned in to him and whispered in his ear. "Meet me out back."

In spite of the din of the room, Bobby heard his words as clearly as if they had been etched in glass. There was something chilling in the man's controlled tone. He didn't seem to be especially upset, yet the words he spoke . . . Did he want to fight, or was this about something else? In any case, Bobby was ready for a fight, even though not yet primed with ale. *So much the better,* he thought; his reflexes would be keener, while his opponent's would be slowed by alcohol.

He waved at his friend Mickey, who had caught his eye and was gesturing madly for Bobby to join him. Ignoring the puzzled look on his friend's face, Bobby slipped through the crowd and out the side entrance. The pub was separated from its neighboring buildings by an alley—one of Edinburgh's many wynds and closes—a wynd being wide enough to accommodate a cart, whereas a close was an even narrower passageway. This one was a close, judging by the distance between its stone walls, which felt barely wide enough to contain Bobby's broad shoulders.

The thick stone walls filtered out much of the noise of the pub, the street curiously quiet as Bobby turned into the narrow passageway. The rain had temporarily abated, leaving only a thin, steady drip of water from the eaves into a rain barrel at the back of the building. The sound was rhythmic and mesmerizing—*plunk, plink, plunk, plink*—and somehow ominous. Somewhere a dog howled. A tightening in Bobby's stomach and constriction in his throat sounded a warning in his head.

Bobby considered turning back. He might have returned to the pub, claiming to himself that the allure of alcohol was stronger than the need for a fight. But he did not turn back. He took a deep breath as he reached the end of the alleyway and turned the corner into the dimly lit rear of the building. He had come out tonight for a fight, and a fight he would have.

It was the last mistake he would ever make.

CHAPTER ELEVEN

Derek McNair was in a bad mood. His friend Freddie Cubbins was late—again. Derek could see the faint glow of dawn in the eastern sky over Holyrood Palace. If the boys were to gather a decent Saturday breakfast from the rubbish bins behind Edinburgh's restaurants and pubs, it was best to start early, before they had been picked over by the city's army of street urchins and other vagrants. The storm that had pounded the city all night was lifting, the cobblestones glistening from days of rain.

Derek paced back and forth in front of the Tron Kirk, their appointed meeting spot, hands shoved into his makeshift trousers—a pair of men's work pants, far too large for him, clasped round his thin waist with a piece of twine he had stolen from a ragpicker's wheelbarrow. His shoes were equally ill-fitting, being several sizes too large, but they were thick-soled and in good condition. He had come by them through the Sisters of Charity's annual jumble sale; he found if he lingered until the sale was nearly over, the nuns would take pity on him and give him free clothing—and cakes if he was lucky.

His short woolen jacket and cloth cap were also from the nuns; Derek's clean features and keen, dark eyes made him a favorite of the more softhearted members of the gentler sex. He had learned what expressions to assume in order to wring pity and compassion from them, what to say, and how to say it. Indeed, there were many things a clever boy of ten might glean from a life on the streets.

Other boys of his age might have pondered the irony of living in a city boasting not one but two palaces scarcely a mile from each other and yet being forced to pick through trash bins in search of food. But Derek McNair was a practical sort of boy, not given to philosophizing or bemoaning his fate. His father was a drunkard and his mother a prostitute, and that's all there was to it. He had never known a stable home or a new pair of trousers, so he couldn't miss what he had never had. At least, that was the way Derek presented himself to the ragged set of urchins who also slept in alleys and doorways, living off what they could beg, borrow, or steal. If what went on in his head in quieter moments was somewhat more complex, he knew better than to share it.

Derek looked up and down the street, fingering the smooth stone in his pocket. He always kept a stone in his pocket. He never knew when it might be useful—in a fight, for breaking a shop window, or tossed to distract a fruit seller while plucking an apple from his cart. But mostly he kept it because he liked to roll it between his fingers when he was agitated or nervous.

He peered down the street again, but the only person in sight was Cob, the milkman, making his rounds with his big chestnut, Timothy. Derek liked Cob—he sometimes gave the boy a cup of milk in exchange for holding the reins—but the boy liked Timothy even more. Derek had a way with horses. When he stole apples, he would try to nab two—one for Timothy—and slip the horse the juicy treat while he held the reins as Cob delivered milk to his customers.

He had no apples in his pocket now, he mused as his stomach contracted with another hunger pang. Where the blazes was that good-for-nothing Freddie Cubbins? As Derek contemplated what he would say to his friend when he arrived, he heard quick footsteps and turned to see Freddie running toward him. Though they were both ten years old, Freddie was taller and half a stone heavier than Derek, with sandy hair and a foolish, friendly face. Derek was small and wiry and dark, and the undisputed leader of the two. Freddie was like a big, gangly puppy, whereas Derek was reserved and watchful. Arms crossed, he stood, frowning as Freddie approached, quite out of breath.

"Where ha' ye been?"

"I'm sorry, Derek, really I am. I overslept."

"Well, let's get to it afore there's naught left."

"Right," Freddie said, following Derek down the steps leading to the cluster of pubs underneath South Bridge. The weary winter sun was just cresting over the Firth of Forth as they began scanning the back alleys of Stevenlaw's Close.

"Oiy—over here!" Freddie called out as Derek pawed through a barrel of discarded oyster shells. "Come on—I got a good one!" Derek hurried over to where his friend was, in back of a pub. "Look at this, then!" Freddie said triumphantly, pulling back an oilcloth to reveal two only slightly chewed loaves of bread and half a nice, fat sausage.

"Wait," said Derek, pointing to what appeared to be a sack of clothes. "What's that?"

"It's a shoe," Freddie said, poking it. Then he turned pale. "Christ. It's . . . it's—"

"Jesus," said Derek, his face grim.

There, between the rubbish bins and the rain barrel nestled against the back wall, a man lay on his back, his sightless eyes staring up at the newly dawning day. Neither boy had ever seen a dead person before, but they both knew instantly what they were looking at.

"W-we 'ave tae get someone," said Freddie.

"We will," Derek replied as he backed slowly away from the corpse, all thought of breakfast vanished by their terrible discovery.

The boys scampered off, unaware they were being watched by a silent observer standing in the narrow space between two buildings in the back of the alley. Hidden in the shadows, the onlooker trembled with pleasure and pride at the sight of the body. It was hard to tear himself away from the scene, but the police would be arriving soon. He shivered with the thrill of it all. *Oh, there was so much evil in a man, one hardly knew where to begin . . .*

CHAPTER TWELVE

DCI Crawford couldn't believe it. He had barely sat down at his desk, and here was DI Hamilton, turning up again like a bad penny—on a Saturday, for Christ's sake. Crawford rubbed his eyes, burning from lack of sleep, hoping it was an apparition from his overwrought brain, but no—before him stood the infernal detective, bright eyed and eager.

"Good Lord, man, don't you ever sleep?"

"My 'little life is rounded with a sleep,' sir."

Crawford ground his teeth. "*Hamlet?*"

"*The Tempest.* You're not looking terribly chipper, sir, if you don't mind my saying so."

"I do mind," Crawford growled, pouring a cup of tea from the cracked blue ceramic pot on his desk. He had come in on his day off to clear up a bit of paperwork, and so far the station house was quiet as a tomb. The only sound penetrating the building's thick stone walls was the city's church bells tolling the hour. Ten o'clock. Crawford sighed as he stirred his tea. "I don't like you nearly as much as you might imagine, Hamilton."

His remark had no discernible effect upon the detective. "Have you seen the morning paper, sir?"

"I haven't even had my tea, for Christ's sake." To make the point, he took a large gulp, nearly scalding the skin off his tongue. He swallowed hard and glared at Hamilton. "Well? Are you going to tell me what is so very interesting *in* the paper, then?"

"I brought one so you could see for yourself, sir," Hamilton said, slapping a copy of the *Scotsman* upon the desk. There, on the front page, the headline screamed out:

MAN GARROTED AT THE HOUND AND HARE. GRISLY FIND BEHIND LOCAL TAVERN. ANOTHER CHALLENGE FOR EDINBURGH CITY POLICE—HOLYROOD STRANGLER STRIKES AGAIN?

Crawford quickly perused the rest of the story. The body, hidden behind a trash bin, was discovered early that morning by a couple of street urchins scrounging about for scraps. They claimed to have dutifully alerted the nearest constable, but evidently not before they went to the newsroom of the *Scotsman* to sell the scoop to the highest bidder. It wasn't the first time local reporters had word of a crime before the police, and Crawford figured it wouldn't be the last. All the reporters had informants on their payroll, many from the less savory strata of Edinburgh society.

"That's just what we need," he said, pushing the paper away. "A public panic. 'The Holyrood Strangler'—good Lord."

"What if the two deaths *are* related?" said Ian.

"We don't even know how this poor blighter died, for Christ's sake! It's bad enough that those damn reporters sacrifice facts in favor of cheap sensationalism—don't you make the same mistake, Hamilton."

Just then Constable Bowers stumbled into the room, his cheeks beet red. He was a very pale young man with blond eyebrows and a matching mustache. "Sir, there's been a mur—" He stopped, seeing the newspaper on Crawford's desk. "But I just—"

"Never mind, Constable," said the chief inspector, fighting the urge to giggle. While there was something comical about Bowers' red face and wild expression, Crawford suspected his impulse was more a result of his exhaustion. Laughing at a time like this would be utterly inappropriate, which only made the urge harder to resist. Digging his thumbnail into his palm, the chief inspector assumed a scowl. "Those wretched urchins raced to cash in on their knowledge before someone else found the body. Lucky for them, they seem to have arrived just before the paper went to press. No doubt they were well compensated. Is someone watching over the crime scene, Bowers?"

"Constable MacQuarrie, sir."

"I have a couple of questions, if you don't mind," said Ian.

"Are you putting yourself in charge of the investigation, Hamilton?" Crawford inquired drily.

"I feel certain the cases are linked."

"'There is no such uncertainty as a sure thing,'" Crawford muttered, taking another sip of tea.

"Robert Burns, sir?"

"Yes."

"Well done, sir."

Crawford sighed. Hamilton got on his nerves, yet something about him aroused fatherly instincts Crawford had never had occasion to express, being childless all these years. Much as he tried to dodge the emotion, he felt protective toward the damn fellow. And yet he was so . . . *irritating*. "Very well, Hamilton—get on with it so Constable Bowers can return to his post."

"What about the boys who found the body?" asked the detective.

"I'm right 'ere," came a voice from behind Constable Bowers.

The owner of the voice was a lad of about ten, with dark hair and deep-set eyes in a pale, intense face. The boy appeared curiously self-possessed for one so young. Though he was dressed in a mishmash of ill-fitting clothing obviously plucked from trash bins and charity shops, and in dire need of a bath and a haircut, there was something dignified and solemn about him.

"And who might you be?" DCI Crawford inquired sternly.

His attempt to intimidate failed. The boy met his gaze. "Derek McNair," he replied calmly. "I found the body along with me friend Freddie Cubbins."

"Did you now?" Crawford said. "And where is this Freddie Cubbins, may I ask?"

"He don' like coppers," Derek replied with a glance at Constable Bowers, whose flush deepened as he fidgeted with the brass buttons of his uniform.

"But you do?" said Crawford.

"Oh, I just love 'em."

The chief inspector leaned back in his chair and crossed his arms. "Well, that's good to hear. Isn't that a relief, Constable?" he added with a glance at Bowers.

The policeman looked at Ian with a pleading expression, then back at Crawford. "If you say so, sir."

"Oh, yes," said Crawford, rising from his chair. "One fears that street urchins like Master McNair here have an adversarial relationship with us, yet he assures us that isn't so. How very jolly—it warms the cockles of me heart, it does," he said, imitating the boy's accent. "It seems you have an equally delightful relationship with the press, giving them a chance to write about a murder before you bother to report it *to the police.*"

Derek shifted his feet and looked uneasily at Hamilton, who took a step forward.

"As the chief investigating officer in the Wycherly case, sir, I would like permission to question Master McNair."

Crawford wiped a few beads of sweat from his forehead and plopped himself back down in his chair. "Have at it, Hamilton—but mind he doesn't feed you a load of bosh and bunkum."

"Yes, sir."

"And while you're at it, see if you can persuade the little ruffian to inform the constabulary of a crime *before* he goes running off to the nearest two-bit newshound, would you?"

"Aye, sir," said Hamilton, laying a hand on the lad's shoulder. "Come along—we'll get you a hot cup of tea and some biscuits. Would you like that?"

The boy nodded warily, his dark eyes watchful. Crawford suspected he missed little—to survive on the streets, a boy needed his wits about him.

Crawford turned to Constable Bowers. "MacQuarrie is watching over the scene?"

"Yes, sir—the press are swarming over it like blackflies."

"Why don't you join him—and do your best to keep them away, Bowers."

"I'll be along shortly," said Hamilton. He led the boy from the room, leaving Constable Bowers behind.

Hands fluttering nervously at his sides, Bowers swallowed hard before saluting awkwardly. "I'll be off, then, shall I, sir?"

"Mind you close the door on your way out."

"Right you are, sir," said Bowers, closing the door behind him.

Crawford rubbed his temples and gazed out the window. The cobblestones glistened in the timid morning sun as it crested over the stolid stone buildings of the Old Town. Maybe Hamilton was on to something after all—this damn city had more secrets than it did alleyways. He shivered and pulled his jacket closer around his shoulders as he turned his attention to the pile of paperwork on his desk.

CHAPTER THIRTEEN

Ian Hamilton studied the intense young boy hunched over his mug, greedily slurping down cup after cup of strong "builder's tea." After going through half a tin of biscuits, he wiped his mouth, took a deep breath, and leaned back in the chair, thin hands crossed on his lap. He was a slight lad, his feet well off the ground as he perched upon the thick oak office chair, legs swinging back and forth underneath. They were in a little side office off the main room used for interrogations, small meetings, and—when the constables could get away with it—naps. Apart from a simple oak desk and matching chair, the room's only amenities were a cot beneath a single window overlooking Old Fishmarket Close, and a worn green hooked rug. The smell of orange peels and boiled turnips snaked through a crack in the yellowing windowpane.

"There now," Ian said, leaning against the desk, arms crossed. "Feel better?"

"Yer mate don' like me much," the boy remarked, wiping his mouth with his sleeve.

"DCI Crawford thinks you should have informed us before selling your story to the newspapers."

Derek licked his fingers. "At least they *pay* me fer information."

His lack of contrition was not surprising. The relationship between the constabulary and Edinburgh's lower classes left much to be desired. Ian sympathized with the lad, but he knew it would be a mistake to show it—the boy would just think he was weak, and try to manipulate him.

"Do you give them many stories?" he asked.

The boy shrugged. "A few, now an' then. None good as this 'un, though—makes me wish there were more murders, so help me God," he added, crossing himself.

"You're Catholic?"

Derek nodded. "I know it's wicked t'have such thoughts, but I can eat fer a week wi' what they paid me for this, and my mate Freddie as well."

Ian knew that was no exaggeration, and a pang of anger shot through him as he gazed at the boy's grubby face and mismatched clothing. *Scottish Enlightenment be damned,* he thought; Edinburgh could not even take care of her dispossessed children.

"Where is your friend now?"

"Can't say, really—could be anywheres. Though round about now, I expect he's havin' a bloody good nap."

"So you discovered the body at approximately what time?"

Derek cast his eyes hungrily about the room, as if looking for something else to devour. "It were just gone half past six."

"You're English—from the West Country?" England's west coast had a peculiar and unique accent, as rugged and twisty as the inlets staggered along its cliffs and beaches.

The boy studied his filthy hands, the nails blackened and cracked. "What's it to ye?"

"Your parents—where are they?"

Derek shrugged. "If you run into 'em, don't let on you've seen me."

Ian decided to test his indifference to see how much of it was real. If he gave the boy some personal information, Derek might reciprocate.

"My parents are dead."

"Yeah?" Derek said, swinging his legs faster beneath the chair. "I'd a been better off if someone 'ad taken a cudgel to me old man." He smiled. "But someone may yet—ye never know."

"Mine died in a fire."

"Decent, were they?"

"They were."

"Must be nice," the boy said without self-pity. Ian imagined life on the streets would knock that out of anyone soon enough.

"So what about you and Freddie—Cubbins, is it?" Ian said. "You get along on your own?"

The leg swinging resumed. "We do all right, with our other mates. Freddie an' me are pals, but there's others like us, y'know."

"Yes, I know," Ian said. He declined to mention that his aunt Lillian volunteered twice a week at the local charity, or that his parents had given generously to the Dean Orphanage. "So you found this—gentleman—a little after six thirty this morning?"

"That's wha' I said, weren't it? And he weren't no gentleman, neither."

"How do you know?"

"Them what goes to the Hound an' Hare are rough trade."

"Can you take me there?"

"Yer blokes took the body off to the morgue, but I can show ye where I found 'im."

"Good."

"Oh, I 'most forgot—found this near the body," the boy said, digging in the pockets of his oversized pants. "Here it is," he said, removing a soiled playing card and placing it on the desk. It was the four of clubs, with the same unusual design of frolicking skeletons as the card found on Stephen Wycherly. Ian snatched it up and slid it into his pocket. His head felt light as his brain spun. At the very least, the two victims were linked—that much was clear. Whether they shared the same killer

75

had yet to be determined. His hand shook as he reached for the tin of biscuits and held them out to his young visitor.

"Why don't you take another or two for the road?"

The boy peered hard at him, then grabbed a handful and shoved them into his pocket. "Right," he said. "What're we waitin' fer, then?"

Ian was not prepared for the scene outside the station house. A crowd had gathered, completely blocking the pavement in front of the building and spilling out into the High Street. He estimated it was well over a hundred people, mostly working class, with a few expensively dressed citizens sprinkled in. Some of them clutched copies of the *Scotsman*, which they waved at Ian, yelling and clamoring for his attention.

"Oiy! What're you lads gonnae do aboot the Holyrood Strangler?"

"The streets aren't safe nae mere!"

"When're ye gonnae catch 'em?"

"Good Lord," he muttered, pushing his way through, taking deep breaths to stave off the familiar panic. He hated crowds even more than enclosed spaces. *You are not going to pass out, Hamilton,* he told himself. *Keep breathing.* Just as he had nearly cleared the throng, a heavy hand clamped upon his shoulder, pulling him back in. Terror swept over him like a bolt of electricity, and he reacted blindly. Without looking, he spun and let loose a right hook, felt his knuckles collide with the bridge of a nose, heard the crunch of cartilage. A fist connected with his jaw, sending him to the cobblestones. The last thing he remembered was his head meeting the curb so hard that it bounced off as the din of voices receded into the blackness.

CHAPTER FOURTEEN

"Well done, Hamilton. Not only did you manage to get yourself knocked unconscious, but you started a street brawl."

Even with his eyes closed, Ian knew the voice belonged to DCI Crawford. He hoped if he didn't stir, the chief might leave him in peace, but Crawford was on a roll.

"I was just thinking we didn't have enough on our plate at the moment, and a good street fight would be just the ticket. You've out-done yourself this time, Hamilton."

Ian opened one eye. He was lying on the cot in the little back room where he had questioned Derek McNair, but there was no sign of the boy. Looming over him was DCI Crawford, and behind him stood a worried-looking Sergeant Dickerson. Ian's hand went to his forehead, where an egg-shaped lump was forming.

"Does it 'urt much, sir?" said Dickerson.

"I should bloody hope so," Crawford muttered. "Well, what are you standing there for? Get him a towel and some ice," he commanded the sergeant.

Dickerson scampered off to obey, and Crawford ran a hand through his sparse ginger hair. "Christ, Hamilton."

"I'm sorry, sir. It was—I mean, I was—"

"I *know* what happened," Crawford said. "There were plenty of eyewitnesses."

"Was anyone badly hurt?"

Crawford shook his head. "They dispersed before our lads could round up the troublemakers. That's what comes of freedom of the press," he said glumly. "That damn rag of a paper has everyone terrified of the bogeyman." He sat wearily on the side of the bed. "I hear you took a swing at someone."

"Yes, sir."

"Why?"

"Felt like I couldn't breathe, and I panicked."

"I asked you this once before, and I'm going to ask you again. Do you think that your—*problem*—will continue to interfere with your ability to function as a police officer?"

Ian opened his mouth to answer, but Crawford interrupted him. "It's no use saying that it doesn't, because it already has. The question is, will you be able to control it in the future? Because if not—"

"Yes, sir, I will."

"How?"

"I'll find a way."

"But—"

"I will *find* a way."

Crawford looked at him with something like pity, then sighed. "You're not the only one who looks bad if you fail."

"I understand that, sir."

He started to sit up just as Sergeant Dickerson returned with a towel and a bucket of ice.

"Lie down," Crawford commanded. "You're not going anywhere for at least thirty minutes. That's an order," he added before Ian could object. "And if you had any bloody sense, you'd go straight to hospital." Heaving himself to his feet, the chief inspector lumbered from the room.

"Here y'are, sir," said Dickerson upon his return, handing him the towel.

"Thanks," said Ian, lying down again.

Precisely thirty minutes later, he left the station house via the back entrance, and was surprised to see Derek McNair slouching against the side of the building, waiting for him. The boy grinned when he saw Ian's forehead.

"Oiy, ye got a nice one, din' ye?"

"How long have you been waiting?"

"Long enough ta miss tea. Ye can buy me somethin' t'eat."

After two helpings of fish-and-chips from a street vendor, the two wound their way through the streets of Old Town to the Hound and Hare. The back alley of the pub yielded little of interest, having been well trodden and picked over by members of the press. Ian didn't spy any of them loitering about—the body had already been taken down to the morgue pending further investigation.

"Where exactly did you find the body?" he asked Derek.

"It were right here," the boy replied, pointing to a spot between rubbish bins and a rain barrel.

"Was it covered in any way?"

"Nope, it were just lyin' out in the open, like."

So, Ian thought, no real effort had been made to hide the body— another similarity to the Wycherly case. Was the killer in a hurry, reckless, or just arrogant? Or maybe he enjoyed the idea of people finding his handiwork.

"Let's go inside," he said.

The pounding in his head was growing worse as he entered the pub, young McNair in tow. They picked their way across the unswept floor, last night's discarded peanut shells crunching beneath their feet. A couple of tables were occupied by middle-aged couples enjoying a quiet lunch—quite a different scene from the rowdy nighttime crowd.

The barkeep was a muscular, bald fellow with a thick Glaswegian accent—which is to say, he was nearly unintelligible.

"Afore ye ask, I dain't know who kilt yer fren," he said when he saw Ian, wiping down the counter with a soiled cloth. His lips did not move perceptibly when he spoke. Aunt Lillian had grown up in Glasgow, but years in Edinburgh had softened her accent considerably.

"He says he didn't notice yer friend leavin'," said Derek. Perched on a bar stool, legs swinging idly, he traced the stain patterns on the bar with his index finger.

"I speak Glaswegian," Ian replied curtly, though in truth he was struggling to make out the bartender's guttural dialect. The man swallowed his vowels, which sounded much like his consonants, swirling together deep in his throat.

Derek shrugged and helped himself to a pickled egg from a jar on the counter, swallowing it in two gulps.

"Oiy!" said the bartender, snapping his towel at the boy.

Ian dug a penny from his pocket and flipped it onto the counter. "And he isn't my friend—he's a murder victim."

The bartender pocketed the coin and began polishing beer mugs with the same grimy cloth. "'At's as may be—seen 'im 'ere afore, though."

"He's a regular?"

"Fridays, mostlah, yeah."

"Do you know his name?"

"Bobby, I thaink . . . yeah, 'at's it—Bobby. Dunno 'is last name."

"Did you see him speak to anyone while he was here?"

The bartender twisted his rag around the inside of a beer mug as he considered the question. Ian imagined the interior of the glass when he finished, filthier than before his ministrations. He had an aversion to dirt and disorder, something Lillian teased him about. He did his best to hide it from his fellow officers in the Edinburgh City Police, where anything could be a target of ridicule. Personal quirks were best kept to one's self.

"It wa' crowded, always is of a Friday," said the barkeep. "He spoke wi'a fellow I 'adn't seen afore. Can't say fer sure wha' aboot."

"Can you describe the man?"

"Dadn't get much of a look. Pale eyes, I 'member that."

Ian pulled out the playing card Derek McNair had given him and held it up for the bartender. "Have you ever seen this card before?"

Peering at it, the man shook his head. "Nay. That's from a right strange deck o' cards, mate."

"And you've never seen it before?"

"I tol' ye already, I nair seen it afore. I'm no' likely ta ferget a card lak that."

The door was flung open, and Sergeant Dickerson burst into the pub. The handful of patrons who were settled in for an early lunch glanced up apprehensively at the sight of a uniformed policeman.

"Beg pardon, sir," Dickerson panted, "but thought you might like t'know the victim has been identified. His name is—"

"Tell you what, Sergeant," Ian said, gripping him firmly by the arm, "why don't you and I take a stroll outside?"

He drew the baffled policeman to the front door and pushed him through, closing it behind him. The cooler outside air seemed to ease the incessant throbbing in his head. The wooden wheels of a passing vegetable seller's cart threw a spray of water from a nearby puddle at them, and Ian pulled the constable beneath the eaves of the pub. A feeble sun struggled to poke out from a dense cloud cover, but the rain had stopped—for now, at least.

"S-sir?" stammered Dickerson, his blue eyes wide.

"I imagine the patrons trying to enjoy their meal would appreciate not hearing the details of last night's murder. But more to the point, it's best not to reveal that information to the general public until we've had a chance to notify the poor blighter's family."

"Sorry, sir," said the sergeant. He looked as if he were about to cry. Ian figured he was about twenty-four years of age, but his pale complexion and ginger hair made him appear even younger. He remembered his own first year or so on the force, and laid a comforting hand on the sergeant's shoulder.

"Never mind—just remember next time, will you?"

"Right you are—sorry, sir."

"So what *is* his name, then?"

"Oh, right!" the sergeant exclaimed, flustered. He extracted a notebook from his pocket. "His name is Robert Tierney. His sister identified the body. Saw 'is picture in the paper an' all, y'know."

"Do you have an address for him?"

"She said he lived on the London Road."

"Well done," Ian said. "After we're through here, we'll—"

He was interrupted by an explosion of activity from within the pub—loud, angry yelling followed by the sound of chairs and tables being overturned. The door banged open, and Derek McNair shot through it, followed by an elderly man with a napkin still tucked into his shirt collar. It fluttered beneath his chin like a deranged clerical garment as he charged after the escaping street urchin, who dashed toward the heart of Old Town as fast as his thin legs would carry him.

"Stop, thief!" the man cried, waving a fist in the air. Seeing Hamilton and the sergeant, he yelled, "That boy picked my pocket!"

Ian and Sergeant Dickerson gave chase, but Derek ducked into the twisting warrens of alleys and wynds leading down to the Lawnmarket. Finding anyone in that maze was next to impossible. Ian and Dickerson gave it their all before admitting defeat and trudging back up the hill to the pub. The irate customer stood waiting, the white linen napkin still dangling beneath his chin like a flag of surrender.

"That wretched urchin stole my wallet!" he sputtered.

"If you'd like me to, I can accompany you to the station where you can fill out a report," Sergeant Dickerson said, panting heavily from the burst of exertion. Ian too was out of breath, and his headache had returned.

The old gentleman's face turned scarlet. "No, I do *not* want to fill out a 'report'! I want my bloody wallet back—now!"

"How much was in it?" Ian inquired, fearing the elderly fellow might succumb to a fit of apoplexy.

He glared at Ian. Startled wisps of hair stood up from his nearly bald pate, wind-borne like small gray sails. "Ten shillings tuppence."

"Very well, here you are," Ian said, fishing money from his pockets. Counting out that amount, he handed it to the bewildered gentleman.

"I can't take this," the man said.

"Think of it as a loan," said Ian, "pending the return of your wallet."

"When it's found—*if* it's found—there'll be no five quid and change in it," Sergeant Dickerson muttered, but the man grinned, showing a broad set of teeth as gray as his hair.

"You are a scholar and a gentleman, sir, and I am forever indebted to you," he said, giving a little bow.

The bartender emerged from the pub, his face scarlet. "I'll gae the blighter a skelpit lug!"

"You'll have to catch him before you can cuff his ears," the elderly man remarked dourly before following him back into the building.

Dickerson shook his head, still breathing heavily. "You can't cover fer that little ruffian forever. I've seen 'is kind afore, and—"

"Please, Sergeant, not now," said Ian. His head ached, his legs were wobbly, and he yearned for the sanctuary of his flat—to close the curtains, lock the door, and be alone.

He headed toward the pub as Dickerson muttered something under his breath. Ian spun around. "Tell me something, Sergeant."

Dickerson's eyes widened, his face slack. "Yes, sir?"

"Have you had occasion to live on the streets?"

"Well, no, sir—"

"Then do me the favor of allowing me to conduct this investigation in my own way."

"A'course, sir—sorry, sir."

Ian marched back into the pub, leaving the sergeant standing in the street amidst the clatter of horses' hooves and the call of fruit vendors and vegetable peddlers.

"Get your fresh cress—two bunches a penny!"

"Figs—plump and ripe! Figs for sale!"

"Neeps an' tatties—freshest in the land!"

After a moment, Dickerson brushed himself off, straightened his uniform, and followed Hamilton back inside the Hound and Hare.

From across the crowded street, another pair of eyes watched—seeing yet unseen, taking advantage of the anonymity a city like Edinburgh could provide.

CHAPTER FIFTEEN

Ian went straight from the Hound and Hare to the morgue to examine Bobby Tierney's body. The smooth, even bruise on the neck indicated ligature strangulation. Carefully measuring the ligature mark, Ian noted that it was exactly the same as on Stephen Wycherly's neck, just under an inch wide. The deep purple indentation was regular and smooth, which meant the weapon used was not a belt or anything with a buckle or a pattern that could be transferred onto the skin.

Tierney was powerfully built—even in death, his muscular body seemed to bulge with menace. Edinburgh was full of Bobby Tierneys—angry young Irishmen with nothing much on their minds except getting pissed and pummeling somebody. And yet someone had gotten the better of him—rather quickly, by the look of it. Examining the body closely, Ian found no indication of a prolonged struggle, no other bruises, cuts, or contusions.

Looking at Tierney's face, the skin chalky white in the pale light streaming in from the tall windows, Ian felt hollow inside. Here was youth, strength, vitality—reduced to a lump of flesh on a slab in a damp city morgue. His initial exhilaration at being the lead detective in the case melted as he pondered the mystery of who would take such a life—not only who, but also how and why. Tierney was a bar brawler, the kind of man who might be on the receiving end of a beating, if he was unlucky enough to meet his match, but this was something different. Whoever killed him had done it quickly, coldly, and, Ian suspected, had come prepared. Was Bobby targeted, or simply unlucky?

Ian pondered the question as he headed to his meeting with George Pearson at the White Hart Inn, a venerable establishment just north of the Grassmarket. Popular with both students and dons at the University of Edinburgh, the White Hart was Edinburgh's oldest public house, dating back to the early 1500s, though it was allegedly much older.

The din of voices was as thick as the smoke hanging in the air of the saloon bar when he spied Pearson sitting alone in the far corner, a pint at his elbow. He was engrossed in a thick book with an ancient-looking green leather cover, his prominent eyes appearing even larger behind wire-rimmed spectacles.

The clientele at the White Hart was as varied as the conversation. Ian wove his way past tables of people, catching snippets of conversations on politics, sports, business, and love. In addition to university students and professors, the darker corners of the room were occupied by courting couples. A few barristers in crisp suits hovered over a table near the bar, arguing amidst a thick blue haze of tobacco.

Pearson spotted Ian through the crowded room and waved him over. "I say, I rarely come here on Saturday—it's rather an assault on the ears, isn't it?" Pearson observed as Ian took a seat across from him.

"It is a bit loud."

"What happened to you?" the librarian said, indicating Ian's head.

"I had occasion to test the law of gravity. I am happy to report it is intact."

The librarian gave one of his curious, high-pitched giggles. "Allow me to buy the first round. What are you having?"

"Same as you—heavy ale, is it?"

"Coming right up," Pearson said.

Ian watched the librarian shoulder his way to the bar. A young couple at the next table with a small white terrier at their feet smiled at Ian, their faces soft with the flush of young love. Would they look back on the sweetness of this day years hence and wonder how it had evaporated so quickly? Sweeping dark thoughts aside, he watched Pearson weave through the crowded tables.

Pearson was a strange fellow, but Ian saw his potential as a resource. Ian's first instinct was to distrust his enthusiasm—but there was something endearing about him, an innocence and complete lack of guile. Of course, he wanted a little too much to be of assistance—Ian would have to prevent the librarian from inserting himself too deeply into his investigation.

Pearson returned with two foaming pints, setting them on the thick oak table before sliding his bulky form into his seat. To say he was stocky would imply an athletic build; it would be more apt to call him pudgy. Everything about him suggested softness: his white hands with their dimpled knuckles, his round cheeks, and full lips. Even his eyes were soft as a doe's—large, round, and golden brown, with thick lashes. He carried himself with the air of one unaccustomed to physical exertion, his belly protruding, sunken in the chest.

"So," he said, placing a pint in front of Ian, "I brought you a nice selection from my personal library. Perhaps you think I'm foolish—"

"'A fool thinks himself to be wise, but a wise man knows himself to be a fool.'"

Pearson beamed. "*As You Like It*, act five, scene one! Pardon me for saying so, but I wouldn't have expected a policeman to be conversant in the works of the Bard."

"My mother was a schoolteacher, and my father rather fancied himself an amateur actor." Ian didn't mention his own literary ambition; it might sound pretentious to a librarian.

"You used the past tense. Your parents are . . . ?"

"Both dead."

87

"Mine as well."

"What did you bring me?" Ian said, gulping down some ale, cool and bitter and tasting of the earth. He wanted to avoid a personal discussion—naturally wary of intimacy, Ian liked to keep his worlds separate. And the subject of his parents' death had sharp, pointed edges he did his best to avoid.

"I thought we might begin with this one," said Pearson, extracting a book from a leather satchel at his feet. He opened it, gently turning the pages. No lover caressed a woman with more tenderness than George Pearson touching the pages of his book. He gazed at it, his eyes glistening. "I found this in a secondhand bookshop in London. It's quite rare—I doubt the chap knew what he had."

Ian looked at the frontispiece, the title engraved in a florid script. *Inside the Criminal Mind*, by Guillaume de La Robert.

"He was a colleague of the great François Vidocq. This is the book I mentioned yesterday."

"What makes it so unusual?"

"It is practically impossible to find any extant copies. As for the rest—well, perhaps you'd better have a look at it and tell me what you think. I hope it doesn't disappoint you."

"'Expectation is the root of all heartache.'"

"Ah—that quote is of doubtful attribution, I'm afraid. Many ascribe it to the Bard, but it doesn't appear anywhere in his works."

"You are a fount of information, Mr. Pearson."

"In all modesty I must remind you I am a reference librarian," Pearson said, reaching into his satchel. "I brought some other books as well."

"Why don't we just stick with this one for now?"

"As you wish," Pearson replied, sounding a bit put off.

"I do want to see the others," Ian assured him, "but I doubt I'll have much time for reading."

"Because of the case you're on?" Pearson said in a low voice, as though someone might be listening in. "The Holyrood Strangler?"

Ian took a long draft of ale, surprised at how much he wanted—needed—it.

"That's what the press are calling him, but that's not—"

"I read in the paper there's been another murder—terrible thing." Pearson shook his head, but his eyes shone. "Do you think they're connected?"

"I can't really comment."

His face keen with interest, the librarian leaned in so close, Ian could see the broken capillaries on the bridge of his nose. "There's a madman out there," he said.

"And I'm going to stop him," the detective answered confidently.

But the words had a hollow ring. In spite of the crisp, bitter ale, the comfortable background din of voices, the crackling of logs in the fireplace as they shot sparks into the air, to be sucked up the chimney, Ian was seized by an unwelcome thought: he might very well fail to apprehend this killer before he struck again.

CHAPTER SIXTEEN

A crowd had already gathered at the Theatre Royal by the time Lillian Grey climbed out of a hansom cab, clutching her ticket to the night's event. She was glad she had bought hers in advance when she saw the throng of people at the box office, pushing and craning their necks, some shouting in their fervor to acquire a ticket.

They had little chance, judging by the "Sold Out" sign plastered on the front of the building. Beneath the black-and-white banner was the colorful promotional poster displaying the cause of all the hubbub. It was Saturday night, but that alone would not account for the box-office frenzy. The reason for the mad rush leered down at his fans from the poster, five times larger than life, his perfect teeth and dark lacquered hair reflecting the dazzling white of his shirt collar and raven-black frock coat.

MONSIEUR JACQUES LE COQ, HYPNOTIST EXTRAORDINAIRE!
MASTER OF OCCULT ARTS AND HUMAN HEARTS
ONE NIGHT ONLY
COME IF YOU DARE! (NO CHILDREN OR LADIES PRONE TO FAINTING, PLEASE)

Lillian shook her head at the flowery prose, calculated to titillate—what better way to attract ladies prone to fainting than to caution them against coming? Perhaps this would be an evening to remember after all, she thought as she gathered the skirts of her gown to climb the front staircase. The wicked weather plaguing the city for the past week had lifted. It was a brilliant night, a wide, grinning moon casting its white light on the neoclassical architecture of New Town. The buildings were ghostly in the pallid light, hovering over the gleaming cobblestones as if waiting for something. A shiver slithered up Lillian's spine as she ascended the wide steps. The theater had been rebuilt just three years ago; the gold trim on its wide columns glittered, the gilt frames on the giant mirrors in the lobby shone, and the plush crimson carpets were deep and soft underfoot.

Inside, the aroma of expensive perfume hung in the air, mingling with the clinking of bracelets and champagne glasses, and the rustle of silk. Patrons bustled about the lobby, purchasing last-minute glasses of spirits or sweets from the refreshment kiosk, their faces glistening with excitement. Lillian was quite caught up in the mood as she picked her way through the crowd to her box seat, in a private booth over the stage. Alfie had been on the board of the Theatre Royal, and everyone had treated her kindly since his death, insisting she keep their box seats. They did not need to insist—Lillian loved the theater and performances of any kind.

What a pity her nephew was unable to join her—he had sent her a message saying that with a strangler loose in the city, he needed to work. *All work and no play, that boy,* she thought as she settled herself into the red velvet seat. In fact, she was rather put out by his abrupt cancellation, though she would not breathe a word of it to Ian. She was a woman who rarely minced words, but the one impression Lillian Grey wished to avoid giving—even to her own nephew—was that she was a lonely old woman.

Still, she thought as she raised her opera glasses, it was a shame Ian wasn't here to take in the colorful crowd. They were not all the glittering and glamorous. In addition to Edinburgh's intellectual and cultural elite in their furs and silks, there were merchants, innkeepers, and bankers, all dressed in their Sunday best. Some of the younger fellows looking miserable, half-choked in stiff white-shirt collars. The back stalls were filling up with a rougher sort—tradesmen, blacksmiths, dockworkers, their hands as rough and callused as their voices, scraped raw by years of wind and salt air. Among the women, Lillian spotted a few who looked like ladies of the night. Their cheeks were too vividly painted, the ribbons in their hair too gaudy, their laughter burst from throats burned by whisky.

The orchestra members finished tuning their instruments as latecomers hurried to their seats. The din of voices dimmed to hushed expectation as the conductor took the podium, resplendent in black tails and white tie. He peered at his musicians sternly, lifting his baton to give the downbeat, and the orchestra struck up a popular march. That was followed by a darkly mysterious waltz Lillian did not recognize. She fancied it was from the Continent—French perhaps.

As the dying strains of the waltz lingered in the air, the heavy crimson curtain covering the stage drew back to reveal a lone figure silhouetted in a single blue spotlight. The crowd sat mute, transfixed, all eyes upon the man standing at the back of the stage, his features obscured by the darkness around him. He took a step forward, and suddenly the stage was illuminated in a flash of brilliant hues—azure, indigo, gold and amber, vermillion and amaranth—all blinding in their intensity. The women gasped, and the men sat up straighter in their seats. By the time the man onstage had taken two more steps forward, he had them.

The spell had begun.

CHAPTER SEVENTEEN

Four pints later at the White Hart, Ian's intention to leave early had disappeared in a haze of alcohol. Now guilt and remorse seized him—he had canceled an engagement with his aunt, to jabber away with a man he barely knew.

"I regret that I must be going," he said, rising unsteadily to his feet. He felt fuzzier than usual, perhaps due to his head injury. He suspected it had been unwise to drink with such abandon.

"May I accompany you to your destination?" Pearson said eagerly. "Where are you headed?"

"Just home."

"Where is that, if you don't mind my asking?"

"Victoria Terrace," Ian replied, the four pints of Scottish ale washing away any caution he might have had about revealing his address. After all, the man *was* a librarian, he thought as he donned his cloak.

"Capital! It's on my way. I'll walk with you, if that's agreeable."

Ian could think of no reasonable objection, so the two men ventured forth into the chill February night.

Like many great cities, Edinburgh had a variety of moods. It could be warm and welcoming, in the boisterous, dangerous way of Scottish cities, sly and beckoning as a sloe-eyed whore, or grim and foreboding.

Tonight there was a feeling of expectation in the air, which had turned blustery and cold. A winter storm was brewing in the eastern sky, and as they walked, the wind from the Firth of Forth blew in gusts, curling around the stone buildings like a cat in search of a soft place to rest.

The two men wound their way through the streets, tugging at their cloaks to keep the wind from yanking them away. Conversation became impossible as the blizzard increased its fury, blowing patches of snow at their faces, whipping their half-closed eyes. It was too late for the omnibuses to be running; Ian looked around for a hansom cab, but they were all taken.

When they reached South Bridge, he bade Pearson good night. He supposed the librarian would like to be invited in for a cup of tea, but they lived in different directions, and Ian had had enough company. His tolerance for other people was limited; he longed for the solitude and quiet of his flat. Still, he didn't envy the poor fellow as he watched his bulky figure retreat into the darkness.

Safely inside, Ian pulled the heavy drapes on the front window closed before taking a lighted taper out to the pantry. Alone at last, he took what felt like the first deep breath of the day, savoring the feel of the plush carpet under his feet.

He had decorated the rooms carefully, with Aunt Lillian's help, filling the place with Turkish fabrics and Persian rugs. It was a source of comfort and pleasure, a retreat from the hustle and bustle of the city. He had chosen Victoria Terrace for its central location but relative isolation—nestled in the side of the rocky hillocks of the Old Town, the terrace was accessible from the Grassmarket via a steep stone staircase. The narrow pavement in front of the crescent of buildings carried no traffic other than the residents of the terrace. The closest thoroughfare for carts, carriages, and horses was Victoria Street, fifty feet below.

His throat parched from wind and alcohol, Ian needed a drink of water. He also realized he was ravenous. Clutching the candle in its pewter holder, Ian opened the door to the kitchen and stepped inside.

As he reached up to light the gas lamp, he was aware of something out of the corner of his eye. He turned around. Sitting upon the counter and nibbling at a few stray bread crumbs was a small gray mouse. Ian blinked at the sight; it was not a rat—Edinburgh had legions of those—but a bloody *mouse*. It looked up at Ian calmly, as if taking measure of him.

Ian gazed at the creature, realizing he was still quite drunk.
The mouse resumed eating.
Ian raised a declamatory hand and began to recite Burns.

"Wee, sleekit, cow'rin, tim'rous beastie,
O, what a panic's in thy breastie!"

The mouse finished eating the bread crumb and moved on to the next one. Ian continued his recitation.

"Thou need na start awa sae hasty
Wi bickering brattle!"

The mouse regarded him without rancor, chewing contemplatively.
"There's no panic in your breastie," Ian muttered, thinking how pleased Lillian would be that he could still recite the opening stanzas in the original Scots dialect. He had learned it back in school, but he had a curious ability to retain and remember almost everything he heard.
The mouse sat on its haunches, sniffing the air.
Ian took a step toward it. The mouse glared at him, flicking its tail irritably, its cheeks stuffed with bread crumbs.
"So," Ian mumbled to himself, "a mouse's home is its castle, eh?" He seized a loaf of bread from the bin and a cold joint of beef from the icebox, and left the kitchen. The mouse watched from its perch on the counter.

"There are some scones in the bread box," Ian said as he closed the door behind him. "Enjoy them, because tomorrow I'm getting a mousetrap."

Soon the fire was blazing in the grate, and after his repast, Ian settled into an armchair with the book George Pearson had given him. Outside, the storm raged on. Sheets of sleet hurtled themselves against the windows, clattering like the tapping of devilish fingers upon the glass. Ian got up and pulled the drapes more tightly closed, but he could still hear the sleet pummeling the windowpanes. *Rat-a-tat-tat, rat-a-tat-tat.* He settled back in the armchair and opened the book. He perused the first paragraph, but his eyelids were heavy, and he struggled to stay awake. It had been a long day roaming about in the damp, chill air, and now that his body was at rest, sleep worked hard to claim him. The leaping flames in the fireplace were mesmerizing, the room was warm, the chair soft—even the rattle of sleet upon the windowpanes added to the soothing atmosphere. *Rat-a-tat-tat . . .*

The fire was everywhere, all around him, and yet he felt no heat. He was standing in the front parlor of his parents' house, the conflagration already in full fury. The flames roared and danced, licking as high as his head, and he stood there as if he had been nailed to the spot. He could hear his mother's voice calling him, and strained to make out what direction it was coming from.

"Ian! Ian, help me, please! Where are you?"

He started off in one direction, but as soon as he did, the voice seemed to be coming from behind him.

"Ian, darling, help! Save me!"

He wheeled around and headed toward the voice, only to hear her cries coming from a completely different part of the house. Windowpanes burst and exploded from the heat; great timbers crashed down from the walls, blocking his path, but still he seemed immune to the flames all around him. A blazing ceiling beam tumbled down above him—he ducked in time to avoid it hitting his head, but the burning wood grazed his shoulder, knocking him to the ground. He fell beneath it, trapped by its weight, the fire searing his left shoulder and back as his ears filled with the sound of his own screams. Through the gathering flames, he saw his mother walking slowly toward him.

Ian sat up abruptly in the chair, wide awake, expecting to see his mother standing in front of him. But the room was empty, the fire in the grate having burned down to glowing embers. His shoulder ached and throbbed, and as he reached to rub it with his right hand, the second stanza of the Burns poem popped into his head.

I'm truly sorry man's dominion
Has broken Nature's social union,
An' justifies that ill opinion
Which makes thee startle
At me, thy poor, earth born companion
An' fellow-mortal!

The only sound other than the occasional crackle of the dying fire was the storm outside, as the wind whistled and rattled the windowpanes. Had man's dominion broken Nature's social union in Edinburgh? he wondered. Or was Nature herself to blame, and man just a part of a wider circle of savagery?

Anger swept over him. He realized with a shock that his fury was directed not at the person responsible for his parents' death, but at *them*. He was furious at them for dying, for leaving him behind to worry about his emotionally crippled brother. At that moment, he despised

Donald, too—might it have been better if his brother also had perished in the fire? Or even Ian himself?

He reproached himself for such thoughts. He recalled the sweet, carefree years in the Highlands. Were they, too, just an illusion, seen through the mist of time and memory? The story of his family's life seemed to be missing chapters. Ian rose from his chair and pulled aside the curtains, peering into the darkness. Snow swirled around the gas lamps on Victoria Terrace, creating a halo of white around the yellow flames.

One thing was certain: time did not move backward. He could never reclaim those days; all he could do was hold them close and lurch into the future. He had but one thing, he thought grimly: the chase. While he was engaged in the pursuit of criminals, everything else fell away, and he experienced a sense of purpose. He gazed into the darkness and waited for the coming dawn.

CHAPTER EIGHTEEN

The man on the stage of the Theatre Royal spread his arms wide as he stepped into the glare of the spotlight. Tilting his head back so the beam focused directly upon his glistening black hair, he peered into the darkened theater. Every woman in the audience felt he was looking directly at her, and every man shifted uncomfortably in his seat. Monsieur Jacques Le Coq greeted his captivated audience with a smile, the light glinting off his broad whalebone-white teeth. Every woman in the room felt her heart flutter, and every man felt his sink. The hypnotist was a fine figure of a man, elegant in his black tails and crisp white cummerbund. His hair was thick and glossy as a colt's coat, his shoes polished to a dazzling sheen. But it was more than that. His presence onstage commanded attention. Lillian herself was quite taken by the man's seductive power, caught up in it in spite of herself.

"How many of you believe in the power of the human mind?" he said, his voice low and rich and heavily accented, showing its Gallic roots.

A murmur rippled through the audience. He held up his hand, and silence fell over the crowd.

"No state is so natural to the human condition as that of longing," he declared, strolling to the right side of the stage. "When we are hungry, we long for food—and as soon as we are sated, we think wistfully of our next meal. Poetry, theater, and song exist because of longing—our myths and stories are full of separated lovers, ambition-crazed kings, and nobly striving heroes. Longing ignites the poetry in our souls like nothing else—not love, not Nature, not domestic tranquility. Many of you are here tonight because you long for something, though you may not know what it is."

He gazed upon the ladies in the front row, who tittered and blushed. He strode to the other side of the stage and looked up at the box seat where Lillian sat. She felt the heat rise up her own neck, her cheeks burning.

"But the power of the human mind has not been sufficiently explored," he continued. "It has the power to overcome not only longing but also pain and suffering and a multitude of life's travails. Who among you believes in the power of the human mind?"

"I do!" shouted a young man in the third row, and all eyes turned toward him. He was seated next to a very pretty young woman in a light blue dress, her face garlanded with ringlets of light brown hair. It was obvious he meant to impress her. There were titters among the audience members, and several of the ladies fluttered their fans in front of their faces, hiding all but their eyes.

Monsieur Le Coq smiled. "And what might your name be?"

"Phillip!" the young man replied, his voice faltering as people twisted around in their seats to get a good look at him.

"A name fit for a king," the hypnotist remarked drily, his audience responding with a burst of nervous laughter. The young man joined in, but his eyes showed more apprehension than amusement.

"Would you like to help me demonstrate the power of the human mind, Phillip?" Monsieur Le Coq inquired genially, rubbing his hands together.

"I should be delighted!" Phillip responded a bit too loudly, his voice tight and high with tension.

"Very well," the hypnotist replied, rewarding the ladies with another dazzling smile. "Come right on up here, if you would, Phillip."

Phillip rose from his seat, straightened his cummerbund, and drew a hand over his already impeccably combed hair. Seizing his young lady's hand, he kissed it with a flourish before squeezing between the seats of the other patrons to get to the aisle. Some of the ladies around him sighed at the gallant gesture, while their husbands frowned at its theatricality. He was a nice-enough-looking young man, if a bit slight, with a firm chin and a fine, aristocratic nose. As he ascended the steps to the proscenium, he caught the toe of his shoe and tripped, but quickly regained his balance, climbing briskly to the stage.

Monsieur Le Coq met him with a firm handshake and a friendly pat on the shoulder. "Ladies and gentlemen, our first brave volunteer of the evening—Phillip!"

The audience responded with a smattering of applause. Tension hung in the air, thick as an Edinburgh fog. The audience leaned forward, a great curious beast, its attention focused upon the proscenium, as a stagehand carried a simple, straight-backed chair onto the stage. Monsieur Le Coq nodded, and the stagehand withdrew silently into the wings.

Next to the hypnotist, with his powerful shoulders and leonine mane of dark hair, Phillip looked spindly and ill-nourished. Lillian thought that some of Monsieur Le Coq's effectiveness derived from his impressive, muscular build. He seemed to dwarf the young man who stood before him, gaining in stature as the other appeared to grow smaller.

"Now then, Phillip," he declaimed in his deep, resonant voice, which carried with ease to the back stalls, "how are you this evening?"

"Very well, thank you," the young man replied, though he was looking less well by the minute. His left knee was shaking, and his jaw was clenched; beads of sweat dotted his forehead.

"Relax!" Monsieur Le Coq commanded, clasping both hands upon Phillip's shoulders. At first the gesture appeared to startle him, but as the hypnotist's eyes met his, all the tension drained from the young man's body. Lillian feared he might fall if not for the firm grasp of the hypnotist holding him upright.

He continued to gaze into Phillip's eyes, until the young man's face relaxed and his eyelids began to droop. His eyes closed and his body went limp as he fell forward. A gasp rose from the audience, but Monsieur Le Coq caught him, adroitly lowering his insensate form into the chair. The hypnotist turned to the audience, ignoring the seemingly unconscious Phillip, who sat slumped over as if asleep.

"The power of the human mind is a wondrous thing. Even now, we can only begin to imagine what it is capable of."

In the third row, the young woman in the blue dress and light brown curls bit her knuckles, but Monsieur Le Coq gave her a reassuring smile.

"I assure you, no harm will come to the young man you see before you. He is neither asleep nor unconscious; he is merely in a state of deep relaxation. In such a state he is highly open to suggestion. Allow me to demonstrate." He turned to the man in the chair. "Phillip, do you know any poetry by heart?"

Phillip nodded, his eyes still closed.

"Would you mind reciting it for me?"

Without opening his eyes, Phillip raised his head and recited in a loud, firm voice.

> "That fawn-skin-dappled hair of hers,
> And the blue eye
> Dear and dewy,
> And that infantine fresh air of hers!
> To think men cannot take you, Sweet,
> And enfold you,

Ay, and hold you,
And so keep you what they make you, Sweet!"

"Robert Browning, if I'm not mistaken?" the hypnotist asked with a smile.

Phillip nodded.

"Well done, Phillip," said Monsieur Le Coq. "Would I be correct in assuming that these lines apply to your charming young lady?"

Again Phillip nodded without opening his eyes.

Lillian gazed down at the young woman in the third row, who was blushing furiously, trying to hide her face with her handkerchief.

"You may open your eyes now if you wish," said the hypnotist. The young man did so, staring blankly in front of him, his gaze unfocused, as if he were in a trance. "Very good so far, Phillip—you are an excellent subject. Would I be correct in assuming that you are able to bark like a dog should the occasion arise?"

Phillip nodded.

"Would you be so kind as to do so?"

Without hesitation, the young man emitted a series of short, percussive barks, such as might be made by a terrier or a spaniel. Several people in the audience tittered.

"And might you also cluck like a chicken?" inquired Monsieur Le Coq.

The young man immediately favored the onlookers with an imitation of a chicken, clucking and cooing quite credibly.

"I should like to see you move like one as well—can you do that?" asked the hypnotist.

Phillip sprang from his chair and moved about the stage in a crouched position, waving his arms like wings, pecking and scratching at the stage as if it were the dirt floor of a chicken coop. The audience roared with laughter as the hypnotist pretended to feed him a fat, juicy worm, which Phillip sucked greedily into his mouth, swallowing it with gusto. The young woman in the third row was not so amused, however; she wore an expression of astonished horror.

"Well done indeed!" said Monsieur Le Coq. "And now, one final test, with your permission." He withdrew a long, thin needle from his frock coat. "Would you allow me to insert this into your arm?"

A gasp arose from the crowd—several women cried, "No!"

The hypnotist raised his hand for silence. "I promised earlier that Phillip would come to no harm, and I beg you to trust me." He turned back to the young man onstage. "Do I have your permission to insert this needle into your flesh?"

Still staring straight ahead, Phillip nodded. The hypnotist whispered something into his ear, and he nodded again.

"What I have just told him," Monsieur Le Coq said to the audience, "is that this will not hurt one bit. And now allow me to demonstrate the power of the human mind. Phillip, would you mind removing your coat and rolling up your sleeve?"

The young man did as he requested, exposing a thin white forearm. The hypnotist said firmly, "As I said, you will not feel this at all."

With that he brandished the needle with a flourish, the thin steel flashing silver in the bright stage lights. A murmur went up from the crowd as he carefully inserted the needle into Phillip's forearm. To Lillian's surprise, there was no bleeding save for a tiny droplet of blood that the hypnotist wiped away with a clean white handkerchief. He pushed farther until the needle went clear through Phillip's arm and out the other side. All the while, the young man's face remained passive and his body showed no signs of distress. He neither flinched nor grimaced as the needle pierced his flesh.

"Now then," said Monsieur Le Coq, "how do you feel?"

"Fine, thank you," he replied in a flat but clear tone.

"Very good, Phillip—well done," said the hypnotist, drawing forth the needle carefully. He turned to the crowd. "Ladies and gentlemen, please give a warm round of applause to our brave volunteer, Phillip!"

The ovation was loud and sustained, an expression of relief as much as approbation. People grinned and elbowed one another, glad to be rid of the anxiety of worrying about the man onstage, the surrogate for everyone in the room.

The rest of the act was variations upon the initial demonstration. Monsieur Le Coq called up volunteers, singly and in groups, to recite poetry, sing songs, or do various foolish things. Occasionally he had someone stand on a chair and pretend it was a cliff, demonstrating how the person experienced real fear.

"Ladies and gentlemen, these are not actors—they are people very much like yourselves. What you are witnessing is the untapped power of the human mind. If you *believe* something is so, then it is so."

Lillian watched the entire performance with interest, though to her nothing had quite the power of the needle going through a man's arm without his seeming to feel any pain at all. She wondered if there might be an application in the field of medicine, to lessen the suffering of patients in pain. But then, she reasoned, the whole thing might very well be a trick, with a fake needle, and Phillip could be an accomplice. Still, she was sorry when the show was over, and applauded enthusiastically with the rest of the audience, feeling that it was indeed a pity her nephew had to miss this . . .

Back in his dressing room, the hypnotist's shoulders drooped as the fervor that had animated his body drained away, leaving him limp and pale with exhaustion. He removed his elegant frock coat, loosening his cummerbund, soaked with sweat. Unbuttoning his damp shirt, he peeled it from his body and tossed it upon the green velvet love seat in the far corner of the room. He sank into a chair in front of the dressing room mirror, lit a cigarette, and stared at his own reflection. His eyes were dead; he could see no soul behind them.

Oh, there was so much evil in a man, one hardly knew where to begin . . .

He sucked on the cigarette, inhaling deeply and closing his eyes as the drug flooded his system. Tobacco was his one consolation, his sole comfort in a wicked world. There was a knock upon the door, and he took another deep drag before answering.

"Yes?"

"It's Calvin, sir."

"Go away." The French accent was gone, replaced by a north-London dialect.

"But you have some well-wishers waiting—"

"Get rid of them."

"What shall I say?"

"Anything—tell them I'm sick; tell them I'm dying. Whatever you want."

There was a pause, then the sound of retreating footsteps. He drew more tobacco into his lungs before leaning back in his chair, head thrown back, eyes closed.

How could he be dying, he wondered, when he was already dead?

CHAPTER NINETEEN

"I seem to have . . . an adviser, I suppose you'd have to call him," Ian said to his aunt. They were having their usual Sunday afternoon tea in the parlor, in front of a roaring fire. Having gorged on roast beef, they were enjoying tea and shortbread while Lillian did Ian's mending, which she insisted on doing for him once a month. He pretended to protest, and she pretended to believe him.

"Oh?" Lillian said, peering at the needle she was attempting to thread. She was farsighted but refused to wear glasses. Holding it up to the light, she squinted as she tried to push the thread through the tiny hole. Ian knew better than to offer to help. "What sort of adviser?"

"He's a librarian."

"How did you come to meet him?"

Ian smiled; Aunt Lillian loved a good story. "I'm sorry to disappoint you with the rather unextraordinary fact that I met him at the library."

"Ah, well, these things can't be helped," she said, finally passing the thread through the eye of the needle.

He told her about Pearson, carefully omitting their meeting the night before. But he did make the mistake of revealing that Pearson was English.

"Ach, the English!" She spat the words out contemptuously. "They're a pallid group o'weaklings. Can't even manage to measure a proper mile."

Ian helped himself to more tea and shortbread. "Auntie, we've not had Scots miles since you were a girl."

"Because the English are too feeble to walk them," she said, biting off the end of the thread after tying it up.

Aunt Lillian seldom missed an opportunity to malign the English, whom she despised with a passion. The longer Scots mile—based on the Royal Mile in Edinburgh—was obsolete, having been replaced by the official English system of measurement for the last time in 1824 (though there were still places in Scotland where the residents obstinately refused to use the English system).

"So your friend is English. I suppose we'll have to forgive him for that." She sighed.

"How very kind of you," he remarked drily. He sometimes wondered if her political attitudes were more pose than conviction.

Lillian shot him a sharp glance as her fingers deftly simple-stitched a button on one of his shirts. "You missed quite an evening last night."

Ian frowned—did she know he had been with Pearson? "I'm sorry," he said. "I thought you'd easily find a friend to join you."

"Well, I didn't, and you would have enjoyed it, being 'a student of human nature,' as you like to call yourself."

"I should love to hear your account of it," he said to mollify her. It was also unlike Lillian to get snippy like this.

"It was most extraordinary," she said, brightening. "He really did seem to have the power to make people ignore pain. He had them do silly things as well, but it was the needle through the arm that really impressed me."

"Tell me about it," Ian said, intrigued.

She recounted the hypnotist's act from beginning to end, and when she had finished, he leaned back in his chair.

"Such abilities could be a wonderful or terrible thing," he said. "To have such power over people could be a source of great good or great evil."

"He insisted that he was doing nothing save 'liberating' the person's innate abilities, but I'm not sure that's accurate. In every case, they did as he suggested."

She went on about Monsieur Le Coq's presence and charisma, until Ian had to smile. "Why, Auntie, I do believe you are smitten."

"Don't be ridiculous!" she snapped. "At my age—*really!*"

But her eyes sparkled, and the color in her cheeks was more than just the heat cast off by the fire in the grate. Ian regretted his decision to forgo the performance—anyone who could make his aunt Lillian blush like a schoolgirl was a man to be reckoned with.

"I'm glad the citizenry has a distraction. The papers are outdoing one another to cause mass hysteria over these murders."

"I heard there was a brawl in front of the police station."

"Where did you get that information?"

She put down her mending. "I assume that's where you received that bruise on your forehead."

"The editors of the *Scotsman* took it upon themselves to give the killer a lurid name," he said, ignoring her remark.

"Ah, yes—the 'Holyrood Strangler.' You must admit, it does have a certain ring."

Ian groaned. "Not you, too!"

"I'm only pointing out it's an appropriate name. Did Chief Inspector Crawford like my photographs?" she said, adroitly changing the topic.

"Yes, and he wanted me to give you a message."

"Yes?" she said, biting off the end of the thread. Aunt Lillian constantly misplaced her sewing scissors, using them to cut peonies and twine and to do numerous other household tasks. Ian had offered many times to buy her a second pair, but she always refused, insisting that she liked the ones she had. But they never seemed to land in her sewing kit, so she invariably resorted to biting off the ends of the thread.

"Detective Chief Inspector Crawford asked if you would consider working with the Edinburgh City Police as a photographer."

"Did he, now?" she said casually, a little smile playing at the corners of her mouth. "Fancy that."

"Would that interest you?"

"I never thought about turning my talents to crime solving—but then, neither did you, until . . ." She bit her lip and looked away. "But that's all you seem to think about now. It wouldn't kill you to have a lady friend, you know."

"'Love is a smoke raised with the fumes of sighs.'"

Lillian wrinkled her nose. "I hope you don't do that in front of your superior officer."

"What?"

"Quote Shakespeare."

"I don't see why I shouldn't."

"I'm sure he finds it very irritating."

"And I enjoy irritating him."

"It sounds like an ideal relationship," she said, selecting a new spool of thread from her sewing kit.

"Can I ask you something?"

"Of course," she said, pouring herself another cup of tea.

"Were my parents . . . happy together?"

She rose stiffly and fetched a torn tablecloth from the bottom drawer of the rosewood armoire. "I don't suppose you'll take some advice from your old aunt Lillian."

"Ah, Auntie, we should all be as young as you." It was flattery, and he knew it—and knew she thrived on it.

"Oh, gae on with ye," she said, reverting to her Glaswegian roots. "What's the advice?"

"Let the dead rest in peace. You're only tormenting yourself with it."

"You sound just like DCI Crawford."

"Then he's a wiser man than I gave him credit for."

He stood and went to the window, pulling back the curtain to gaze at the cold, heartless moon grinning down at him from its remote perch, high in the night sky. "You may as well ask the moon not to shine, Auntie."

She shook her head. "You're Emily's boy, bless her soul. She was as stubborn a Scot as ever lived."

He turned to face her. "And you?"

She raised an eyebrow and drew herself up in her chair. "I'm *persistent*. There's a difference."

He threw back his head and laughed. "I know you don't believe in God, but God bless you all the same."

She smiled and began threading another needle. "And you—are you a believer?"

"The whole question strikes me as irrelevant."

"What about the existence of good and evil?"

"I don't see why God should enter into it. If you are being virtuous only to enter into heaven and avoid damnation, then aren't you just thinking of yourself?"

"Does your brother share your beliefs?"

He looked at her sharply, but she was concentrating on her work— perhaps to avoid meeting his eye. "I couldn't tell you."

"He was such a brilliant young man," Aunt Lillian said, crossstitching the hem of the tablecloth.

"He's a bloody genius," Ian muttered. "That doesn't excuse him."

"Must you be so harsh on your brother? He suffered so when the fire took your parents."

"And I didn't?"

She laid down her sewing and put a hand on his arm. "Donald doesn't have your strength of character. He was always high-strung, overly sensitive. He has your father's darkness in him. You're more like your mother—she was the rock in the family."

"Donald's far cleverer than I am."

Lillian smiled sadly. "Sometimes being clever makes it more difficult to be happy."

"It's not about being happy—it's about doing what needs to be done."

She put down her sewing and laid a hand on his shoulder. "Perhaps Donald is doing what needs to be done right now, for him."

He looked into her clear blue eyes, so full of concern and compassion, and sighed. "Oh, Auntie, if only everyone in the world were more like you."

"Well!" she said. "I'm glad you finally realized that. And you can tell your boss that I should be delighted to work for him. Now then, how about some more tea?"

CHAPTER TWENTY

The man standing alone in the darkened street gazed up at the lighted turrets of Edinburgh Castle, glowing dimly through the fog. His left hand tightened around the silk scarf in his pocket. Sunday, not a good night for hunting—and the rain pelting the city for the past week had left everything soggy and damp and smelling of mildew. Weary of battling the inclement weather, people were staying home. Instead of venturing out to the pubs, they were bundled up in front of their fires, sipping tea laced with whisky or hot buttered rum. *Useless sods,* he thought as a fat rat scuttled out from behind a trash bin and down a sewer grate.

He stepped into a covered alley as the rain began to spit from the sky again, coming down in thin, sharp shards. Standing next to a rain barrel filled to the brim, he shook the droplets from his coat and leaned against the cold stone wall of the near building. He fingered the scarf in his pocket with longing. Plying his trade on a night like this was too risky; the city was too quiet, and someone was likely to spot him. When the streets were filled with roaming hordes of revelers, he was much less likely to stand out or be remembered. Discretion was part of his code, being very much the better part of valor.

If someone were by chance to see a prostrate form lying in some deserted wynd or close, it might at first appear to be another drunken hoodlum, hardly worth a second glance. He liked to keep a vigil near the corpse, reliving his triumph. And when somebody took the trouble to look closer, he would be there to see the expressions of astonishment and horror as his handiwork was discovered. But by the time the police were summoned, he would be well away—no point in pushing his luck.

He sighed and rested his head against the wall, thinking of the last one. Not nearly as pretty as Stephen Wycherly, but fresh and sturdy and so very strong, like a young ox. Not strong enough, of course—none of them were, in the end. Brimming with anger—oh, how the young man had wanted a fight! He closed his eyes now, feeling the muscular flesh against his as the victim struggled. His groin tightened at the thought of the taut, firm body he had held the power of life and death over. One more twist of the ligature, and he could extinguish that life as easily as blowing out a candle. He almost felt regret, recalling a fleeting impulse to let this one live—not from pity or compassion, but from a desire to prolong the experience.

His groin swelled, pressing against the cloth of his linen pants, his breath deepening as his grip on the scarf tightened. With his other hand, he liberated his engorged flesh, stroking it as he contemplated his latest conquest. He thought about the young man's breath, so hot and hoarse in his ear, and how he pressed his face against the fellow's cheek as he twisted the scarf tighter around his neck. Just as his victim was about to lose consciousness, he released his grip, allowing him to breathe for a while before pulling the ligature taut again . . .

Sweetness flooded his limbs, and he shuddered with spasms as his seed spurted out, mingling with the rain as it fell upon the already drenched cobblestones. He watched it trickle into the gutter, to be carried into the city's underground sewer system to mingle with the sins of an entire populace. A smile lifted the corner of his mouth as he splashed his hands in the water gushing from a spout above the rain barrel.

He closed his eyes again, but this time his father's voice rang in his ears.

"*Useless!* How can anyone be so *weak and useless?*"

His forehead burned with shame at the memory, and he tried to shake it from his brain, but that just made it burrow in deeper, like an evil parasite.

"Why can't you be a proper man like your brother? What are you? A weak old *woman!* Pick yourself up and come at him again!"

The alley he was standing in vanished, replaced by the fenced-in yard behind the crofter's hut of his childhood. He could feel the sod beneath his feet, soft and slippery, so hard to get a firm footing in. He saw the white plumes of his father's breath in the damp air, heard his brother's wheezy breathing, as he inhaled the sour smell of his own terror. Wiping the sweat from his clammy forehead, he staggered toward his brother, fists flailing. From the corner of his eye, he caught a glimpse of his mother's white, terrified face peering out from the kitchen window.

He was eight years old, his brother two years older.

He moaned like a wounded animal at the memory, clutching his head as the darkness threatened to swallow him. *Oh, there was so much evil in a man, one hardly knew where to begin . . .*

CHAPTER
TWENTY-ONE

When Ian arrived at the station house early Monday morning, he was greeted by Constable Bowers.

"Boss wants to see you, sir," he said, jerking a thumb in the direction of Crawford's office.

"What about?"

"The letters, I expect," Bowers replied, buttoning his overcoat.

"Letters?"

"You haven't heard?"

Ian looked around the room. Everyone was staring at him expectantly. "Apparently I'm the only one who hasn't," he said. "Thanks, Constable."

"Good luck, sir," Bowers replied before ducking out through the double doors leading to the main staircase.

Ian's knock on Crawford's door was greeted by a muffled grunt that might have been "Come in," "Come bin," or "Corn bin." Crawford evidently had a cold—not a good sign.

The chief inspector was seated behind his desk, staring disconsolately at an untidy pile of correspondence in front of him.

"Bowers said you wanted to see me, sir?" said Ian.

"Close the door behind you," said Crawford, blowing his nose into an enormous white handkerchief.

"You seem to have caught a cold, sir," Ian remarked as he closed the door.

"Your stunning powers of observation have not been exaggerated," Crawford muttered, stuffing the kerchief into his breast pocket.

"Sir?" Ian said, beginning to lose his patience but intent on not showing it.

"Well, what are you standing there for? Here they are," he said, grabbing a fistful of letters. "Come have a look."

"What are they, exactly?"

"Letters from every crackpot in the city purporting to be the strangler. And a few useful suggestions on how to improve our job performance."

"Could any of them be authentic?"

"That's for you to decide—you're the lead detective," Crawford said, pushing the pile toward Ian. "Now, if you don't mind, I'd like my desk back."

Ian threw open the door and called out into the main room. "Sergeant Dickerson, would you bring me a box?"

Moments later the sergeant appeared with the requested item. Scooping the letters into the box, Ian left Crawford's office and returned to his own desk.

"Blimey, sir," said Dickerson, staring at the box full of correspondence.

"Roll up your sleeves, Sergeant," said Ian. "They aren't going to sort themselves."

There were dozens of letters, all shapes and sizes, some just scribbled notes on bits of scrap paper, others carefully penned on good-quality paper. Some were typed. Several were from women; one wanted to meet with the strangler, claiming she could mend his evil ways. Another offered to marry Ian.

One letter stuck out from the rest. Written in a firm, masculine script, with good-quality blue ink, it was on Waterloo Hotel stationery and said simply, *Catch him before I kill him.*

There were no other identifying marks of any kind—it was unsigned and undated.

"What do you make of this?" Ian asked Dickerson.

The sergeant frowned and scratched his chin. "How can he kill t'strangler unless he knows who t'is?"

"My thoughts exactly."

"D'you s'pose this fellow is stayin' at the Waterloo? It's a fancy place."

"It's possible—but equally likely he used this stationery to throw us off the track."

"So is there anythin' we can do?"

"Not at the moment, I think," Ian said, but he folded the letter carefully and slid it into his vest pocket.

Ian spent the rest of the day chasing down leads in the death of Bobby Tierney. His attempts met with failure—Tierney's sister was not at home, and the neighbors were either away or uncommunicative. He hoped Sergeant Dickerson had met with better luck, having been dispatched to the other end of town to ferret out information in the Wycherly case.

Ian turned up at the station house shortly after five, disappointed and weary. The shift had just changed, but he found the ever-faithful Dickerson at his desk, working. A smile crossed the sergeant's freckled face when he saw Ian, but a frown quickly replaced it when he saw the detective's expression.

"Bad day, sir?"

Ian flung himself into the chair next to Dickerson's desk. "'I wasted time, and now doth time waste me.'"

"That's very . . . poetic, sir."

"Shakespeare has that reputation, Sergeant."

"I were just puttin' down a few remarks. Miss Harley weren't t'home, but I told her maidservant we'd call again tomorrow."

"Ah, yes, the niece who was in love with young Wycherly."

"Come again, sir?"

"Wycherly's employer, Eugene Harley, thought his niece was sweet on Stephen."

"That could give matters an int'resting twist, sir."

"Have you managed to locate any stationery shops in Edinburgh selling playing cards with that unusual design?"

"Not as yet, sir. Per'aps we should look at some specialty shops."

"Good idea."

Ian looked out the window. Night had fallen, and a blank-faced moon was already rising in the eastern sky.

"Let's examine the elements of the crimes. What is one constant in both cases?"

"Assumin' the two dead men are victims of the same killer, sir?"

"Yes."

"Well, I s'pose it's that both victims are men."

"Write that down—make a column called 'Victims.'"

Dickerson complied, biting his lower lip in concentration. His handwriting was precise and small, the letters perfectly symmetrical.

"Good," said Ian. "Now, what is the other constant in both cases?"

"The fact that they were both killed th' same way, y'mean?"

"Ah, not just any way—they were *strangled*. The constant is *method*, Sergeant. That's another column. Use capital letters."

Dickerson wrote *M E T H O D* and drew a line beneath it.

"This tells us something about the relationship between victim and murderer."

Dickerson's bland face went blank. "Sir?"

"Strangulation is a very personal method of killing someone."

"I'm 'fraid I don' take your meaning, sir."

"It's not the easiest way to kill. What if the victim fights back, or manages to escape? It would be far simpler—and more reliable—to simply shoot someone, or knife them, or even bang them over the head."

"But if there's no weapon t'hand, might it not be a killer's only choice?"

"Young Wycherly was pushed off the cliff *after* he was strangled, when the fall alone surely would have killed him. As you yourself said, why not just push him and be done with it?"

Dickerson smiled. "I did say that, didn' I?"

"More often than not, the killer will have a personal relationship with a victim he chooses to strangle."

"So y'think Stephen Wycherly knew his killer, then?"

"I think it quite likely."

Constables on the evening shift were shuffling into the station, stamping snow from their boots, chatting and laughing as they headed for the tea caddy. It was the kind of bitter cold that made a hot cup of tea seem positively medicinal.

Ian leaned forward and lowered his voice.

"For some time now, Sergeant, I have made a study of certain . . . deviant personalities, people who are different from the average run-of-the-mill criminal. They are not different in degree, but in *kind*—they are a subspecies, as it were, not motivated by mere greed, jealousy, or revenge. Their deeds spring from a darker place."

Dickerson's eyes grew wide. "Are you sayin' the killer is mad, sir?"

"He isn't a raving lunatic—he might appear quite unremarkable to most people, perhaps even forgettable."

"What I don' understand is why some'un would trudge all the way t'top of Arthur's Seat just to—"

"Perhaps because the place had some special significance to him."

"I don' follow, sir."

"Mountaintops are symbolic places. If he lured Wycherly all the way up there, he may have had a reason."

"Per'aps Wycherly encountered 'im by chance."

"I don't think so. He wasn't dressed for a hike. I think the killer lured him up there with the express purpose of taking his life. And by doing so, took a tremendous chance. The two men might have been seen together, he might have failed to kill Wycherly, leaving him alive to testify against him. Wycherly was a strong young lad, and might even have managed to turn the tables."

"So why take such a chance?" Dickerson said, chewing on the tip of his pencil.

"Exactly! I'm convinced that's a key element to finding our man."

"Beg pardon, sir, but we are sure it's a man?"

"A woman of such Amazonian strength? Possible, but unlikely, I think."

"Or two men—what if th'bloke has an accomplice?"

"Well done, Dickerson. Always question assumptions—that's Hamilton's First Rule of Investigative Procedure."

"An' what's the Second Rule, sir?"

Ian stood up from his chair as the castle clock struck six. "Always make time for a pint or two."

Dickerson grinned. "That's more like it, sir—first round is on me."

Just then, Constable Bowers approached Hamilton and Dickerson, accompanied by a stringy little man with lank gray hair and an oily complexion, dressed in a yellow sou'wester and thick-soled Wellingtons.

"Beg pardon, Sergeant, but Frank here says Mrs. McGinty's pig's broke out of its pen again."

Sergeant Dickerson frowned. "Not my problem, Constable—I got more important fish t'fry."

Bowers shifted his feet and coughed. "Frank here says you have a way with the pig—that you, er, know how to talk to it."

The fair skin on Dickerson's neck flushed a mottled red. "An' just how does one talk to a pig, Constable?"

The stringy little man stepped forward. "Ach, ye jes whisper in her ear, and she'll do anythin' ye want—I've seen ye do it!" His voice was rough as a metal grate.

Several of the other constables snickered, and Ian glared at them. Dickerson flushed a deeper red and sprang from his seat.

"Come along—let's get this over with! I'll join you shortly, sir," he told Ian, "after I deal wi' this wretched pig."

Hamilton smiled. "'There is nothing either good or bad, but thinking makes it so,' Sergeant."

"It's all very well for you t'say, sir," Dickerson grumbled as he shoved on his hat. "You might feel different if it were you herdin' a bloody pig."

He stomped out of the station amidst stifled laughter from his colleagues. Throwing on his cloak, Ian mused that even Edinburgh's police force needed a good belly laugh now and again. He didn't much feel like laughing himself as he followed the others from the warmth and light of the station house into the waiting night.

CHAPTER
TWENTY-TWO

Sergeant Dickerson looked around uncomfortably as he pushed open the thick front door of the Hound and Hare later that evening, nicked and scarred by centuries of kicks, cuts, and fists. He didn't protest when Hamilton suggested they meet there—he knew it was pathetic, but he desperately wanted the detective's approval.

William Chester Dickerson—Billy Boy to his friends in Lancashire—was of meek disposition. Places like the Hound and Hare intimidated him. It catered to rough trade, the sort of fellows who bullied him at school, putting nettles in his trousers or hanging him upside down from the nearest low tree branch. One sadistic Irish hooligan by the name of Charlie Higgins liked to pour treacle into his desk, drowning his books and papers in the sticky stuff.

Seared by his boyhood experiences, Billy Dickerson attempted to conquer his fears by moving to Edinburgh to join the police force. He was shocked to find it filled with the kind of men he left Lancashire to avoid—rugged, rough-spoken Highlanders with blunt manners and loud voices. Some were thugs, of course, but others, like DI Hamilton, seemed truly interested in justice.

He found the detective standing just inside the entrance. He acknowledged Dickerson's arrival with a nod.

"Try not to act like a policeman," Hamilton said, pressing through the maze of bodies toward the bar.

"Yes, sir," Dickerson said, trailing behind like a faithful spaniel, wishing he were in uniform instead of the street clothes Hamilton insisted he wear. At least when he was in uniform, he was treated with some respect—in regular clothes, he was just a short, pudgy fellow with ginger hair.

"If we want information on who killed Robert Tierney, our best bet is to mingle with the regulars."

"Right you are, sir," the sergeant replied, sidestepping a puddle of spilled beer near a table full of ruffians in football jerseys.

After just a few days working with Hamilton, he had come to regard the detective with a reverence Dickerson himself knew was absurd. His stern purity inspired the sergeant to feats beyond his usual scope. The climb up Arthur's Seat was an example—hardly a prime specimen of manhood, Dickerson, anxious to please, had huffed uncomplaining up the hill at the punishing pace Hamilton had set.

Now he stood at the bar, viewing the room and its occupants with dismay. It was one thing to come here in the afternoon, but quite another to dive into the nighttime uproar and chaos. A beady-eyed ruffian with thick shoulders caught Dickerson looking at him and pressed his face close to the sergeant's.

"What're ye lookin' at, boyo?" he growled, his breath stinking of tobacco, herring, and stale beer. He was dressed like a dockworker, in a stained shirt and overalls.

"He's looking at your lady friend," Hamilton replied calmly, "wondering if she's better in bed than your sister."

The thug stared at him blankly, the words taking some time to register in his dim excuse for a brain. Then his face went scarlet, and he roared like a wounded lion, his meaty hands clawing toward Hamilton's face.

Hamilton sidestepped him easily. "What do you say we take this outside?" he said with a smile.

His would-be attacker wheeled around, ready to advance again, before thinking better of it. By now they had caught the attention of several other people, including the bartender, who nodded sternly toward the rear exit. Fights were common in the Hound and Hare, but the back alley was the preferred place for brawls if you ever wanted to set foot in the place again.

As Hamilton headed for the rear exit, Sergeant Dickerson looked wildly around, thinking perhaps to corner an ally, but most of the patrons had lost interest, returning to the real business of the evening—drinking. A couple of them laughed and patted Hamilton's antagonist on the back as he charged past them.

"Mind ye don' knock 'is teeth out, Jimmy, or ye'll have tae pay the dentist bill!"

"Oiy, Jimmy! It's early yet fer a fight, innit?"

These remarks were followed by guffaws and shoulder slapping as the three of them pushed through the crowd toward the exit. Dickerson swallowed hard as he followed the others out. Hamilton's adversary had at least a two-stone advantage and looked mean as a cornered badger. Dickerson noticed a small chap with a neat little black mustache break off from his companions and follow them as they left the pub.

"Terry McNee," the little fellow said, extending his hand as they made their way through the narrow wynd leading to the back of the building. "Most people call me Rat Face. I'll be Jimmy's second. And you'll do likewise for your friend, I suppose?"

His voice was light and high and educated, minus the dull, mindless aggression of the pub's other clientele. Dickerson wondered what he was doing at a place like this.

"William Dickerson," he said, shaking the man's hand, smooth and soft as a woman's, the fingernails neatly trimmed.

"Right, Willie, let's see what your friend has to say for himself," McNee, alias Rat Face, said pleasantly. Dickerson tried to apply Hamilton's methods to figuring out what kind of person this fellow was. Clearly not a menial laborer—but why would a respectable office worker be hanging around with the brutish Jimmy?

The alley behind the pub was squalid and smelly, bordered by a pigsty on one side and a penny tenement on the other. The odor of rotting cabbage and sour cheese assailed Dickerson's nostrils as he watched Jimmy remove his coat, muscles bulging against the fabric of his flannel shirt. The brute rolled up his sleeves, exposing muscular forearms scored with colorful tattoos. Hamilton did the same, and Dickerson noticed with disappointment that his figure was considerably less bulky than his opponent's. Though a tall man, DI Hamilton looked scrawny next to the massive Jimmy. Dickerson hoped the detective's intellectual edge would count for something. He shivered at the thought that one dead body in the back of the pub was already more than enough.

He glanced at Rat Face, whose sharp features registered eager anticipation. Dickerson saw how he got his nickname—there was something feral about the long nose, small eyes, and receding chin. The way he brushed his tiny mustache with his long, tapered fingers was like a rat cleaning its whiskers. Rat Face extruded a long, thin piece of what appeared to be hardtack from his pocket and held it out to Dickerson.

"Beef jerky?"

"Thank you, no," Dickerson said, realizing how dry his throat was. He dearly wished they had imbibed a pint or two before trudging out to this godforsaken alley. His stomach contracted as the two men squared off and a light rain began to fall. He had no idea what was required of him; he had never been a participant in a bar fight. He looked at Rat Face for a clue, but his counterpart was calmly chewing his beef jerky. The sergeant took a step toward Hamilton.

"Sir—"

The detective shook his head. "Later, Sergeant. Well, shall we?" he said to his opponent, who resembled a bull about to charge. His small eyes were narrowed slits, his broad shoulders puffed up and hunched forward, body tensed and ready for combat.

With a grunt, Jimmy launched his massive form at Hamilton. The two men collided with a dull thud, and Dickerson closed his eyes, expecting to hear the crunch of bone as Hamilton collapsed under the weight of the beast. When he opened them again, he was relieved to see the detective had his opponent in a headlock. One wiry arm was wrapped around Jimmy's neck, while the other grasped his elbow, pulling it tighter.

Jimmy's face deepened from scarlet to vermillion as he tried to throw off his opponent. Raising his right arm high, he drove an elbow hard into Ian's back, dropping them both to their knees. Taking advantage of the moment, Jimmy twisted his body and wrenched free, rolling to the ground. The two staggered to their feet, breathing hard and facing each other.

"C'mon, sir," Dickerson muttered, fists clenched. He longed to enter the fray, but he knew better. This was a fight between the two of them, a test of courage as much as skill.

Jimmy ran at Ian again, head down, in what looked like an attempt at a rugby tackle, but the detective managed to sidestep his opponent, whirling around like a matador evading a bull. This only enraged the big man, who came at Ian with a roar, fists flailing. Again, Dickerson was afraid to look as the two exchanged punches. Jimmy was bigger, but Ian had the advantage of being more nimble and evaded more blows than he caught. An uppercut to the face appeared to daze him, though, as blood burst from his nose. He staggered backward, leaning against the alley's stone wall.

Jimmy lunged toward him, and Dickerson had a sinking feeling as the two locked shoulders like wrestlers, sweat dripping from their faces.

He could hear their labored breathing as they each tried to bring the other to the ground. Surely the larger man would prevail now, with his superior weight and might.

Suddenly Ian rolled to the ground backward, throwing his opponent off balance, so that Jimmy somersaulted over his head in the direction of the wall behind them. His momentum took him into the wall headfirst, and Dickerson flinched at the sound of bone thwacking against stone.

As Jimmy crumpled to the ground, Ian stumbled over to lean on the rain barrel sitting beneath the building's eaves. Bloodied and shaken, he didn't look much better than his opponent. The sergeant watched as Jimmy slowly pulled himself to his hands and knees. Steam rose from his back as he hung his head between his shoulders, his breath coming in thick, hoarse gasps.

Dickerson looked at Rat Face, whose mouth hung open, a look of astonishment on his ferret-like features. No one spoke as Jimmy slowly got to his feet. Hands on his knees, he took a few more deep breaths hunched over, then straightened up slowly, painfully, like an old man. Stretching his spine to its full length, he took a step toward his opponent and extended a hand. Dickerson tensed as the two men clasped hands, fearing it was a trick.

But Jimmy's aggression had drained away. Without a word, he fished a grimy handkerchief from his pocket and handed it to Ian. It looked filthy, but Ian took it and wiped the blood dripping from his nose.

"How'd ye learn to fight like that?" Jimmy asked in a raspy voice.

"I did a bit of wrestling in school," Hamilton replied, massaging his right forearm.

"More than a bit, I'd say," Rat Face remarked.

"If I were you, I'd have someone check out your head injury," Ian said to Jimmy. "It could be serious."

"Don' be daft, man," Jimmy scoffed. "Ye think it's the first time I've had a poundin'?"

Ian smiled. "I suppose not. Still—"

"Why'd ye wan' tae fight? Because ye knew right enough ye were bound tae win?"

"I figured it was the best way to gain an introduction."

The big man looked perplexed. "Why on airth would ye—"

"Well," ventured Rat Face, "they're coppers, obviously."

Dickerson stared at him. "How did you—"

"You smell like coppers."

"So, what d'ye wan' from us?" asked Jimmy.

"You're clearly the most feared man in that establishment," said Hamilton, "and your friend here is the most intelligent."

His flattery had the intended effect. Jimmy crossed his arms, a lopsided smile on his broad face.

Rat Face wasn't so easily convinced. "Why not just talk to us?"

Hamilton smiled. "Come now, Mr. McNee."

Rat Face frowned. "You know me?"

"You are, I believe, the most skilled pickpocket in Edinburgh."

"Indeed." His attempt to look innocent did not suit his features.

"So tell me," said Hamilton. "Would you have answered my questions twenty minutes ago?"

"I suppose not," said the pickpocket.

"I assume you would have told me to bugger off?"

"Correct."

"What makes ye think we'll talk to ye now?" said Jimmy, rubbing his neck, which was still red.

"Because I was willing to risk a thrashing to get what I want."

"It's aboot tha' fella wha' was killed a coupla days ago, innit?"

"Yes," said Dickerson, clearing his throat officiously. "I am Sergeant William Dickerson of the Edinburgh City Police, and this is Detective Inspector Ian Hamilton. We're investigating—"

"What's in it for us?" asked Rat Face.

"For starters, I won't arrest you or tell the gentleman in the green tweed cap that you picked his pocket," said Hamilton. "Though I would appreciate it if you returned his wallet before leaving tonight."

Rat Face blanched. "How did you . . . ?"

Hamilton smiled. "You have a 'tell,' which I won't reveal to you, because I'd rather not make you more proficient at your vocation."

Rat Face stared at him, then laughed. "By God, you are a clever copper! Go ahead—ask me whatever you want."

"Were either of you at the Hound and Hare this past Friday?"

"That's the night the fella wa' killed?" Jimmy asked, scratching his head.

"D'you know anything about it?" said Dickerson.

"Wha' if we do?" Jimmy said. "What's it worth to ye?"

"It's more a question of what it's worth to you," Hamilton replied. "Numbers running may be common in Edinburgh, but it's still frowned upon, I'm afraid."

"Give it up, Jimmy," Rat Face said. "This fellow knows more about us than our own mothers, though I'll be damned if I know how he got his information."

Dickerson stared at Hamilton, confounded. He was as much in the dark as the other two.

"It's not difficult to see that you gentlemen are partners in more than just bar fights," Hamilton said. "So the question becomes where in the underworld is one most likely to find a need for both brains and brawn? Several answers occurred to me, including burglary, but Mr. McNee doesn't have the look of a safecracker. A pickpocket is likely to be a cardsharp, and possibly a bookie. And every bookie needs someone to collect money from reluctant clients."

Rat Face laughed again, showing a row of pointed gray teeth. "I declare, Detective Inspector—Hamilton, is it? I really must congratulate you. I do pride myself on a certain facility with a deck of cards, though I would never turn my skills to the service of crime."

"Of course not," Hamilton replied with a smile.

Rat Face extracted a toothpick from his pocket and planted it in the corner of his mouth, chewing on it delicately. "So, what can we do for you, gentlemen?"

Dickerson cleared his throat. "Were you acquainted with th' late Robert Tierney?"

"Do you have a photograph of the fellow in question?" said Rat Face.

Dickerson frowned. "His picture was in the paper for two days."

"Alas, I'm somewhat lax in my reading habits."

"I know 'im," Jimmy said. "Comes in of an evenin', usually lookin' fer trouble. Me and him 'ave had a go or two in the past. Fights dirty, likes to bite."

"I see," said Dickerson. "And last Friday . . . ?"

"I weren't here."

"Might I ask where you were?" said Hamilton.

Jimmy looked at his shoes. "Helpin' me mum."

Dickerson started to laugh, but the expression on Jimmy's face cut him off short.

"It's true, gentlemen," Rat Face said. "Jimmy's a good son to her—aren't you, lad?"

"She's me mum, ain't she?" Jimmy mumbled, still staring down at his shoes, scuffed and caked with mud.

Dickerson turned to the pickpocket. "So were *you* at the Hound and Hare last Friday?"

"Sergeant," he replied, pulling his collar up as a thin, cold rain began to fall again, "before continuing, do you suppose we could retire to the comfort of a corner booth and a pint of ale?"

CHAPTER
TWENTY-THREE

The atmosphere inside the Hound and Hare had heated up. Dickerson nearly choked on the cloud of tobacco smoke billowing out the door when he opened it. The air inside was worse. A thick blue haze lay over the room, the noise was deafening, and the floor was slick underfoot. The sawdust sprinkled on the boards wasn't enough to soak up the puddles of spilled beer. Harsh laughter competed with drunken singing and the clatter of beer mugs as they pushed toward the back of the room. Dickerson rubbed his eyes, burning from the dense layer of smoke hanging like mist in the air. He looked at Hamilton to see if he, too, was suffering, but the detective appeared oblivious to the foul atmosphere.

They squeezed their way to a booth in the far corner. Sitting alone with a pint in front of him was a man who looked so out of place that Dickerson would have noticed him even if he hadn't been waving at Detective Hamilton.

"You *know* him?" the sergeant asked, bewildered.

"I'm afraid so," Hamilton said, frowning.

The man rose and greeted the detective warmly. Dressed in a frock coat complete with vest and cravat, he had a soft, plump build and a refined air that was utterly out of place in the Hound and Hare. He looked like a tailor or a law clerk, at sea among dockworkers, bootblacks, and thieves.

"What a pleasant surprise, seeing you here!" he exclaimed, shaking Hamilton's hand warmly as Jimmy looked on sullenly. Rat Face had taken advantage of the distraction to disappear.

"I didn't take this to be your sort of establishment," Hamilton said.

The other man winked. "Scene of the crime and all that, eh?"

Hamilton turned to Dickerson. "Sergeant, may I introduce Mr. George Pearson."

The sergeant shook Pearson's hand; the fingers were plump and soft.

"A pleasure to meet you, Sergeant—"

"Dickerson."

"Anything I can do in the interest of justice—"

Hamilton interrupted him. "And this is Mr. Jimmy—"

"Snead," the big man said. "Jimmy Snead."

"A pleasure," said George Pearson. "Any friend of Detective Hamilton's is a friend of mine."

Jimmy shifted his weight to the other foot. "We're not exactlah—"

"Please," said Pearson, "allow me to buy the first round."

Jimmy brightened as Hamilton looked around the room. "Your friend seems to have taken a powder."

Jimmy shrugged. "Maybe 'e has business tae attend to." He turned to Pearson. "Now, what were ye sayin'?"

"What can I get you?" Pearson replied genially.

"A pint o' heavy," Jimmy said, wiping his nose with his sleeve.

"Capital!" Pearson said, rubbing his hands together. "And you, gentlemen?"

Hamilton did not look pleased, and Dickerson hesitated.

"I'll, uh, have the same."

"For you, Detective?" Pearson asked cheerfully.

"The same," Hamilton replied, gazing at a group of drunken footballers singing bawdy songs at the other end of the bar. "Now then," he said to Jimmy as they settled into the booth, "what can you tell me about Robert Tierney?"

Jimmy shrugged. "Ye could set yer watch by 'im of a Friday night—come in by eight, regular as clockwork."

"So is it safe to assume he was in here last Friday at about that time?"

"Ye'd have to ask them what was 'ere that night, but I 'spose so, yeah."

"You said he liked to fight," said Dickerson. "With anyone, or just certain people?"

Jimmy looked him up and down and smiled. "I ne'er saw 'im pick on a runt like you."

Dickerson felt his face redden, but Hamilton laid a hand on his arm.

"You mean he liked to fight with people his own size?" said the detective.

"Righ' enough. Like I said, him an' me's had a few scuffles in our time."

"You said he fought dirty," said Dickerson. "Were anyone out to get 'im for that—someone angry at him, maybe?"

Jimmy threw his head back and laughed, the red bruises around his throat still visible. "Ye 'aven't been around here much, have ye?"

Dickerson took a deep breath and tried not to choke on the smoke-filled air. "Enlighten me."

"Ev'ry man in this place fights dirty. Some worse 'an others, but there's not a sod in 'ere what wouldn't bite yer ear off if he could git away wae'it."

"Then what made Tierney stand out?"

Jimmy put his face close to the sergeant's, the gaslight glinting off his narrowed, bloodshot eyes. "Bobby wasn't just *willin'* tae bite—he was lookin' fer any chance. An' it weren't only ears, either—he once bit off a poor sod's finger."

Dickerson felt a little sick. The combination of close, smoky air swirling with the fetid fumes of Jimmy's breath was beginning to turn his stomach.

Just then, George Pearson arrived with an armful of beer mugs, lowering them awkwardly onto the thick oak table, scarred with years of promises deeply carved into its surface. In front of Dickerson were the words *Death to the English*. He hastily slid his glass over it to obscure the message.

"Here we are," Pearson declared cheerfully, sliding in next to Jimmy Snead, whose surly expression softened at the sight of alcohol. "I got two for you. You're a big fellow, and you look thirsty."

Snead closed his thick fingers around the glass and lifted it in a toast. "Here's tae yer health."

"Cheers," Pearson replied, lifting his drink.

Dickerson drank greedily, savoring the cool, bitter brew. He had waited a long time for this and was determined to enjoy it. DI Hamilton sipped at his without relaxing his watchful, guarded expression.

"How is the investigation proceeding?" George Pearson asked, his large, liquid eyes shining as he leaned forward.

Hamilton frowned. "Mr. Pearson, have you been following me?"

Pearson's soft body deflated like a balloon losing its air. "I just want to be of assistance."

"I would appreciate it if you would do your 'assisting' from the—"

He was interrupted by a commotion at the table of footballers. Angry shouting was followed by a loud thud and the crashing of broken glass as the table was upended. Glassware, ashtrays, and coins slid to the floor as the yelling became louder.

The other patrons turned to look as one of the footballers squared off with a much smaller opponent. Dickerson saw to his surprise that it was Rat Face.

"Goodness me," said George Pearson, "I do believe they're about to have a row."

Dickerson frowned at Jimmy. "Your friend's about t'get pulverized."

"Not if I can 'elp it," the big man replied, getting to his feet.

Hamilton laid a hand on his shoulder. "Allow me."

Jimmy tried to push his arm away, but Hamilton tightened his grip and looked him in the eye. "I have a score to settle."

Jimmy cocked his head to one side and frowned. "Have it yer way."

"What score is that?" Pearson asked Dickerson as Hamilton removed his coat and shouldered his way past the other patrons.

"I've no idea," said Dickerson. He watched the detective push through the crowd as the bartender lumbered toward the two combatants, shouting.

"Oiy! Take it outside!"

But Hamilton was closer and had almost reached them, when the football player threw a punch at Rat Face. The little man tried to dodge the blow, but it landed on his ear, throwing him off balance. The football player, who was big and blond, grinned as the mob pressed forward, egging them on.

"C'mon, Rat Face, go after 'em!"

"Oiy, Tony, why don' ye pick on someone yer own size?"

"Pummel tha' bastard, Rattie!"

The football players supported their teammate with their own catcalls.

"G'wan, Tony, crush the little bugger!"

"Annihilate the wee rat, Tony boyo!"

Tony wiped spittle from his mouth and raised his fist to strike another blow at Rat Face, who had staggered back into the fray.

He never got the chance. Ian Hamilton launched himself at the man, arms wrapped around Tony's waist in a rugby tackle. The two went down hard, knocking into a table and crashing to the floor amidst broken beer glasses and peanut shells. Dickerson sprang to his feet, craning his neck to see over the heads of the crowd.

"Oiy!" the bartender shouted, having reached the brawlers. "I said take it outside, or I'll call the police!"

Hamilton rose unsteadily to his feet, blood trickling down his face from a new cut on his forehead. "I *am* the police." He fished a badge out of his shirt pocket and waved it at the barkeep. "Detective Inspector Ian Hamilton, Edinburgh City Police. I'm arresting this man for creating a public nuisa—"

He turned to where his opponent had been moments ago—just in time to hear the pub's back door slam.

"The bugger got away!" cried one of the other patrons.

"Slipped oot th' back," another said.

"For sure 'e's gone now," declared another. "Ye'll never find 'im on a night like this."

Hamilton's face was hard as stone as he handed the bartender a card. "If he shows his face here again, or if you hear a whisper of him causing trouble any time of night or day, call me."

The barkeep pocketed the card and pointed to the broken glass littering the floor. "Who's gonnae pay fer this?"

Without a word, Hamilton tossed a handful of coins on the nearest table, then turned and headed back toward the corner booth. Dickerson watched the crowd part for him. They had gone quiet, though the sergeant couldn't tell whether it was because Hamilton was a policeman or because of his quiet anger.

"Much obliged," Rat Face called after him, but Hamilton didn't turn around.

When he reached the table, he handed another card to Jimmy Snead. "I may wish to talk to you again. Where can you be reached?"

The big man looked at him with a mixture of admiration and apprehension. "Ye can find me 'ere mos' nights. Ask anybody here—they'll tell ye."

Hamilton grabbed his coat from the back of the chair where he had left it, his face still grim.

"I say, aren't you going to stay awhile?" George Pearson asked, twitching uncomfortably.

"No," the detective replied. "Good evening, gentlemen." Without another word, he ducked through the same back exit Tony had used for his escape. Sergeant Dickerson hastily gulped down his beer before scrambling after him.

As he left the pub, a woman with painted cheeks and a slash of vermillion on her lips sauntered up to Dickerson, attaching herself to him like a river leech. Wrapping her arm around his, she pulled herself close to his ear.

"Would ye like a bit o' fun tonight, ducky?" She was not young, and her breath smelled of cheap whisky and lye soap. "I like little fellows," she purred, her hand sliding down his torso. "Bet you're big where it counts." He pulled away, but her hands found his, her jagged nails digging into his flesh. "Promise I won't tell yer wife."

Hamilton, several steps ahead of them, turned around. "Not tonight, Sally."

She let go of Dickerson abruptly. "Sorry, Detective—didn't see you there." She laughed. "I nearly frightened yer wee boyo here senseless. You'd better get him hame tae bed so he kin get t'school tomorrow."

"Very amusing," Dickerson muttered. He almost remarked that she was old enough to be his mother, but it was unmanly to insult a woman, even one like her.

"It's too cold a night for you to be out, Sally," said Hamilton. "Why don't you go home?"

Sally snickered. "Right. I'll just tell me maid to light the fire an' fix me a nice rum toddy, eh?"

Hamilton pressed some coins into her hand. "Don't spend it on whisky. For God's sake, find a place to sleep."

"Thanks, Boss," she said. With a leering glance at Dickerson, she turned and melted into the darkness.

The night wrapped itself around the city in a comfortless embrace, starless and black as pitch. Dickerson hurried after Hamilton, jogging and quick-stepping to keep up with his long strides. After a few blocks he worked up the courage to speak.

"Excuse me, sir, but wha' happened back at pub?"

Hamilton kept walking.

They continued on for a while, their breath coming in thin wisps in the crisp air. The temperature had dropped, and rainwater had crystallized in frozen puddles, patches of slick ice between the cobblestones. The buildings of Old Town loomed above them, seeming to lean in as the streets twisted and wound around one another. Most of the windows were dark, though the occasional gas lamp still flickered behind curtains.

As they neared the Lawnmarket, Dickerson tried again. "Who were tha' chap, sir?"

"Someone who should be swinging at the other end of a rope."

Dickerson felt as though a spoon had scooped out his stomach. "Beg pardon, sir?"

Hamilton stopped walking. "He's a known arsonist, Sergeant, too clever by half to get caught red-handed—at least so far."

Dickerson cleared his throat. "D'ye think—I mean, were he the one who—"

"No, he was behind bars when the fire killed my parents. I just hate all arsonists."

"Sir?"

"Let's leave it at that, shall we? It's late and I'm tired."

"Will ye be all right, sir?" Dickerson said, pointing to the thin river of dried blood on Hamilton's face.

"It's nothing. Good night, Sergeant."

"G'night, sir."

He watched Hamilton's long form lope toward Victoria Terrace before he headed in the direction of his own flat, blowing on his hands to keep them warm as a wicked wind whipped between the buildings of the Old Town. The sergeant turned around for one last glimpse of the detective, but he had already disappeared into the night.

CHAPTER TWENTY-FOUR

Henry Standish Wright stood before the hotel bedroom mirror late Monday night, gazing at his own reflection. The face looking back at him was handsome, well featured, the olive skin smooth, with a noble brow and full, curved lips. It was a face that made women swoon and men burn with envy. Along with his elegant, tapered figure and measured, mellifluous voice, it made him nearly irresistible.

But anyone looking at him more closely could see that his eyes were vacant. Large and liquid, ringed with dark lashes, they should have been the eyes of a lover or an artist, as captivating as the rest of his flawless figure. Onstage they glimmered in the glare of the footlights, as brilliant and shiny as the dreams of his admirers. But like his act, it was only a charade, a hoax to trick the naïve spectator. In reality, his eyes were as empty and blank as those staring out of the sockets of the dead fish stacked in rows of baskets in the Lawnmarket.

Henry Wright, alias Monsieur Le Coq, turned away with disgust from the sight of his own face just as a short, sharp rap sounded at the parlor door. With a weary sigh, he crossed into the next room and opened the door to admit the man who smiled at him with taunting familiarity. His visitor sauntered into the room, settled himself upon the French Empire love seat, and crossed his legs, displaying muddy, scuffed boots. His frayed shirt collar was open, his hair was uncombed, and his eyes were bloodshot.

Henry glared at him and lit a cigarette, inhaling deeply. "You look like something the cat dragged in."

His guest looked at the silver tray of crystal decanters on the sideboard. "Aren't you going to offer me a drink?"

Henry waved a hand toward the cabinet. "You know where it is."

His visitor strolled over to the sideboard and plucked the stopper from the lid of one of the bottles, pouring a generous amount into a cut-glass tumbler. Holding it up to the light of the chandelier, he swirled the tawny liquid in the glass, catching the glow of gaslight. "Lovely, isn't it?" he said, gulping down half the glass before settling languidly onto the love seat. "Don't you want to know where I've been?"

"No!" Henry declared with a shudder.

"You know, I didn't even plan the last one. It just happened. Though it was quite exciting, I must say."

"Shut up," said Henry.

"But I thought you liked my little stories."

"Just stop talking."

His visitor shrugged. They sat, silence heavy as chains between them, the only sound in the room the mechanical ticking of the mantel clock.

Finally Henry said, "Why did you come here? What do you want?"

"Tut-tut—is that any way to speak to your own flesh and blood?"

"You want money? An alibi? A change of clothes?" he added, with a glance at the bloodstained shirt.

His guest helped himself to a cigarette from a silver box on the end table. "I'm disappointed in you. I drop by for a friendly visit, and this is how you treat me. You wound me deeply, Henry."

Henry rose abruptly from his chair and went to the window, pulling back the crimson brocade drapes to gaze into the street below. "This can't go on, you know," he said finally.

"What are you referring to? The inclement weather, this hotel—your engagement at the Theatre Royal?"

"You know very well what I mean."

"Then why don't you turn me in? Afraid of the adverse effect the publicity would have on your glittering career?"

Henry wheeled about with such a look of fury and loathing that the man on the sofa shrank back. Regaining his composure, he smiled arrogantly. "Tut-tut, Henry—or should I call you Monsieur Le Coq? I can plainly see what you're thinking, but do you think you could get away with killing me? You're bound to botch it in the end, and then you'll be the one with a life behind bars."

Henry clenched his fists and hissed through his teeth, "It would be worth it, by God, to rid the world of the likes of you."

The other man laughed softly. "You're not the killing type, Henry. Why don't you leave it to those who are?"

Henry fixed his gaze deliberately upon his visitor, locking eyes with him. For a moment, the man on the sofa met his stare, his face blank. His shoulders relaxed, and his eyes began to glaze over, his cigarette dangling loose from his fingers, as though about to fall to the plush carpet beneath his feet.

"You do not really wish to kill anyone," Henry said slowly. "You are sorry for those you have injured, and you will never hurt anyone again."

His visitor grinned and sat up straight. "Do you really think your technique will work on *me*? How pathetic. I know all the tricks, better than you do!"

Henry turned away in disgust and looked out the window. People hurried along the street below, caught up in the mundane minutiae of their lives. He felt so removed from them, barely able to recall life's everyday pleasures—a warm fire at the end of a day, a hot cup of cocoa

on a winter's night, the soft touch of a woman's hand. He was an automaton going through the motions of living, as if he were on the other
side of a mirror, looking in. Everything he had formerly enjoyed felt
mechanical and meaningless. His only comfort now was cigarettes.

"You know," his visitor remarked, "you have no right to scorn me.
After all, someone had to play the villain. You should be grateful to me."

"Don't be absurd," Henry hissed without turning around.

"It's all his handiwork, you know. All those years, putting us at each
other's throats. What could he possibly expect—"

"Stop it!" Henry cried.

"Don't tell me you 'loved' him!" he snorted. Cocking his head to
one side, he gave a scornful smile. "You did! You actually cared for him,
didn't you? That's disgusting. He was a monster."

"*You're* the monster," Henry rasped, his voice thick with emotion.
He wheeled around abruptly and strode over to a small safe secreted
behind a romantic oil painting of a thatched cottage. Pushing the painting aside, he twirled the tumbler with trembling fingers, pulling open
the heavy door. He fumbled inside and withdrew several bundles of
bank bills.

"Here," he said, thrusting them at his visitor. "Take this. Do what
you will with it—but don't come back."

The other man crossed his arms and leaned back into the plush
sofa cushions. "So now you're going to buy me off. What about your
own guilty soul—can you buy that off, too? Would any amount of
money stop the nightmares, the dark thoughts, the river of sin that
flows through your blood?"

Henry Wright bowed his head, anguish gripping his heart with
a cold, hard grasp. His ears buzzed, and spots danced before his eyes.
When he spoke, it was through clenched teeth, his voice harsh and
raspy, the words wrung out of him. "Take the money. I don't want to
know what you're doing or where you are; just leave me in peace, for
God's sake!"

The other man drained the last of his whisky before rising from his seat. Taking the bills, he stuffed them into his coat pockets. "Very well," he said stiffly, though Henry had the sense he was putting on an act, incapable of true emotion. "I will not darken your doorstep again—unless you do something foolish, of course."

"You have made promises before," Henry cried. "See that you keep this one!"

Without another word, his visitor slipped out of the room and into the night. In two strides Henry crossed to the window and closed the heavy drapes. He stood for a moment, staring blankly into space before pouring himself a stiff drink, which he downed in one gulp. Lighting another cigarette, he sank into the armchair by the fire and gazed at the licking orange flames with an expression of utter defeat and horror, as if he were staring into the fires of hell itself.

CHAPTER TWENTY-FIVE

The next morning, Ian called upon Catherine Harley, niece of Eugene Harley, Esq., the late Stephen Wycherly's employer. After calling in on her uncle first, Ian learned that Tuesday was her day off. The old man had delicately hinted that she might be sufficiently recovered from her shock at young Stephen's death to answer questions. Ian showed up at her doorstep at precisely half past nine.

He was bustled into an elegant foyer full of hunting prints by a personage of considerable girth who appeared to function as lady's maid, nanny, cook, and heaven knew what else. She wiped her hands on the tea towel at her waist before shoving a stray hairpin into her unruly red hair, all the while muttering to herself. The whole performance seemed geared toward giving the impression that he was an unwelcome complication to an already busy day.

"Wait here, Mr.——"

"Detective Inspector Hamilton."

She eyed him suspiciously. "Detective Inspector, is it, then?" Her accent sang of the rolling hills of County Cork.

"I am here on the matter of Stephen Wycherly's death."

She rolled her prominent eyes and shook her head tragically, causing the recently fastened hairpin to free itself from her forest of ginger curls and clatter to the floor. "That was a sad affair, so it was," she said, bending to pick it up. "Miss Catherine was quite prostrate with grief. Such a lovely young man, so well-spoken and polite he was."

Her monologue was interrupted by the appearance of a waifish young woman upon the central staircase just off the foyer.

"Bernadette? Who's there?" she called in a thin voice.

"It's a *detective*, miss," she replied, unable to hide the thrill in her voice.

"Show him into the parlor. I will be down presently," she said, withdrawing into a second-floor bedroom.

The redoubtable Bernadette did as requested, pressing tea and cream cakes upon Ian, watching his reaction as he bit into one.

"It's me grandma's secret recipe," she declared. "Made with real vanilla."

"It's very good," Ian said, and so it was. It wasn't hard to see how Bernadette had attained her impressive size, if the tea cakes were any indication of her kitchen skills. They were creamy and light, with just a touch of lemon. Ian was contemplating eating a second one as a handsome pair of Siamese cats sauntered into the room. Eyeing him with their cool blue gaze, they leapt gracefully onto the settee, one at each end. Closing their eyes, they appeared to be napping, as cats do, without entirely relaxing into sleep. He supposed they were Eugene Harley's partners in law, Wickham and Clyde, though they were so much alike, he wondered how anyone could tell which was Wickham and which was Clyde.

The mistress of the house joined him after about ten minutes, floating down the stairs in a flowing white dress. She resembled an apparition in an old-fashioned wedding gown. Catherine Harley was a tremulous young woman, thin and pale, with a vague, distracted manner. Her voice was hollow, as though someone had scooped out its center, her light blue eyes rimmed with lashes pale as wheat. She wore her white-blond hair in an upswept chignon; the only touch of color on her person was a pair of ruby earrings. A simple gold locket dangled from her neck, and a silver signet ring adorned her right hand. Ian couldn't help thinking that she would have been an attractive girl if she had more vitality. But her hesitant manner and slow, dreamy movements made her seem older than she was.

She refused Bernadette's offer of cakes, though she did consent to sip languidly at a cup of tea. She gave the impression of one who needed neither food nor drink, as a spirit who walks the earth would have use for neither.

"So," she said, resting a teacup upon her thin knee, "you're the detective they've sent to investigate Stephen's death. It says in the papers he was murdered. Is that true?"

"I'm afraid it is."

She shrugged her narrow shoulders as if trying to dislodge the idea. "But who would want to kill Stephen?"

"I was rather hoping you might help me answer that question."

"I'll do what I can," she said, casting her eyes upon a handsomely framed photograph upon the mantel. "That's Stephen and me in happier times." She sighed.

Ian rose and went to the fireplace to inspect the picture. Dressed in plaid knickers, Stephen Wycherly stood leaning on a golf club, a smiling Catherine Harley by his side. Even in the badly focused photograph, her face held a vitality it lacked in the flesh.

"That was on holiday in Perth two years ago. My uncle went to play the course at St. Andrews, and took Stephen and me along."

Ian tried to imagine the crooked Mr. Harley swinging a golf club, but the thought made his own spine ache. "Your uncle said you were quite fond of Mr. Wycherly."

"And I like to think he was fond of me."

Ian cleared his throat. "Were you—"

"Lovers?" she said, surprising him with her frankness.

"Well, I—"

"That is what you were going to ask, isn't it?" she said, a sad smile playing at her lips. "Whether we were lovers, sweethearts, courting—whatever you wish to call it."

"Yes."

She folded the napkin on her lap into a tiny square. "We spent enough time together that had he wished to make an overture—one that a young lady of breeding might accept—well, he must have known I would have been receptive to such a proposal."

"But he never did?"

She shook her head, dislodging a few wisps of blond hair from her chignon. "He was always a perfect gentleman, polite and affectionate—but not in that way."

"And yet you say he was fond of you."

"He gave every indication of it. He often sought my company and, upon occasion, my advice."

"May I inquire as to what matters in particular he sought your advice upon?"

"If it will help you bring to justice the person or persons responsible for his death."

"I cannot guarantee it, Miss Harley; I can only say that the most insignificant-seeming detail is often the key to solving a crime."

She lifted the lid of the teapot and peered inside it. "More tea, Detective?"

"Yes, thank you," he replied, not because he wanted more but because, in his experience, the more time witnesses had to mull over a response, the more salient details they were likely to include.

Catherine Harley picked up a small silver bell from the tea table and rang it, summoning forth the stalwart Bernadette, who appeared so quickly, Ian wondered if she had been listening at the parlor door.

"More tea, please, Bernadette," said Miss Harley.

"Right away, mum," the lady replied, seizing the tea tray in her plump hands. "More tea cakes, sir?" she asked Ian.

"Yes, please," he said. "They are quite excellent."

Catherine gave another of her wan smiles when Bernadette had gone. "She's a treasure—she has been in service with my uncle ever since I was a girl. Of course, she's a terrible gossip, and adores eavesdropping, but she would do anything for us."

Ian made a mental note to have a chat with Bernadette—servants were often better informed than masters about what went on in their households.

"You said Mr. Wycherly often asked your advice. Was there any conversation in particular—"

"Yes, as a matter of fact. The most recent one was a strange affair indeed. It involved a letter Stephen received."

Her account was interrupted by the arrival of a beaming Bernadette, who laid the fresh plate of tea cakes upon the table with the flourish of an artist unveiling his latest masterpiece. She stood hovering over them until Ian picked up a cake, took a bite, and nodded his approval. Grinning broadly, Bernadette turned and trundled out of the room.

"You were saying?" Ian prompted.

"It was a letter he received," Catherine replied, pouring a cup of tea from the steaming pot.

"Did you chance to read it?"

"No, but I was there on Wednesday when Stephen opened it," she said, handing the cup to him. "He went quite pale. I saw the letter in his hand and surmised it was the cause of his disquiet."

"Did you happen to notice whom it was from?"

"I never saw the envelope. He folded it along with the letter and tucked it into his vest pocket. A little later he asked me what I would do if someone were attempting to blackmail me. Naturally I thought of the letter, but he refused to give me specifics, even when I pressed him for more information."

"And what did you tell him?"

"I said that I would hope not to stoop to gratify a blackmailer, but that I supposed there were circumstances where I might have no choice."

"And that seemed to satisfy him?"

"For the time being, I suppose, though he still appeared greatly troubled. And then he was dead."

"Did your uncle know of this letter?"

"He was there when it arrived, but he had no idea of its contents, which Stephen expressly forbade me to mention to him. Oh, Detective Hamilton," she said, twisting the silver ring upon her right hand, "do you think there's a connection?"

"I believe it's quite possible, Miss Harley."

Several cups of tea and three tea cakes later, Ian had gleaned all the information he could from Eugene Harley's niece. He resolved to return to the Harley residence to interview the ever-attentive Bernadette, but first he had someone else to see. After thanking Catherine Harley profusely, he stepped forth into a dull gray morning to pay another visit to Wycherly's former landlady.

He could add another chapter to the story of the law clerk's death, but there were pieces missing. Stephen Wycherly was being blackmailed by someone—but by whom, and why? At some point, the plot lines of his death and Bobby Tierney's intersected, but Ian still couldn't see the thread connecting them. He had glimpsed the beginning of Wycherly's story, and he knew the sad end, but the middle remained a mystery.

CHAPTER
TWENTY-SIX

When he rang the doorbell at 22 Leith Walk, Stephen Wycherly's landlady recognized Ian immediately, giving him a broad smile. Mrs. Sutherland was the kind of woman who gave the impression of never having been truly young, and who would never be truly old. She seemed to exist in an eternal state of vigorous middle age. Her mouse-colored hair was streaked with tinted blond strands, her sturdy figure thick around the middle, solid as the trunk of an oak. The backs of her hands were spotted with freckles and old scars, but her lively hazel eyes and rosy cheeks gave her an air of vitality reinforced by her quick, youthful manner.

"Why, hello to you, Detective Hamilton," she said, opening the door to admit him inside. Before closing it, she gave the dust mop she carried a quick shake into the street, releasing a billow of cat hair into the wintry air. She closed the door and ushered him down the hall and into the sitting room next to the kitchen. "Now then," she said, tucking the mop into a closet, "what can I do for you?"

"I have a few more questions in the matter of Stephen Wycherly's death, if you don't mind," Ian replied as an enormous black-and-white cat sauntered into the room and settled its bulk upon a low-lying hassock. He doubted the cat was capable of defying gravity enough to jump up onto the sofa.

"Scat, Bacchus—go away!" Mrs. Sutherland said, waving at the cat, which ignored her. Curling comfortably into a ball, Bacchus closed his eyes and purred loudly. The landlady sighed. "Whatever you want him to do, he does the opposite," she said, settling herself on the sofa.

"I know some people like that."

She laughed, revealing strong, even teeth. "Please, sit down," she said, indicating an overstuffed armchair across from her.

He did, and almost immediately the softness of the cushions and the warmth of the room made him drowsy.

"Cup of tea?" she offered, perhaps seeing his drooping eyelids.

"Thank you, no," he replied, yawning. "I've drunk quarts of it already."

"Bad night?" she asked.

"I did sleep rather poorly." The previous night had brought disquieting dreams; the investigation was taking its toll on him.

"Why don't you tell me why you're here; then you can go home and have a lovely nap," she suggested in a soothing voice, absently petting the disobedient Bacchus, who responded by purring louder. Something about Mrs. Sutherland reminded Ian of his aunt Lillian, though his aunt was keener, her edges less rounded.

Ian stretched and rubbed his eyes. "I was wondering if Mr. Wycherly ever mentioned a letter he received shortly before his death."

Mrs. Sutherland cocked her head to one side. "What sort of letter?"

"I'm afraid I don't know what was in it."

She nodded thoughtfully. "Does it relate to his death somehow?"

"It may have contained some reference to blackmail."

"Goodness!" she said, straightening up in her chair.

"Did you notice any particular agitation in the days leading up to his death?"

"Not especially—though I saw little of him the last couple of days. He took most of his meals out and came home late."

"Was that unusual?"

"If there was much work at the law office, he was likely to come home at all hours. I naturally assumed he was busy at work, until—" She broke off as two fat tears slid down her cheeks. "Forgive me," she said, wiping them with her apron. "He was so young, so like my own Michael."

"Your son?"

She smiled shyly. "Yes. He's at university in London, studying to be a lawyer, bless him."

"You must be very proud."

"If only his father could be here to see it, God rest his soul." She wiped away another tear and returned to petting Bacchus, who rolled over onto his broad back, nearly tipping off the hassock.

"So Mr. Wycherly never referred to a letter of any kind?"

"No. Did he receive it here?"

"It was sent to him at Mr. Harley's chambers."

"I see." She studied her hands, which were broad and strong, the nails cracked and jagged. "The papers said he was strangled. Is that true?"

"You mustn't believe everything you read in the papers. Did any of his acquaintances strike you as odd?"

"Several of them were—different, you might say, but none looked violent."

"Different in what way?"

She bit her lip. "Others may disagree, but I believe a young man has a right to his privacy."

"It's all right, Mrs. Sutherland—anything you tell me will be kept quite confidential."

"Mr. Wycherly's friends were . . . Well, let's just say that he never entertained young ladies." She gave Ian a meaningful look. "If you take my meaning."

"Oh," he said. "I see."

"There's some who believe it's wicked, but God made us all, and if there's some he made a little different, I daresay he had a reason for it."

"That's very broad-minded of you, Mrs. Sutherland."

"Perhaps," she said, scratching Bacchus behind the ears. The cat closed its eyes and purred more loudly, a rumbling engine of contentment. "I was a schoolteacher in my youth, and I saw plenty of children who were—different. Never could bring myself to hate them, so I don't see as how I should be hating them now."

"You wouldn't happen to know how I could contact any of Mr. Wycherly's acquaintances?"

"Not really. I wish I could be of more help."

"You've been considerably helpful already, Mrs. Sutherland," he said, to which she blushed and looked away. "One more thing—do you still have any of Mr. Wycherly's clothing?"

"Only what you saw when you went through his rooms last time you were here."

"Have you disturbed anything in there?"

"I've been so busy with my other tenants, I've not run so much as a dust rag through that room."

"May I have another look?"

"Certainly, Detective—anything you like," she said, lowering her eyes and blushing. Her hands fluttered to her head as she tidied her hair. Was it possible Mrs. Sutherland was a tiny bit sweet on him? Ian wondered.

He climbed the stairs to the second floor. As before, what struck Ian about Stephen Wycherly's room was that it was so tidy. The bed was impeccably made, the spread smoothed out with barely a wrinkle on it, and the small writing desk beneath the window clear of clutter. Ian couldn't help wondering how Wycherly had been able to endure the messy collection of papers in Eugene Harley's law office. Ian himself liked order; chaotic surroundings gave him a headache.

The closet was no less a model of organization. A brace of brown oxfords nestled next to a sturdy pair of hiking boots. How odd that Wycherly had ascended the summit of Arthur's Seat in oxfords, leaving the hiking shoes in his closet—he must have been in a terrible hurry. He examined the shoes and each piece of clothing hanging neatly above them before turning to the simple pine dresser along the opposite wall. The neatly folded vests in the second drawer yielded no stray bits of paper—the pockets of all his clothing were empty. Disappointing, perhaps, Ian thought as he closed the dresser drawer, though hardly surprising, considering the young man's passion for order. Ian himself was given to emptying his pockets upon returning home in the evening; it made him sad to reflect that Stephen Wycherly was a kindred soul.

Further examination of the room was no more rewarding, and as he opened the door to leave, an object hanging on the wall caught his eye. It was a leather dog leash, presumably purchased for the recently acquired puppy.

Downstairs, the smell of beef and root vegetables simmering on the stove made him quite faint with hunger. A glance at his watch revealed that it was half past two. Following the aroma of beef stew, he found Mrs. Sutherland in the kitchen, standing over a cast-iron pot of promising capaciousness. She turned as he entered the room, the color leaping to her cheeks as she saw him.

"Have any luck?" she asked, stirring the pot.

"I'm afraid not. Mr. Wycherly was very orderly, wasn't he?"

"He was a model tenant, poor dear," she said, stooping a little to taste a bit of stew, scooping it out with a ladle and blowing on it before taking a sip. She made a pensive face. "More sage," she declared, striding over to the spice cupboard.

"What happened to his puppy? I found the leash upstairs," Ian said, holding it up.

"He's in the laundry room for now," she said, plucking the bottle of sage from the spice shelf. "But he can't stay there. Bacchus will tear him apart if he ever gets into the room."

Ian pictured the cat hurtling its bulk at the offending canine, claws flying.

"Would you like to have him?" Mrs. Sutherland asked, shaking a liberal amount of sage into the stew, the herb's pungent fragrance filling the air.

"I can't take care of a dog," Ian said.

"I'll take 'im," said a voice behind them.

They turned to see Sergeant Dickerson standing in the doorway, quite out of breath.

"Sergeant?" said Ian. "What are you doing here?"

"We 'ave a suspect, sir," Dickerson replied. "He's at station house. Thought you might like t'know."

"What are we waiting for?" Ian said, already halfway down the hall. "Come along, Sergeant! Thank you, Mrs. Sutherland!" he called over his shoulder. "We'll be back for the dog later!"

They were out on the street before the landlady had replaced the lid of the sage bottle.

CHAPTER
TWENTY-SEVEN

"How did you manage to locate me?" Ian asked as he strode along Leith Walk, Sergeant Dickerson scurrying to keep up with him.

"I went along t'Miss Harley's house, and she mentioned you were tryin' to locate a letter Mr. Wycherly had received. I thought it were th' most logical place t'look."

"Excellent reasoning, Sergeant."

"Thank you, sir," Dickerson replied, grabbing his hat as a gust of wind attempted to lift it from his head.

"Now, what's this about a suspect?" Ian said, sidestepping a vegetable cart piled high with root tubers—potatoes, turnips, carrots, and parsnips. The cart's wooden wheels clattered on the paving stones as the vendor labored up the hill toward the Grassmarket. "Have you arrested someone?"

"Not as yet, sir, but I thought ye might like t'interview him."

At the intersection of Leith Walk and the London Road, they hailed a hansom cab and soon were rattling into the heart of the city.

"Who is this person, and why is he a suspect?" Ian asked as the cab wheels splashed through puddles of melted snow and ice.

"Turned himself in," Dickerson replied. "Just showed up unannounced and said he were the Holyrood Strangler."

"Did he give you his name?"

"He said he wanted t'speak with you."

"Curious," Ian mused. "I wonder how he knew who I am."

"It were in th' papers, sir," Dickerson replied, turning to stare out the window at a gaggle of schoolgirls in plaid skirts and white blouses, their legs thin in black woolen stockings.

"Sergeant!" Ian said sharply.

"It's naught like that, sir—that's my sister's school, and I were just tryin' t'see if I could spot her."

"My apologies. How old are you?"

"Twenty-three, sir."

"And your sister?"

"Pauline just turned fourteen. I try t'look after her, y'see."

"Very commendable. Which paper published my name?"

"The *Scotsman*, sir. Said you were lead investigator in t'case."

The cab pulled up in front of police headquarters, and Ian paid the driver while Dickerson alighted from the cab and opened an umbrella. The rain had started again—a thin, perfunctory drizzle washing away the remnants of snow still clinging to the cobblestones.

An air of expectation greeted them inside. Evidently word had gotten around, and eyes followed them as Ian and the sergeant entered the main room. Threading through the desks and filing cabinets, they proceeded down the narrow hallway toward the holding cells. The floorboards creaked as they entered the cellblock, containing a dozen or so cramped but relatively comfortable compartments.

Seated on the bunk in the first one was a small, rather elderly man in a tweed hunting jacket. He looked up and smiled expectantly when he saw Ian.

"Detective Inspector Hamilton, I presume?"

"And you are . . . ?"

"Whitaker Titterington the Third."

"I see," said Ian as Sergeant Dickerson let them both into the cell, opening the thick metal gate and clanking it closed behind them.

"Please, won't you sit down?" inquired Whitaker Titterington III, indicating a chair in the corner of the cell.

Ian complied, leaving Sergeant Dickerson standing rather stiffly by the door, as if he expected the prisoner to leap up and flee at any moment. "So, Mr. Titterington, you claim to be responsible for the death of Mr. Robert Tierney on the night of Friday last?"

"I am indeed."

"Do you mind answering a few questions?"

"Are you going to hold me overnight?" he asked eagerly.

"If we find it necessary."

"Oh, it is most necessary, I assure you."

"Perhaps you can tell me how and why you came to kill Mr. Tierney."

"Certainly. It was during a bar fight."

"Over what, exactly?"

"He insulted me."

"What did he say?"

"He called me a henpecked bantam cock."

"And so what did you do?"

"Well, I killed him."

"How, exactly?"

Titterington looked down at his shoes. "I, uh, strangled him."

"With your bare hands?"

"Yes."

Ian rose from his chair. "Mr. Titterington, I should arrest you for lying to a policeman and wasting our time, but since you seem to be so keen to be incarcerated, I'm going to let you off with a warning." He turned to Sergeant Dickerson. "Would you be so kind as to let this gentleman go so he can return home?"

The sergeant blinked twice, then unlocked the metal cell gate and swung it open.

"You're free to go, Mr. Titterington," said Ian.

"Oh, no, this isn't right at all," their visitor said, wringing his hands. "I'm a cold-blooded killer! Think of the ravage I could wreak upon society, the innocent lives I could destroy!"

"Feel free to return if the urge to kill strikes you again."

The little man continued to protest. "But—"

"Good day, Mr. Titterington," said Ian as the sergeant led him away.

Ian closed the cell door behind him and made his way back through the corridor to the main room of the station house, where Dickerson was waiting.

"I'm sorry, sir, I thought—"

"There are a great many crackpots in this town, and a few will inevitably confess to crimes they did not commit. Apart from hardly being capable of strangling someone like Robert Tierney, he doesn't even know what method the killer used."

"Right—he didn't know there were ligature involved," Dickerson answered sheepishly.

"Now you see the value of keeping certain details from the general public."

"Sorry, sir."

Ian laid a hand on his shoulder. "Never mind, Sergeant—live and learn, eh?"

"But why would he confess t'crime he didn't commit?"

"A desire for publicity, perhaps, to be thought of as more dangerous and grander than he is. He might wish to escape a nagging wife, or debts—or any number of unpleasant situations."

"But to risk bein' hanged, sir?"

"I suspect he didn't really think it through. He probably thought the real criminal would be caught before the hangman's noose reached his own neck."

Dickerson shivered. "I still don' get why bloke'd do sommit like that."

"There are all sorts in this world, Sergeant." Ian yawned and stretched. "I'm going home. Why don't you do the same? It's been a long day."

"Thank you, sir—good night, sir."

"Good night, Sergeant."

Ian left the station house, ignoring the amused looks from the other constables, who had observed Mr. Titterington's abrupt exit.

"He looks like a ruthless killer, all right," murmured one of the beat cops.

"Can't believe you let him go," said another. "Cold-blooded murderer if ever I saw one." Several others snickered and looked away.

Let them have their fun, Ian thought. He suspected this killer would not be a wild-eyed, drooling monster. When he did catch the strangler, they might all be in for a surprise.

CHAPTER
TWENTY-EIGHT

Ian stepped into the street and drew his cloak closer before turning in the direction of his flat.

"That were quick," said a voice behind him. He turned to see Derek McNair standing in the shadows beneath the building's overhanging eaves.

"When did you get here?"

"I been followin' you fer a while. Long enough t'get bloody cold—I can 'ardly feel me fingers." He took a step forward, the gaslight reflecting cold and pale on his dark hair.

Ian frowned. "Why the blazes aren't you wearing a hat?"

"I ain't got one."

"I'm surprised you haven't stolen one." Ian plucked the tweed cap from his own head and tossed it at the boy. "Here, put that on."

"Much obliged, Guv'nur," Derek replied in mock subservience.

Ian shoved his hands into his pockets, feeling the wind cold and sharp on his bare head. He shivered and started off down the street.

"Oiy—wait up!" Derek cried, running after him. "I ain't told ye why I was waitin' fer ye."

"I presume you can walk and talk at the same time," Ian said without slowing his pace.

"'Course I can," Derek replied, scurrying along at his side.

"It won't do, you know—you can't get away with stealing forever. Sooner or later you'll get nicked and end up in prison."

"How else am I ta live?"

"That's not my concern."

"So d'you wanna hear what I got ta say or not?"

"I'm not stopping you," Ian said as he stepped over a pile of horse manure.

"What's it worth to ye?"

"Depends on what it is."

"How 'bout a hot meal?"

"Most places are closed now."

"Yer place, then."

Ian looked down at the boy, taking in his secondhand coat and threadbare trousers, his filthy face and grubby hands with their blackened nails. There were children like him all over the city, but Derek was here, now. To turn his back on the lad would be worse than hardhearted; it would be heartless. "Very well," he said. "You can sleep on the sofa."

Derek tried to mask his surprise and delight at the offer, but an extra skip in his step gave him away. "I ain't slept indoors in weeks."

"You do have family, I believe?"

"My father's a poor excuse for a da, and I dunno if me mum's alive or dead. I ain't seen her in a while."

"There's the shelter run by the Sisters of Charity. Why don't you sleep there?"

Derek kicked at a stray rock, sending it scuttering across the cobblestones. "They're always gassin' on about God and faith and little baby Jesus. Makes me head ache."

Ian had to smile in spite of himself—Aunt Lillian had complained about the nuns' sanctimonious piety on more than one occasion.

Derek peered at him through lank, greasy bangs, a sly smile on his face. "Sounds like ye've had dealings wi' the sisters, too?"

"My aunt is involved in some of their charitable works."

"Aye, so she's told ye what they're like."

Ian stopped walking. "Look here, I've no doubt you have your reasons for sleeping in the street—that is, if you're telling the truth."

"So 'elp me, Guv'nur," Derek said in a Cockney accent. "Cross me 'eart an' hope t'die."

"Why don't you drop the pathetic-street-urchin act? You're a clever lad—I'll wager you can talk posh if you choose to."

Derek scowled, his face darkening under the layers of grime and dirt. Then he burst out laughing. "By God, I like you, mister! You're a sharp one, you are." His accent had disappeared, his enunciation clear and crisp as a university don's.

"So, what were you so anxious to tell me?"

"I talk better on a full stomach," he said, resuming his native West Country dialect.

"Very well," said Ian, and they spent the rest of the walk in silence. Here and there the yellow glow of gaslight shone behind French lace curtains; somewhere a dog barked. The rain had broken, and the sky was dotted with the cold glimmer of distant stars.

"You live *here*?" Derek said as Ian ushered him into his flat on Victoria Terrace.

"No, I just thought I'd break into the home of a perfect stranger," Ian replied, throwing his keys on the foyer table.

Derek paused to admire himself in the hall mirror. "This hat looks better on me than it does on you," he said, pulling the brim lower.

"Keep it," Ian said.

"Nice cloak," Derek remarked as Ian hung it up. "Where'd ye get it, a costume shop?"

"It belonged to my uncle."

Lillian had given Ian the cloak upon Alfred's death. Made of heavy, good-quality wool, it was old-fashioned, but Ian liked the way it hung all the way to his knees, shielding him from even the wickedest wind. It was rain repellent, and the high collar kept his neck warm. He even liked its quaint look. It made him feel mysterious, and he was touched that Lillian had honored him with her beloved Alfie's favorite garment.

"Now let's see about getting you some supper," he said.

The boy followed him down the front hall to the kitchen, peeking into the parlor as they passed. He reached for the pennywhistle on the side table.

"Leave it," Ian said.

"Ye play that thing?"

"Don't touch anything—I don't like having my things disturbed."

Derek took in the Persian carpets and silk drapes and whistled softly. "Ye can afford all this on a policeman's salary?"

Ian smiled. Aunt Lillian, a tireless shopper at jumble sales and estate liquidations, was responsible for much of his flat's furnishings. "You like lamb chops?"

"Ye bet I do!"

"Right," said Ian, turning up the gas lamps. "Lamb chops it is." He took a step into the kitchen—there, sitting on the kitchen counter, was the mouse. It returned his gaze, flicking its tail irritably. It looked decidedly well fed, plump, and sleek.

"A pet mouse!" said Derek. "Yer not so borin' after all."

"Go on," Ian told the mouse. "Go away."

The mouse sniffed the air.

Ian took a step toward it. *Go away.*

The mouse began industriously cleaning its whiskers.

"GO!" Ian shouted, waving his arms.

With a dismissive shake of its tail, the creature waddled to the other end of the counter and disappeared behind the stove.

"Tomorrow I buy a mousetrap," Ian muttered.

"So it's not yer pet, innit?" said Derek, hopping up to sit on the counter.

"No."

"Why don't ye kill it?" he asked, scratching behind his ear.

"Why don't you go take a bath while I make dinner? There are clean towels in the linen closet, and a bathrobe."

"Ye have a *bathtub*?"

"Go along, then."

He listened for the boy's retreating footsteps before lighting the gas under the skillet. By the time Derek emerged from the bath, pink and scrubbed, Ian had the meal set out on the carved mahogany table in the parlor. A brace of pewter candlesticks bookended a perfectly browned lamb chop smothered in potatoes and turnips.

"Where'd ye learn to cook?" the boy asked as he stuffed his cheeks full of lamb with neeps and tatties. With his dark complexion and black hair, he looked like a Middle Eastern prince in the oversized Turkish bathrobe.

"My uncle ran a restaurant," Ian said, opening a bottle of pale ale.

"Lucky you. He still 'ave it?"

"He's dead."

"Kin I have a beer?" Derek asked, wiping his mouth with his sleeve.

"Oiy!" Ian said, thrusting a napkin at him.

The boy took it. "How 'bout a beer?" he asked, eyeing Ian's bottle.

"What are you—nine, ten years old?"

"Sixteen."

"You are not."

"I'm small fer me age."

"No, you may not have a beer. You may have a sip of mine."

"Thanks, mister!" Derek said, gulping it down greedily.

"That's enough," Ian said, wresting it from him.

"My da used t'let me drink whenever I wanted."

"And what a fine specimen of manhood he is. Now then, what did you want to say to me?"

Derek burped loudly. "It's more in the way of a business proposition."

"I'm listening."

The boy put his elbows on the table and leaned forward. "It's like this, see. I got mates, all over town, what could be of help—"

"*Who* could be of help."

"Ye get what I'm sayin', innit? We could be your eyes and ears, so tae speak, an' keep ye informed about what's goin' on."

"I assume your sudden passion to aid law enforcement comes with a price."

Derek grinned. "I'm sure we can think a somethin', Guv'nur."

"It's late. We'll do our thinking tomorrow."

"Right," said Derek, scooping the last bit of food from his plate with a piece of bread.

After dinner, Ian made a bed for the boy on the sofa, giving him a pillow from his own bed. Derek threw himself on the couch and sank into the soft cushions, sighing with contentment. "This is what I call livin'. Play me a tune, will ye?" he said, eyeing the pennywhistle.

"It's late."

"Just one, mate? It'll help me sleep."

"What do you want to hear?"

"Sommit sad an' mournful. D'ye know 'The Minstrel Boy'?"

Ian played the song through slowly, and Derek sang along softly.

"The minstrel boy to the war is gone,
In the ranks of death you'll find him;
His father's sword he has girded on,
And his wild harp slung behind him"

crash. The pot smashed to smithereens, biscuits rolling across the floor toward all corners of the room. The sergeant leapt to his feet, his face crimson. "I'm so sorry! Are ye all right?"

"Quite all right, thank you," Caroline replied. "All the tea spilled on the floor."

"I think we can conclude this interview for now," said Ian, rising from his chair. "If you think of anything else, Miss Tierney, please get in touch with me."

"Certainly, Detective Inspector," she replied, rising gracefully and pulling on her cloak. "Thank you for the tea."

Dickerson muttered something in response as he bent to pick up the shattered pieces of crockery. A few of the other officers snickered as he scurried to collect the escaped biscuits.

After escorting Miss Tierney from the station house, Ian returned to a crestfallen Dickerson.

"I'm sorry, sir. That were most clumsy," he said, sweeping up the remaining pieces of the broken teapot.

"Perhaps we can take a lesson from this, Sergeant."

Dickerson looked up from his whisk broom and dustpan. "Wha' might that be, sir?"

"Objectivity is the first rule of crime solving. A good investigator must never allow the interview subject to put him off his game."

Dickerson stopped sweeping. "What're you implying, sir?"

"We'll speak no more of this, Sergeant. I have no wish to embarrass you further."

Without replying, Dickerson returned to his task, his jaw set. Ian felt for him, but he couldn't allow his sympathy to eradicate the natural barrier between them—or worse, relax the standards required of a police officer. Dickerson was young, a smitten puppy, but the sooner he learned the importance of discipline and emotional distance, the better for him. Ian, too, had taken note of Miss Tierney's charms, but she might as well have been a lovely statue as far as his emotional response was concerned. A nagging voice at the back of his head told him that was unnatural, that there was something wrong with him, but he forced his mind onto other things.

Consulting his watch, he saw it was long past time to leave. Aunt Lillian had invited him over for the evening, and he seldom refused an offer from her. He walked quietly to the coatrack, slid on his cloak, and left the station house.

CHAPTER
THIRTY-THREE

A wicked wind whipped in from the west as Ian stood on the narrow pavement, pulling on his gloves. Exhaustion hung on his body like a heavy cloak, but Lillian was his most valued sounding board, and he looked forward to mulling over the case with her.

As he started down the street, he heard a familiar voice.

"Hullo, Guv'nur!"

"Hello, Derek," he said without turning around.

"I've come ta report in," the boy said, scurrying along beside him.

"Very well," Ian replied without breaking stride.

"I brought me friend along."

Ian stopped walking. Next to Derek stood a lanky boy of roughly the same age with fair hair and frank blue eyes.

"This is me mate Freddie what I told ye 'bout."

"Hello, Freddie."

"'Lo, mister," Freddie replied with a glance at Derek, who was clearly the leader of the two. "Is it true you're the copper what's catchin' that mad killer?" Freddie asked, gazing at Ian with wide eyes.

"I'm doing my best," Ian replied, resuming walking.

"Don' ye wan' t'hear what I got ta say?" said Derek, striding to catch up with him.

"Do I have a choice?"

"If that's the way ye feel, I'll slip away into the night and darken yer doorstep nae further."

Ian stopped walking. "'Darken my doorstep no further'? Where did you pick up that kind of language?"

"Books, Guv'nur," Derek replied, fishing a battered tome from the depths of his overcoat.

"You can read?" Ian asked, looking at the book's title. "*The Pickwick Papers*, by Charles Dickens. You read *this*?"

"He's not so bad—writes 'bout fellas like me, y'know," the boy replied, snatching it and shoving it back into his pocket.

"I am aware of the work of Mr. Dickens."

"I'll bet ye went to a swanky school, eh, mister?" said Freddie.

"Not especially. But I did like to read."

"But you don' anymore?"

"I have to be somewhere," Ian said as a gust of wind nearly swept away his hat.

"So do ye wan' my news or not?" asked Derek.

"If you can keep up with me," Ian replied, resuming walking.

"I have a message from Mrs. Sutherland."

Ian stopped abruptly. "Stephen Wycherly's landlady?"

"The same."

"What were you doing talking with her?"

"Part a' my job is ta know where you go, innit?"

Ian frowned. "I don't remember inviting you to do that."

"Jes hang on a minute, will ya? So I stops by to see if there's anythin' she forgot to tell you, and she tells me there is something. Only she'd rather tell you in person, see? So I says I'll pass that message along to you."

"She didn't say what it was?"

He was surprised the boy knew all the lyrics. When he finished, Derek sighed happily. "That were great—do another."

"I said one. Now go to sleep," Ian said, bending down to tuck the quilt around the boy's feet. As he did, Ian's dressing gown slid slightly, exposing some of his left shoulder.

Derek looked up at him. "Oiy—what happened to yer shoulder?"

Ian drew the robe closer, covering the exposed shoulder. The skin was red and bumpy, like bubbling lava. "I was in a fire."

"Same one what killed yer folks?"

"Yes."

"That's a rough break, mate."

"It's time for bed."

"Do it hurt?"

"Go to sleep."

"No wonder ye seem kinda angry all th'time."

"I should warn you, I'm a light sleeper. If you rob me, you'll regret it," Ian said, heading toward his bedroom. "Good night."

"'Night, Guv'."

As Ian lay in bed, his shoulder throbbed, as it did in damp weather. He wondered if his injury was the real reason he avoided women—or was it just an excuse, as Lillian had suggested? He did fear they would find it repulsive, but there were darker forces that made him shy away from the fairer sex. He went to bed at night hugging his anger, holding it close as a lover. He feared if he let go of it, he would have nothing. He knew he was holding on to his pain, worrying it as one might pick at a scab, but it gave him a perverse sense of comfort.

He rose from his bed and padded across the green Persian rug, pulling back the lemon silk drapes Lillian had hung over the French windows overlooking Victoria Terrace. So many of his comforts he owed to her. Stunned by his parents' death, for a while he had existed in a daze, barely able to dress himself or eat. His brother had disappeared even before the funeral, leaving Ian alone with his grief and confusion.

He did not know what might have become of him if Lillian had not swooped in and scooped him up in her embrace, transferring onto him the fierce love she had given Alfie. He gazed out at the sleeping city, its inhabitants tucked safely into their beds. It was his job to protect them, to see no other family was savaged by tragedy as his had been. It was a quest worthy of Don Quixote, but it was reassuring to be at his post day after day.

He thought of the boy sleeping on his couch, taken unawares by the swelling in his throat, the moisture collecting on his cheeks. Ian kept his emotions so tightly in check that when one escaped, it was startling. Edinburgh had many Derek McNairs, sleeping on hard cobblestones rather than cushioned sofas. Ian realized he had more in common with the boy than he might care to admit, knowing what it was to be dispossessed. Flicking away unfamiliar tears, he returned to his bed and slipped in between the sheets. His shoulder pulsed and throbbed as he turned onto his right side, the bedsprings moaning and creaking.

That night he dreamed of following a faceless murderer through the streets of Edinburgh as the city burned. The leaping flames danced all around as he trailed him down wynds and alleys, until he cornered the man in a basement. Ian started down the cellar steps, thinking he would finally see the killer's face, when he awoke abruptly from the dream. A thin gray dawn hung outside his bedroom curtains, and he watched the light gather before sinking into an uneasy sleep.

CHAPTER
TWENTY-NINE

The solitary figure standing beneath the shadow of Castle Rock gazed at the city, which lay lost in midwinter slumber. He did not like this time of year. The winter his mother succumbed to cholera, a life that had been bearable became a living nightmare. His father took him and his brother to the city, opened a chemist shop, and never smiled again. The more he tried to avoid his father, the more the old man zeroed in on him for abuse. The barnyard fights were moved to the building's basement, beneath the apothecary shop, strewn with straw from the horse stalls next door.

Shoving his hands into his pockets, he walked along the High Street, following the route traversed by centuries of warriors and wizards, monks and merchants, saints and sinners. But he was not thinking about any of them; he was remembering the night everything changed forever. It was only a few weeks after his mother's death, and grief had settled over the house like a grim visitor, encasing the three of them in its miserable cocoon.

Having dragged both boys out of bed on one especially nasty night, his father was muttering drunkenly to himself, twisting his belt around his hands. If the boys didn't fight well enough, they would feel the belt on their backs. He knew this, and knew his father's rage had grown and festered in the past weeks until it threatened to destroy them all.

He decided that night not to fight his brother. It was time to stand up to the old man, and he felt if he didn't now, he never would. He refused to fight, and his father's taunts failed to move him.

"Nancy-boy! Weakling! *Useless old woman!*" his father shouted, weaving drunkenly around the room and brandishing the belt, while his brother cowered in the corner.

He steeled himself for the blows, but to his surprise, they did not come. Instead, he felt the leather belt being wrapped around his throat quick as a flash. Before he could cry out, he heard his father cursing in his ear, his face so close, he could smell his whisky breath.

"*You think you can cross me?* I'll show you what happens to boys who try that, you miserable little insect!" he hissed, pulling the belt tighter.

He felt the life drain from his body along with his breath, and his last thought was that he was glad it would finally be over. The next thing he remembered, he was lying on the basement floor, his brother, looking worried and terrified, standing over him. His father was nowhere to be seen. Instead of relief at being alive, he felt tremendous disappointment that his suffering wasn't over after all. What he didn't know was that it was only just beginning.

CHAPTER THIRTY

A loud pounding on the front door awakened Ian on Wednesday morning. Cursing, he threw off the pile of blankets and heaved himself to the floor, the wide wooden planks icy beneath his feet. As he felt around for his slippers, the knocking continued relentlessly.

"Jesus, Mary, and Joseph," he muttered, using the curse his mother had always uttered, and grabbed his red plaid dressing gown. By the time he threw open the bedroom door, the banging had stopped. He entered the foyer to find a sleep-tousled Derek McNair standing at the open front door and chatting with a cheerful-looking George Pearson.

"Good Lord, do you have any idea what time it is?" Ian demanded.

"Indeed I do," Pearson replied. "It is precisely half past six."

"Is he ta come inside?" Derek asked, giving Pearson an appraising look.

"I have something of interest to impart to you," the librarian said, his prominent eyes shining.

"For God's sake," said Ian as an icy gust of air swirled in. "Come in, and close that blasted door!"

Derek admitted Pearson without relinquishing his hold on the doorknob. Once inside, the boy gave the heavy door a mighty shove and stood leaning against it, arms crossed, as though on guard in case Pearson should suddenly make a break for it.

"What is so urgent that you drag me out of bed at this hour?" said Ian.

"I apologize for my untimely entrance," the librarian replied. "I took you for an early riser."

"So what is this vital information you have?"

Pearson glanced at Derek and raised an eyebrow. "Who is this young fellow?"

"Master McNair is my houseguest. He was just about to go to the kitchen and put the kettle on," Ian added with a meaningful look at the boy. Derek frowned, but Ian clasped him firmly by the shoulder and pushed him toward the kitchen. "Please, don't let us interfere with your tea making. I am sure we are all parched for a cup."

Derek wrested himself from Ian's grasp. "But—"

"I'm sure you wouldn't want to jeopardize our working relationship."

McNair's sharp face broke into a wide smile. "Comin' right up, Guv'nur!" he said, skipping into the kitchen.

"What an odd child," Pearson commented, watching him go.

"Now then, Mr. Pearson, what coaxed you out of a warm bed at this ungodly hour?"

The librarian pulled a carefully folded newspaper from the pocket of his overcoat. "I was going through the stack of old newspapers, preparing to discard them, when I came across this." It was a copy of *Le Figaro*, the French daily.

"This is two months out of date. Why—"

"Look at the article below the fold on the first page," Pearson urged.

Ian's eyes fell upon the article's headline.

LE MYSTÉRIEUX ÉTRANGLEUR A ENCORE FRAPPÉ!

The librarian read over his shoulder. "It says—"

"I understand French. It's an article about a mysterious strangler in Paris."

"Read on," said Pearson. "You'll find that the crimes are similar to the Edinburgh stranglings."

Scanning the article, Ian realized Pearson was right. He looked at the librarian, who was fairly bursting with excitement. "The man you seek may have already committed crimes on the Continent!" Pearson proclaimed.

Derek McNair entered the room, carrying a tea tray piled so high with biscuits and scones, his thin arms could barely support it. "Tea's up!" he chirped. "I found some boiled eggs, too," he said, setting the tray on the dining table.

Pearson eyed it greedily. "Why, thank you—don't mind if I do."

Lighting the gas in the grate, Ian sat down to the meal McNair had prepared. Sandwiched between his two unwelcome guests, he felt cranky and out of sorts.

"So, what do you think of my discovery?" said the librarian, slathering butter on a scone.

"Many people travel back and forth from the Continent. I don't see how this helps us locate the perpetrator."

"You kin talk to the French coppers, fer one thing," suggested Derek, stuffing his cheeks with raisin scones. "Two heads is better 'an one, innit?"

George Pearson regarded the boy with some alarm, then extended his hand. "George William Pearson, chief reference librarian, University of Edinburgh Library."

Derek brushed the crumbs from his fingers and shook Pearson's hand. "Derek McNair, professional pickpocket."

Pearson giggled. "Your nephew is quite the jokester."

"He's not joking. And he isn't my nephew."

The librarian gave Ian a puzzled look. "Why on earth has a pickpocket taken up residence with you?"

"He's leaving today," Ian replied with a meaningful look at Derek, who frowned and bit his lip. "I just let him stay the night in exchange for—"

"Fer help on 'is case!" the boy declared.

"Indeed?" said Pearson. "What kind of help?"

"Not to be rude," Ian said, rising from the table, "but I need to report in at the station house. I'm sure you have somewhere to be as well, Mr. Pearson—"

"Not really," Pearson replied cheerfully, helping himself to a boiled egg. "It's my day off."

"Then when you have both finished breakfast, would you kindly—"

"I'll wash up," Pearson said genially, "since our miscreant friend here prepared the meal."

"Much obliged, I'm sure," Derek mumbled through a mouthful of scone.

Realizing he was outnumbered, Ian turned and headed for his bedroom.

"Oiy—got any more cream, mate?" McNair called after him.

"No," Ian said, already regretting his decision to let the boy stay the night. *No good deed goes unpunished,* he thought glumly, closing the door behind him.

CHAPTER
THIRTY-ONE

By the time Ian was dressed and ready to leave, Pearson and Derek were on their second pot of tea. The boy was persuaded to leave through bribery with scones, which he stuffed into his pockets before making his exit. Pearson was more difficult; after trying unsuccessfully to coax case information out of Ian, he finally prepared to make his exit.

"I'll leave the newspaper, shall I?" he said, lingering at the door. "Just in case you want to have a go at contacting the French police."

"Thank you, Mr. Pearson."

Pearson tugged his hat lower and leaned against the door. "You will follow up on this, won't you?"

"I'll see what I can do."

Pearson's chubby face fell. "I rather thought you'd find this useful."

"Thank you for bringing it to my attention."

"You will drop by the reference desk this week?" Pearson said moodily. "I want to know what you thought of that book I gave you."

"I'll do my best."

"Good day, then," said the librarian, and Ian watched through the window as he trudged toward the steps leading down from Victoria Terrace.

After quickly downing a final cup of tea, Ian slung his cloak over his shoulders, grabbed a hat, and ventured down the steep, narrow staircase. Victoria Street was one of the oldest roads in Edinburgh, looking very much as it had four hundred years ago. Four- and five-story buildings hugged the narrow street as it curved and rose toward Castle Hill, round chimneys poking up from the roofs like candles on a cake.

The city was still slumbering when Ian turned onto Princes Street toward the telegraph office. When he entered, the bell on the door tinkled to announce his arrival. He wasted no time scribbling out his message, handing it to the sleepy window clerk.

INVESTIGATING STRANGLINGS SIMILAR TO PARIS CRIMES TWO MONTHS AGO. ANY ADDITIONAL INFORMATION USEFUL. CONTACT DI IAN HAMILTON, EDINBURGH CITY POLICE.

"I'd like to pay for a reply, please," he said, sliding the message underneath the brass bars of the window.

"Very good, sir," replied the clerk, eyes heavy beneath his green visor.

"Have it delivered here," Ian said, writing out the address of the station house. He handed it to the clerk along with a one-pound note.

"Right you are, sir," said the clerk, counting out his change.

Ian was out the door before the clerk had closed the cash drawer. Leaning into a strong wind, he made his way to the station house, arriving just in time for the morning shift change. Sergeant Dickerson came in moments later, rubbing his hands together and blowing on them.

"Forgot me blasted gloves," he said, settling down at his desk. "Anythin' new, sir?"

Ian handed him the newspaper *Le Figaro*.

Dickerson squinted at it. "I don' speak French. What does it say?"

Ian told him.

The sergeant leaned back in his chair and studied the newspaper. "Assumin' this is the same perp'trator, how does this help us catch 'im?"

Ian sat across from him. "It tells us some things about him."

Dickerson frowned. "Per'aps I'm a bit thick, sir, but what, exactly?"

"He gravitates toward large cities. He is comfortable in both Edinburgh and Paris, and doesn't stand out as unusual or suspicious; he may be employed in some capacity in both places. He is likely to be a man of some means, and rather worldly. He is likely educated, clever, and articulate, and probably speaks French."

Dickerson scratched his chin. "Beg pardon, sir, but how do ye get all that?"

"Whoever committed these crimes didn't call attention to himself—at least not enough to alert his victims until it was too late. That means he managed to blend into his surroundings."

"How d'you know he's 'comf'table' in Paris an' Edinburgh?"

"Offenders tend to commit crimes where they feel at home, places they know. Someone familiar with Paris and Edinburgh is likely to be worldly and well traveled."

"But why educated? The Hound and Hare isn't a place for tha' kind a bloke."

"The Hound and Hare aside, someone who can afford to travel between major cities is more likely to have an education and come from a good family. He's clever and articulate enough to have lured Stephen Wycherly to his death on Arthur's Seat."

Dickerson shivered. "I dunno, sir—the more ye talk about this fellow, the less I think we're likely to catch him any time soon."

At that moment, a young boy in a square-brimmed cap entered the station house. "Telegram for Detective Inspector Hamilton," he announced in a thin, reedy voice, holding up a piece of paper.

"I'm Detective Inspector Hamilton," Ian said, fishing in his pocket for change.

"Ta very much," said the lad, taking the tuppence.

Ian scanned the message eagerly.

TAKING FERRY TONIGHT. ARRIVE LONDON TOMORROW MORNING. FIRST TRAIN TO EDINBURGH. STAYING AT WAVERLEY HOTEL ON PRINCES STREET. CHIEF INSPECTOR LOUIS GERARD, SURETE NATIONALE.

"Who's it from?" asked Dickerson, trying to peer over Ian's shoulder.

"My French doppelganger."

"Beg pardon, sir?"

Ian handed him the telegram. "It seems we're about to have a visitor."

CHAPTER
THIRTY-TWO

The second surprise arrived later that day in the person of Bobby Tierney's sister, Caroline, clutching the business card Ian had left at her flat when he tried unsuccessfully to call on her. Having awakened before dawn, Ian was just contemplating a nap when the duty sergeant ushered her into the room.

"Detective Inspector Ian Hamilton?" she asked timidly, avoiding the stares of constables seated at their desks or standing in small groups in front of the duty-roster board. Ian had to admit they had something to stare at. Miss Caroline Tierney was a young woman of unusual beauty, with white skin framed by lustrous black hair. Her eyes were green as jade, and he imagined many a young man swooned at the thought of kissing those tremulous red lips.

He indicated a chair next to his desk. "Please, take a seat."

"Thank you," she replied, a becoming blush spreading across her rosy cheeks. "I must apologize for not coming earlier, but I've been very occupied—preparing for Bobby's funeral, and seeing to his possessions. I'm his only living kin, you see."

"I'm very sorry about your brother. I won't take much of your time."

She dabbed at her eyes with a perfumed lace handkerchief. Ian was struck by how unlike her brother she was—from all accounts, Bobby was a bar brawler and ruffian, whereas Caroline seemed the very picture of feminine propriety.

Ian cleared his throat. "Now, then, Miss Tierney—"

He was interrupted by the appearance of Sergeant Dickerson, who had been filing papers in the back of the station. The sergeant swung around the corner of the glass divider and was nearly at Ian's desk when their visitor turned to see him. Ian had never seen a person receive an electric shock, but he imagined it would look very much like Sergeant Dickerson's reaction to Caroline Tierney. His eyebrows shot up, and his mouth dropped open. There was a sharp intake of breath as his entire body froze.

"Meet Miss Caroline Tierney," Ian said. "This is Sergeant Dickerson," he told her. "He's assisting on your brother's case."

Caroline extended a dainty hand. "Pleased to meet you."

Dickerson hesitated, and Ian wasn't sure whether he was going to shake it or kiss it. He appeared utterly unhinged at the sight of her. "P-pleased to meet ye, miss," he said finally, grasping her hand and giving a deep bow. Releasing her hand, he looked at Ian desperately for help.

"Why don't you take notes while I interview Miss Tierney?" Ian said.

"Certainly, sir," Dickerson replied in a voice an octave higher than usual. "Right you are." He plunked himself down in the chair on the other side of the desk and busied himself writing in his notebook. He printed *Interview with Miss Caroline Tierney*, then underlined it, pressing so hard on the paper, Ian thought he would tear it.

"You said you were Mr. Tierney's only family?" Ian asked.

Her green eyes welled with tears, her lips swelling and trembling in a way that made her even more attractive. "Both our parents are gone, you see, so it was only me and Bobby." She dabbed at her eyes with her handkerchief. "And now it's just me."

Ian glanced at Sergeant Dickerson, whose own face expressed such misery as he gazed at her that Ian thought it best to snap him out of it.

"Sergeant?"

Dickerson turned to him with an expression like a scolded puppy's. "Sir?"

"I expect Miss Tierney could use a cup of tea on a raw day like this. Why don't you—"

"Yes, sir!" Dickerson responded, jumping up from his chair. He paused, frowning. "What about the note taking?"

"I'll manage on my own until you return."

"Right you are, sir," Dickerson said, lurching off toward the tea service in the back of the room.

"Now then, Miss Tierney," Ian said. "What happened to your parents, if I may ask?"

She looked down at her elegantly gloved hands. "Pa died of a heart attack shortly after the famine, and Ma died of grief."

"I'm very sorry to hear it."

"Bobby never got over it. Always angry, he was. There was nothing in County Cork for us anymore, so we came here. One of Bobby's schoolmates set us up with a flat on the London Road."

"Near Leith Walk?"

"That's right."

Ian scribbled *London Road/Leith Walk* in the notebook. That meant that the two victims lived very near each other. "And how was it working out for you?" he asked.

"Bobby could always find work on the docks, and I'm a decent secretary. Between us, we made a go of it, I s'pose."

"Pardon me if this is too personal, but you sound quite well educated," Ian remarked.

"Our mother was a schoolteacher. Our home was never lacking in books. Guess I took to them more than Bobby did, bless his soul."

Sergeant Dickerson came wobbling toward them with a heavily laden tea tray. He had managed to find a tin of biscuits and some crystallized ginger.

"Here we are," he said, nearly toppling everything as he leaned over the desk.

"How very kind of you," Caroline said.

"I'll pour, shall I?" he said, wiping the sweat from his palms and loosening his shirt collar. Irritated, Ian bit his lip. He supposed Miss Tierney was used to having an effect on men, but Dickerson's reaction was extreme.

"Can you think of anyone who might want to harm your brother, Miss Tierney?" Ian asked as Dickerson handed her a mug of tea.

She smiled sadly. "It's rather a question of who wouldn't want to, I'm afraid. My brother had a habit of finding trouble. After a while, trouble had a habit of finding him."

"Is there anyone your brother had a disagreement with recently?"

She sipped delicately at her tea and rested the mug in her lap. "He often came home with battle scars but spoke little about them."

"Did he have a sweetheart?"

"He had a girl back in Ireland, but she tired of his drinking. He truly cared for her, I believe, but couldn't seem to control his love of the bottle."

"And your brother's friends, Miss Tierney? What were they like?"

"Most of his 'friends' were angry young men with a chip on their shoulder."

"More tea, Miss Tierney?" Sergeant Dickerson asked, reaching for the pot without taking his eyes off her. The tray wobbled dangerously as his sleeve caught on the edge before tumbling to the ground with a crash. The pot smashed to smithereens, biscuits rolling across the floor toward all corners of the room. The sergeant leapt to his feet, his face crimson. "I'm so sorry! Are ye all right?"

"Quite all right, thank you," Caroline replied. "All the tea spilled on the floor."

"I think we can conclude this interview for now," said Ian, rising from his chair. "If you think of anything else, Miss Tierney, please get in touch with me."

"Certainly, Detective Inspector," she replied, rising gracefully and pulling on her cloak. "Thank you for the tea."

Dickerson muttered something in response as he bent to pick up the shattered pieces of crockery. A few of the other officers snickered as he scurried to collect the escaped biscuits.

After escorting Miss Tierney from the station house, Ian returned to a crestfallen Dickerson.

"I'm sorry, sir. That were most clumsy," he said, sweeping up the remaining pieces of the broken teapot.

"Perhaps we can take a lesson from this, Sergeant."

Dickerson looked up from his whisk broom and dustpan. "Wha' might that be, sir?"

"Objectivity is the first rule of crime solving. A good investigator must never allow the interview subject to put him off his game."

Dickerson stopped sweeping. "What're you implying, sir?"

"We'll speak no more of this, Sergeant. I have no wish to embarrass you further."

Without replying, Dickerson returned to his task, his jaw set. Ian felt for him, but he couldn't allow his sympathy to eradicate the natural barrier between them—or worse, relax the standards required of a police officer. Dickerson was young, a smitten puppy, but the sooner he learned the importance of discipline and emotional distance, the better for him. Ian, too, had taken note of Miss Tierney's charms, but she might as well have been a lovely statue as far as his emotional response was concerned. A nagging voice at the back of his head told him that was unnatural, that there was something wrong with him, but he forced his mind onto other things.

Consulting his watch, he saw it was long past time to leave. Aunt Lillian had invited him over for the evening, and he seldom refused an offer from her. He walked quietly to the coatrack, slid on his cloak, and left the station house.

CHAPTER THIRTY-THREE

A wicked wind whipped in from the west as Ian stood on the narrow pavement, pulling on his gloves. Exhaustion hung on his body like a heavy cloak, but Lillian was his most valued sounding board, and he looked forward to mulling over the case with her.

As he started down the street, he heard a familiar voice.

"Hullo, Guv'nur!"

"Hello, Derek," he said without turning around.

"I've come ta report in," the boy said, scurrying along beside him.

"Very well," Ian replied without breaking stride.

"I brought me friend along."

Ian stopped walking. Next to Derek stood a lanky boy of roughly the same age with fair hair and frank blue eyes.

"This is me mate Freddie what I told ye 'bout."

"Hello, Freddie."

"'Lo, mister," Freddie replied with a glance at Derek, who was clearly the leader of the two. "Is it true you're the copper what's catchin' that mad killer?" Freddie asked, gazing at Ian with wide eyes.

"I'm doing my best," Ian replied, resuming walking.

"Don' ye wan' t'hear what I got ta say?" said Derek, striding to catch up with him.

"Do I have a choice?"

"If that's the way ye feel, I'll slip away into the night and darken yer doorstep nae further."

Ian stopped walking. "'Darken my doorstep no further'? Where did you pick up that kind of language?"

"Books, Guv'nur," Derek replied, fishing a battered tome from the depths of his overcoat.

"You can read?" Ian asked, looking at the book's title. "*The Pickwick Papers*, by Charles Dickens. You read *this*?"

"He's not so bad—writes 'bout fellas like me, y'know," the boy replied, snatching it and shoving it back into his pocket.

"I am aware of the work of Mr. Dickens."

"I'll bet ye went to a swanky school, eh, mister?" said Freddie.

"Not especially. But I did like to read."

"But you don' anymore?"

"I have to be somewhere," Ian said as a gust of wind nearly swept away his hat.

"So do ye wan' my news or not?" asked Derek.

"If you can keep up with me," Ian replied, resuming walking.

"I have a message from Mrs. Sutherland."

Ian stopped abruptly. "Stephen Wycherly's landlady?"

"The same."

"What were you doing talking with her?"

"Part a' my job is ta know where you go, innit?"

Ian frowned. "I don't remember inviting you to do that."

"Jes hang on a minute, will ya? So I stops by to see if there's anythin' she forgot to tell you, and she tells me there is something. Only she'd rather tell you in person, see? So I says I'll pass that message along to you."

"She didn't say what it was?"

"She found somethin' she wants ye t'see."

"Would you run along and tell her I'll call on her first thing tomorrow?"

"Righto, Guv'nur," Derek said, but didn't move.

"Well? What's keeping you?"

"Dashin' all 'round town builds up an appetite. An' Freddie's hungry too—aren't ye?"

Freddie nodded vigorously.

"Fine," Ian said, fishing half a crown from his pocket. "Here."

"Thanks, Guv'nur," Derek said, slipping it into his pocket.

"Now get along. And stop calling me Guv'nur."

"Whatever you say, Guv'nur."

The boys darted off, laughing. Ian tugged the brim of his hat lower, pulling his collar up against the chilly night, and continued in the direction of his aunt's town house.

The air smelled of salt and seaweed as he trudged up the hill. The wind was shifting, bringing in sea air from the Firth of Forth to the northeast. Born in the arctic waters of the North Sea, the firth cut a deep slash into Scotland's east coast, bifurcating the land at the narrow stretch boasting its two greatest cities, Glasgow and Edinburgh. Lying at almost the same latitude on the map, they were the last two metropolitan hubs, beyond which lay the wild expanse of the Highlands and the outer islands scattered along Scotland's shores like broken pieces of birthday cake.

Tugging tired children behind them, pedestrians plodded by, laden with packages. Everyone seemed sunk in gloomy contemplation, struggling silently up the hill in the early February darkness.

Ian was relieved to see the gaslights blazing brightly in the front windows of his aunt's town house. He was glad he had accepted her offer—more like a commandment—to join her for a drink. Though a midweek meeting was not one of their established rituals, it was doubly welcome after the past few days. His glum mood brightened when

Lillian's front door swung open, bringing the welcome sight of her face, wreathed in smiles. In her left hand was a bottle of cream sherry.

"Ach, you're just in time for a wee dram."

He kissed her cheek, soft and crinkled as tissue paper.

"Hello, Auntie."

"Come in and close the door behind you—no need to heat the whole outdoors," she said, trundling down the hall as he followed obediently behind.

"So," she said as they settled in front of the fire, "tell me how your case is going."

"Not well. And today Sergeant Dickerson made a fool of himself over a pretty face."

"Dear me. What happened?"

As he recounted the incident involving Caroline Tierney's visit, he saw his aunt trying unsuccessfully to suppress a smile.

"Your sergeant is a red-blooded young man," she said, laying a hand on his. "You mustn't be so hard on him—allow him some of the foolishness of youth."

"We can't afford foolishness when lives are at stake."

"But you were only interviewing a young woman whose brother had the misfortune to be a victim."

"A crime investigator must learn to cultivate objectivity."

"Dear me, that's harsh."

"You can't always know whether the charming person sitting opposite you is a murderer."

"Is that why you have no one special in your life?"

"We're not discussing my personal life," he replied stiffly.

"Do you consider it less important than your professional life?"

"Yes, as a matter of fact."

She shook her head sadly. "What a pity. All the flowers of Edinburgh going unplucked because you feel you have to remain 'objective.'"

"'Love looks not with the eyes, but with the mind, and therefore is winged Cupid painted blind.'"

She gave a dismissive wave. "Ach, Ian, don't use your intellect as a weapon."

"I know you had an idyllic marriage to Uncle Alfred, and I'm very glad for you. But the 'flowers of Edinburgh' will manage to struggle on without me."

"Is it because of your shoulder?" she asked softly.

"I'd really prefer not to discuss it," he replied, feeling the heat rise to his face.

She sighed and pulled her aged limbs out of the armchair. Ian saw her effort to disguise the discomfort, but she couldn't entirely mask the stiffness in her bones. Flooded with remorse, he laid a hand on her arm.

"Forgive me, Auntie—it's been a trying week."

"There's nothing to forgive, dear boy," she said, reaching for a new bottle of sherry in the liquor cabinet. "It's just that I want so much for you to know the deep pleasure of true love."

"Maybe I will someday," he said. "Don't give up on me just yet."

But even as he said the words, he didn't believe them.

"So the case, then?" she said eagerly, pouring them each a second glass.

"I can't find a link between the victims. They seem so different, yet there *must* be something connecting them."

"Is it possible they were killed by different people?"

"No."

"How can you be sure?"

"If I tell you, it must not leave this room. We're not releasing this detail to the public."

"You have my word."

He told her about the strange cards found on each victim. She drained the rest of her sherry. "Dear me," she said, tapping the empty glass with her finger. "Could the link be gambling?"

"I have no evidence to suggest that."

"Maybe the only connection is that they both knew their killer."

"I'm not convinced of that, either."

"But why kill a perfect stranger?"

"I'm convinced there's logic there, but I'm missing pieces of the puzzle. Once I find them, the story will flow as fluidly as—"

"As the Greek myths you used to love as a boy?" Lillian said softly.

"I loved all sorts of stories, especially ones my mother read to me."

"I liked the ones you wrote yourself best—full of heroes and mythical creatures and marvelous adventures. I always thought you were going to be a writer, in fact. We all did."

Ian thought about telling his aunt about his poetry but decided against it. He stared into the fire, the flames greedily licking the air, yellow as a dragon's tongue. He longed for the certainty and safety of fiction—in real life, monsters weren't always vanquished, and heroes didn't always win.

CHAPTER
THIRTY-FOUR

The streets were nearly deserted when Ian left Lillian's. He wove his way home, waving off cabbies who tipped their hats to offer their services. It was a short walk, and he was soon at his flat on Victoria Terrace.

The moment Ian reached his front door, he knew someone was there. He had not left the gaslight on in the parlor, yet a yellow flame flickered in the front window. His body stiffened as he eased the door open slowly, taking a single step into the foyer. He smelled onions frying, and the sound of whistling came from the kitchen. The tune was familiar, an old reel his mother used to play on the piano. He reached for the umbrella in the stand next to the door; as his hand closed around the handle, he heard approaching footsteps. He raised the umbrella, ready to strike, as the intruder stepped into the front hall. Seeing Ian wielding a weapon, he took a step backward.

"I know it's been a while, but I didn't expect to be greeted with a thrashing."

Ian lowered the umbrella. Standing in the front hall was his older brother, Donald, a dish towel wrapped around his ample waist.

"Good Lord," Ian said, wiping the sweat from the back of his neck. "How the devil did you get in?"

"I have a key, remember?" his brother replied, holding it up between his thumb and forefinger. "You really should change your lock, you know—this place isn't safe."

"Edinburgh, or this neighborhood?"

"Both—either. Take your pick. Nowhere is really safe these days. I hear you're pursuing a madman. How's that going?"

"What are you doing here?"

Donald frowned and pushed a lock of hair from his forehead. His face was long and aquiline, like his brother's, with the same keen gray eyes, but his hair was blond, his body soft and given to fat. He had put on a stone or two in the years since Ian last saw him. Taller than his brother by a couple of inches, Donald Hamilton was a substantial physical presence.

"You could at least pretend to be glad to see me."

"Sorry, fresh out of pretense today," Ian said, shoving the umbrella back in its stand.

His brother crossed his arms and cocked his head to one side. "Really, little brother, you wound me."

"I haven't heard from you for years, and you suddenly show up without warning. Why are you here?"

"Well, most immediately, to cook you dinner. I'm making my specialty, haggis under glass," he said, flicking the dish towel onto his shoulder.

"Seriously, Donald, it's late and I'm tired."

His brother met his gaze. "Seriously, then?"

"Aye."

Donald held out a trembling hand. The long, tapered fingers everyone had predicted would belong to a great surgeon someday shook with a visible tremor. "I'm done with it, Ian—finished. No more drinking for me."

For a moment, Ian's heart leapt. That was followed by a hollow thud in his chest. He had heard it all before—the vows, the promises, the declarations of sobriety. It had never come to anything. The bottle had always proven stronger than his brother's will.

He cleared his throat. "Can't you get sober in Glasgow?"

"Everything I care about—and fear—is here. You should know that better than anyone," he added, his gray eyes burning into Ian's. They were red-rimmed and swollen, and Ian suspected it wasn't from frying onions. "If I can't face Edinburgh, I can't shake the bottle."

"And the gambling—are you giving that up as well?"

"I know what you're thinking," Donald said. "You've heard it all before. But this time I'm determined. It's not too late to go to medical school; I could still get a degree, you know."

"You could," Ian said, keeping his voice steady and uninflected. He didn't want to provoke his brother into one of his rages. Though they usually happened when he was drunk, Ian had too many memories of Donald's rants, and had learned to be wary.

"You don't believe me."

"It's not up to me," Ian replied carefully. "The important thing is that you believe—"

"Don't condescend to me!" his brother hissed, and Ian instinctively backed away. "I'm sorry," Donald said quickly. "I'm afraid I'm a bit out of sorts—no booze and all that, eh?" he added with a little laugh.

"Of course," Ian replied. "Now then, you said you're making dinner? Let's have it, then—I'm famished."

His brother's face brightened. "Right!" he said, brushing away the rogue lock of hair. "I was joking about the haggis—I made shepherd's pie."

"Beef or lamb?"

"Both. Hope you're hungry. If I recall correctly, your appetite was not always up to snuff."

"No fear of that. I'm famished."

Ian followed his brother toward the kitchen, relief flooding his limbs. Donald was sober—for now, at least, so there would be no drunken rages, no descent into self-pity and maudlin monologues.

At the kitchen door Donald turned to him. "D'you know there's a wee mouse in here?"

"Did you kill it?"

"Couldn't catch the little bugger. I can get you a trap tomorrow."

"I'll get one," Ian said, wondering if he meant it.

"Suit yourself. And now, behold!" Donald said, opening the oven and drawing forth a golden-brown shepherd's pie. A waterfall of saliva cascaded into Ian's mouth—it smelled wonderful, and he remembered what a good cook his brother was.

Donald set it on a pineapple-shaped brass trivet on the kitchen table, standing back to admire it. "I haven't lost my touch in the kitchen—or so I hope. You can give me the report when you've had some."

The report was favorable. Ian was soon on his second helping, the two of them seated before the fire in the parlor, Donald sipping a ginger beer. He leaned back in his chair and surveyed the flat—the Turkish cushions, mahogany armoire, and rich fabrics.

"You've done well for yourself, by the look of it."

"This is all Lillian's work," Ian replied, tearing off a chunk of bread to sop up the sauce on his plate.

"How is dear Lillie?"

"She has arthritis and thinks she's hiding it from me."

"Always the sharp-eyed one, Brother Ian. It must feel strange to be in the same harness as our dear old da, eh?"

Ian wiped his mouth with a monogrammed linen napkin. "I seem to have a knack for it."

"Good on ye, as they say in Glasgow."

"How is life in Glasgow?"

"Crude, rude, profane. Inebriated. I felt right at home. Do you ever miss the Highlands?"

"I dream about it sometimes."

"Remember the smell of heather in early spring?"

"Aye, and the wild mountain thyme."

"'And we'll all go together,'" Donald sang softly. "Remember when we used to sing that?"

"I remember it all."

"And yet here you remain," Donald remarked. Lighting another cigarette, he tossed the match carelessly in the direction of the fire. It landed short of the grate, falling upon the carpet.

Ian leapt from his chair and swept it quickly into the fireplace. "Be careful! You could have burned the rug—"

"Or started a fire?" Donald suggested.

Ian clenched his fists and turned away.

"I saw the way you peered at me when I lit that cigarette. I've also noticed you don't smoke."

"It's bad for your health," Ian muttered without turning around.

"Surely as a 'medical man' you ought to know that."

"But that's not why you don't smoke, is it?"

"If your idea of a jolly evening is discussing the reasons behind my personal habits, I suggest we call it a night," Ian replied tightly.

"Not another word—promise. Hand to heart, hope to die."

"Let's have no more talk of dying. I'm well enough sick of it."

They sat staring at the leaping flames in the fireplace, their hungry orange tongues licking the air.

"Your shoulder still bother you?" Donald asked.

"Not too bad," Ian lied. He didn't want anyone's pity, least of all his brother's.

"Mum would be proud of you, you know," said Donald.

"What about Father?"

"What about him?"

"Wouldn't he be proud as well?"

"Perhaps he wasn't everything you imagined he was."

"What do you mean?"

Donald stretched and sighed. "This is no time to malign the dead. Forgive me."

"Are you referring to the rumors about him being corrupt? Because I don't believe them."

"Quite right you are. I'm sorry I said anything, truly."

They stared into the flames for a while longer, as drowsiness settled over the room.

"Well," Donald said with a yawn, "it's late and I'm knackered. Being sober does that to you." He rose and stretched himself, padding across the carpet in the direction of the bedrooms. At the doorway, he turned and smiled—not the weary, ironic smile of the man, but the sweet, shy smile of the boy Ian remembered. "Just like old times, eh, Brother?"

Ian knew that no matter how much they pretended otherwise, those days were gone forever. Looking at his brother's face, shiny with sweat and hope, he didn't have the heart to say so.

"Aye," he said. "Just like old times."

CHAPTER
THIRTY-FIVE

Elizabeth Sutherland, known to her friends as Betty, bustled about her kitchen with more energy than usual Wednesday evening. Though the death of her tenant was upsetting, she was now the object of curiosity and sympathy, a state she found most gratifying. Her neighbors were treating her with unusual deference—even bossy Mrs. Porter who ran the rooming house next door had laid a hand on her arm, clucked her tongue, and said, "Poor dear—how *are* you getting on?" To which Mrs. Sutherland had replied she was doing as well as could be expected under the circumstances, and that it was most disturbing to have a tenant *murdered* under your own roof (she felt justified including that last detail, untrue though it was, since Mr. Wycherly *had* lived under her roof, even though he wasn't actually killed there).

The next morning, a lemon cake with real buttercream frosting arrived with a thoughtful note from Mrs. Porter expressing her sympathy, saying if there was anything she could do—anything at all—to please let her know. Other expressions of sympathy and concern arrived from other friends and neighbors—tins of sweets, notes and cards, and even a bouquet of flowers from elderly Mr. Grant, who owned the barbershop on the corner.

Being a kind soul, Betty Sutherland was of course saddened by Mr. Wycherly's untimely demise, but she didn't feel herself to be in any danger. She and Mrs. Porter (of the luscious lemon cake) had reached the conclusion he had probably been killed over a gambling debt or some other character flaw. He had seemed such a nice young man, but you never knew about people—she had run a boardinghouse long enough to know the most genteel exterior could hide a dope fiend, dipsomaniac, or inveterate gambler. Though she continued to encourage the impression that the murder had happened *under her own roof,* she didn't really believe the killer would turn his eye upon her. She was merely the unlucky lad's landlady, nothing more.

And so, Wednesday evening when the doorbell rang, she bustled down the hall to answer it in high spirits, thinking it was perhaps another cake, or a vase of flowers. Just to be safe, she lifted the lid to the letter slot and peered through, to find herself staring into the eyes of the urchin who claimed to be working with that handsome detective inspector Hamilton. Though doubtful as to the boy's veracity, she had sent a message to the detective. If the message reached him, she knew the boy was on the level—it wasn't uncommon in Edinburgh to pay street Arabs a few pence to carry information to and fro.

"Mrs. Sutherland?" the boy said. "I got a reply from Detective Inspector Hamilton."

"What is it?"

"Kin I come in?"

"Are you alone?"

"Aye."

She unlatched the door and admitted him into the foyer. He was a scrawny fellow, small for his age, she judged, without knowing exactly how old he was. Though he was slight in stature, his eyes shone with keen intelligence. At least his face and hands weren't too grimy, she thought; he appeared to have bathed in the last week or so.

"Wipe your feet," she said, and he complied, removing his cap respectfully. "I expect you'd like some soup." The city was awash with boys like him, and a body couldn't take care of all of them. But she had noticed him licking his lips as the aroma of cabbage soup wafted in from the kitchen, his stomach rumbling loudly.

"Thank you, mum," he said as he followed her down the hall.

"So, what's this message, then?" she asked once he was settled in the corner nook of the kitchen, loudly slurping down leek and cabbage soup and stuffing his cheeks with hunks of brown bread.

"Detective Inspector Hamilton says he'll call on ye t'morrow."

"Very well," she said, hoping he didn't notice the flush spreading from the base of her neck upward. The thought of another visit from the dashing detective made her go a bit wobbly in the knees. "Did he say anything else?" she asked, turning to stir the soup to hide her reaction.

"No, mum," her visitor mumbled through a mouthful of bread.

"Don't gulp your food," she said. "It will give you indigestion."

"Yes, mum," he replied, swallowing with a loud gulp. "Sorry, mum."

She turned around and peered at him. "Derek, is it?" He nodded, spoon halfway to his mouth. "Please tell the detective inspector he's welcome to stay for a bite to eat if he comes in time for breakfast. I've just bought some fresh cress, and I can make him an omelet."

"Very good, mum," Derek responded. "Or," he added slyly, "ye could jus' give me what ye got an' I'll give it to 'im."

She frowned. "I'm not sure that's wise. Things can get lost so easily in transit."

"You kin rely on me, mum."

"It would be better if I gave it to him myself." In fact, she wasn't all that certain the object she had found was of any use—but it was an excuse to see the handsome detective inspector again.

"Suit yerself," said Derek, shoving more bread into his mouth.

Before the boy left, she gave him a couple of old shirts and a pair of darned socks. She tried not to think about where his mother might be or why a lad like him was on his own as she watched him head off down the street, but she had to admit there was something heartbreaking in the cockiness of his stride. The fact that he wasn't seeking her pity made her that much more inclined to give it.

She retired back to her kitchen, to have a bit of soup herself before bed, when there was another knock at the door. Thinking the boy had returned, she hurried out to the hall. But when she peered through the mail slot, she saw a face she recognized.

"Oh, it's you," she said, opening the door. "What on earth brings you here at this hour?"

Her visitor smiled enigmatically as she closed the door behind him. "I came to see how you were faring after the dreadful news."

She sighed. "It was quite a shock—to you as well, I imagine."

"Yes, poor fellow."

"You were a good friend to him, I know."

"Yes, yes," he replied, his eyes wandering the room restlessly. "Have you—"

"Yes, dear?" she said, giving the soup a stir.

"Have you gone through his room yet?"

"The police were here a few nights ago. They poked around a bit."

"Oh? Did they take anything?"

"No, but they were very keen to find a letter," she said, wiping her hands on her best towel, creamy linen with blue stripes. "Something about blackmail."

"Did they find it?"

"No."

"Do you mind if I have a look around?"

Her face softened. "Do you want a keepsake, then, something to remember him by?"

"Yes, that would be nice." He paused, suddenly alert. "What's that sound?"

She listened, and could hear whimpering and the sound of soft scratching coming from the back of the house. "Oh, that's Stephen's dog. He's sleeping in the laundry room, but he must have heard you come in. Would you like to take him, by any chance?"

His face registered displeasure. "No, thank you."

She sighed. "That young sergeant said he would take the dog, but he hasn't been back since then. Anyway, just go on up—you know which is Stephen's room."

She busied herself in the kitchen, humming as she tidied the counters and turned down the flame under the soup. After a few minutes, her visitor returned, looking disappointed.

"Did you find something, then?" she said.

"No," he replied, his eyes scanning the room and coming to rest on a scrap of paper protruding from her cookbook. "What's that?"

"Oh, this? Just something I found in poor Stephen's room," she said, plucking the card from between the pages. "I don't suppose it's anything, but I thought I'd give it to the investigating detective all the same."

"What an unusual design."

"It had fallen behind his dresser and was lodged in a crack in the wall. I wouldn't have seen it if I hadn't been doing a thorough cleaning."

"Do you know where it came from?"

"Not a clue. He didn't even play cards, as far as I know."

"So you have no idea where he got it?"

"I don't—but perhaps the police will be able to find out. Would you care for some cabbage soup? I just made a fresh pot."

"That would be lovely."

"Have a seat there," she said, leading him into the kitchen.

"It smells wonderful," he said, following her, the same enigmatic smile on his face.

Twenty minutes later, he emerged from the building, fists shoved in his pockets, the card clutched in his right hand. After a quick glance up and down the street, he strode briskly toward the center of the Old Town. He was angry with himself—the card had been missing for some days now, and after turning his hotel room upside down, he had finally gone to the only place he could think of where it might be.

He remembered the night he must have left it there. He and Stephen had gone on a bender, ending up at Leith Walk—and like a fool, he hadn't been able to resist showing off for Stephen. He didn't even know the card was missing until just last night, when he'd happened to thumb through the deck.

He stepped around a sleeping vagrant in front of Waverley Station, resisting the urge to give him a kick as a train thundered out of the station, belching black smoke into the night air. He took the ramp to North Bridge, still cursing himself for being so careless.

It was shortly after that evening he decided Stephen must die. He felt a little bad about the landlady, but glad he had come prepared. It would seem like a death from natural causes. Poor old thing—she reminded him a little of his mother. He bore no ill will toward kindly landladies; she was simply in the way. And he was not a man to let anything—or anyone—stand in his way.

CHAPTER
THIRTY-SIX

Dawn slunk timidly through the streets of the city the next morning, as if afraid of what it might find. The pale sun filtering in through the gingham curtains in the kitchen of 22 Leith Walk fell on a pathetic sight. The woman seated in the kitchen nook stared out at the thin light with unseeing eyes, her head resting upon the table as if she had fallen asleep. A bowl of cabbage soup sat next to her, long gone cold, as had the pot on the stove. A large black-and-white cat rubbed against her shins, complaining vocally that she had not yet stirred to feed it.

The cat would go unfed for most of the day. The poor woman was finally discovered by her lone boarder, a university student who stumbled sleepily downstairs after a night of studying. Expecting a hot meal, he was startled and shaken to find his landlady's lifeless body. After collecting himself, the boarder turned his footsteps in the direction of the police station, arriving disheveled and wild-eyed, to the bemusement of the constables on duty. Detective Inspector Ian Hamilton was summoned to the town house, accompanied by the stalwart Sergeant Dickerson.

"Sir?" the sergeant whispered, hovering next to DI Hamilton, who stood, staring at the dead woman in front of him, arms crossed, lips compressed in a frown. Sergeant Dickerson sighed. It had been nearly a quarter of an hour since they arrived at the boardinghouse, and the detective had spoken scarcely half a dozen words to him. Hamilton seemed to be burning with inner rage, clenching and unclenching his fists and muttering as he examined the scene. Dickerson tiptoed from the room into the hallway, where a pair of uniformed officers stood guard.

"What's this all about, sir?" asked one of them, a chunky young fellow with close-cropped blond hair. "Why are we treating this like a crime scene? Looks to me like the poor lady had a heart attack."

The sergeant removed his cap and ran a hand through his own head of increasingly shaggy red hair. His next haircut was long overdue. "It's like this, lads," he said. "This is where that dead fella lived—young Wycherly."

The blond constable's eyes widened. "The one what was strangled?"

Dickerson nodded with the satisfaction of possessing knowledge the others didn't. "The same."

"So did his killer do her as well?" asked his companion, a young lad with such smooth cheeks, he didn't look old enough to grow a beard, let alone wear a uniform.

"That's what DI Hamilton is trying to determine," Dickerson replied, feeling rather important. "Best leave him alone when he's workin'."

"I hear he's like a bloody bulldog," said the pudgy blond constable. "Once he gets ahold of a case, he don' bloody let go."

"Ye heard right," said Dickerson. "And one thing t'remember 'bout bulldogs—stay away from their teeth."

The constable's snicker was interrupted by Hamilton's voice from the next room. "Sergeant! Would you come in here now?"

Startled, Dickerson dashed off to the kitchen, leaving the constables murmuring to each other in low voices so that DI Hamilton's wrath would not descend upon them.

He entered the kitchen to find Hamilton staring down at a yellow hound mix racing around the room. The dog, less than a year old, was madly cavorting around the kitchen, sniffing in all the corners and trying to lick the detective's shoes.

"That must be the puppy she were talkin' about earlier," Dickerson said. "I near forgot I said I'd take 'im."

"Meanwhile, would you please remove this animal before it contaminates the entire crime scene?"

Dickerson hastened to obey, scooping the dog up in his arms. The puppy was heavier than it looked; it squirmed and wriggled so energetically trying to lick Dickerson's face that the sergeant nearly dropped it.

"What shall I do wi' him, sir?"

"Just get him out of here."

The sergeant lugged his unwieldy burden down the hall, locating an empty laundry room in the back of the house. He deposited the dog in the middle of the floor and made a break for the door, which the puppy took as an invitation to a jolly game of chase. The dog easily beat Dickerson to the exit; standing in the doorway, it wagged its tail and grinned happily.

"All right, you," the sergeant muttered. Finding a rope in the cupboard, he tied the dog to the legs of the clothes wringer and left the room, pulling the door closed behind him. Plaintive yelps followed him down the hall as he retraced his steps, wiping the sweat from his forehead.

As he passed the staircase leading to the second floor, he was greeted by a young Indian man descending the steps. His smooth dark hair gleamed in the gaslight from the wall sconces.

"I say, is there any chance that you chaps could interview me so I could be getting to my classes? I have an exam today." His accent was educated, with just a hint of his Eastern origins.

"Uh, I'll see wha' we can do, Mr. . . . ?"

"Singh. Rabindranath Singh."

"Jus' a moment, please, Mr. Singh." Dickerson ducked into the kitchen, where he found Detective Hamilton sniffing at the half-eaten bowl of soup in front of Mrs. Sutherland. "Excuse me, sir—"

Hamilton silenced him with a wave, then motioned him over to where he stood. "Lend me your nose, would you, Sergeant?"

"Sir?"

"I want you to see if you can smell something."

"Anythin' in particular, sir?"

"Give this a whiff."

Dickerson complied, stepping close enough to Mrs. Sutherland that he could see the whites of the deceased woman's eyes. His skin felt clammy and his muscles weak as he bent over the table. William Dickerson did not like dead bodies, a fact he contrived mightily to conceal. He willed himself not to faint or otherwise humiliate himself in front of Detective Hamilton.

As he bent over the congealed soup, his stomach lurched, threatening to rebel. He inhaled a faint but distinctive aroma of almonds, bitter at the edges. He turned to the detective. "Smells like burnt almonds, sir."

"Are you sure, Sergeant?"

Bending lower, Dickerson took another whiff. "Yes, sir—I s'pose that's what ye'd have t'call it. It's like almonds, only kinda gone off, like."

To his surprise, Hamilton clapped a hand on his shoulder. "Well done, Dickerson—well done indeed!"

"Thank you, sir, but what's this all about?"

"Only certain members of the populace have the ability to detect the distinctive aroma of bitter almonds in cases of poisoning by cyanide salts. Fortunately for us, you are a member of that select group."

"I see, sir."

"I immediately suspected Mrs. Sutherland was the victim of foul play, and now, with your help, I hope to prove it."

There was a knock upon the kitchen door, and Rabindranath Singh poked his head into the room.

"Begging your pardon, sir, but I should like to be interviewed as soon as possible."

"My apologies for keeping you waiting," said Ian. Dickerson's triumph seemed to have lightened his mood, and the tightness had drained from his face. "Please come in."

The tenant complied, but as he stepped into the room, there was a sound like the report of a pistol in the back of the house. All three men instinctively ducked, but as he heard the rapid scurrying of approaching paws in the hallway, Sergeant Dickerson realized the pistol shot was actually the laundry room door banging open. The guilty culprit appeared at the kitchen door, tail wagging, a chewed piece of rope still tied around its neck. The puppy jumped up on Mr. Singh, attempting to lick his face.

Hamilton glared at Dickerson, but there was no real fury in his gaze; the sergeant had scored too big a victory for him to be truly angry.

"Come along," Dickerson said to the dog.

"Where are you taking him, Sergeant?" asked the detective.

"Well, sir, seein' as he's so stuck on me, I thought I'd take 'im home, like I promised."

"We're not finished here yet. Put him back where you had him. There's a leash upstairs you can use—and this time, *lock* the door, why don't you?"

"Yes, sir," said Dickerson, picking up the gnawed end of rope dangling from the dog's collar. "Come along, Prince."

"That's not his name," Mr. Singh offered.

"It is now," Dickerson called out as he disappeared down the hall.

CHAPTER
THIRTY-SEVEN

"Sit down, for God's sake—you're giving me the willies standing there like a bloody statue. Have a drink with me."

"But sir—"

"First a drink, then you can tell me whatever it is you're so keen to say."

"I don't want—"

"Sit."

Ian Hamilton complied, settling his lean body in the chair opposite DCI Crawford's desk. Crawford fished a bottle from the drawer, poured two shots, and handed one to the detective, who looked surprised, but took it. It was early evening, and the station house was quiet, with only the desk sergeant on duty at his post near the front door. Darkness had fallen like a sentence from heaven, with freezing rain thick enough to discourage even the most stouthearted miscreants.

Crawford took a sip of scotch, enjoying the burn as it slid down his throat. He settled back in his chair and rested his feet on the desk. Outside, the sky was slinging down sleet in thick, long shafts that caught the light from the gas lamps, shining like the tails of tiny comets hurtling from the night sky. Crawford shivered and took another swig, pointing at Hamilton's untouched drink.

"Drink up. No use in wasting good whisky."

Hamilton took a sip, a distracted expression on his maddeningly handsome face. He leaned back in his chair, letting the glass dangle from his hand.

"Now see here," Crawford said. "The death of young Wycherly's landlady is not on you."

"If I had gone to see her last night, instead of going to my aunt's, she might still be alive."

"We don't know yet that any foul play was involved. Didn't it look to all indications like a heart attack?"

"That's what I came to tell you, sir. I suspect cyanide poisoning."

"Because . . . ?"

"There was a distinct aroma of bitter almonds."

"Which you yourself smelled?"

"Sergeant Dickerson detected it."

Crawford's bushy eyebrows furrowed into a frown. "Dickerson? What is so special about him?"

"Only a certain percentage of the population can detect the scent of bitter almonds in the presence of cyanide salts. Dickerson belongs to that group—I, alas, do not."

"Even if the coroner proves you right, it's still not your fault," Crawford insisted.

Hamilton ran a hand over his forehead and reached for a refill. "I'll never know what she wanted to tell me."

"Did the tenants hear anything, see anything?"

"The medical student who resides in the room nearest the front of the house says he thought he heard two visitors. The first one sounded like a child."

"Any idea who that might be?"

"Not really."

"How odd," Crawford commented. "Because I think I know. Oh, aye, I've seen him loitering about waiting for you," he added in response to Hamilton's look. "You can't trust boys like him, you know."

"I don't have to trust him," said Ian. "I only have to make him useful."

"You have some romantic notion of the poor, beaten-down urchin—and no doubt the lad's life has been hard. If it weren't for bad luck, he'd have no luck at all, and all that. But you'd best be careful, or—"

"What exactly are you cautioning me against, sir?"

"The wrong mistake can cost you your career."

"The kind of mistake my father made?"

Crawford downed the rest of his glass and poured himself another. "I had nothing against your father."

"Then you were in the minority, sir."

"Look, Hamilton, I don't see the point of digging up old grievances." He shook his head and rubbed his forehead with his thumb and forefinger. Blasted headache—it had been with him all day and was getting worse. "Why don't you update me on the case?"

"We know a few key elements about our man," said Ian.

"Such as . . . ?"

"He's a fellow of some size and strength. Likely educated, perhaps bilingual."

Crawford took another swig of scotch. "That's something, I suppose."

"I have reason to think that his relationship to Mr. Wycherly was of a personal nature."

"What are you getting at?"

"Strangulation is a very personal way to kill someone. Absent a monetary motive, which we have yet to uncover, it points at something more insidious and disturbing."

"Revenge, perhaps?"

"Perhaps."

"And what about this French detective?"

"He should arrive in Edinburgh shortly."

"Bring him here tomorrow, why don't you? Show him round the station house, that sort of thing. I'd quite like to meet him myself."

"Very well, sir."

Fighting one of his unaccountable urges to giggle, Crawford leaned back in his chair and put his feet up on the desk. It wasn't an especially comfortable pose for a man of his size, but he was trying to show Hamilton that he could be informal and relaxed, even while projecting what he hoped was an aura of gravitas. "'Man's inhumanity to man makes countless thousands mourn,'" he declared.

"Robert Burns, sir?"

How irritating that Hamilton not only recognized the quote, but he didn't even consider that Crawford himself might have come up with it.

"You know, when I joined the force, I had the same ambition as you," he said, trying to project a fatherly tone.

Hamilton drew his thick black eyebrows together. "What might that be, sir?"

"To change the world—make things better for the common man; all that bosh and bunkum."

"What gives you the impression—"

Crawford laughed—a long, somber sound closer to a sob. "Come, now, Hamilton—haven't I been around long enough to be able to read a man? Take my advice—save yourself some sleepless nights and give up your fancy notions of justice. It will only cause you grief in the end."

Hamilton stiffened. "Sir?"

"For Christ's sake, man, can't you see I'm trying to help you? Loosen up before you burst a blood vessel!" Crawford thought of his wife's admonitions to avoid becoming overly emotional. Moira insisted it was bad for him, though it was her health he worried about now.

DI Hamilton drained the rest of his whisky in one gulp. Crawford winced—that was no way to treat a decent single malt. He tried not to dwell on what he had paid for that bottle.

Hamilton placed the glass on Crawford's desk and stood up. "I appreciate your taking me under your wing, sir, but I—"

Crawford banged a fist on the desk. "Under my *wing*? What do you think this is, a boys' school? I'm merely offering you some much-needed advice—take it or not." Aware his reaction was excessive, Crawford leaned back in his chair and took a deep breath. "See here, Hamilton, I've taken an interest in you."

The detective frowned. "What are you getting at, sir, if I might ask?"

"Blast you bloody Highlanders and your pigheadedness," Crawford muttered, shivering as sweat trickled down his shirt collar. "It's like this, Hamilton. If you throw yourself headlong into this damn job, it will eat you from the inside out. Trust me; I know what I'm talking about. Now, a lot of the lads around here just take it as all in a day's work. They go home to their fat little wives and snotty-nosed children; they have pensions to look forward to and all the rest of it. You see?"

"What are you suggesting, sir?"

"Get yourself a fat little wife and a couple of snotty-nosed children, Hamilton. Go home at the end of the day like a normal, sane man. Stop prowling the streets at all hours, following dubious information given to you by some ratty little street Arab." Crawford leaned forward in his chair, until his protruding belly touched the oak desk. "Your father was a Highlander, too."

Most of the original members of the Edinburgh City Police were Highlanders—Crawford himself was no exception, hailing originally from Pitlochry. He folded his fingers as if in prayer and cleared his throat. "There is a fierce kind of honor up there. Men may be violent and cruel, but they are straight with you. They mean what they say and do what they promise; their words match their deeds."

"Have you forgotten the Glencoe Massacre?"

"Tut-tut, man—that was centuries ago! And that was the fault of the bloody English." Hamilton raised an eyebrow, but Crawford waved him off. The detective chief inspector lowered his voice, even though the only other soul in the station house was the duty sergeant, two rooms away. "This place—this city—is not like that. It is dark and close, slippery as an eel. Secrets live within its walls. It has always been thus, Hamilton—neither you nor I nor any man can change it."

As he spoke, a sheet of rain hurled itself against the windows, rattling the panes, as if trying to break into the station house.

"'Stars, hide your fires; Let not light see my black and deep desires,'" Hamilton murmured.

Crawford groaned. "If you *must* show off your book learning, Hamilton, at least pick a proper Scottish writer."

"Yes, sir. 'Firmness in enduring and exertion is a character I always wish to possess. I have always despised—'"

"'The whining yelp of cowardly resolve,'" Crawford finished for him. "I know the quote."

"Then you know it is Robert Burns."

"Nobody likes a show-off, Hamilton."

"But you said—"

"Good Lord, man!" Crawford sat back heavily in his chair and gazed at him with such longing and sadness that Hamilton lowered his eyes. The chief inspector turned to look out the window at the battalion of raindrops assaulting the town. "Go home," he said. "Go home to your empty flat and your cold supper."

"It's not exactly empty, sir."

"You have a paramour?"

"No, sir."

"A pet—a dog or a cat?"

"Not exactly."

"What, then?"

"A mouse."

"You have—*a mouse?* I suppose I shouldn't be surprised. Go home to your mouse, then, Hamilton."

Ian gave a little salute, something Crawford had never seen him do before. "Thank you for the whisky, sir."

"Next time you might consider not swilling it down so quickly."

Crawford thought he saw a smile tug at the corner of the detective's mouth.

"Yes, sir."

He turned on his heel and left the station house, the click of his boots crisp against the polished floor. Crawford sat staring out the window for some time before rising stiffly from his chair and shrugging on his coat. He plucked his green tweed hat from the coatrack and perched it atop his balding pate. The hat was a gift from his wife, who was neither fat nor little, bless her. Her long hands were cool and dry, and he longed to feel them on his forehead. But even her touch couldn't smooth the churning in his stomach, he thought as he nodded to the desk sergeant on his way out—and all the rains of heaven couldn't wash the stink of sin from the streets of Edinburgh.

CHAPTER THIRTY-EIGHT

Ian arrived at his flat to find all the lights burning brightly. As he removed his cloak, his brother called to him from the parlor.

"You're back late."

Ian entered the parlor to find Donald in front of the fireplace, feet propped up on the grate, a book on his lap. He wore Ian's crimson dressing gown, though due to his size, it didn't come all the way round his middle.

"I stopped at the station house, and DCI Crawford offered me a scotch," said Ian.

"Was it decent?"

"He seemed to think so."

"Lucky you, being able to drink. Oh, before I forget, a small urchin of dubious origin stopped by—said he had a message for you."

"Oh?" Ian said, his exhaustion vanishing. "What was the message?"

"He said he tried to collect something from the landlady, but she insisted on giving it to you in person."

"Did she tell him what it was?"

"I'm afraid not."

"Damn! Her stubbornness may have cost her her life."

"How on earth do you know such a fellow?"

"That's my dressing gown," Ian replied, ignoring the question.

"It looks so good on me, I supposed you would want me to have it."

"That robe belonged to Uncle Alfred. Lillian gave it to me."

"She wouldn't want you to be stingy," he proclaimed, drawing the coat around his bulky frame.

"May I point out that you are seated before *my* fire, reading *my* book—"

"It's jolly interesting, too," Donald said. "*Inside the Criminal Mind*, by Guillaume de La Robert. Where did you get this?"

"From an odd fellow I met at the library."

"Are you in the habit of frequenting the library for companionship? How tragic."

"I was doing research. He's a reference librarian."

"Well, he knows what he's talking about. This book almost makes me want to be a criminologist. Oh, don't worry," he added in response to Ian's look, "I have quite enough on my plate reapplying to medical school."

"Do you still have total recall of everything you read?"

Donald fingered the tie of the dressing gown, and Ian noticed his hands trembled. "Another reason to give up the bottle—it was beginning to affect my memory. Can you still remember everything you hear?"

"Sometimes I wish I could forget some of the things I hear."

"A gift and a curse," Donald said, stretching himself. "By the way, can I stay with you for a while? It would be a pity to let that extra bedroom go to waste."

Ian looked down at his brother, trying to appear careless and casual. He could feel Donald's nervous energy. "Yes," he said. "But the dressing gown stays with me."

"If you insist." Donald shrugged, projecting unconcern, but Ian knew it was to maintain his fragile equilibrium. Lillian was right—Donald was the weaker of the two, torn apart by the intensity of his emotions.

"Is there anything to eat?"

"There's a cold joint and some roasted potatoes in the icebox," Donald replied. "I thought you might come home hungry."

"Stay as long as you like if you continue to make yourself useful," Ian said, going out to the kitchen. He stopped in the doorway, astonished at the sight that greeted him.

Perched on top of the counter, looking very much at home, was Mrs. Sutherland's black-and-white cat. Ian turned and charged back into the parlor. "What on earth is that animal doing in my—"

"Oh, I forgot. A little redheaded chap brought him round earlier—Sergeant Snickers—"

"Dickerson."

"He said you needed help with a mouse problem, thought maybe the cat would be a solution."

"He has some cheek—"

"Do you?"

"What?"

"Have a mouse problem?"

"Well, yes, but—"

"There you are, then—problem solved."

"I never—"

Donald rose and stretched himself. "I know, little brother, you don't like other people making decisions for you. But maybe in this case it's a turn of fortune. What's the creature's name?" he said, wandering into the kitchen.

"Bacchus," Ian said, following him.

Donald clapped him on the shoulder. Ian winced from the impact against his injured flesh, the burned area still sensitive to touch.

His brother didn't notice, turning away to rummage through the kitchen cupboards. "Perfect! The Greek god of sensual pleasure. God knows you could use more of that in your life."

"How do you know?"

"A brother can sense these things. Ah, this looks decent," he said, pulling a jar of plum chutney from the cupboard. "Now let's see about that joint of beef, shall we?"

After devouring a good-sized portion of roast beef and boiled potatoes, Ian felt quite anesthetized. He sank down in a chair in front of the fire, staring into the glowing embers, and felt his head begin to droop.

Donald was sprawled on the couch, his head buried in the book George Pearson had given him. "Fascinating stuff, this. I was just reading the chapter on motives for murder."

"What did you learn?"

"They run the gamut, but the Seven Deadly Sins are a good place to start—greed, revenge, jealousy. What about your fellow—any ideas?"

"I'm leaning toward revenge, though I'm having trouble connecting the dots."

"Dear me." Donald lit another cigarette. "Still, how convenient to have miscreants and murderers walking among us, so that the rest of us may lead virtuous lives. They're like the pustules in an otherwise healthy body, siphoning off the toxins of society."

"That is a rather bold theory."

"It seems to me that the amount of good and evil in the world remains more or less constant. If you take that view, you'll see the criminals play their part—just as my failure has contributed to your brilliant success."

"Are you suggesting there could be only one 'successful' brother between us?"

"I'm suggesting the forces of light and dark exist in a relationship of delicate balance, and that murderers appease the bloodlust of humanity. They perform a double duty: first, by expressing mankind's desire to kill, and second, as appropriate victims of slaughter when they are brought to justice."

"Do you believe the thirst for blood runs in all our veins?"

"When you look into your own soul, do you not find a shadowed corner that takes secret delight at the suffering of others? The Germans even have a word for it—*Schadenfreude.*"

Ian frowned. "I am aware of German propensities."

A smirk spread over his brother's face. "So you don't believe a true, hearty Scot is capable of such corrupted desires?"

Ian gave a curt laugh. "This town alone is rife with pickpockets, thieves, and blackguards."

"Ah! I'm not speaking of crime for profit. Surely anyone can understand that—and even a thief might have a conscience, a soft spot in his soul. I'm talking about evil for evil's sake—that cold, hard edge of the soul that admits neither compassion nor tenderness toward one's fellow creatures."

"I'll grant you some wretches have such a life—but most, I think not."

"I think you'd find that subset of our citizenry to be larger than you imagine, Brother." He rose to give the fire in the grate a poke. "Why, our own father—" At that moment a spark shot out from a green log, the glowing ember landing on the Persian rug. Ian leapt to his feet and stamped on it so violently that his brother stared at him.

"Steady on. It's only a bit of cinder, you know."

"Maybe to you," Ian said tightly, "but that shows how little you know of me."

"Perhaps you should consult an alienist. After all these years, you are clearly still suffering—"

"At least I'm not drinking myself into an early grave."

Donald went pale. "Do you imagine I was somehow unaffected by the tragedy?"

"I couldn't possibly say, because you weren't there that night."

"Oh, that's how it lies, is it? You still blame me—"

"Don't be absurd!" Ian cried, turning away.

His brother was right, though—Ian did blame him, especially in the early days, when he felt he would go mad, and Donald was nowhere to be found. He wheeled around, his face hot with fury. "How can you know what it is like to be haunted by their eyes night after sleepless night, pleading with me to save them?"

"Was it my fault that I was out—"

"Out *drinking*."

"I was—"

"You were pub-crawling!"

"Surely I am not the first undergraduate in history to spend an evening with my fellow students in an Edinburgh tavern! You might have been out drinking if you knew what I knew—"

"How like you, to avoid taking responsibility for anything!"

"It was bad luck, but I fail to see how that makes me responsible for our parents'—"

The logical side of Ian's brain knew his brother was right, but that part of his mind was underwater, flooded by the intensity of emotions flowing over him.

"Since when have you cared about anyone but yourself?"

When he saw the look on his brother's face, he knew he had gone too far. Donald's eyes went cold, hard and gray as steel. Ian tried to think of a way to take back what he had said, but it was too late; the damage had been done. Without another word, his brother slipped out of Ian's dressing gown, threw on his coat, and stalked out of the flat, slamming the door behind him.

Perhaps drawn by the commotion, Bacchus sauntered into the parlor. Stunned by his own cruelty and lack of self-control, Ian stared at the cat. Dangling from the animal's mouth was a very fat, very dead mouse. The sight of the unfortunate creature's demise was the last straw. Sinking into the nearest armchair, Ian put his face in his hands and wept.

CHAPTER THIRTY-NINE

Kerry O'Donohue sipped his pint of ale and threw a sideways glance at the well-dressed man in the corner of the basement nightclub. The rake was trying not to appear interested, but Kerry knew well enough when someone was looking him over. It was early, and the club wasn't as crowded as it would be later. There were still empty stools at the bar; Kerry could afford to take his time. The damp, low-ceilinged room with its stone walls and flickering wall sconces held enough light to make out the dozen or so sinuous forms draped over couches or slinking furtively in darkened corners. In an hour there would be threefold as many, the stones themselves seeming to sweat in the blue haze of tobacco and opium.

Kerry pulled a silver cigarette case from his hip pocket, slid one out, and shoved it between his lips. Looking through all his pockets, he pretended to search vainly for matches, though there was a new box in his vest.

When a flame appeared before his face, he didn't even turn to see whose hand held the match. With a sly smile, he leaned forward and inhaled deeply, sucking the tobacco into his lungs and savoring the smoky aroma of Virginia's finest. Kerry didn't have a lot of money, but he spent what he had on decent tobacco. The silver case had belonged to his grandfather back in Ireland. In his more grandiose moments, Kerry fancied himself a gentleman, though in reality he was nothing more than the son of a Dublin blacksmith.

"Ta," he said, offering the man a cigarette.

His seducer took one and lit it before sliding into the seat next to him. That was the way Kerry liked to think of the men he met at the Owl's Nest—as seducers. His relationship to his own sexuality was such that he could enjoy the illicit encounters he craved only if he imagined himself an "innocent" partner in debauchery. No matter how fiercely he was attracted to any man he met in his nightly escapades, he always cast himself in the role of the unworldly ingénue, seduced and swooning over an older and more experienced Don Juan.

"Haven't seen you here before," the man remarked. His voice was a smooth, rich baritone, definitely English, probably from around London.

"Nor you," Kerry replied, giving the man a glance before returning to his pint. In that brief moment, he managed to take in most of the details about his appearance: the pale, deep-set eyes; square cheekbones and long jaw; the sensual mouth, with a suggestion of cruelty in the downward twist of the lips.

His loins tingled at the thought of pressing his own face against this stranger's handsome one, the hint of menace making him even more intriguing. Kerry was not immune to the allure of danger—he was not entirely averse to "rough trade," and had enjoyed more than one furtive, furious encounter in alleyways with the city's less savory citizens.

This stranger was hardly a member of that class—he was dressed as a gentleman, his black frock coat woven from the finest gabardine, black boots polished to a high sheen. Kerry recognized quality when he saw it, and knew his companion had spent more on his wardrobe than Kerry made in a year. He had the hands of a gentleman, too—smooth and well cared for, so unlike Kerry's own, weathered and rough from years of working the docks at Leith.

"So what's yer name, then?" he ventured, hoping the man wouldn't find his accent off-putting—not that his origins were any secret. Even if he had wanted to hide his Dublin roots, it would have been impossible; as his ma always said, the map of Ireland was stamped all over his broad, freckled face.

"I'm Harold," the man replied.

Kerry laughed and signaled the bartender for another pint. "Ye don't look like a Harold."

"And what does a Harold look like, pray tell?"

"Not the likes of you."

"So, what's your name—something equally unconvincing?"

Kerry took a long swallow of ale before answering. "Brian."

Harold—if that was his name—smiled. "You don't look like a Brian, so I suppose we're even."

"D'you want to go to the back, then?" said Kerry, with a glance toward the far corner of the room. A narrow passageway led to a secluded chamber where all manner of sin and debauchery could be had—for a price. A slim young Adonis with chestnut curls emerged from the hallway on the arm of an older, dignified gentleman. The younger man's eyes were glazed over, his stare vacant and dreamy. The older man's cheeks were glowing, his eyes shining with lust and pride.

Harold glanced at them and shook his head. "No, I prefer somewhere more . . . private." He drew a pack of playing cards from his frock coat and fanned them wide with a single smooth gesture. "Pick a card."

Kerry tilted his head to one side. His brain was already fogging as the noise in the room blended into an impressionistic soup of sound. The rise and fall of voices, the clink of glassware, the shuffle of leather soles, all combined to form a background hum, a cocoon that enclosed him in the moment, as if his arms were woven to his sides, encased in silk. He stared at the perfect semicircle of cards.

"Go ahead," Harold said. "Any card."

Kerry reached forward and plucked a card from the group. It was the five of clubs. "What now?" he said. "Are you going to guess which one it is?"

Harold laughed. "No—it's for you to keep."

"What for?"

"Just for the fun of it."

Kerry knit his brow and studied the card. Five skeletons grinned up at him; two of them wore fezzes, their bony limbs askew as they danced jauntily upon the face of the card. "This is an unusual design, so it is," he said.

Harold laid a hand on his shoulder, and Kerry felt the heat of it through his woolen frock coat. "You're an unusual man."

The back of Kerry's neck tingled with the possibilities of the evening ahead. His companion radiated confidence, with none of the shame or diffidence Kerry had seen in other denizens of the Owl's Nest. He exuded something else, too, thick as musk and even more intoxicating: danger. The slow, deliberate movements, the way he looked at Kerry, studying him as one might examine a dissected body upon a laboratory table—it all made the young Irishman's knees go wobbly. His head swam and he felt dizzy.

"What d'ye have in mind, then?" he said as the sweet, sickly smell of opium drifted in from the narrow corridor leading to the back room. "Sure you don't want ta go to th'back?"

"Quite sure," Harold replied, taking his elbow. "Why don't we leave this den of iniquity and find somewhere more secluded?"

Kerry shrugged, trying to appear unconcerned, though he felt anything but. Spots danced before his eyes, and his cheeks burned with the heat of desire and adventure.

"I've got this covered," Harold said, tossing a few coins onto the bar. "Come along, let's go."

Kerry slid off his stool, a bit unsteady on his feet, but Harold's firm hand on his arm guided him across the room, through the door, and into the night.

CHAPTER FORTY

"Very well, I shall simply wait until he returns," snapped Chief Inspector Louis Valeur Gerard, crossing his arms over his compact torso. He had appeared early Friday morning at the Edinburgh police station, asking to speak with Detective Hamilton, who hadn't yet arrived. Sergeant Dickerson's attempts to placate the Frenchman met with firm Gallic resistance. The sergeant stood, hands dangling helplessly at his sides as he tried frantically to think of something to appease Gerard's mounting displeasure.

"Per'aps you would like a cup of tea—"

The French policeman gave a dismissive wave of his hands, elegantly clad in impeccable white gloves. "*Non, merci*—I do not see how you British can drink of this—this dishwater you seem to so much enjoy. Why do you not enjoy the far superior *café*, eh?"

"We do enjoy coffee, but it's more expensive and harder to come by," Dickerson explained. "And I'd advise you not t'call the lads here 'British.' They're most of them Highlander Scots, and they won't take kindly to it."

A frown spread over Gerard's long face. With its high cheekbones, heavy-lidded eyes, and protruding lips, it was a caricature of a classic Gallic countenance. "Hmm!" he said, pulling at the thin mustache that emphasized the thickness of his lips. "Scottish people are also British, are they not?"

"It's a bit more complicated," Dickerson replied. Feeling a sneeze come on, he tried to stifle it, but it exploded from his nose just as DI Hamilton entered the station house.

"Are you quite all right, Sergeant?" Hamilton said, hanging up his cloak.

"I'm 'fraid Dogs make me sneeze, sir."

Hamilton frowned. "Dogs?"

"I took Prince—that's the dog at Mrs. Sutherland's—home wi' me, remember?"

"Perhaps not the wisest thing if they make you sneeze."

"I'll get used to it, sir," Dickerson replied, stifling another sneeze.

"Which reminds me, I don't recall requesting a feline companion."

Dickerson felt himself redden. "Beg pardon, sir, but you mentioned having a mouse problem, and I thought—"

"Never mind; I know it was well intentioned."

"Yes, sir. Meanwhile, this is Inspector Gerard—"

"*Chief* Inspector Louis Valeur Gerard," the Frenchman interrupted, stepping forward. *"À votre service."*

"Detective Inspector Ian Hamilton," Ian said, extending his hand. "I hope you had a pleasant journey."

"No journey can be pleasant when such *sauvages* are abroad," Gerard replied sternly, giving his hand a stiff shake.

"Well said, Chief Inspector. Shall we get down to business, then?"

"I perceive you are somewhat lax in discipline," Gerard said with a glance at a pair of constables strolling into the station house, laughing and joking between themselves. They stopped and stared when they saw the Frenchman, before continuing, snickering and murmuring to each other. Chief Inspector Gerard frowned. "You allow your officers to wander in whenever they feel like it?"

Sergeant Dickerson's ears buzzed. The impudence of this French fop! Why, if he could only speak his mind, he'd show him a thing or two . . .

To his surprise, Hamilton just smiled. "I'm sure there are many differences between us, but I hope that doesn't mean we can't work together."

"No, of course not," the Frenchman replied stiffly, with a brisk tug at his crisp uniform. His brass buttons were polished to a bright sheen, the crease in his dark blue trousers razor sharp. Most amazing to Dickerson were the creamy white gloves, without a single stain upon them. He didn't know how anyone could pass through the streets of Edinburgh without attracting any of the soot, grime, and filth spitting forth daily from its chimneys, foundries, and slaughterhouses.

Gerard glanced around the room at the constables seated at their desks or loitering about the tea station. "Is it possible to speak somewhere more private?"

"Voudriez-vous passer à une autre chambre?" Hamilton said.

The Frenchman's face cracked into a stiff smile. *"Vous parlez français?"*

"Un petit peu."

"I am glad to see the language of philosophers is not entirely without representation among the barbarians."

Sergeant Dickerson glared at their visitor. He was about to regale Gerard on the subject of Scottish philosophers, when Hamilton threw him a warning glance. Dickerson pursed his lips but remained silent.

"I daresay you may be surprised by what you find here," Ian remarked calmly.

Dickerson was amazed at Hamilton's composure in the face of French insolence as he followed them to the small room at the back where the lads enjoyed the occasional furtive nap. Dickerson himself had fallen asleep on the little cot more than once.

"Here we are," Hamilton said, offering Gerard a chair while he perched on the side of the room's only desk. "We can talk here undisturbed." Sitting on the cot was out of the question, so Dickerson had to content himself with leaning against the wall, which only increased his rancor toward the Frenchman.

"*Bon,*" Gerard said, removing his gold-braided cap before lowering himself into the chair. "I see no reason the entire constabulary of Edinburgh need hear our conversation, *n'est-ce pas?*"

"I understand that you have a series of crimes bearing a striking similarity to our recent stranglings."

Removing his gloves, Gerard smoothed a hand over his perfectly oiled hair, giving off a whiff of peppermint pomade. "I have studied your newspaper accounts, and they bear every mark of ours as well. I must say, your journalists are given to rather—baroque expressions."

"Do you believe the Paris and Edinburgh crimes to be the work of one man?"

"*C'est possible.* Perhaps two men—or women."

"Ye can't be serious," said Dickerson. "A woman's not capable of—"

"One must never come to a premature conclusion," Gerard responded, pulling a small notebook from his jacket pocket. "I have here the details of our murders—there were three in all, within the space of two months, last autumn."

"And then they stopped?" said Ian.

"*Complètement.* We hoped the perpetrator had died or been imprisoned for another crime. *Alors,* I am sorry to learn he may have simply crossed the Channel."

"May I see that?" asked Dickerson. Gerard raised an eyebrow before handing it to him. Seeing to his dismay that the writing was of course in French, the sergeant handed the notebook to Detective Hamilton. "Can ye translate this, sir?" he asked as he failed to ward off another bout of violent sneezing.

"You might want to reconsider your dog acquisition, Sergeant," Hamilton remarked as he gazed at the document. "I see one of the crimes took place in the neighborhood known as Pigalle—the red-light district?"

Gerard nodded. "Any manner of dissipation or vice you wish can be found there for a price."

"Men as well as women?"

"*Bien sûr,*" Gerard replied, his face expressing distaste. "But the victims were respectable men, one of them a banker with three children, another a well-known doctor of medicine."

"The French newspaper accounts make no mention of playing cards left at the scene of the crimes."

Chief Inspector Gerard smiled. "Ah, yes—some information must always be kept from the public, do you agree?"

"Indeed."

"So *did* he leave cards?" Dickerson asked, about to burst from curiosity.

The French detective gave a secretive smile and reached into his inside breast pocket, drawing forth two playing cards, which he placed on the desk: the ace and two of clubs. The design was identical to the ones in their evidence room—the same leering skeletons, one for each number on the card.

"*Et vous?*" Gerard said. "What do you have?"

Ian's unsmiling eyes met his. "The three and four of clubs."

"And the design?"

"The same."

Chief Inspector Louis Valeur Gerard threw up his hands. "*C'est ça.* It's the same killer."

"But you said you had three victims—yet only two cards?"

"He left nothing on the first victim. And yet all of the other aspects of the crimes are identical."

"I believe you are correct, Chief Inspector, in believing it is the same perpetrator."

"But why leave no card on the first victim?"

"It may be he was in a hurry, fearing discovery. Or perhaps he had not yet conceived of leaving his 'calling cards,' as it were."

The conversation continued, but Sergeant Dickerson barely heard them. He was too busy staring at the cards on the desk in front of him, the skeletons dancing and cavorting as he tried to imagine what kind of fierce joy this fiend found in the strangling of young men.

CHAPTER
FORTY-ONE

There existed in Edinburgh a tribe of men and women who plied their trade in darkness, whose livelihood depended upon the setting of the sun. Their movements were illuminated by gaslight, half in shadow, glimpsed from the corner of the eye by their fellow citizens, as in a dream. They had their own rules, regulations, and rituals, known only to them; secrecy was their constant companion, silence their motto.

They were the lamplighters and night watchmen, thieves and brigands, pickpockets and prostitutes, and they lived in the spaces between waking and sleeping, their existence as deep and still as a held breath.

Jamie McKenzie was a member of this tribe, having at least a nodding acquaintance with many others. One of Edinburgh's vast army of leeries, he ventured forth upon the heels of daylight, tramping through the town as twilight deepened into dusk, the instrument of his trade held aloft as he approached each gas lantern atop its cast-iron post.

The sun was just slipping behind Castle Rock as Jamie set out from his home in Craig's Close, past the Isle of Man Tavern, where poet Robert Ferguson once rubbed shoulders with the notorious Deacon Brodie, as members of the famed Cape Club. Jamie wasn't much given to socializing. The left side of his face was disfigured, making him wary of encounters with his fellow man. He had been so since the age of six, when he wandered too near to a horse his father was shoeing. The gelding was skittish and delivered a kick to the side of young Jamie's face, caving in his cheekbone and leaving him blind in one eye. He had developed a preference for nighttime; for him, the lamplighting profession was ideal.

But Jamie was well-known around town, regarded fondly by citizens accustomed to his familiar figure as they trudged home from their day's labor. There was something comforting in the sight of his long, spidery form wending through the alleys and wynds, his flint held aloft, a scarred but stalwart Prometheus. They called him Long Jamie, for he was well over six feet and as thin as a parson's gruel. Children sometimes danced behind him, making up rhymes and songs about him. Sometimes they were cruel, children being what they are, but most often they were stories of his nightly adventures—which, seen through a child's eye, were romantic indeed.

On this night, no packs of children followed him; though the rain had abated, a stiff wind whistled along Cockburn Street. Jamie didn't mind—he enjoyed solitude, and if the cold wind caused the denizens of Edinburgh to hide behind closed shutters, so much the better.

He spied Sally McGrath huddled beneath the eaves of the Hound and Hare. Though the fancy ladies of the New Town referred to her as a "fallen woman," Sally was lively and kind, often sharing her profits with her fellow night travelers. On more than one occasion she had treated Jamie to a bowl of stew or tatties and neeps at local eateries.

But Sally was well past her prime, and times were hard for an aging prostitute—dangerous, too. Jamie imagined she needed the money badly to venture out on such a chill night. He tipped his hat, indicating there were no policemen nearby—had he seen a copper, he would have whistled. She smiled at him and drew her cloak closer.

As he trudged up the hill, Jamie sang a popular ballad, "My Highland Laddie." Enjoying the sound of his own voice, he stopped to light the lamp at the intersection of Cockburn and Lyon's Close. He was just about to begin the second verse when something lying in the alley caught his good eye. Thinking it was one of the town's many inebriates overcome by alcohol, Jamie ventured into the narrow passageway to rouse the man.

"Oiy!" he said, prodding the still form with his toe. "Git up wi' ye—time t'gae home."

He gave the man another poke, dislodging his coat collar and revealing his face. With a sharp intake of breath, Jamie McKenzie realized what he was looking at was not a drunken man, but a corpse. Jamie staggered backward, his knees turned to butter. Hardly aware of what he was doing, he flung down his pole and lurched down the street in the direction of the police station.

CHAPTER FORTY-TWO

Ian returned to his flat on Victoria Terrace to find it dark and still. As he reached to light the flame on the gas lamp, something brushed against his leg. Startled, he gave a yelp. At that moment, it occurred to him his brother might be playing a trick on him, as he had so often when they were children. Donald loved to scare people, and Ian, two years younger, was his prime target. His heart leapt at the thought his brother had returned. Guilt had nagged at him all day for his treatment of Donald the night before. Ian knew he had allowed the years of worry and resentment to build up into the outburst against his brother. In spite of his intentions, his better self had not prevailed, and more than anything he wished he could take back every harsh word.

"Donald?" Ian said, grasping for the matches he had dropped on the floor. His hand touched something furry, which began to purr loudly, and he realized what had rubbed against his leg. "Good Lord," he said. "What are you doing scaring me half to death?"

The cat responded with a plaintive cry Ian recognized as a demand for food.

"Come along, then," he said, finally managing to light the lamp. "Have you run out of mice to eat so quickly?"

The cat looked at him quizzically. There was a black smudge on its nose, as if the feline had been poking around behind the stove. Ian had to admit there was something fetching about the animal's aquiline visage, with its long nose and round eyes—it was a rather uncatlike face. Bacchus accompanied Ian to the kitchen, swerving back between his feet as though trying deliberately to trip him.

"Steady on," Ian muttered. "If I fall and break my neck, you won't be having your dinner."

He pulled some meat from the previous night's roast and put it in a bowl on the floor. Bacchus sniffed at it and crouched over the bowl, pecking delicately at the meat.

"That should hold you for a while," Ian said. "You're not staying, you know," he added. Candle in hand, Ian explored the rest of the flat for any signs of Donald. He was disappointed to find all the rooms dark and silent. He opened the closet in the spare bedroom, searching for his brother's belongings, but he wasn't sure whether Donald had arrived with luggage. His coveting Ian's dressing gown was entirely in keeping with his character; Donald always enjoyed giving him a hard time.

Finding a rucksack in the back of the closet, he pulled it out to examine it. Inside were two pairs of trousers, a handful of shirts, and various toiletry items. Hope danced in Ian's chest—perhaps Donald would return for his things, and Ian could apologize. As he lifted the pack to return it to the closet, a deck of cards tumbled out of the front compartment. He bent to pick it up but recoiled as if stung.

The skeletal faces on the cards, by now too familiar, grinned up at him, mockery in their terrible, empty eyes. He counted the cards with trembling hands—to his relief, they were all accounted for. But the discovery was deeply troubling. He slipped the deck back into the rucksack, threw on his cloak, and set out in the direction of his aunt's town house. Lillian would know what to do.

She greeted him warmly as usual, a woolen shawl wrapped around her shoulders. He recognized the tartan as his uncle Alfie's Clan Grey.

"What brings you out on such a night?" she asked, drawing the curtains on the cold, thin rain spitting from the sky. "Come sit by the fire and have a wee bowl o' leek and potato soup."

As they ate, he told her the story of Donald's abrupt arrival and even more precipitous departure.

"Dear me," she said. "You were rather harsh with him, weren't you?"

"There's more," he said grimly, and told her about the pack of cards.

Lillian shook her head. "Surely you don't think Donald could—"

"I don't want to, of course! But is it mere coincidence that he shows up at the same time as the—"

"The Holyrood Strangler?"

"Blast the press," Ian said, biting his lip. "Causing public hysteria with their sensationalistic claptrap."

"Did Donald mention being on the Continent?"

"He's not been especially forthcoming about his whereabouts, and I haven't pressed him."

Lillian laid down her soupspoon. "Don't you find it disturbing that we're sitting here calmly discussing whether your brother is a murderer?"

"As a policeman, I have to believe anyone is capable of anything."

Lillian rose to clear the table. "Well, I'd better keep my nose clean so you don't haul me in for questioning."

Ian rolled his eyes. "I should have said *nearly* everyone—obviously not *you*, Auntie."

"Under the right circumstances, I've no doubt I'd be capable of killing someone."

Before he could respond, there was an urgent pounding at the door.

"My goodness," his aunt said. "Perhaps that is the prodigal nephew returning already."

"Stay where you are," said Ian, bounding to the door. He peered through the window to see a bedraggled Sergeant Dickerson, rain dripping from the end of his nose, hatless, in a long yellow sou'wester.

"Ta very much, sir," he said when Ian opened the door to let him in. His cheeks and nose were ruddy, and he was quite out of breath.

"How did you know where to find me?" Ian asked.

"Since ye weren't to home, I thought t'look for ye here," he replied, rubbing his hands together.

"Well done, Sergeant. We'll make a detective out of you yet."

Dickerson responded with a violent sneeze. "Beg pardon, sir," he said, pulling a damp handkerchief from the pocket of his oilskin coat.

"Goodness—you'll catch your death out there," said Lillian.

"It's just allergies, mum," Dickerson replied.

"Come in and stand by the fire," she said.

"I don' want to drip all over your carpet. I'm soakin' wet."

"Nonsense," Lillian insisted. "It's just an old rug, for heaven's sake."

"What was so urgent that you needed to find me?" Ian asked Dickerson.

"Well, sir—"

"Take off that wet coat and come have a hot bowl of soup," Lillian interrupted.

"I'm afraid I can't stay, mum," Dickerson said as she pulled at his elbow. "I've just come to tell DI Hamilton that—" He paused and looked at Ian.

"Go ahead, Sergeant. Whatever it is, I'm sure my aunt is up to hearing it."

The sergeant's response was interrupted by an even more violent sneeze. He blew his nose loudly into the handkerchief.

"Well?" said Ian. "It must be important if you came out on a night like this."

"I'm afraid there's been another murder, sir."

"Good heavens!" said Aunt Lillian.

"What happened?" Ian asked.

"I was just about to leave fer the night, when Long Jamie rushes into t'station, shoutin' that someone's been murdered in Lyon's Close." He paused, glancing nervously at Lillian.

"Go on, Sergeant," Ian urged. "I presume you asked him why he believed the man was murdered."

"I did, aye. An 'e just says that the man's eyes was buggin' all outta his head, red an' swollen like. So I'm thinkin' that's what the eyes look like on someone who's been strangled."

"So you came straight here?"

"Straightaway, sir, after I dispensed a coupla constables to keep watch over the body."

"Sorry, Aunt Lillian," Ian said, "but I must go."

"Ach, get on with ye—no need to apologize," she replied, drawing her shawl around her thin shoulders. "But you could use a hot bowl of soup and a mustard plaster, young man," she said to Dickerson. "You'll catch your death if you don't take care."

"Yes, mum," the sergeant replied, trying unsuccessfully to stifle another sneeze. "Sorry," he said sheepishly, wiping his nose with the now very soggy kerchief.

"Perhaps my aunt is right," Ian ventured. "You'll be of no use to anyone if you contract pneumonia."

"If it's all the same t'you, sir, I'd like ta go wi' ye to view the body."

"Very well, if you insist."

"At least take a fresh handkerchief," Lillian said, fumbling through her pockets. "Here you are," she said, extracting a clean embroidered handkerchief, neatly folded. The hand-stitched monogram, in gold thread, read *LRG*. "My initials," Lillian explained as she handed it to him. "Lillian Rose Grey."

"Oh, I couldn't, mum. It's much too fine."

"Just *take* it, Sergeant," Ian said, "so we can be on our way."

Dickerson turned beet red. "Thank you, mum," he mumbled, stuffing it into his pocket.

This time they were luckier in finding a cab and soon were seated in the back of a hansom, rattling through rain-slickened streets.

"Is Long Jamie still at the station house?" Ian asked, peering out the window as they careened around the corner of Niddry Street. A couple of merrymakers swerved their way down the High Street, on a Friday night pub crawl, an Edinburgh tradition that even the foulest weather couldn't dampen.

"Yes, sir," Dickerson replied. "I left one of the lads in charge of 'im. Poor fella looked quite shaken."

"I want to interview him after we have a look at the crime scene."

"Yes, sir," said the sergeant, with another shuddering sneeze.

Ian regarded him with a mixture of sympathy and impatience. "Perhaps you should reconsider accompanying me."

But Dickerson remained steadfast. "I'm keen t'ave a look at the poor chap what was killed, sir."

"But I thought you found dead bodies . . . disturbing."

Dickerson straightened his shoulders and gave his nose a mighty blow. "Th'only way to overcome a fear is to face it, innit?"

"Good on ye, Sergeant," Ian said as they pulled up in front of Lyon's Close. "Though I'm not sure it's worth risking pneumonia."

Ian paid the driver and approached the two waterlogged constables keeping watch over the body, which they had draped with an oilcloth. After dispatching one of them to the coroner's office, Ian took a lantern and knelt down to examine the victim.

He recognized the man immediately. "This is Kerry O'Donohue," he said. "He was brought up a few months ago on charges of licentious behavior in public. I believe he was fined and released the next day."

"What exactly were he accused of, sir?" Dickerson asked, bending over the body.

"Sodomy," said Ian.

Dickerson cleared his throat. "Might we regard that as potential clue, then?"

"We might indeed," Ian replied, turning his attention to the dead man. He remembered seeing Kerry O'Donohue in the police station—a spirited, strikingly handsome fellow, with yellow ringlets and cheerful blue eyes. The inert form lying on the sodden ground was a sad remnant of that energetic lad, all the life drained from his staring eyes. Upon closer examination, petechial hemorrhaging was clearly visible—the tiny red blotches indicative of burst blood vessels in the eyes. Kerry's open collar displayed the deep purple indentations of ligature strangulation.

"I've seen enough," Ian said, handing the lantern back to the constable.

"What about the, uh, playin' card, sir?" asked Dickerson. "Shouldn't we look for it?"

"Good idea. Please do."

Dickerson swallowed hard. "Right you are, sir." He bent over the body, swaying unsteadily. Clearing his throat, he reached for the coat pocket of the dead man. His hand never found its mark—before he could touch it, his legs gave way, and he crumpled slowly toward the cobblestones.

"Damn," Ian muttered, reaching out to catch him. Lowering the sergeant to the ground, he turned to the bemused constable. "I'm afraid he's not well—seems to have contracted a case of influenza."

The policeman took a few steps away from them. "Hope it's not cholera. Nasty stuff, that is."

"Different symptoms," Ian replied, patting Dickerson's cheeks. "Come along, now, Sergeant—wake up."

Dickerson's eyes fluttered. "I—I do apologize, sir," he said, struggling uncertainly to his feet.

"Think nothing of it," Ian replied, with a glance at the constable, who had backed off to a safe distance. "You should be in bed with that influenza of yours."

"But I—oh, right," Dickerson answered, catching on. "I am feelin' a bit worse."

"Never mind," said Ian. Bending over the body, he sniffed at it, inhaling deeply.

"What on earth is he doin'?" said the constable, scratching his head.

"*Shh,*" replied the sergeant. "He's workin'."

Ian rifled through the dead man's pockets. Sure enough, there it was, in the left breast pocket—sodden but unmistakable. He withdrew it and held it up to the lantern.

"Is it the five of clubs, sir?" asked Dickerson.

"Aye," Ian replied. "It is indeed."

The constable stared at the sergeant as if Dickerson were bewitched. "How on earth did you know that?"

Dickerson shrugged. "Just lucky, I guess."

CHAPTER
FORTY-THREE

"The look on that poor constable's face!" Ian said as they sat in the back of a hansom cab. The driver put the horse into a brisk trot, its hooves resounding smartly on the paving stones, a counterpoint to the rain pelting onto the vehicle's roof.

"Poor chap did seem spooked," the sergeant replied. Ian was beginning to reevaluate Dickerson; the man had more guile than he had given him credit for. "Figured I needed t'regain fella's respect after faintin' dead away like that. Ta very much for coverin' for me, sir."

"It's the least I could do, after making you search the dead man's pockets. I forgot about your . . . . aversion."

"Bloody embarrassin'."

"We all have something, Sergeant. No one is without their Achilles' heel," Ian said, thinking of his brother's drinking and his own aversion to fire and enclosed spaces. "Yours is a very natural revulsion, actually."

"Sometimes I wonder why I became policeman, bein' as how I can't stand being 'round dead folks," the sergeant mused, staring out the window.

"Why did you join the force?"

"I s'pose I were after security for me an' my sister, sir."

"Pauline, is it?"

"Aye, that's her—my little Pauline. She's all I have in t'world."

"What happened to your parents?"

"They were taken by cholera when we were young, sir."

"Who took care of you?"

"I were fourteen when they died, old enough to support us both. Worked in't mines till I saved enough to get away. I always wanted to live in proper city, so we came here."

"You brought up your sister?"

"Aye. It's been just two of us for long time now."

They rode in silence the rest of the way. Ian felt a newfound respect for the chubby sergeant, as well as envy. He didn't have anyone to look after—there was Lillian, of course, but she looked after him more than the other way round. Ian supposed he should feel lonely, but he didn't—he loved his solitude. Did that mean he was abnormal? He had had a chance to look after Donald, and yet had chased him off within a couple of days. Guilt and shame wrung a sigh out of him as he gazed out the window.

"Y'all right, sir?" said Dickerson.

"Yes, thank you." Ian had no desire to discuss his personal problems with the sergeant. Lillian was his one true confidant, but there were things he wouldn't reveal even to her.

They arrived at a nearly deserted station house, its only occupants a sleepy desk sergeant and Long Jamie, who appeared quite agitated. He leapt to his feet when he saw them, wringing his thin hands.

"Did ye find the poor fella?" he asked. "Right where I said 'e was?"

"He was there all right," Ian replied. "Do you mind answering a few questions, Mr. McKenzie?"

"Call me Jamie—everyone does," the leerie replied. "I don't s'pose I might have another cup o' tea, seeing as how I'm gonnae stick around fer a while?"

"Certainly," said Ian. "Sergeant, would you be so kind?"

"Right away, sir," said Dickerson, ducking behind the glass partition in the back of the room.

"Please, have a seat," Ian said, indicating a chair opposite his desk. The lamplighter folded his stork-like body into the wooden chair, crossing his long legs. Ian reckoned they were close to the same height, but that he weighed at least two stone more than Jamie, who was so excessively lean that his right cheekbone jutted out from his face, sharp as a razor. The left one was caved inward, giving his face a lopsided look. He did not seem to be in any discomfort from it, however, and gazed at Ian with his good eye, which was large and brown.

"Now then, if you would tell me everything you observed, leaving out no detail, no matter how insignificant," said Ian, pulling a notebook from the desk drawer.

"Well, I was gaein' aboot me rounds—just startin' out—when I sees what I took tae be a drunkard lyin' in the alley." He shuddered and clasped his hands together, leaning forward. "I stepped a bit closer and saw 'twas a poor dead fella. I dain't like the look of 'im, so I hightailed it 'ere straightaway. That reminds me—I were so taken back, I dropped me lamp-lighting pole. D'ye have it, by chance?"

"No, but we'll get it back to you."

"That's a first—I never let go a' me pole afore."

"So you didn't disturb the body in any way?"

"Not me, no—I couldna git away fast enough."

"Did you notice anything else?"

"Such as wha'?"

"Perhaps something out of the ordinary?"

The lamplighter scratched his head, causing white flaky bits to float from his scalp and settle on his shoulders. "Naught out a th'ordinary, no . . . Hang on a minute, there was one thaing."

Ian leaned forward. "What?"

"The smell a' cigarette smoke. It struck me at the time, because there were no one else aboot, and it were already rainin'—but there it was, hangin' in the air, like someone just 'ad a smoke. And it weren't the usual, either—it were thicker, sweet and heavy, like."

"Did you ever smell this particular tobacco before?"

"It smelled expensive. Might 'ave come across it once or twice in the New Town, I s'pose, outside the fancy homes."

"Thank you—you've been very helpful," Ian said, rising from his chair.

"Wha' about m'tea?"

"Just comin' up, sir," said Sergeant Dickerson, rounding the corner and balancing a tea tray with three mugs and a plate of biscuits. "Thought you might do with some as well, sir," he said, laying it out on the desk. "It promises to be a long night."

"Thank you, Sergeant." Ian sighed. When he was hard on a case, he often considered food and drink unwelcome distractions, and had no desire to engage in idle chitchat over tea.

Taking the cup the sergeant offered, Ian snagged a couple of ginger-snaps, stuffing them into his pocket. He intended to walk home; something about the forward motion seemed to loosen a part of his brain.

"Well, I'm off," he said, gulping down the last of his tea so quickly, he nearly scorched his throat.

"I'm free t'go, then?" Long Jamie asked, clearly disappointed.

"Please provide Sergeant Dickerson with your address in case we need to interview you further."

This seemed to cheer the lamplighter up. "I will, ye can rest assured," he said, nodding vigorously. "Any time o' day or night, ye kin count on Long Jamie."

"See you tomorrow, Sergeant," Ian said, heading toward the door.

"Uh, sir . . . ?" Dickerson said, scurrying after him.

"What is it?"

"Tomorrow's Saturday."

"Need I remind you that criminals don't take holidays?"

Dickerson shuffled his feet, looking miserable.

"What is it, Sergeant?"

"It's my only chance to spend time with my Pauline, an' I—"

"Very well, if you must take the day off—"

"Per'aps just the mornin'?"

"I'll see you here at one o'clock promptly."

"Thank you, sir—ta very much indeed." Seized by a sudden fit of sneezing, he pulled the monogrammed handkerchief from his pocket and wiped his eyes when he was through.

"Get to bed, Sergeant—take my aunt's advice and put on a mustard plaster. And see that you get him out of here," he added with a nod toward Long Jamie, who was inspecting the photographs on the bulletin board of wanted criminals.

"Leave it t'me, sir," Dickerson said, beaming.

Hamilton threw his cloak over his shoulders and pushed open the heavy oak door, which closed behind him with a decisive thud.

CHAPTER
FORTY-FOUR

The walk home provided no hoped-for insight; Ian came up with a dozen theories and discarded them all. His mind kept spinning around the smell of expensive tobacco, and the aroma he had detected on the corpse, most certainly opium. Opium dens in Edinburgh were seedy establishments catering to the down-and-out as well as the city's Asian population, who were more likely to smoke cheap tobacco. Where might he find a place catering to a clientele favoring costly tobacco?

When he arrived at Victoria Terrace, sitting on his doorstep was George Pearson. "Mr. Pearson," Ian said, "what are you doing here?"

The librarian leapt to his feet. "I have some information that may interest you."

"You could have left me a note," Ian replied, unlocking the door.

"I don't trust that form of delivery when something is important. As a reference librarian, I know information can disappear more easily than you might imagine." Eyes shining, he stood on the doorstep expectantly, like a big round puppy.

"Come in, why don't you?" Ian sighed, tossing his keys on the foyer table. A plaintive meowing, followed by loud purring, greeted him as Bacchus darted into the room and rubbed against his leg.

"I say—you have a cat?" Pearson said. "But you didn't before."

"Things happen, Mr. Pearson," Ian replied, "sometimes without being wished for." He hoped the librarian would take his meaning, but it fell short of the target.

"He's quite a handsome fellow," Pearson said, scratching the cat behind the ears. Bacchus responded by wrapping himself around the librarian's shins.

"He catches mice," Ian remarked, "which makes him useful."

"I believe he is asking to be fed."

"In a minute," Ian said, hanging up his cloak before heading for the kitchen, followed closely by Bacchus and Pearson. There was still no sign of Donald, which was a relief and a disappointment. Ian was still perplexed about the playing cards in his brother's rucksack.

"Have you never owned a cat before?" Pearson asked.

"My mother hated cats," he said, pulling a joint of mutton from the icebox.

"How does he do his—business?"

Ian stared at him.

"The—er, water-closet business."

"I let him outside for that."

"I can make you a cat door."

"What's that?"

"A small swinging door he can use to go in and out—I can cut it out of a corner of this one," he said, pointing to the back entrance in the rear of the kitchen leading to the alley behind the building. "You're lucky you live on the ground floor."

"Thank you for the offer, Mr. Pearson," Ian said, filling the cat's bowl with cream. "Now then, what is it you wanted to tell me?"

"I have found the establishment where your—er, strangler may have purchased those singular packs of playing cards."

"In Edinburgh?"

"Yes. It purports to be a milliner's, but is in reality a shop catering to magicians, illusionists, and other specialty stage performers."

"How on earth did you know that?"

"I have a minor interest in such things myself, and I stopped by today to inquire. The gentleman behind the counter said they sell quite well, in fact."

"What is this establishment?"

"It's called the Magic Hat. Here is the address," Pearson replied, handing him a slip of paper covered with his neat, precise handwriting.

"I am in your debt," Ian said, folding it before placing it carefully in his pocket.

"Think nothing of it," the librarian replied, though Ian noticed he was eyeing the roast hungrily.

"Would you like some cold mutton and a glass of beer?"

Pearson coughed delicately. "If you're having some."

"By all means," Ian said, realizing he was ravenous.

An hour later, Ian was stretching his legs in front of the fire, listening to the sounds of sawing and hammering from the kitchen as Pearson busied himself making the agreed-upon cat door. After providing him with the necessary tools, Ian was shooed off to the parlor, where he nodded off in front of the fire. Pearson was handier than Ian expected; before long he appeared at the door, his face glistening, sleeves rolled up, a hammer in his hand.

"There—finished! Come have a look-see."

Ian dragged himself from the armchair into the kitchen. "That really is quite ingenious," he said, pushing on the small wooden flap Pearson had cut from the back door. Attached by hinges, it swung back and forth smoothly.

"Now we must introduce it to your feline friend," the librarian said as Bacchus slipped around the corner into the kitchen.

Pearson grasped him firmly around the middle and placed him in front of the cat door. After giving it an introductory sniff, Bacchus pushed his head against it. When it gave, he initially backed away, but caution soon gave way to curiosity. Before long he was dashing through it to the alleyway and whatever lay beyond.

"How do we know he'll come back?" said Ian.

Pearson smiled. "Cats like a ready source of food, which he already associates with you."

His response made Ian feel a bit put out, and he realized with some surprise that he wanted to be more to the cat than a source of food. In spite of his ambivalence about the animal, the cat door seemed to have sealed the deal. He was surprised at how uncharacteristically passive he had been about the whole affair, being bullied first by Sergeant Dickerson, and now George Pearson.

"It's late," the librarian said, eyeing the decanter of brandy on the sideboard hopefully. "I really should be going."

"Just one more thing, Mr. Pearson," Ian said as his guest buttoned his coat.

"Yes?"

"How did you know about the cards?"

The librarian reddened. "Why, you must have told me."

"But I didn't."

"Are you quite sure?"

"Quite."

"I really must be going. Good night," Pearson replied, ducking quickly out the door.

Ian supposed Pearson had wheedled the information out of Sergeant Dickerson, but . . . no, he thought, the heart of a killer could not beat in that fleshy chest. He gazed out the window as a waning moon rose in the sky. The number of people he could trust seemed to be shrinking daily.

What if Donald was right? Did evil really exist in equal measure in every man's heart? Ian had spent his career convinced there were good men and bad, and it was his job to protect the former from the latter. Was it just a matter of circumstances, then—and under the right conditions, even a good man could become corrupted, like the monster he pursued so doggedly? He paced the front parlor restlessly, the wan moon casting shadows on the forest-green Persian rug, with its intricate pattern of vines twisting around one another in a never-ending dance.

The idea was unthinkable. If his brother was right, fate toyed with people like a cat tormenting a mouse, and mankind was at the mercy of a cruel and indifferent universe. He had spent the past seven years struggling to wrest some order in the midst of chaos, but now . . .

His hands twitched, and he longed for something to hold in them. His eyes fell upon the cigarette case Donald had left on the mahogany end table. Trembling, he seized it and snapped open the gold clasp. Pulling out a cigarette, he inhaled the sharp aroma of tobacco. Placing it between his lips, he struck a match and watched it flare as he held it to the end of the cigarette. Inhaling deeply, he tossed the match into the center of the fire, where it was devoured by the flames.

CHAPTER
FORTY-FIVE

Ian awoke from a dreamless sleep to bright sunshine pouring through the front window. The weather had been dark and gray for so long, it took him a moment to adjust. He attempted to sit upright in bed, but a weight on his chest prevented him from moving. He looked down into the half-closed, glassy green eyes of his newest houseguest.

"I don't recall inviting you to join me," he said.

The cat purred loudly and stretched a languid forepaw toward his head, its fishy breath cold on his cheek.

"Off you go," he commanded. "Now!"

Bacchus rolled over, exposing his wide white belly.

"Right," said Ian. "That's it." Throwing off the covers, he swung his legs off the side of the bed. The cat clung to him like treacle, digging its claws into his thigh. "Ow! Bloody hell," Ian muttered, disengaging the claws to pull the animal away from his body. "Can't you take a hint?"

Bacchus stood amidst the disarray of bedclothes, flicking his tail irritably.

"Good Lord," said Ian. "You're worse than the wee bloody mouse."

The cat responded by rolling onto its back and purring.

"I don't have time for this nonsense," Ian said as he slid into his clothes, shivering. He longed for a hot bath, but the angle of the sun told him it was late morning already. Bolting down a crust of bread and a piece of sausage, he tore off a piece of the meat and put it in a bowl for the cat, placing another one of cream next to it. Bacchus sniffed at the sausage, flicked his tail, and lapped greedily at the cream.

"So you don't like sausage," Ian muttered, pulling on his boots. "Just remember, beggars can't be choosers," he added as he pulled on his cloak and slid out the door.

After weeks of gray weather, the sunlight was disconcerting. Overnight, the tempo of the city had changed. The dank cold had lifted; the streets swirled with warm pockets of mist, the sun penetrating corners and crannies that had been dark for days on end. Everyone walked with straight shoulders and open faces, their limbs relaxing in the balmy air.

Ian felt his own muscles loosen as he strode up the High Street, Edinburgh Castle glimmering high atop its rocky crag. Even the voices of the vendors on the Grassmarket sounded cheerful, blending with the noise of their lowing cattle and bleating sheep. Saturday was the weekly livestock market, as farmers drove their herds through the Cowgate from the east and through the West Port to the west. The last public hanging had taken place in the Grassmarket more than fifteen years earlier. Nowadays unlucky sinners were sent to meet their Maker in the privacy of the prison yard—though crowds of curious spectators sometimes gathered on nearby Calton Hill to gape at executions of more celebrated criminals.

Ian picked his way carefully across the cobblestones, avoiding the inevitable specimens left by scores of farm animals. The musty smell of manure was harder to avoid, floating up from the pens down in the marketplace. Breathing through his mouth, he hurried past the area toward the police station.

A crowd had gathered in front of the building, and as Ian approached, several people turned and pointed at him.

"There he is!"

"Oiy, when are ye gonnae catch the strangler?"

"We're not safe in our beds!"

"What kind o' police are ye, to leave a madman at large?"

The crush of bodies advanced toward him. Acid fear flowed through his veins, making his legs go weak. He didn't see a way around the crowd—to enter the building, he would have to go through them. His brain raced to find a solution.

"Ladies and gentlemen, citizens of Edinburgh!" he declared. "I want to assure you we are doing everything we can to catch this miscreant. In fact, due to some recent developments, we are very close to capturing him!"

"Why should we believe ye?" yelled a stocky fellow in a butcher's apron.

"What are these 'developments'?" shouted a well-dressed man in a rust-colored frock coat.

"I cannot tell you that, but I will say that upon my honor and my life, we will bring this monster to justice!" Surprised by the passion in his own voice, Ian was relieved to see the effect on the crowd. Several nodded, while others, who had been angry a moment before, looked placated. He took a chance and continued toward them. "And now, if you'll excuse me, I'd like to go do my job."

To his surprise, several people began applauding, and others joined in, stepping aside for him to pass. As the sweat slid down his face, it occurred to Ian that Moses was no more pleased at the parting of the Red Sea than he was at the sight of this crowd making way for him. He knew he did not deserve the applause, but all that mattered was getting inside the building.

As he entered the foyer, he was greeted by the sound of angry yelling. Removing his cloak, he strode down the short hallway leading to the central chamber. A few constables cowered to the side of the room, pretending to be busy with paperwork. In the center of it stood Chief Inspector Louis Valeur Gerard, crisply dressed in his immaculate uniform, his face purple as a plum.

"But why wasn't I called? It is *inexplicable—inconceivable!*"

The target of his tirade, DCI Crawford, stood a few feet away, a weary expression on his heavy face. "Look, Inspector Gerard—"

"*Chief* Inspector—"

"Chief Inspector, I myself only just found out about it."

"*Mais pourquoi?* What kind of organization have you here, eh? That you would not know is *vraiment incroyable.*"

Crawford shot Ian a supplicating look, as if pleading to be rescued from this mad Frenchman.

"I think I can answer that," Ian said, approaching them.

Gazing at Ian gratefully, Crawford said, "This is Detective Inspector Hamilton."

"We have met already," Gerard replied, wheeling around to face him. "Why do you fail to contact me when this new murder occurs, *monsieur?*"

"I apologize," said Ian. "It was very sudden, and I wasn't sure how to reach you."

"But I inform you in my telegram that I stay at the Waverley Hotel."

"My sincerest apology, Chief Inspector—we were all taken off guard."

The Frenchman let out a breath, and his forehead relaxed a bit, though he still wore a peeved expression. "*Alors*, if you allow yourselves to be *distraits* every time this killer strikes, you will never catch him. You must not play by his rules, eh?"

"This is not a game, Chief Inspector," Crawford said evenly, but Ian sensed his anger was mounting. "May I remind you that you are here as our guest, in a nonofficial capacity, and while we appreciate any help you can give us, that doesn't mean—"

"Look here," Hamilton interrupted, "why don't I tell you both what I know?"

Chief Inspector Gerard pursed his lips and frowned. "Very well—I am listening."

"Why don't we go into my office?" Crawford said. "The toxicology report on Mrs. Sutherland just came in."

"What does it say?" Hamilton asked, following him and Gerard past a group of relieved-looking constables.

Crawford closed the office door behind the three of them. "See for yourself," he replied, plucking a file folder from his desk and handing it to Ian.

Ian opened it, searching eagerly for the phrase that would confirm his suspicion. There it was, bold as day, on the first page:

Cause of Death: CYANIDE POISONING

"So," he said, looking up at DCI Crawford, "he's not only a strangler, but a poisoner as well."

"Hang on a minute," replied his boss. "We don't know the same person is responsible for poisoning Mrs. Sutherland."

"Who is she?" asked Gerard. "And why was she poisoned?"

"She knew something," Ian replied. "Or he believed she did."

"But why not just strangle her?" said Crawford.

"I think he intended to disguise her death as natural."

"And it might have worked, if not for your persistence," Crawford mused, absently twisting a piece of string between his fingers.

"And Sergeant Dickerson's nose," Ian added.

"What about last night, then?" asked Crawford.

Ian filled them in on the details of the previous night.

"Someone should have fetched me," Crawford said, handing Ian the early edition of the *Scotsman*. "The eyes of the town are upon us."

The newspaper screamed out its headline:

Murderer Runs Rampant Through City Streets!
Police Baffled by Ruthless "Holyrood Strangler"—
Is a Lust Killer at Large?

Ian groaned. "Isn't that just what we need now—more lurid journalism."

"They got one thing right—they do have elements of lust killings," said Crawford.

Ian frowned. "That's an element, but I think it's more complicated than that."

Gerard frowned. "But this latest victim was a—"

"Yes, but Bobby Tierney was not."

"You said this club, the Owl's Nest, was hard to find," said Crawford. "How would the killer know about it?"

"I think Stephen Wycherly took him there."

Chief Inspector Gerard looked at the headline with distaste. "Our Paris newspapers would never stoop to such depths of fearmongering."

"Bully for them," Crawford growled. "But you're in Scotland now, and the sooner you get used to it, the better."

The Frenchman's eyes opened wide with astonishment, and for an instant it looked as if he might explode in fury. But then he laughed. "Never fear, Monsieur Chief Inspector; I have not forgotten it for one moment. Even if I wanted to, it would be impossible—the cuisine has reminded my poor stomach ever since I arrived."

"Our food may not equal yours, but I'll wager you a meal at Edinburgh's best restaurant that before you leave, you will be impressed with our police force."

Inspector Gerard gave a pinched smile. "I can only hope you are right, *monsieur*."

Ian held up the toxicology report. "Can we keep this from the press?"

Crawford crossed his arms. "Make the official cause of death natural causes, you mean?"

"To avoid public hysteria."

"Agreed. Public faith in the constabulary is eroding as it is."

"If the strangler did poison Mrs. Sutherland," Ian observed, "it makes him even more dangerous."

Gerard crossed his arms. "I fail to see how he could be more dangerous than he already is."

"What makes you say that?" Crawford asked Ian, ignoring the Frenchman.

"It shows a level of premeditation. He arrived prepared, and carried off his plan without being seen. He is not a man who makes mistakes."

"*Mais* he makes the mistakes sooner or later," Gerard said. "The trick is to catch him at it."

"Easier said than done," Crawford grunted, sitting heavily behind his desk.

"But why wait until now to kill her?" Gerard asked.

"He must not have realized she was a threat earlier."

"What do you think she was going to tell you?"

"I'm afraid we'll never know."

Crawford pointed to a bulletin board containing pictures of all the victims, in the order they were found. Beneath them were the cards found upon each body. "What do you make of these playing cards—what do they signify?"

"They are quite the rage in Paris," said Gerard. "It's the *danse macabre*—the dance of death."

"So he might have brought them over with him," said Crawford.

"Perhaps the cards are a clue to his profession," Ian suggested.

"He is taunting us," Gerard remarked.

"That much is clear," Crawford replied, "but beyond that, what do they tell us about his identity?"

Gerard cocked his head to one side. "He seems to be trying for—what do you call it in poker . . . *la quinte flush*—a straight flush?"

"You're right," said Ian. "And if you include the two Paris killings, that makes five total, so—"

"His hand is complete," said Crawford.

"Oui," Gerard agreed. "Which leaves the question, what will be his next hand?"

"That depends upon what cards he still holds," Ian remarked.

As he gazed at the late-morning sunlight slanting in through the high window, it occurred to him that they didn't hold much of a hand at all.

CHAPTER FORTY-SIX

Derek McNair paced restlessly in front of the intersection of Candlemaker Row and George IV Bridge. Freddie Cubbins was late *again*. Derek had just about had his fill of waiting for his friend, who never seemed to arrive on time. It was market day, and they planned to join the milling crowds on the Grassmarket, pretending to mingle while looking for pockets to pick. Saturday was their most lucrative day of the week—folks were so busy haggling, they failed to notice their wallet was no longer in their coat pocket until Derek and Freddie had vanished into the crowd.

Being small and slight, Derek seldom attracted attention. Assuming he was younger than he was, people didn't see the threat until it was too late. His slim, delicate hands were like quicksilver; he could lift a purse from a lady's handbag and slip away through the crowd before anyone was aware of his presence. Freddie was not as skillful, and being larger, was more likely to draw suspicious glances or catch a policeman's eye. Derek didn't need Freddie to have a profitable day, but the two had been mates ever since Freddie defended the smaller boy from attacks by bullies, and Derek prided himself on his loyalty.

Still, he thought as he paced the same blocks for the tenth time, there was a limit to his patience. Just as he was about to give up, he saw Freddie. Hatless and out of breath, he was dashing down the street as if being chased by demons.

"Sorry I'm late! Almost got nicked by a copper fer stealin' fruit and 'ad to lie low until he gave up the chase." He stood panting and sweating, his big, friendly face anxious for approval. His big-boned hands protruded from a tweed wool jacket several sizes too small for him; his trouser cuffs hung a good five inches from the ground. While Derek hardly seemed to grow from year to year, Freddie had shot up like a blond beanpole sprouted from magic seeds.

"I 'most gave up on ye," Derek said, starting down the stone stairs leading to the Grassmarket.

"Oiy—wait up!" Freddie cried, a lock of sandy hair falling over one eye as he scrambled after his friend in his awkward gait, ungainly as a young colt.

"We'll have t'make up fer wasted time," Derek called over his shoulder as he darted nimbly around a plump dowager struggling down the stairs, encumbered by an enormous shopping basket on her fat arm.

"Where we gonnae start?"

"We'll dig in't the crowd around the livestock pens."

Local Midlothian farmers came to town on Saturdays with livestock, homemade jams and jellies, and everything in between. The wide avenue was packed with slaughterhouse men and butchers, as well as housekeepers looking to stock their pantries. The square was lined with all manner of stores—grocers, victual dealers, clothing and candy shops, all doing a brisk trade on market day. The coffee shops were packed with drovers rubbing shoulders with servants of society ladies looking to stock their pantries.

Like most Scots, Edinburgh residents were a thrifty lot, but once seized by the desire to spend, their frenzy could last all day. The one common element was cash, and plenty of it—which was where Derek and Freddie came in, their aim being to relieve their fellow citizens of as much of the cumbersome stuff as possible.

"Look sharp," Derek cautioned as the boys swung round the corner onto the broad avenue, already filling with merchants and shoppers. The air rang with the high, plaintive bleating of sheep and goats, and the throaty rumble of cattle, as animals' earthy odor floated into the city's already fetid air. Looming above them, Edinburgh Castle perched like a brooding hen upon its stone nest, guarding the entrance to the city as it had for centuries.

Derek glanced around for any sign of their competition. Pickpockets of all stripes were drawn here on market day. The best plied their trade with ease, while the less skillful drew the attention of the police and created warier victims. Across the street he spied Terry McNee, alias Rat Face, loitering in the shadows and sizing up potential marks. McNee was so skillful at his trade that he even commanded the respect of the local constabulary. They had yet to nab him in the act, though he was once imprisoned on the testimony of a pawnshop owner he had commissioned to "reset"—fence—a gold watch.

"See anyone?" Freddie said, following Derek's gaze around the assembled crowd. Sometimes he seemed to have no will of his own, mimicking everything Derek did.

"Rat Face is here already. I don't s'pose he'll cause us any concern."

"What about that mate of 'is—Jimmy Snead?" Freddie asked nervously. He had good reason to be frightened of the big man, who had once spied the boys encroaching upon what he regarded as his friend's territory. His attempt to scare the boys off succeeded. Derek could still feel the great beast's fingers around his throat, and Freddie had been so terrified, he'd wet himself.

"No sign of Snead anywheres," Derek replied. "Let's get ta work afore the amateurs show up an' spoil it fer us."

"Right," Freddie replied without enthusiasm. The sight of Rat Face had spooked him, and he followed close behind Derek, casting nervous looks from side to side as they shouldered their way through the crowd.

Derek's technique, developed from years of practice, was to head for the center of a group. People on the outer edges tended to be more wary, since they assumed (erroneously) that a pickpocket would immediately abscond after snatching a purse. In fact, Derek enjoyed casually relieving a person of his valuables, often standing next to his victim for some time afterward. Occasionally he even ventured a friendly remark or two. When the time came to slip away into the crowd, the boy was like an eel, slithering between bodies with astonishing agility.

He slid between a couple of lawyers in white wigs engaged in a heated exchange about the nature of Scottish independence—a much-discussed but little-acted-upon topic in Edinburgh. Freddie lingered a few yards behind, doing his best to emulate his friend, but without his talent. His journey was spotted with epithets, exclamations, and excuses as he trod on toes, jostled elbows, and bumped into fellow burghers.

"Oiy—watch it, why don' ya?"

"Hey—look where you're goin'!"

"'Scuse me, really sorry—beg pardon, sorry."

Derek sighed as his friend's incompetence trailed behind him like the tail on a comet. He knew being clumsy wasn't Freddie's fault, but sometimes Derek wished to be rid of the encumbrance. Freddie was so clueless. Derek held his breath and slipped between a couple of comely, chattering housemaids with wicker baskets dangling from their arms, running a casual hand over their bottoms. The girls were so engaged in giggling and gossip that they didn't even notice.

One reason Derek liked the center of a crowd was that people were less wary of physical contact, being used to a certain amount of jostling. Pickpocketing was that much easier—and so was the opportunity to caress plump buttocks or gaze with impunity at a lavishly displayed bosom. Derek could graze a lady's bottom with such a featherlight touch, she wouldn't be aware of it. And if by chance she did feel something, her accusatory glare would invariably fall upon the closest grown man—after all, who would suspect a ten-year-old boy of such licentious public behavior?

But Derek was incorrigibly randy; the mere whiff of a tea-rose sachet or the ruff of a lady's bonnet could catapult him into frenzied infatuation. Not so Freddie—he loped along behind Derek like a big friendly golden retriever, good-natured and eager to please.

Derek was studying the frock coat of a prosperous-looking gentleman of middle years, wondering how much cash his wallet was likely to yield, when he heard a commotion behind him, near the outer edges of the crowd. Turning, he saw the same rotund dowager he and Freddie had passed earlier. Red-faced and furious, she was thrusting a fat finger at his friend.

"Thief! He tried to steal a loaf of bread from my basket!" she shouted at anyone who would listen.

Freddie froze, wide-eyed and trembling, as if bolted to the spot. Derek realized he must act quickly or his friend would be seized by the first spectator to get his wits about him. Shoving roughly through the crowd, he grabbed Freddie's wrist and turned to face his accuser.

"Me poor brother is a dumb mute idiot," he said, tears springing to his eyes. In addition to his other talents, Derek was an excellent impromptu actor. "Please forgive 'im. Poor lad is probably hungry and didn't know how t'ask fer food."

The good woman's face softened. She shook her head, her own ruddy cheeks moistening with tears. "Oh, dear me, I am ever so glad you told me. Here—take the bread," she insisted, shoving it at Derek.

"Oh, no, mum, I couldn't," he replied, but she thrust it into his hands.

"I insist! You're a good lad to take such care of your brother," she said, ruffling his hair. "Here's half a crown for the both of you."

Derek took the piece of silver and muttered his thanks. Freddie stared at them both with such a stupid expression, Derek wasn't surprised the good lady had bought his story about him being an idiot. She smiled at them beatifically before continuing on her way toward the shops lining the main square. After some head shaking and a few muttered remarks of sympathy, the crowd lost interest in the boys, returning to the purpose of the day—haggling and buying.

Derek grabbed Freddie by the wrist and dragged him to the other side of the street.

"Ye've gone an' ruined an entire day—over a loaf of *bread*!" he sputtered, waving the offending item in Freddie's astonished face.

"I was hungry," he replied meekly.

"We can't stay here an' work now. Everyone's had a bloody good look at us. We' done fer the day," he said, disgusted.

"W-what'll we do, then?" Freddie asked, close to tears.

"I don' care what ye do," Derek declared. "I'm goin' somewheres else where I kin do a decent day's work. Here," he added, tossing Freddie the half crown. "Go buy yerself another loaf o' bread."

And with that, he stalked off without looking back, the rage boiling in his ears drowning out the voice of his conscience.

CHAPTER
FORTY-SEVEN

The magician hummed to himself as he set up his equipment on the street corner at the Grassmarket. The plaza buzzed with activity as Saturday shoppers and vendors came together in a timeless ritual of bartering and buying. He enjoyed doing magic on the street—it was more of a challenge than performing in a theater, more honest and raw. He liked the close contact with his audience, being able to see the awe and wonder in their eyes when he fooled them. No, not "fooled"— *enchanted* them. He drew them into a world of mystery and marvel, where anything could happen, and they entered it willingly.

He did a few tricks with metal rings and silk scarves to warm up— basic stuff, which he did well, having studied the techniques of the best, from Herrmann the Great to Robert-Houdin. His patter was smooth, his movements mesmerizing, and his good looks didn't hurt, either— plenty of couples passed by, the women craning their necks to get a better look at him, the husbands tugging at their wives impatiently to move along. Constant practice had refined his innate gift for "presti-digitation," as it was known on the Continent—what people here called "sleight of hand."

He produced a bouquet of flowers from a tiny Chinese lantern, which he lit by blowing on it, tossing the flowers to a young lass in a red-and-green tartan. She caught them gracefully, batting her eyelashes at him before her husband pulled her along the pavement. The magician loved the effect he had on women, but he enjoyed the reactions from husbands even more.

He cut a fresh white length of rope in half, then quarters, making it whole again by blowing on it. He pulled half crowns from behind the ears of astonished boys and made a dove appear beneath the hat of a young girl. He made bright silk handkerchiefs disappear into his clenched fist and reappear in the purses of fashionable ladies, who blushed and tittered and lowered their eyes before his searching gaze. He did all of this and more, gathering quite a crowd around him, as shoppers leaving and entering the market were drawn by the increasing number of spectators straining to see over the heads of the people in front of them.

It was all a prelude, an overture, to the main event, the skill he truly excelled at: card tricks. He was a wizard with a deck of playing cards, and could make them dance and leap as though they were alive. His hands, always supple, moved with lightning swiftness; buoyed by his constant stream of commentary, he could fool even the keenest eye.

"Who would like to pick a card?" he asked, tossing an entire pack into the air, flipping them over one by one with lightning speed so that they returned to his hands like fifty-two boomerangs. Jaws dropped among his spectators, who burst into enthusiastic applause, followed by excited chattering.

"Did ye see that, Mary?"

"'At fella's a wonder, he is!"

"I never seen anythin' like it."

"Lord Almighty in heaven!"

"More like the devil, if ye ask me."

He smiled and fanned the cards out in front of him in a perfect half-moon. "Go ahead—pick a card, any card." He looked over the crowd, their faces as open and trusting as children's. He had them— they were truly in his power now. He took a deep breath and smiled at his subjects, catching the eye of a grubby, sad-faced street Arab. The boy frowned and shoved his hands into his pockets. The magician beamed at him. "What's your name?"

"Freddie," the boy replied, gazing down at his shabby shoes.

"Pick a card, Freddie. Don't be afraid. I'm not going to bite."

Hesitantly, the boy reached for a card, and the magician felt a surge of pleasure. It was going to be a good night.

CHAPTER
FORTY-EIGHT

Long after the firing of the One O'Clock Gun high atop the volcanic Castle Rock, the shadows were lengthening in the Edinburgh police station. After shining bravely all morning, the weary February sky had finally surrendered to a mottled cloud cover threatening to cast the city into another midwinter gloom. The three men huddled in DCI Crawford's office poring over evidence hardly noticed the change in the air, so intent were they on unraveling the puzzle of one man's identity.

"It would be a great help to us, Chief Inspector, if we could locate the shop where those cards were purchased," DCI Crawford remarked.

"*Malheureusement*, they are very common in Paris," the Frenchman replied. "We look already, of course, though with no result *définitif*. But I must return to Paris. I will try to turn over more stones, eh?"

"My sources have located a shop in Edinburgh that sells them," Ian said.

Crawford looked at him curiously, his bushy eyebrows drawn together. "And what 'sources' might those be?"

"Sergeant Dickerson," Ian lied. He had no desire to explain George Pearson or his interest in the case to DCI Crawford.

"Where the blazes *is* he, by the way?"

Ian considered telling the truth about the sergeant's whereabouts but decided against it. "Interviewing potential witnesses, sir."

Crawford grunted and slid into his chair. "Very well—if you can trust him not to muck it up."

"Dickerson's a good man. There are one or two other points I intend to investigate."

"Such as . . . ?"

"I detected the aroma of opium on Kerry O'Donohue."

"Indeed?"

"I have some ideas as to where he may have procured the opium."

Chief Inspector Gerard raised a thick black eyebrow. "*Vraiment?* I would like to stay, but I take the train to London this evening. Before I leave, would either of you care to join me for a late lunch, as my guest?"

"Very kind of you, but I must be getting home to my wife," Crawford said. "Another time, perhaps."

"*Certainement. Et vous, monsieur?*" Gerard asked Ian.

"Thank you, but I have another interview to conduct this afternoon."

Inspector Gerard shook his head. "I must say, I fail to comprehend the Scottish indifference to food. In France, we consider meals to be *sacro-saint*—what is your expression for this?"

"The same," said Ian. "Sacrosanct."

"*Oui, c'est la même chose.* To us, it is very important, the eating of good food, the sensual *plaisir*, you know?"

"Blame Scottish Presbyterianism," said Crawford. "We're a bunch of bloody stoics. Though we do like our sweets," he added, popping a biscuit into his mouth.

"*C'est important* to refresh the mind and body, no?" said Gerard.

"I envy your Gallic sensuality," Crawford said, "but I'm too old to change. Go and enjoy your lunch."

"*Merci*. It has been a privilege working with you," Gerard said, offering his hand, which Ian and Crawford shook warmly. In spite of the initial friction between them, Ian would be sorry to see the Frenchman go, and he suspected the chief inspector felt the same. "I call on you tomorrow," said Gerard, putting on his hat and coat.

"Tomorrow is Sunday," said Crawford. "I'll be at church in the morning."

"*Et vous, monsieur?*" Gerard asked Ian.

"I usually spend Sundays with my aunt."

"And when will that aunt of yours give me an answer about the photography?" Crawford said. "'Hope springs exulting on triumphant wing.'"

"My apologies, sir—she said she would be delighted."

"You could have told me earlier," Crawford grunted. "Tell her I'm glad to hear it."

"I'll also convey your excellent knowledge of Robert Burns. She is also a devotee of his writing."

"Good on her for appreciating a proper Scottish poet."

"You will please contact me if there are further developments?" Gerard interrupted impatiently.

"We will," said Crawford. "Goodbye, Chief Inspector, and thank you." After Gerard had gone, Crawford ate another biscuit and offered Ian the tin. "Sorry about yesterday. My wife . . . She's not well."

"I'm sorry to hear that, sir," Ian replied, taking a biscuit. "Nothing serious, I hope?"

"I'd rather not go into it. Thanks for carrying on without me."

"Not at all, sir. And now I'd like to get out on my interview."

"Take another biscuit for the road."

"Ta very much," said Ian, taking one. As he approached the stairs leading down to the ground floor, he heard a familiar voice.

"Hullo, Guv'nur!"

He turned to see Derek McNair, his face even grimier than usual, leaning on the banister. "It's about time you showed up," said Ian. "Where the hell have you been?"

"I've got a livin' to make, y'know. I left a message with yer brother."

"I need to know exactly what the landlady said to you," Ian said as they walked down the stairs and out of the building. Heading east, he turned south onto Stevenlaw's Close.

"You mean Mrs. Sutherland?" Derek replied, scurrying to keep up.

"Yes."

"She were real good to me—gave me soup an' all."

"She's dead."

Derek stopped walking. "Wha' happened?"

"She was poisoned."

"She were fit as a fiddle when I left 'er," Derek said, his voice shaky. "What could . . . Wait—the soup! You don't s'pose—why would anyone kill a nice lady like her?"

"I want you to repeat exactly what she said to you."

"She said she foun' somethin'."

"Did she say what?"

"No."

Ian resumed walking, the boy following. "Did you see anything while you were there?"

"Like what?" Derek replied, kicking at a stone in his path.

"Did you notice anyone or anything suspicious?"

"Not as I can remember. Like I says, she were fine when I left."

"Anyone on the street, loitering about as you left?"

"No . . . wait, there was this one fella, looked like he were waitin' fer someone."

"Where did you see him?"

"On't pavement, in front of 'er house."

"What did he look like?"

"He were a handsome fella, with black hair and curious pale eyes, dressed like a gentleman."

"How tall?"

"'Bout regular height. Not nearly so tall as you."

"And you had the feeling he was waiting for someone?"

"Yeah."

"Did he see you?" Ian said, turning onto Cowgate.

"He looked straight at me, like as to bore a hole right through me."

Ian stopped walking. "You could be in danger."

Derek snorted. "Who'd want ta go after a scrappy little street urchin like me?"

"He wouldn't hesitate, if he thought you knew something."

"Or," Derek said, "maybe he were jes' a nice gentleman waitin' fer a lady to join 'im."

"But you said he looked directly at you."

Derek laughed. "Mister, if I'd half a crown fer every bloody person what gives me looks on the street, I'd be as rich as Solomon."

"But hardly as wise."

Derek shrugged. "Try livin' as I do, an' see how ye fare. There's all kinds 'a wisdom."

"I don't doubt it," Ian replied, heading south on Guthrie Street.

"So where're ye headed?"

"To interview a young lady."

Derek whistled. "Sounds romantic."

"It's nothing of the kind."

"Ha! I've heard that afore."

"What do you know about women, at your age?"

"Not as much as I'd like. But when I'm old enough, I'll give the ladies a run fer their money, I swear it."

"Look," Ian said, stopping in front of Eugene and Catherine Harley's town house. "You need to have a care for your safety. Don't involve yourself in this any further."

"But I was enjoyin' bein' part of the law instead of runnin' from it all the time."

"Where's your friend Freddie? It's safer if you have someone else around."

Derek scuffed his shoe on the curb and picked at his blackened nails. "Me an' him's had a fight."

Ian fished four sovereigns from his pocket and handed them to Derek. The boy stared at them, his mouth hanging open in astonishment. "It's all I have right now," Ian explained. "But I'll give you more if you'll promise me you'll have nothing further to do with this."

"Kin I work on yer next case?"

"Right now I just want your word that you'll mind your own business and be careful."

"Seems like I get paid more fer not helpin' than fer helpin'."

"I must go inside now," Ian said. "Why don't you spend some of that getting a bath somewhere?"

"Oh, the nuns'll give me a bath," Derek said with contempt. "I jes' don' care for 'em."

"The nuns or the bath?"

"Both."

Ian laughed. "Go on with you, before you get into trouble." He watched the boy swing jauntily around the corner before rapping on the front door of Eugene Harley's elegant town house. His knock was answered by the redoubtable Bernadette, looking even more imposing than he remembered, in a dark blue dress with white cuffs and collar and a matching white apron.

"Good day to you again, Detective Inspector," she said, her Irish accent thick as her considerable girth. "What can I do for you, now?" she asked, wiping her hands on a dish towel. They were covered in flour, which Ian thought was a promising sign. He had not forgotten her cream cakes—and his stomach was reminding him it was long past lunchtime.

"Is Miss Harley home?"

"I'll just go and see, sir."

"Much obliged, Bernadette."

She gave the briefest of nods. "Please wait here."

"Thank you," he replied, stepping into the foyer with its paintings of bucolic English landscapes complete with huntsmen on galloping horses, baying hounds underfoot. Eugene Harley didn't strike him as the horsey type—nor, in fact, a likely candidate for any sort of athletic endeavor, in spite of his alleged fondness for golf.

He listened to Bernadette's heavy tread upon the stairs and the first-floor landing as she lumbered to Catherine Harley's bedroom. The sound of her knocking was followed by low voices—strain as he might, Ian couldn't make out the words. Shortly afterward, he heard the return of footsteps down the steps, and the maid reappeared at the foyer entrance.

"Miss Harley is indisposed at the moment," she announced, avoiding his gaze. "Perhaps if you'd like to leave your card—"

Her speech was interrupted by the sound of a door opening upstairs, followed by a muffled cry.

"Excuse me, sir," Bernadette said, alarm spreading over her broad face. "My mistress—"

At that moment Catherine Harley appeared on the staircase, clad as before all in white, but this time she wore an ivory nightgown. She stumbled down the steps, one pale hand clutching the banister, the other pulling at her unkempt hair. Bernadette bustled to her aid, clucking like a red-crested laying hen.

"My lady, what are you doing? You are not well. I implore you, go back to bed!"

Catherine Harley shook off Bernadette's fumbling attempts to shepherd her back upstairs, staggering down the stairs in what appeared to be a drunken state. Seeing Ian, she stretched out a thin arm toward him.

"Ah, you've come back, Stephen—thank God! I thought you were dead. How I've missed you!"

Her vacant stare and halting gait shocked Ian into a sudden realization. He wondered how he had not recognized it earlier.

Catherine Harley was an opium addict.

CHAPTER FORTY-NINE

Passengers swirled through Waverley Station like drops of cream in an unstirred cup of tea, forming geometric patterns so intricate that the man in the dark overcoat standing in the majestic main room could only watch in fascination. As much as he loved solitude and dark, secluded streets, he appreciated the charms a city like Edinburgh could provide. Such variety, so many endless possibilities! *Oh, there was so much evil in a man . . .*

He leaned casually against the wall next to the tea canteen, scanning the crowd. He enjoyed the chase more than anything—the moment before was so delicious, so luxurious, he wanted to prolong it. That was one reason he had not yet gone after that pesky Edinburgh detective. He smiled as he lit a cigarette—his time would come, just not today. He was saving the best for last, when the attack was least suspected. Today, though, he had another victim in mind.

He didn't have long to wait. As the last rays of daylight faded behind the tall latticed windows, a trim, dapper figure appeared, stood in line at the ticket booth, then advanced toward him, heels clicking smartly on the polished floors.

The man in the dark overcoat followed at a discreet distance, his face impassive, until they reached Platform 18. Burying his face in a newspaper, he waited next to the well-dressed gentleman until the train heaved into the station, white smoke billowing from its single stack. Obscured by the spreading smoke, his hands shot out to give a quick, sharp shove to the small of the back of the trim gentleman. Turning quickly, he didn't even see the man clawing the air in a futile effort to arrest his fall into the path of the oncoming train.

Slipping back into the main room, he blended into the crowd as the screams from Platform 18 caused everyone to stop what they were doing and freeze in horror. Anyone observing the scene would have noticed that as everyone in the station surged toward the commotion, he alone moved quickly in the opposite direction. By the time anyone knew what was happening, he was walking briskly along George IV Bridge, to be swallowed up in the bowels of the Old Town.

CHAPTER FIFTY

Bernadette's distress was evident, and her attempt to protect her mistress was touching. Seeing the recognition in Ian's eyes, she hastened to escort Miss Harley back upstairs, but the lady was having none of it. She lurched into the foyer and wrapped her arm around Ian, tugging him toward the parlor.

"Come tell me where you have been all this time, my poor dear Stephen," she said, stroking his cheek.

He allowed her to draw him into the next room, as Bernadette fussed and cajoled her mistress. "Now, now," she said, "does this gentleman look like Mr. Wycherly to you?" as Catherine pulled him down next to her on a gold French settee.

"Why, he is the very image of dear Stephen!" her mistress replied, hanging on to Ian's arm as though it were a life preserver.

Bernadette shook her head, tears springing to her frank green eyes. "Shouldn't you return to your room until you feel better?"

"Nonsense—I fee-el f-fine," Catherine responded, though her eyelids drooped, and her mouth was having trouble forming words. Her lank hair hung in disarray upon her bony shoulders; the diaphanous dressing gown she wore failed to conceal her skeletal form. She looked even thinner than the last time Ian saw her, just a few days ago.

"Did you b-bring me some . . . medicine?" she asked, tapping him on the shoulder.

He glanced at Bernadette, but she averted her eyes.

"I did," he replied. "And I'll give it to you later."

"I want it *now*," she said, pushing out her lower lip like a petulant child.

"Tell you what," he said. "Why don't you go upstairs and get dressed, and we'll go riding together?"

"Oh, Stephen!" she said, taking his head between her hands. "That would be lovely! But c-can you give me my medicine?"

"After you're dressed, you can have your medicine."

She gazed at him searchingly, as if she didn't believe him, but rose unsteadily from the settee and tottered out of the room upon wobbly legs, throwing him one last glance as she started up the staircase. Even with her halting gait, Ian had the odd sensation she was floating up the stairs, her strangely ethereal quality enhanced by the effect of the drug.

When she had gone, he turned to Bernadette, whose solid body sagged with defeat. "Laudanum, is it?"

She blinked at him and shook her head of massive red curls. "Begging your pardon, sir?" she replied, doing her best to sound offended.

"Your loyalty to your mistress does you credit. But surely you must see that hiding her addiction is no help to her."

"I really don't take your meaning, so I don't," she said, turning away. But he heard her sharp intake of breath, which was followed by a sob that caught in her throat.

"It's not your fault," he offered.

"D'you think I don't know that, then?" she cried bitterly, wheeling around. "Isn't it me who stayed up of a night with her when she couldn't sleep?"

"Your mistress is indeed lucky to have you."

"So she is, at that," Bernadette replied. "Though I don't know what good it's done her."

"When did it start—the addiction, I mean?"

Bernadette sat heavily upon the couch, the springs groaning beneath her broad posterior. Ian was a little surprised to see her sitting so freely in his presence, but her distress had evidently erased any class distinction between them.

"She were always high-strung, but the real trouble started after the death of her mother—a sweeter lady never trod the earth, so help me God," she added, crossing herself. "You have to forgive Miss Harley; she has suffered so much."

"It's not up to me to judge her. I truly hope she finds the strength to conquer her affliction before it is too late."

The loyal Bernadette could not suppress a shudder. No doubt she, too, had glimpsed the vacant-eyed wraiths who succumbed to the noxious drug. They could be seen wandering the back alleys and wynds of the Canongate. Those without means turned to prostitution to support their habit.

"It seems Stephen was her supplier—until recently," Ian ventured.

"Yes, sir. Though Lord knows where he got it."

"Does her uncle know?"

"I don't see how he could miss it, though he never speaks of it to me, bless his soul."

"Where is he now?"

"In his law chambers. He hasn't yet found a replacement for Mr. Wycherly, so the poor dear is working even longer hours than usual."

"Bernadette," he said, "I want you to think—hard—where Mr. Wycherly might have procured this substance. A great many lives may depend upon it."

"The laudanum, you mean?"

"Laudanum is a derivative of opium, as you must know."

"Er, yes—now that you mention it, sir."

"So if you have any idea as to how Mr. Wycherly might have come by opium, I implore you—"

"Hang on a minute," she said. "Mr. Wycherly did like to go to a certain place, and sometimes he would stop by here afterward, rather—er, under the influence, as it were."

"Where did he go?"

"He mentioned . . . an owl, I think it was, sir. I took it to be a pub, o' course, but maybe it was something else?"

"Anything else you remember?"

"He talked about a Chinaman called Pong. I remember it struck me because the name is so much like the game, Ping-Pong. You know," she said in response to his blank look, "also called whiff-whaff."

"Ah, yes—table tennis."

"Right you are, sir."

"Thank you, Bernadette!" Ian cried, kissing her upon the forehead. "You have been most helpful."

The good lady blushed and waved her flour-coated hands at him. "I just hope you can use what I told you to solve poor Mr. Wycherly's murder."

"Take care of Miss Harley, will you?"

"I'll do my best, sir."

By the time Ian left the Harley residence, he was faint with hunger. His head felt light as a balloon; he had an odd floating sensation as he walked down the street, as though half levitating, like a magician's assistant. He bought a meat pie from a street vendor and gulped it down so fast, he nearly choked. Wiping his fingers on his handkerchief, he strode with purpose toward the Canongate, the epicenter of all that was shady, vile, and unlawful.

CHAPTER
FIFTY-ONE

George Pearson stood at his window overlooking the Royal Terrace, a steaming cup of tea on the sill. There was little free space in his large but cluttered seven-room flat, so windowsills often served as impromptu tables. The steam rising from the cup fogged the lower portion of the glass, but George could see the street well enough. He watched the pedestrians on the pavement three stories below. He could make out the faces without being seen himself, his stocky body tucked behind green brocade window drapes.

He had always felt more comfortable hiding behind things—reference desks, curtains, doorways. Out in the open, he felt his body was exposed, dangling like a useless appendage and waiting for instructions to a language George had never fully understood.

And so George collected. China, furniture, doilies, histories of the world—it hardly mattered. Surrounded by his objects, he felt safe, protected. Collecting filled a yearning inside him, like a giant maw, a hunger that knew no satiation. The objects were the physical representation of something much deeper and keener. He could not bear the thought that all the world's knowledge would someday be lost. He believed that deep within inanimate objects lay a truth more real and necessary than the merely corporeal world.

He reached for his tea and took a sip, grimacing as he swallowed. He had forgotten to buy sugar, and on top of it, let the pot sit too long; the expensive blend of oolong he favored turned bitter quickly. He set the cup back down on its matching bone china saucer, a delicate robin's egg blue. George was feeling restless. Even the sight of his exquisite—and expensive—Royal Doulton china failed to placate his jittery nerves. He had spent his Saturday afternoon reading—not his usual history texts or books on botany; he had turned his attention to crime in all its gory and salacious detail.

Crime was his passion, and when he became interested in a subject, he immersed himself in it. And, to be honest, he was more than a little taken with DI Hamilton. His fine figure and keen gray eyes had cast a spell on George Pearson.

He took another sip of bitter tea and gazed at a young couple strolling arm in arm along the pavement, the girl leaning into her companion and pressing her shoulder into his side. The bonnet she wore prevented him from seeing her face, but every aspect of her attitude and movements telegraphed her happiness. The two of them were not especially well dressed, so George knew they hadn't much money, but they looked so happy that his heart swelled with envy. He knew such public affection would never be part of his own life—his desires were aberrant in the eyes of society. He could alleviate his bodily cravings in such low, degrading establishments as existed in Edinburgh, but the idea was abhorrent to him.

In spite of his cluttered flat, George Pearson was a fastidious man, and the thought of groping strangers in dark and dingy rooms was more than he could bear. He was a natural romantic, given more to love than to lust, longing for soulful union rather than rude, animalistic coupling. And so he lived in a state of continual desire, tormented by the vision of love all around him. But there was something in the longing itself, a sharp sweetness he had come to believe was better than nothing at all.

When he met DI Hamilton, George resolved to make himself useful to the young detective. He gazed at the pile of books stacked on the floor next to his favorite wing chair, its venerable armrests covered with tattered doilies. The one he had been reading lay on the cushion, open to the chapter on motive. That was the tricky aspect of these killings, George thought. He wondered if he had more in common with the murderer than he would care to think.

George gazed at the book, its pages browning at the edges, and wondered if such a man could be found at one of the places where he had vowed never to set foot. Outside, the light was seeping from the sky as it slipped from cobalt to midnight blue. George bit his lip, standing for a moment undecided, then reached for his coat. The night beckoned, and so did the allure of danger. He felt a thrill in his veins; as he locked the flat behind him, he realized he had never felt more alive.

CHAPTER
FIFTY-TWO

When Scotland's King David I established Holyrood Abbey in 1128, he would no doubt have been mortified to learn its eventual fate as a palace of the British monarchy. As for the neighborhood known as the Canongate (from the old Scots word "gait," meaning road), its destiny was even less savory. Originally named after the clerics of the nearby abbey, Canongate was now the location of all manner of vice and depravity. When a member of Edinburgh's police force needed to track down a criminal, odds were the miscreant would turn up in the warren of dilapidated tenements stacked like chicken crates atop the spiderweb of wynds and alleys weaving between the city's shrugging façades and crumbling walls.

It was to this seedy locale that Ian Hamilton's search took him. If one needed to procure opium without any questions being asked, Canongate was the place to go. Armed with only vague references to an owl and a Chinaman named Pong, he set about to find where Stephen Wycherly might have procured the drug.

On Saturday night, the already considerable level of drinking and debauchery increased several notches. Swells from the New Town seeking a night of illicit companionship roamed the rough-hewn cobblestones alongside the neighborhood's denizens—an unpleasant mix of thieves, ruffians, and pickpockets. Home to most of the city's slaughterhouses as well as a fair number of pubs, the Canongate had a distinctive aroma of warm blood, cold steel, and stale beer. The slaughterhouses were dark, but lights blazed brightly in pub windows, shouts and drunken singing spilling out into the streets along with rowdy bar brawlers. As Ian passed the Hound and Hare, stepping carefully over refuse and piles of horse manure, he heard half a dozen inebriants bellowing the lyrics to a popular bawdy song.

> Big Nell was a woman of parts
> With a face that broke many hearts
> Her bottom was wide, and so soft inside
> You'd best look out for her farts

Ian shook his head—the popular urge to juxtapose the sexual and the scatological had always puzzled him. When he thought of women—and he did his best not to—it was not in conjunction with rude bar songs. Just then, a familiar voice behind him said, "Unpleasant, isn't it—the mindless braying of the great unwashed?"

Startled, he spun around to see a smiling George Pearson, dressed in an Inverness cape and tweed cap.

"What on earth are you doing here?"

Pearson's smile drooped. "May a man not move about freely without being questioned as to his intentions?"

"See here, Mr. Pearson—I appreciate your interest, but you really must stop following me."

"I am not 'following you,' Detective," the librarian replied huffily. "If we happened to meet tonight, it is simply by chance."

"Coincidence does not have so wide a reach as you seem to imagine."

"I did not say it was by coincidence—I said it was by chance."

"I fail to see the distinction."

"Coincidence implies that no cause aligns our mutual presence here. But chance allows for the presence of that cause."

"Which is . . . ?"

"The apprehension of a murderer."

"Mr. Pearson," Ian cautioned, "please refrain from imagining that you are my associate in this matter."

"No thought is farther from my mind, I assure you. I bid you good night," he replied stiffly.

"Good night, then," Ian said, striding off into the night. Before he had gone more than a few yards, he turned to see the librarian following several paces behind. "Why are you following me?" he said, frowning.

"As we seem to be headed in the same direction, I thought I would let you proceed apace so as to not burden you with my company," Pearson replied, lighting a cheroot pipe.

"And exactly where are you going?"

Pearson blew a puff of smoke into the foggy air; it hung suspended for a moment before dissolving into the mist. "I intend to pay a visit to an unsavory establishment."

"What is it?"

"You would not care for it."

"For the love of God, man, what *is* it?"

"It is called the Owl's Nest."

Ian couldn't help the surprise that came over his face. "The Owl's Nest, did you say?"

"Why—do you know it?"

"I intend to."

"I see," Pearson replied without moving.

"Well?"

"Well what?"

"Are you going to show me where it is or not?"

"You want me to take you there after castigating me for interfering?"

Ian took a deep breath and thought of Aunt Lillian. He could almost hear her voice: *Be sensible, Ian. You've always been far too impatient.* He looked at the librarian, who stood puffing on his pipe, the smoke curling around his plump face.

"First I must know the answer to a question."

"Yes?"

"How did you know about the playing cards?"

"The child told me."

"You mean Derek McNair?"

"Yes—over breakfast at your flat, after you left."

Ian frowned. "He shouldn't have told you."

"I didn't realize it was confidential until you mentioned it the other day. Not wishing to get him in trouble, I avoided answering you."

"We never released that information to the public."

"Then how did he know?"

"He found a card when he discovered one of the victims."

"How gruesome," the librarian said with a shudder, but his eyes glistened with excitement.

"Now, would you please conduct me to this establishment?" Ian said.

His companion's broad face relaxed into a smile. "Certainly, Detective—right this way."

He launched his ungainly body forward, striding with such vigor that Ian grabbed hold of his hat to prevent it falling off.

As the two of them disappeared into the fog, they failed to notice a dark figure skulking in the shadows of the row of tenement houses across the road. The figure trailed them at a distance, hugging the buildings on the dark side of the street. Somewhere in the distance, a dog howled mournfully as the fog thickened, wrapping the city of Edinburgh in its murky embrace.

CHAPTER
FIFTY-THREE

The unmarked entrance to the Owl's Nest was impossible to find without knowing precisely where to look. An unlocked iron gate led through a courtyard off Fleshmarket Close—appropriately named, Ian thought grimly as a rat scuttled across the paving stones. At the far end, stone steps led to the basement of a sixteenth-century tenement building. He followed Pearson down the stairs and through a heavy oak door, darkened by years of soot, and into a dimly lit basement cloudy with tobacco smoke.

The only illumination came from a pair of wall sconces and a few candles scattered haphazardly about. A row of men crowded the long bar at the other end of the room, while others loitered in pairs along the bare brick walls on either side. The sickly sweet smell of opium lurked beneath the haze of tobacco. A narrow passageway led past the bar to a back room, which Ian assumed was the source of the aroma.

Their entrance was greeted with searching glances from the men at the bar. Ian felt his breath coming shallow and tight, but to his surprise, the normally awkward Pearson moved through the press of bodies, inserting himself next to a slim young man at the bar. Ian followed, avoiding eye contact with any of the patrons, though he could feel their gaze upon him.

Behind him, a man with a thick Glaswegian accent muttered, "Now 'at's a bit I wouldn't mind gettin' next tae." His companion laughed a throaty whisky laugh, followed by a sputtering cough.

Ian's discomfort was followed by a memory of a conversation he once had with Aunt Lillian about the indignities she had suffered as a young woman from the attention of men. He had not until this moment considered what it must have actually felt like. Ears burning, he slid onto the stool next to George Pearson, who was calmly conversing with the bartender, a heavyset Irishman with one gold earring and a red beard.

"That'll be one shilling," said the barkeep as he slid two glasses of whisky in front of the librarian. "Is he with you, then?" he added with an appraising glance at Ian.

"Indeed he is," Pearson responded calmly.

"Not bad," the Irishman remarked with a grin, showing a set of whalebone-white teeth. He reminded Ian of a pirate—all he needed was a kerchief wrapped around his head to be at home on a schooner flying a Jolly Roger flag.

George held up his glass. "'May you live all the days of your life.'"

"I never heard o' that one," said the bartender.

"Jonathan Swift."

The Irishman smiled. "A Dubliner, God bless 'im!"

"Indeed," George remarked.

Ian was impressed at the librarian's poise. He was clearly more at home and relaxed than the detective, who felt jumpier by the minute.

The bartender smiled widely, displaying his gleaming ivory teeth. "You've decent taste for an Englishman, so you do."

"Why, thank you."

"Your friend's a quiet one, though."

"He's just shy," said George. "But he does have something to ask you."

"An' what might that be, then?"

Ian fumbled around in his jacket pocket for the playing card, afraid he had lost it, until his fingers closed upon it. He held it up to the bartender. "Have you seen this card before?"

"Let's have a look," the Irishman said, leaning his beefy forearms on the bar. He stroked his thick red beard, peering at it in the dim light. "What's it worth to ye, then?" he asked with a sly smile.

Pondering how best to reply, Ian took a deep breath, but Pearson spoke first. "It may be worth a great deal to you if you don't want your establishment to be raided by the Edinburgh City Police."

The bartender's eyes narrowed. "Are ye coppers, then?"

"I am," Ian replied, peeved at Pearson for revealing it.

A slim, nattily dressed gentleman of middle years sauntered over to them. Even in the dim light, his cravat was dazzling white, his gold vest and black frock coat were of the finest cloth, and his boots shone with polish. With his lean face and high cheekbones, he bore a strong resemblance to Ian's father.

"Is there a problem, Nate?" he asked.

The bartender/pirate crossed his arms and leaned back on his heels. "We've a copper in our midst."

The gentleman cocked his head to one side. "Indeed? I certainly haven't seen you here before," he said to Ian. "What's your business here?"

By now many of the other men were watching the conversation at the bar. It was clear the elegant man was a figure of some importance— the proprietor, perhaps.

"I am not here to arrest any of you," Ian replied, uncomfortable with the scores of eyes upon him.

"We are trying to catch a murderer," George declared officiously. He appeared to be thoroughly enjoying himself.

"I see," said the elegant man. "And how might we help you?"

"Does anyone remember seeing this card before?" Ian said, holding it up to the room's occupants. He saw no recognition on any of their faces, until a slight young man stepped forward. Hardly more than a boy, his thick, long bangs fell over dark, wary eyes. His clothing and grimy hands suggested he worked the docks at Leith.

"Jes t'other day," he said in an accent that betrayed his working-class origins, "a fella were doin' a card trick at' bar there, an' used a deck wi' that design."

"What did he—"

Ian silenced George with an elbow to the ribs. "Had you ever seen this person before?" he asked.

"Er, no, come t' think of it. But the lad he showed the trick to were the same one found dead yesterdah."

"Kerry O'Donohue?"

"Don' know 'is last name," the boy replied, looking down at his boots, which were worn and scuffed. "But yeah, 'e called himself Kerry, all right."

"We don't inquire as to people's last names here," the elegant gentleman explained to Ian.

"Did th' card have sommit to do wi' his murder?" the boy asked.

"As a matter of fact—" the librarian began, but Ian trod heavily on his foot. *"Ouch,"* George said, glaring at him.

"I'm afraid we can't comment on an ongoing investigation," said Ian, turning to the boy. "Can you describe the man?"

"Go ahead, Peter," the slim gentleman urged. "It's all right."

"Well, 'e were good-lookin' enough," the boy added, blushing.

"Can you be more specific?" Ian said, feeling the heat rise to his face.

"Let's see . . . not nearly as tall as you; more medium height, and thicker 'round the shoulders. Dark hair, wavy like . . . oh, and the palest eyes—almost like there weren't no color to 'em at all."

"How was he dressed?"

"Like a gentleman—real fancy clothes, wi' a gold watch."

"Peter always notices watches," remarked the pirate behind the bar. "Don' ye, lad?"

Peter coughed and fiddled with his belt buckle.

The bartender laughed, and a few of the other men snickered, but the slim gentleman silenced them all with a stern glare. "Please! Peter is doing his best to aid a murder investigation. He doesn't need any help from any of you," he added, glowering at the bartender, "unless of course you have something to add."

"I weren't workin' that night," Nate replied sulkily, turning away to wash glasses.

"Did you remark upon anything else about him?" Ian asked Peter. "His voice, perhaps?"

"It were educated . . . He sounded English, maybe a bit foreign, though I couldn't swear it." He went on to describe how Kerry had picked a card from the deck offered to him, and that the two of them had left shortly afterward.

"Would you be willing to describe him to a police sketch artist?"

"Uh, yeah, I s'pose."

"Here is my card," said Ian. "Please come to the station house at your earliest convenience."

"I kin come t'morrow after church."

"Thank you," said Ian. "You've been very helpful."

"Can I buy you a drink, Officer . . . ?" asked the elegant man.

"Detective Inspector Ian Hamilton, at your service."

"Detective Inspector, then—would you or your companion care for something from the bar?" he added with a glance at George, who nodded vigorously.

"We must be on our way," said Ian. "Thank you, Mr. . . . . ?"

"Call me Terrance."

"Thank you, Terrance."

"You are welcome anytime," he answered with a slight bow. His courtly manners and fine clothes suggested he was a man of means as well as breeding. Ian wondered what his profession was—lawyer, perhaps, or even a judge?

Dragging a reluctant George Pearson behind him, Ian ascended the dimly lit stairwell, emerging into the courtyard. A pale moon glimmered between the bare tree branches as they threaded their way back through the alley, their breath coming in wisps, mingling with the fog that had settled over the city.

"I don't know why we couldn't stay for one blasted drink," the librarian muttered as they stepped into the street.

"We were there to gather information," Ian replied. What he didn't say was that the Owl's Nest made him extremely uncomfortable. "Thank you for pointing the place out to me. I should never have found it on my own."

"You're welcome," Pearson replied sulkily. "Well, I suppose I'll be off, then."

"Good night."

"Good night." He waited for a moment—perhaps hoping Ian might invite him to join him for a nightcap, but when Hamilton said nothing, Pearson skulked off in the direction of New Town.

Ian was not entirely convinced the librarian had told him the truth about the playing cards. Next time he encountered Derek McNair, he would have some pointed questions for the boy. He watched as Pearson's bulky figure was swallowed by the swirling fog before turning his own steps homeward.

CHAPTER
FIFTY-FOUR

The fog curled like a cat around Ian's feet as he trod westward toward Victoria Terrace. As he passed the Hound and Hare, he saw a slight, wiry form dart into the far alley. Something in the set of the man's shoulders and quick movements looked familiar—and since the fellow was trying to avoid him, Ian decided to follow. He slipped around the corner of the building in time to see his quarry scurry behind the pub. Ian turned and came around the other side, figuring the man would continue in the same direction.

He was right. Beneath the gaslight where the alley met the street, he ran headlong into Rat Face. Shock and surprise registered on his ferret-like features before sliding into an unconvincing smile.

"Why, Detective Inspector Hamilton, what a pleasant surprise."

"Is it? I had the distinct impression you were trying to avoid me."

"Why on earth would I do that?"

"I can think of several reasons."

"One must never be too careful about choosing one's companions," Rat Face replied, drawing Ian into the shadows beneath the building's eaves. "But I would never avoid *you*—on purpose, that is," he added, glancing nervously in the direction of the street.

"Perhaps you mistook me for someone else?"

"No doubt. My eyesight is not the best."

"May I inquire whom you are so afraid of encountering, and why?"

Rat Face coughed delicately. "There was a slight misunderstanding over a card game."

"When you cheat at cards, you must take care to not be found out."

"Your insinuation wounds me," he replied, with a hurt look no more believable than any of his other expressions.

"I believe we have some unfinished business."

"Do we indeed?" Rat Face said, without taking his eyes off the street, as shouts and drunken laughter floated out of the Hound and Hare.

"I seem to recall the last time we met—at this very pub—I rescued you from a thrashing."

"Most kind of you," he said, shifting restlessly and scratching his long nose.

"Perhaps you could enlighten me on a matter regarding my investigation."

"I am always delighted to assist members of the police force, Detective."

"What can you tell me about card tricks?"

"Why do you ask?" he said nervously.

"I'm afraid some details of the case must remain hidden."

"What makes you think I know anything about card tricks?"

"A little mouse told me—your cousin, perhaps."

"How amusing," he said, shrinking back against the building as the wheels of a passing cab threw a spray of muddy water in their direction. "I regret to say I really do have to be somewhere."

"In other words, you need to be away from here."

"Something like that."

"Very well," Ian said. "I know another place not far from here."

Soon they were seated in the back room of the White Hart Inn, a pint of ale at their elbow. The clientele was considerably less boisterous than the patrons of the Hound and Hare—at this hour, mostly university students, more given to quoting Burns and Milton than brawling.

"Well?" Rat Face said, his eyes darting about the room. "What did you want to ask me?"

Ian withdrew the four of clubs from his pocket. "Have you seen this card before?"

"Dear me, what a strange design," he replied, studying the grinning skeletons in their jaunty red fezzes. "I have not. What else do you wish to know?"

"I would appreciate anything you have to say about sleight of hand."

"As much as I am gratified by your interest, I am a busy man."

"I will pay for your time."

A smile snaked across his thin lips, and he leaned forward. "May I assume you will not use anything I say against me in the future?"

"I am in search of more dangerous game."

Rat Face drank deeply, wiping his mouth. "Sleight of hand is an ancient art, invented to beat the house, as it were."

"And the other players."

"Ah, but that can be risky. One must never succumb to the temptation to show one's skill."

"Why is that?"

"Because it is a very good way to court death. Your technique must be invisible, unless you want to die."

"And do the same rules apply to magic tricks?"

"The great Robert-Houdin said magic is cheating for amusement. Your technique should always be secondary to the effect. That is what matters, not your skill."

"How does one acquire this skill?"

"Doing magic is about focusing the audience's attention on what you want it to perceive. There are many ways to accomplish this, but one of the most well-known methods is misdirection."

Ian signaled the waiter for another round. "Please continue."

"Simply put, you give the audience something else to focus on in order to hide the move that is the secret to the trick. Allow me to demonstrate," he said, pulling a deck of cards from his vest pocket. "I always carry these with me just in case—not as colorful as the deck you showed me, but they do the trick. Oh, that's rather good," he added, chuckling. "They *do the trick.*"

He proceeded to shuffle the cards with great dexterity, his long, thin fingers flying over the deck, which he extended to Ian.

"Pick a card, any card."

Ian plucked the four of diamonds from the pack.

"Ah," Rat Face remarked with a sly smile. "I see you have chosen the Ambitious Card."

"Meaning . . . ?"

"No matter where you place it in the deck, it always ends up on top. Allow me to show you what I mean."

He cut the deck deftly in half, placing Ian's card on the top of the bottom half, faceup, pushing it forward from the others so he could see it. "Is that your card?"

"Yes."

"We'll slide that in the middle of the other half—you see?" he said, sliding the card into the top half of the deck.

"I do."

"Now we put the two halves together—and it should be in the middle, correct?"

"Yes."

"And yet somehow it works its way to the top of the deck," he said, turning over the top card—the four of diamonds.

Ian stared at him. "How on earth did you do that?"

"It relies upon a common technique known as a double lift. When I showed you that your card was on top of the bottom half, you noticed I turned it over so you could see the face?"

"Yes."

"That was a misdirection. There was another card on top of it—and *that* was the card I slid into the middle of the top half. That was the double lift."

"Remarkable."

"Child's play. But a trick should work even when it is explained—if it is well done."

"Very impressive."

"I believe you hinted at a more corporeal form of appreciation?" Rat Face said, his eyes hungry.

Pulling out his wallet, Ian handed him a five-pound note.

"Most generous," his companion replied, folding it carefully before sliding it into his vest pocket. "I hope you'll allow me to be of use in the future."

"You may have helped to unlock a key part of the puzzle."

"Would you care to elaborate?"

"I can only say that it involves misdirection," he said, rising and tossing some coins onto the table.

"But—"

"Thank you—I am in your debt."

He scooped up his cloak, hurrying out into the night, leaving his puzzled companion with two half-full pints of amber ale.

Ian was both relieved and disappointed to find the flat empty and dark, save for a very hungry and vocal Bacchus, who proclaimed his displeasure at Ian's absence loudly, weaving in and out between his feet. Picking his way carefully around the cat to the kitchen, Ian tore into what remained of the joint his brother had cooked. He ate standing at the counter, tossing bits of meat to Bacchus, who gobbled them up greedily.

When Ian crawled into bed, the cat snuggled up against him, purring loudly, one paw thrown over his arm. The cat's eyes were half-closed, the expression on its face as close to pure contentment as Ian had ever seen. Why was it so easy for a dumb animal to find peace and happiness in this world, while human beings created wars so they could hack at one another, spending untold hours thinking up new ways to inflict harm?

Why were families, which should offer solace and comfort, such sources of anguish? The story of his family had ended too abruptly, leaving too many unanswered questions. It was like a badly constructed plot, loose narrative threads dangling without closure. He stroked the cat's head absently, and the animal reached a paw up to his face, running it lightly over his cheek. Ian burned with shame and regret. Why was it so much easier to befriend a stray cat than to be kind to his own brother? Was there a missing component in his personality that compelled him to push people away? Self-pity began to flower in his breast; through force of habit, he immediately converted it into anger, a far more acceptable emotion.

The thin sliver of moon stared down from the eastern sky as he pulled the covers up to his chin, but thoughts continued to race through his brain. What had happened to his family was no worse than a hundred tragedies that befell others every day—why linger on the agony? The pain and rage had made a home in his heart, burrowing in like the cat nesting next to him in bed, and he felt powerless to budge it.

Finally he rose and lit the bedside lamp. Rifling through the rolltop desk in the corner, he fished out a few pieces of paper. He scribbled out some lines, without thought as to whether they were good or bad, just to make himself feel better.

> The Hand of God
> is dull, diffident—or worse, indifferent
> How can he demand from us

what he refuses to provide
mocking us with notions of love
he continues to hide
while we stew in shame
like an unwilling bride

He didn't really believe in a Christian God, but he needed a target for his anger. The lines did provide some relief, and when he returned to bed, Ian smiled at the sight of Bacchus stretching a paw out to him, as if welcoming him back to bed.

But when he finally drifted off, sleep was not an amiable companion. He was visited by nightmares of pursuing a killer down dark and crowded streets, through closes and wynds, until a blank brick wall stopped both pursuer and pursued. When the man turned to face him, red and panting, the shock of recognition turned Ian's limbs to stone. There, in the dank and festering alley, was his brother.

"Shocked, are you?" Donald taunted. "Stupid git—the clues were there all along, but you were too dim to see them!"

Ian tried to speak, but no words came—his tongue was as thick and useless as his legs. He watched helplessly as Donald turned into the same hideous skeleton found on the playing cards left by the murderer. His brother danced a jaunty gig, bones rattling, grinning an eyeless grin as Ian looked on, horrified. The scream that finally wrung itself from Ian's throat was drowned out by his brother's mocking laughter.

CHAPTER
FIFTY-FIVE

Lucy Davenport, her head swathed in layers of flannel, staggered down the Canongate, trying unsuccessfully to wring the voices from her head. She hoped that if she wrapped her ears with enough fabric, she could silence the tormenting whispers that followed her everywhere.

Sadly, she was wrong. At the moment, she was engaged in a dialogue with one she called Evil Seth. He was a particularly nasty character who liked to berate her, reminding her of her own worthlessness.

"Small wonder your mother abandoned you," Seth snarled as she lurched past the window of McClennon's Dry Goods. The well-dressed shop ladies inside shook their heads and clucked their tongues at the sight of her—*poor Daft Lucy, out there all alone in this wretched weather.* But Lucy took no notice of the weather—when the voices were upon her, it was all she could do to put one foot in front of the other.

"You're a worthless bampot," her tormentor declared, using the slang word for "idiot." Seth often used vulgar language—yesterday he had called her a "fanny," a double insult meaning both "vagina" and "stupid."

"I am not," she muttered, clutching her ears as she stumbled past an organ-grinder and his monkey. He was hardly a more popular figure on the street than she was; though children loved to see his strange little creature perform its tricks, most people in Edinburgh, when they gave him money, did so in hopes he would move on to another neighborhood. Still, he tipped his hat to her like a gentleman, and she attempted to smile back, even though she couldn't help shrinking away from the ugly little beast with its tiny head, sharp teeth, and sunken eyes. Its shriveled face reminded her of shrunken heads she had seen in London shops as a girl.

Those days seemed a long way off—Daft Lucy, as she was known, had lived in Edinburgh most of her life. The voices had begun around her eighteenth birthday, causing her parents to turn her unceremoniously out of the house. She was now in her midtwenties, though she wasn't sure exactly how old she was. Her parents had died in the last cholera epidemic, along with many of Edinburgh's citizens, and she truly was alone in the world.

But Edinburgh was a city that embraced its oddities, and Lucy was seldom without an offer of a hot meal or a discarded dress to wear. She spent her more lucid days reading in the library, devouring books on everything from history to botany to popular literature. She was well-known to all the local pastors, always welcome in church; sometimes, on the good days, she even helped give lessons to the children in Sunday school.

This was one of the bad days. When the voices came, she could not bear to be still, so she wandered the streets, shaking her head and talking to her invisible companions. Families on their way to church gave her a wide berth, mothers tucking their children's heads close to their skirts to shield them from her.

"Everyone is watching you," Seth said. "They think you're just a daft, useless drudge."

"What do ye know of anythin'?" she muttered, pulling her scarf tighter around her head as she peered into the Daily Bread Bakery. Her mouth watered as she stared at the fairy cakes in the window, tiny round treats with frosting in all colors of the rainbow. They were so beautiful— if only she could have just one . . .

As she stood gazing through the window, she thought she heard a faint moaning coming from Warden's Close, the alley next to the bakery. Thinking it was just Seth trying to trick her, she ignored it—but no, there it was again.

"Where do you think you're going?" he demanded as she crept around the corner into the narrow passage.

"Aw, shut yer trap," she muttered, walking slowly between the buildings and listening for the sound.

Sure enough, there it was again—coming from behind the bakery. She searched the cramped rear corridor for any sign of life. All she spied were a few trash bins, discarded radish greens, and an old set of rusty bedsprings partially covered with an oilcloth. Turning to leave, she heard it again, coming from behind the bedsprings.

Stepping carefully over the piles of rubbish, she lifted the oilcloth and peered around the corner of the bedsprings. There, lying between them and the wall of the building, was a young lad of about ten. He lay very still and appeared to be dead. But was it not his moaning she'd heard coming from the alley? His blond hair was lank and long, his features marred by the purple blotches beneath his eyes, though even with that and the grime on his cheeks, she could see he was quite a handsome boy.

"Get away!" Seth sputtered. "They'll think you killed him, you stupid cow!"

Ignoring him, Lucy reached out to touch the boy's face, and was shocked to see his eyes open as he gasped for air. Startled, she fell backward, hitting the cobblestones hard and smacking her tailbone smartly on the paving stones.

"God take me fer an idjit!" she muttered as tears spurted into her eyes. She didn't pause to rub her bruised limbs, more concerned about the boy in the gutter than her own injuries. Pulling herself onto her hands and knees, she crawled toward him. His eyes were closed again, and she saw no further sign of life. She cradled his head in her lap and stroked his forehead, brushing the long yellow locks of hair out of his eyes. His lips were blue, his skin alarmingly white, the flesh mottled like marble. "Come on, then," she whispered. "Kin ye breathe, then?"

She imagined she should be doing something to resuscitate him, but she couldn't think what it might be. She loosened his collar, revealing the angry purple bruises around his neck. Lucy knew enough about death to recognize the signs of strangulation.

"Who did this to ye?" she murmured, and to her surprise, the blue lips parted in a feeble attempt at speech. She leaned her head over his, her ear to his mouth. "What is it?"

The words were little more than a breath of air, thin with the approach of impending mortality. "Ma . . . magi . . ."

"Louder," she urged. "What are ye tryin' to say, lad?"

But the next breath that left his body was his last. A slow wheezing sound escaped his lungs, and his lips closed forever, leaving Lucy crouched on the unforgiving ground with his cold, lifeless form cradled in her arms.

CHAPTER FIFTY-SIX

Ian Hamilton awoke to a chill and clinging dawn. He closed his eyes again for what seemed like just a moment, but when he opened them again, the gray light had blossomed, intensifying the pounding in his head. From the angle of the sun, it looked to be midmorning. He took a ragged breath and rubbed his eyes, startled by the sound of an engine nearby. He turned his head to see Bacchus staring at him through half-closed eyes, purring loudly. Glad for the animal's presence, he reached out to stroke its fur. The cat leaned into him, rubbing its face along Ian's fingers.

"It's late," he said, throwing off the covers. "Come along, let's get us both some breakfast."

As his feet touched the floor, there was a rapid knocking at the door. Cursing, he threw on his dressing gown and opened the door to see a wild-eyed Sergeant Dickerson, his face still creased from sleep. The disarray of his uniform suggested he had dressed with some haste.

"Dickerson," Ian said. "I thought this was your day off."

"Ye'd better come right away, sir."

"What is it?"

"It's a young lad—done same as t'others."

"Where?"

"Warden's Close, sir, just off the Grassmarket."

"Have you seen the body?"

"No, sir—I came here straightaway soon as I heard."

Ian let loose a low curse. "Fetch a cab—I'll be out directly."

"Yes, sir."

Five minutes later, Ian was out the door, leaving behind a disappointed and hungry cat. Resigned to fend for himself, Bacchus slunk out of the kitchen in search of a live breakfast. Luckily for him, Edinburgh had no shortage of vermin, four-footed or otherwise.

The fetid stench of rotting cabbage assailed Ian's nostrils as he alighted from the hansom cab, striding past the brace of patrolmen guarding the crime scene. Edinburgh was an odiferous city, and the recent thaw had brought out its less savory smells. A crowd of people had gathered, craning their necks trying to peer into the alley. Several individuals, employees of the Daily Bread, wore white bakery aprons. Ian recognized several other onlookers as newspaper men.

"Is it another victim of the strangler, Detective?" one of them called out.

"What can you tell us about the victim this time?" said another.

"How long before you lads catch him?"

Ian ignored them, striding down the narrow wynd leading to the rear of the bakery. The victim lay on his back behind discarded household items, some rusty old bedsprings, and a cracked butter churn. Only the boy's legs were visible from where he stood; he was clad in oversized boots and undersized trousers. Ian turned to the sergeant.

"Who found the body?"

"Daft Lucy, sir."

"Where is she now?"

"Waiting for you at the station house, sir. She were fair upset, so Constable Bowers took her there fer a cup o' tea."

"That's all we need—a delusional madwoman as a witness." Ian took a step toward the body as the pounding in his head intensified. When he saw the fair hair and familiar face, a groan escaped him.

"Oh, no," he moaned. "No, no, no."

"What is it, sir?" Dickerson asked, his freckled face crinkled in concern. "You know this boy?"

Ian knelt beside the body and gently brushed the blond hair from the high forehead, the skin cold and white as ivory in death. "His name is Freddie Cubbins."

"Looks to be a street Arab."

"Quite right, Sergeant." He bent over the boy and gently searched his grubby clothes. He found it right away, slid neatly into the left vest pocket: the ace of diamonds. He held it up for Dickerson to see.

The sergeant peered at the card and frowned. "He's changed suits, sir."

"He's started a new hand."

"Why d'you suppose he did that?"

"He's going for another straight flush." Ian slipped the card into his own pocket and gazed at the dead boy lying on the cold, hard cobblestones. "'Hell is empty and all the devils are here.'"

"Beg pardon, sir?"

"It's from *The Tempest*."

"Shakespeare's last play, weren't it?"

"And by God, I swear this will be this murderer's last victim. Mark my words, Sergeant."

But even as his words were drowned out by the sounds of the city around him, he doubted his own ability to make them come true.

CHAPTER
FIFTY-SEVEN

Henry Standish Wright awoke early Sunday morning from an uneasy sleep—if sleep you could call it—and stared at the ceiling. He felt hungover, yet had imbibed not a drop the night before. Following another sold-out performance at the Theatre Royal, he had crawled into bed, exhausted in mind and body. But sleep failed him, as it had so often recently, and he spent a wretched night wrestling with what was left of his conscience.

He swung his legs over the side of the bed, with its silk sheets and lush brocade spread, setting his feet upon the deep, plush carpet. The luxurious surroundings only deepened his misery, reminding him of his own unworthiness. Others in this town had barely a crust of bread and a cup of foul water for supper, while he dined on oysters and beef Wellington, spending more in a day than they would earn in a year.

He rose stiffly and dragged himself to the water closet; after doing his business, he sat at the vanity next to the poster bed with its grand canopy of plump, laughing cherubs and elegant, winged angels. He stared at his own reflection, shocked at the haunted eyes looking back at him. Here was no fat pink cherub or angel—it was the face of a man pursued by devils. He alone could help end this nightmare, yet he was too weak.

He remembered his brother as a boy, and how sweet and gentle he had been while their mother still lived—like any other boy, really, with his little stick hobbyhorse he was so proud of. He recalled the games they had played together—tag and four corners and mumblety-peg. He had tried to protect his brother from their father's anger, falling upon them like bitter rain. But his brother was always defiant, drawing more than his share of whippings. The enforced boxing matches in the back-yard only served to deepen his rebellious spirit. The more Henry tried to shield him from his father's rage, the heavier his father's retribution, seemingly inexhaustible after their mother's death.

Henry had escaped to school, but no such luck for his brother, who stayed behind to work in their father's chemist shop. In the long hours behind the counter, he developed his skill at card manipulation, delighting customers with his tricks. During that time, the rumors had also started—that he was "different," bullying younger children and responsible for missing cats and dogs. It wasn't something they ever talked about, but somehow Henry knew what his brother was, and perhaps even why. When he came home from school that first spring, Henry saw in his brother's eyes a cruelty he had never noticed before.

Henry pulled on his dressing gown and padded into the sitting room, with its grand chandelier and French Empire furniture. His head ached with the weight of memories. He looked longingly at the sideboard with its gleaming bottles of liquor, steeling himself against temptation. It was important to keep his mind clear. On the carpet in front of the door was the daily newspaper. It appeared each morning, slid beneath his door by a member of the hotel staff, one of many work-ing tirelessly to make his stay comfortable. He leaned over to pick it up, groaning as the bones of his stiff spine protested wearily. The headline slammed into his brain like a rifle shot.

TERRIBLE CRIME IN THE GRASSMARKET — BOY MURDERED!

HOLYROOD STRANGLER STRIKES AGAIN— YOUNGEST VICTIM YET

He sank to his knees and buried his head in his hands, trying to drive his brother's words from his mind, to no avail. Over and over the phrase repeated itself in his head. *Oh, there was so much evil in a man . . .*

CHAPTER
FIFTY-EIGHT

"I've had just about enough of this bosh and bunkum!" DCI Crawford declared, spewing spittle into the surrounding air. Ian took a step backward to avoid the spray, wincing as the droplets landed on his face. "A mere *child* this time? Good Lord, why can't we catch this bastard?"

Ian was silent. Answering the chief during one of his tirades was not advisable—best to wait for it to run its course.

"Well?" Crawford bellowed. "And where the bloody hell is Dickerson?"

At that moment the door to the office swung open, and Sergeant Dickerson burst in, clutching a newspaper, flushed and out of breath. Ian was surprised to see him enter the office without knocking.

Crawford looked as if he couldn't decide whether to chide the sergeant for being late or for neglecting to knock. "What took you so long?" he demanded.

The sergeant thrust out the newspaper he held, his hand trembling.

"What's this?" Crawford said, frowning.

"It's Chief Inspector Gerard, sir," Dickerson said, pointing to a boldface headline on the front page.

Tragic Death at Waverley Station!

Man Crushed by Train

Accident or Suicide—or something Darker?

"Good Lord," Crawford said, scanning the article. "That was just hours after we last saw him." He looked at Ian. "Do you think . . . ?"

Ian nodded, his face grim. "I think it's a likely explanation." He scanned the article. No one claimed to have seen anything, according to Constable McKee, the officer on duty.

"Get McKee in here and grill him," Crawford said. "See if he knows anything."

"Yes, sir," Ian said, turning to Dickerson. "Can you handle that while I interview Daft Lucy?"

"Right away, sir."

Crawford fell back heavily into his chair, the springs creaking beneath his bulk. "Good luck getting anything coherent out of her."

"Where is she?"

His boss flung a fat thumb toward the back of the station house. "Asleep. The lads gave her some tea and she asked to lie down, so we put her in one of the empty cells."

"I'll fetch her before I leave, sir?" Dickerson offered.

"Off you go, then," Ian said.

The sergeant blinked, rocked back on his heels, and fled the room.

CI Crawford ran a hand through his abundant ginger whiskers, absently twisting a piece of string between his fingers. "Do you have anything at all, Hamilton?"

"We may have an eyewitness."

"Haul him on down here!"

"He's promised to come in today. We're likely to get better results if he comes voluntarily."

"Who is it?"

"His first name is Peter."

"And his last name?"

"I don't have it, but—"

"Why not?"

"I know where to find him, sir."

Crawford scowled at Ian. "What about the Arthur's Seat victim—is there a connection?"

"I believe it to be the same killer."

"Why were the other victims all found in alleys?"

"He lured Wycherly to the top of Arthur's Seat either to disguise it as a suicide, or, failing that, to make it appear to be a disagreement that turned lethal. He was attempting to use misdirection to confuse us."

"Why did he not do that with the rest of the victims?"

"He got lazy—or confident. Once he believed he could get away with his crimes, the killings became bolder, more direct. He no longer worked to cover his tracks. And that's how we're going to catch him."

Sergeant Dickerson's face appeared at the half-open office door. "Excuse me, sir—I fetched Lucy, and she's ready to speak with you."

"Thank you, Sergeant," said Ian.

"I'll just be off, then," Dickerson said, holding the door open for Lucy to enter.

Lucy Davenport was long and lean, her weathered face making her look much older than her age, which Ian guessed to be about thirty. She was dressed in a motley pile of clothes heaped on top of one another with no regard to fashion—the layers of tartans alone probably represented half a dozen clans. On her long, thin legs were mismatched woolen stockings, and on her feet a sturdy pair of men's boots. Strips of flannel wound round her head completely obscured her hair. Her skin being the color and texture of tanned leather, she resembled a demented Eastern shah.

"Hello, Lucy," Ian said, offering her a chair. "Won't you sit down?"

She shook her head violently. "Oh, I daren't, sir—he won' let me."

"Who won't?" Crawford asked.

"I cannot speak 'is name, sir."

"I see."

"Can you write it, perhaps?" asked Ian, offering her paper and pen.

"I s'pose so," she replied, carefully scratching out the letters in spidery capital letters: *EVIL SETH.*

"Evil Seth?" Crawford said, his shaggy brow furrowed. "Who on earth is that?"

"Is he the one whose voice you hear in your head?" Ian asked her.

Lucy nodded vigorously.

"And he tells you to do things?"

"Mostlah 'e just tells me how bad I am. I'm no' wicked, am I, sir?"

"No, Lucy, you certainly are not," Ian replied. "In fact, we were hoping you might help us find the person who killed young Freddie Cubbins."

"The boy wha' I found, sir?"

"Yes," said Crawford. "Did you see anyone hanging around the body when you discovered it?"

"It weren't no body when I arrived, sir."

Crawford frowned. "I beg your pardon?"

"He were alive when I got there."

"He was?" The chief inspector could hardly contain his eagerness. Ian hoped he wouldn't frighten Lucy into silence.

"Aye. I asked who done this, and I believe he tried tae tell me, but the poor bairn had nae mere breath left in him than a tiny wisp o' air."

"So did he speak?" Crawford asked, his small blue eyes keen.

"He tried, God rest 'is wee soul."

"What did he say?"

"It sounded like 'Madge.'"

"Madge?" Ian repeated.

"That can be short for Margaret," Crawford said. "I had an aunt Margaret we called Madge."

"Is that what he was trying to say, you think?" Ian asked Lucy.

"I don' rightly know, sir. I just heard 'Madge,' or maybe 'Madgie.'"

"Do you know of anyone named Madge or Madgie?" Crawford asked Ian, who shook his head.

Lucy shrugged. "That's wha' I heard, is all. An' I could get nae mere out o'him. Poor fellow just—" She stopped abruptly and clasped her hands to her ears. "Stop it! Leave me in peace!" she cried in a tormented voice.

The men exchanged looks. "Is Seth bothering you?" said Ian.

"Oh, please!" she wailed, shaking her head from side to side. "Jes' gae away!"

Crawford heaved his bulk from his chair and opened the door to his office. "Sergeant," he called out to the desk sergeant on duty, "will you get Miss Davenport something to eat and escort her out?"

"Certainly, sir," the sergeant replied, hurrying into the DCI's office. "Come on, miss—let's see about gettin' you something t'eat, then, shall we?" he said, taking her gently by the elbow.

Shaking her head fretfully as if trying to dislodge something, she allowed herself to be led from the room.

"I think we've taxed her enough," Crawford remarked to Ian when she was gone.

"What do you make of that? Was the entire story one of her delusions?"

"I shouldn't think so," said Ian. "She seemed very lucid when describing that memory."

"But what can it mean?"

"Maybe he was trying to say 'magician,'" Ian suggested.

"Madge. Madgie. Magician." Crawford pulled at his whiskers. "You think he was killed by a magician?"

"That would explain the cards left on the bodies."

"By Jove, so it does," Crawford said. Ian sensed he was trying not to sound too enthusiastic—the chief inspector preferred to lead in the traditional Scottish way, with an eye to everything that could go wrong. That way, as Ian's father used to say, one was less often disappointed.

"Also," Ian continued, "the scene described by our witness at the Owl's Nest would bear out the idea that our killer is someone familiar with cards and card tricks."

"Then why isn't he here? Skittish about coppers, is he?"

"He's probably also afraid what happened to the others will happen to him if he talks."

"It's more likely to happen if he doesn't talk," Crawford muttered, pulling on his whiskers.

Ian glanced at the clock on the wall behind Crawford's desk. It was a few minutes after noon. "He should be here soon—is there a police sketch artist available?"

Crawford frowned. "Keith McGregor is in Inverness, and Samuel Harrison has a bad case of boils. What about that aunt of yours? Can she sketch?"

"As a matter of fact, she won an art prize at school—"

"Tell her the reputation of the Edinburgh City Police is at stake."

"I usually have Sunday dinner with her. I can go ask her now if you like."

"Off you go, then. If your witness shows up, I'll send a constable to your aunt's to fetch you both."

"Here's her address," Ian said, scribbling it down on a piece of paper.

"And Hamilton," Crawford added as Ian turned to leave, "you can have anyone else you want—whatever it takes to capture this devil."

"Thank you, sir."

"There's not a man on this force who wouldn't be proud to be the one to bring him in."

"I appreciate that, sir."

"Now get on with you—and tell that aunt of yours to fatten you up, for Christ's sake. You look like a bloody scarecrow."

"Yes, sir," Ian replied. Throwing his cloak around his shoulders, he left the station, striding into the wintry gloom of a pallid February afternoon.

CHAPTER FIFTY-NINE

On the other side of the Royal Mile, the luxurious furnishings of the Waterloo Hotel only served to torment the man pacing the elegant parlor, smoking one cigarette after another. Henry Standish Wright was at a crossroads. He could no longer bear the weight of guilt he had lived with far too long. It was like a physical presence, pushing him down, choking the breath from his body. Fear and loyalty had prevented him from taking action until now, but as he gazed out the frosted panes of the French windows, he felt only horror. He could no longer stand by and watch passively as one young life after another was sacrificed to a dark and distorted desire.

What did it mean, this wretched life, if one had no power to right what was wrong, no matter the cost? Henry had no illusions about what it would mean to his career if he went to the police. He lit another cigarette with trembling fingers. Inhaling deeply, he savored the harsh tobacco as it slid down his throat, followed by the calming rush of the drug, which both sharpened his reasoning and relaxed his anguished spirit. Until now, the killer had taken the lives of strong young men who were capable of defending themselves—but this! Surely this latest outrage demanded retribution in this life, if not in the next. He could hardly bear to look at the newspaper sprawled upon the coffee table, where he had flung it when he first read the terrible news.

He took a last drag from his cigarette, then stabbed it out in the crystal ashtray, pressing so hard, he nearly burned his fingertips. He took a deep, ragged breath and straightened his spine. He had come to a decision. He wheeled about and strode to the coatrack, grabbing his coat as his hand closed on the front-door handle. When he pulled it toward him, he was astonished to see the man standing before him in the hall.

"How long have you been standing here?" Henry croaked hoarsely; his voice seemed to have deserted him. "Have you been spying on me?"

His tormentor smiled. "Going somewhere?"

"I need to buy cigarettes," Henry muttered, avoiding eye contact.

"That's strange," the man replied, looking over his shoulder at the fresh pack on the coffee table. "You have a newly opened box right there."

"I need to take some air. Let me pass!" Henry replied tightly, trying to push past him.

His opponent stood his ground, the smile fading. "What's the rush?" He grasped Henry by the wrist, twisting it behind his back.

Henry ground his teeth as the pain shot up his arm. "Let—me—go," he rasped, but the other man was stronger, and forced him back into the room.

"I say, you're not in a very friendly mood," his adversary said, locking the door behind him. His glance fell upon the newspaper on the coffee table and he frowned. "Dear me, have you been reading the paper? You really should stay away from upsetting news—remember your delicate constitution."

Henry attempted to light another cigarette, but his hands shook so violently, he dropped it on the floor.

"You don't look well at all. Are you still having trouble sleeping?"

"I am sleeping quite well."

"You always were a rotten liar," his antagonist replied, advancing toward him. "And you really shouldn't believe everything you read in the paper."

Henry took a step back. "Keep away from me."

His visitor smiled, and in that smile all the evil of the world seemed to reside. "Relax. What are you so afraid of?"

"Just keep your distance."

"I thought that you might react badly to all that lurid newspaper coverage. It appears I was right."

"I have no idea what you mean," Henry replied, but he knew the look on his face gave him away.

"Pity you never learned to lie well—I could have taught you. I am quite good at it."

"Very well," Henry croaked as panic closed off his throat. "Why don't you teach me?"

"I'm afraid it's too late for that now."

Henry backed away, knocking over a Chinese vase, which tumbled from its perch, shattering on the parquet floor.

"I'm disappointed in you," his tormentor said, advancing toward him with the measured stride of a tiger stalking its prey.

Henry's instinct told him to avoid turning his back on his opponent, but he also knew he couldn't fend him off barehanded. Remembering the steel letter opener in the desk drawer, he spun around, pulled the drawer open, and clawed through its contents frantically.

His fingers clutched the pearl handle just as he felt strong hands closing around his neck.

As his breath deserted him, Henry closed his eyes, letting his body go limp and leaning into his fate, inevitable as it was. The last thing he felt, as the darkness overtook him, was relief—relief that it would all soon be over, and at last he would be able to rest.

CHAPTER SIXTY

As the heavy wooden door of the High Street police station closed behind him, Ian Hamilton stepped from the building to see Derek McNair waiting on the other side of the road, leaning against a tethering post, arms crossed. There were stains on his cheeks where tears had scraped vertical lines through the dirt and grime. Derek's eyes were swollen and red, and his chin, though firmly clenched, threatened to give way any moment.

"You've heard, then," Ian said.

"Aye," the boy replied.

"Who told you?"

"It's in all th' papers."

"I'm so sorry. I know Freddie was your mate."

"Yeah," Derek said, compressing his lips tightly. "Right."

"He seemed like a nice boy."

"Lot nicer 'an me, which is pro'bly why e's dead."

"When did you last see him?"

"In the Grassmarket, the day afore he were . . . found."

"Approximately what time?"

"About ten in th' morning."

"Did you see him with anyone suspicious?"

Derek shook his head. "Naw. We was . . ."

"Working the crowd?"

"Don' know what ya mean."

"For God's sake, I'm not going to haul you in for pickpocketing!"

"We was workin' the crowd, yeah."

"Then what happened?"

Derek kicked at a stone in the road. "That's when me an' Freddie had a fight, and I went off an' left him there."

"Anything else you can remember? Was the Grassmarket crowded?"

"Aye. It were market day, an' there were lots a folks out and about."

"Very well," said Ian, heading off down the High Street in the direction of Edinburgh Castle, black and solitary on its slab of rock. Derek fell in beside him, scurrying to keep up with the detective's long stride. They walked in silence before Ian stopped, in the shadow of St. Giles', its Gothic arches hovering over them like great stone arms.

"Well?" he said. "Why are you following me?"

"'Cause you obviously need help."

"Do I?"

"Well, ye need sommit, don' ye?" the boy cried, releasing a torrent of tears and anger. "Else ye would've caught 'im by now—but ye haven't, 'ave ye?"

"No, we haven't," Ian replied. "And since you're so keen on helping me, I have a question for you."

"Yeah?"

"Did you tell George Pearson about the playing cards?"

Derek cocked his head to one side. "Don' know what ye mean, mate."

"You did tell him, didn't you?"

"Wha' if I did?"

"It's privileged police information."

"I'm the one what foun' the card on that poor bloke an' gave it ye."

Ian frowned. "In the future, please refrain from divulging such information to anyone."

Derek kicked a stone out of his path. It skittered across the cobblestones and into the gutter. "Ye coulda told me earlier. But like it or not, I'm in it much as you now."

"Look, I'm really sorry about your friend," Ian said.

Derek shoved his hands deeper into his pockets. "Fellas like him an' me aren't missed much by anyone."

As they passed the National Gallery, a couple of toffs in their Sunday best strolled by. The younger one, a slim, black-haired fellow with an arrogant swagger, raised an eyebrow at Derek, flicking his ivory-handled cane toward the boy.

"I say, Rodney, there's one of your typical Scottish 'raggediers' now." His accent was British, exaggeratedly well-bred.

"Why, so it is," replied his companion, a striking fellow with a neatly trimmed silver beard and ironic blue eyes. "Here you go, lad— here's a shilling for you," he said, tossing a coin at Derek.

It landed at his feet, and both men laughed.

"Well, what are you waiting for? Pick it up," said the one with the raven hair.

"I'm surprised he didn't catch it before the rats could come and carry it off," the other one remarked.

Ian was unaware of having moved at all until he found himself grasping the black-haired man's elegant frock coat by the lapels.

"He doesn't need your stinking charity!" he hissed, his Highland accent thickening as it did in times of stress. He pulled the man's face closer to his, inhaling the lavender pomade wafting from his hair. "If he wanted to, he could take all your money without either of you neeps being any the wiser."

"Look here, my good man," began the silver-bearded one, but Ian wheeled around and shoved his police badge in the man's face.

"If I so much as catch a glimpse of either of you around here again, I'll have you hauled to the police station for disturbing the peace!"

"Now see here," said the other man, but Ian silenced him with a glare that could have burned paint off metal.

"Be on your way—*now*," he said, "unless you fancy spending the night in a cell."

Red-faced, the men sputtered and spewed a feeble protest, but soon took to their heels, striding rapidly away and throwing glances behind them from time to time to see if Ian was in pursuit.

"Guess you showed them," Derek observed when they had gone.

"They had it coming," Ian muttered, resuming his journey along the High Street.

Derek scrambled after him. "Wha's a 'neep,' anyway? I thought it meant a turnip."

"It's Highland slang for 'idiot.'"

"Good one," Derek said, brightening a bit. "Callin' someone a turnip. Gotta share that one with Fred—" He broke off and took a long, ragged breath.

Ian laid a hand on his shoulder. "We'll catch him. By God, if I have to throttle him with my own two hands, he will pay, I promise you that."

Derek dug something out of his pocket and held it out to Ian. "Here, I wan' ye ta have this."

"What is it?"

"It's me lucky stone. Ye might need it."

It was hardly more than a pebble, perfectly round and polished to a sheen from being in the boy's pocket so long. Ian slipped it into his jacket pocket. "You know," he said as a tear snaked its way down the boy's filthy cheek, "it wasn't your fault. It could have happened to anyone—to you, for example."

"It wouldn't a happened ta me 'cause I'm not like Freddie! He were always too trustin' by half—I always told 'im so. I tried ta look after 'im, like, but I weren't there when he needed me."

"Sometimes people have to learn to look out for themselves."

"Is 'at what you think, mister?" Derek said, squinting up at him in the bright, cold-afternoon light.

"Yes," Ian said, but a little worm of doubt began to gnaw its way into his ear as he turned south on Bank Street. He wondered what his brother was up to, and where he was, as guilt burned a little hole in his heart.

CHAPTER
SIXTY-ONE

Ian wasn't surprised when Lillian insisted Derek join them for Sunday afternoon dinner, and even less surprised when the boy eagerly accepted. He was more surprised when Lillian agreed to DCI Crawford's request to fill in for the absent sketch artists.

"It might be fun to get out my charcoals again," she said. "Ever since dear Alfie died, I've been meaning to get back to my art. And I would like to help—this has gone on long enough."

"Can you be available at a moment's notice?"

"I don't see why not."

"The witness said he'd come by after church today. If the boy doesn't show up at the station house by tomorrow, I'll haul him in myself," Ian said as his aunt handed him three warmed plates from the oven.

"I think we'll eat in here," she said, laying out three places on the round table in the parlor. "It's a chilly day, and I won't have to light the fire in the dining room if we dine in here."

Derek looked around the room reverently, as though he had entered a fairy palace, touching the polished ivory keys on the piano and running his hand over the marble fireplace mantel.

"You can wash up through there," Lillian said, pointing the way to the lavatory.

He obeyed, treading carefully on the hall runner carpet, as if he feared he might plunge through it. While he was away, Ian explained to Lillian that the strangler's latest victim was Derek's friend.

She crossed her arms and frowned. "Do you not have room for him to stay for a while? He's just a wee thing."

"Physically, perhaps, but hardly in personality."

"Ach, Ian, would it be so much trouble?"

"What if Donald comes back?"

"Then he can sleep on the sofa. Are you not afraid the boy himself may be the next victim?"

"I suppose it's possible, but—"

"Very well—it's settled, then."

Ian sighed. When Lillian was determined to prevail, there was no point in arguing. He felt overrun by uninvited guests of late—Donald, the cat, and now Derek. Solitary by nature, Ian did not appreciate sharing his space with anyone, let alone a pickpocketing street urchin. The British fop had called the boy a "raggedier," and in spite of his loathing of everything those men represented, Ian had to admit it was a felicitous description.

His heart softened a bit when the raggedier, face scrubbed, appeared in the hallway, surveying the feast Lillian was setting on the table.

"Now then," his aunt said after they had seated themselves, "will it be sausages or fried fish—or both?"

"Both, please, mum," Derek replied, eyeing the food hungrily.

Lillian beamed at him. "I thought so."

"Much obliged," Derek mumbled through a mouthful of bread smeared liberally with sweet creamery butter.

Lillian regarded the boy with fond satisfaction. Ian knew how she loved feeding people, remembering with a pang it was a trait she shared with his mother. "You'd best have a bit o' tatties as well, laddie," she urged the boy, who didn't need to be asked twice.

His aunt had a way of sprinkling her conversation with Scottish words and phrases, as though trying to reinforce her identity. Edinburgh was undoubtedly the country's most cosmopolitan city; at times one could almost forget it was Scottish at all, so filled with visitors from every part of Europe and beyond.

"Do you remember the hypnotist I saw at the Theatre Royal?" Lillian asked as she tucked her napkin under her chin. No one in Edinburgh's polite society would think of doing such a thing—but she was a Glaswegian, born and bred.

"How could I forget? You gushed on about him for days," Ian said, helping himself to boiled potatoes and fried cod.

Derek let out a snicker, which he attempted unsuccessfully to smother in his napkin.

"Young man, it's unseemly to mock your elders," Lillian reproached sternly.

"Sorry, mum," he mumbled through a mouthful of mushy peas.

"Monsieur Le Coq, wasn't it?" said Ian. "Or something similarly preposterous. He's still playing there, I believe."

"I was thinking of going again—that is, if you'd like to join me."

"Hang on a minute," said Derek. "Was he stayin' at the Waterloo Hotel?"

"I have no idea," Lillian replied. "Why do you ask?"

"I passed by there on me way t'meet you," he said to Ian.

"I suppose their clientele offer choice pickings?" Ian remarked.

Derek ignored the barb. "I were passin' by and I 'eard some fellas what worked there standin' jes' outside, sayin' as how this fancy performer had jes' took 'is own life in 'is hotel room, like."

"What—how?"

"These blokes said 'e was found hangin' from the rafters in 'is own room."

"That can't be!" Lillian cried.

"And you're sure this was at the Waterloo Hotel?" Ian said.

"Yep, 'at's what I said."

"I'm afraid you'll have to excuse me," Ian said, rising suddenly from the table.

His aunt looked alarmed. "What's the matter?"

"I need to assure myself of something," he said, hurrying out to the front hall.

Lillian scurried after him, her napkin fluttering beneath her chin like an oversized clerical collar. "What is it, Ian?"

"Don't worry, Auntie—I'm sure it's nothing," he said, kissing her papery cheek. "But I must be certain."

"But your dinner—"

"I'll return later. Don't wait up for me."

"It will get cold," she said forlornly.

"Then I shall have it cold."

"Kin I come?" Derek said from the doorway.

"No," Ian replied firmly, throwing on his cloak. "Stay here and take care of my aunt—and mind you help her tidy up."

He was out the door before either of them could utter another word.

Seated in the back of a hansom cab rumbling over North Bridge, Ian pulled from his vest pocket the letter he had so carefully plucked from all the others. Beneath the elegant crest of the Waterloo Hotel stationery were the words that had so struck him at the time. *Catch him before I kill him.*

Perhaps at last, he thought, all the disparate story elements were finally coming together.

CHAPTER
SIXTY-TWO

All around him, the city lay in Sunday evening stillness, a great sleeping beast at rest before gathering itself for another Monday morning assault. The cab took the turn onto Princes Street, passing the Duke of Wellington statue, gleaming cold and dark in the moonlight, the Iron Duke captured in bronze, forever a young warrior on a charging stallion.

Waterloo Place, the eastern extension of Princes Street, was the city's premier shopping venue, with its elegant stores and well-dressed denizens. The neoclassical architecture of Edinburgh's New Town had no better example than in the Waterloo Hotel, with its grand arches and magnificent view of Holyrood Park.

Ian flashed his badge at the front desk clerk, a sleepy bulldog of a man with muttonchop whiskers attempting unsuccessfully to hide a severe underbite.

"Sir?" said the clerk.

Ian cleared his throat officiously. "Detective Inspector Hamilton, investigating the—incident involving Monsieur Le Coq."

The clerk leaned forward eagerly, his sluggishness vanished. "Oh, you mean Henry Wright. Poor fellow."

"I was given to understand his name was Le Coq."

"That's his stage name. Poor bloke wasn't French any more than I am! He used that as an alias to make his act seem more sophisticated. I heard the ladies went for it."

"Is the body still there?"

"Far as I know—but the lads from the morgue just showed up, so you'd better hurry."

"Thank you," Ian said, turning away.

"Room Two Twelve," the clerk called after him. "Second floor—you can take the lift."

Passing the lift, Ian bounded up the stairs two at a time, arriving at the room in time to see two morgue attendants enter with a stretcher.

"Just a moment," Ian said, pulling out his badge. "DI Hamilton, Edinburgh City Police. I have one or two matters to investigate before you remove the body."

The older of the attendants, a bear of a man with beery eyes and a gut like a bedroll, scowled at him. "The poor blighter offed hisself, mister. Wha' else d'ya need ta know?"

"I'll let you know when I find it," Ian replied stiffly, pushing past them into the room.

The elegance of the suite was marred by the presence of the body lying upon the settee. Ian recognized him at once from the posters in front of the Theatre Royal. The handsome face was pale, the only visible sign of violence the purple discoloration on his neck, just above his shirt collar. A leather belt lay on the floor next to the body. Ian searched the victim's pockets carefully for the usual playing card, but found none. As he was puzzling the reason for this, he heard footsteps behind him.

A reedy, worried-looking man in an elegant frock coat stood over him, wringing his hands. Balding and avuncular, he wore wire-rimmed glasses upon his beak of a nose.

"Alan McCleary," he said, extending a thin hand. "I'm the night manager."

"Detective Inspector Ian Hamilton, Edinburgh City Police."

Mr. McCleary appeared suitably impressed by his credentials. "Dreadful business!" he said, continuing to wring his hands as he paced the plush carpet. "I fear it will bring bad repute upon the hotel!"

The manager's lack of concern about the dead man struck Ian as more than a little callous, but he held his tongue. Mr. McCleary might yet prove useful, and Ian was too much of a pragmatist to scold him and risk losing his cooperation.

He pointed to the leather belt. "Was this used in the hanging?"

"Dear me, yes—shocking, it was! The chambermaid came in with clean linens and found him hanging from the beam in the bedroom! Poor girl, she was quite distraught."

"Where is she?"

"I sent her home."

"You did *what*?"

"She was quite hysterical, Detective."

"I'll need her name and address."

"Why?"

"Because I haven't yet determined the manner of death."

"Surely it's plain as the nose on your face!" the manager exclaimed. "The poor wretch hanged himself. Why on earth would he do such a thing here, of all places? Surely he was satisfied with the service—we gave him no cause for complaint."

Ian stared at him. Did the man really have so little compassion that all he could think about was his hotel? But one look in McCleary's frantic eyes and Ian knew he was in a complete panic, no doubt capable of uttering the most absurd nonsense. Sweat beaded in droplets on his creased forehead, and his sallow cheeks were aflame.

"What do you suppose drove him to do it?" he said imploringly.

"I am not at all convinced he did anything," Ian replied, bending over the body.

"What on earth do you mean by that?" McCleary fretted, his shrill voice rising in pitch.

"I'm not at all convinced this is a suicide."

"Oh, dear," McCleary moaned, sweating even more profusely. "If it wasn't suicide, then could it be—murder? At the Waterloo Hotel? Why, it's unthinkable! Who on earth would do such a thing?"

"That is what I mean to find out," said Ian, looking around the room. Everything was in order, except for the French Empire–style writing desk beneath the far window. The center drawer had been pulled out, the contents in disarray. A pearl-handled letter opener lay on the floor near the desk. He turned to the hotel manager. "Is this as the maid found it when she entered the suite?"

"You mustn't blame her, poor girl—she was out of her wits with terror," McCleary said. "Under normal circumstances, she would have tidied up immediately."

"I'm glad she didn't," said Ian.

"Beg pardon?"

"The disarray suggests a struggle of some kind. If your maid had put everything in order, I should have lost a vital clue."

"I see," McCleary replied, wiping his damp forehead with a neatly pressed handkerchief.

Ian went into the bedroom, McCleary tiptoeing after him as though he were the uncertain guest and Ian the master. As in the living room, everything was in order—Mr. Wright had clearly been a tidy man in life; even in death he left his surroundings largely undisturbed. "Is this the beam he was found hanging from?" Ian asked, pointing to a broad oak rafter stretching lengthwise in the center of the room. An overturned desk chair lay on the ground directly beneath it.

"Yes," McCleary replied with a shudder.

Ian studied the beam, which could easily support the weight of a man's body.

He pointed to the overturned chair. "And this was here?"

"Yes, yes," the manager responded irritably. "But I don't see—"

"Would you do me the kindness of fetching the belt, please?"

Alan McCleary blinked twice, then lurched into the parlor, returning with the belt, holding it outstretched between thumb and forefinger as if it were a venomous snake.

"Thank you," said Ian. Turning the chair upright, he climbed upon it and threw one end of the belt over the beam. Slipping the metal prong of the buckle through the last eyehole, he attempted unsuccessfully to put his head in the loop formed by the buckled belt.

"Dear me!" the manager yelped. "You're not going to—"

"Calm yourself, Mr. McCleary," Ian said, stepping down from the chair. "I wasn't planning on following in Mr. Wright's footsteps. I was simply examining the length of the belt."

He returned to the living room, where the disgruntled morgue attendants stood smoking.

"Look here," said the fat one, "are ye gonnae release this body or what?"

"You can have him right now," Ian said, "if you help me with one last thing."

"What's that?" the attendant asked suspiciously, his small eyes narrowed.

"Stand him upright for a moment."

"What fer?"

"Just do as I ask, and you may have him."

The attendants shrugged and hoisted the unfortunate man to his feet. Rigor mortis had not yet set in, so the limpness of his body made it a difficult task.

"All right," said the fellow with the beer gut. "Now what?"

Ian stood next to the dead man. "Now then, Mr. McCleary, which of us would you say is the taller?"

"Why, you are, by at least an inch or two."

"Thank you," Ian said. "You may take him away now," he said to the attendants, who did as he said, in between some head-scratching and eye-rolling.

When they had gone, McCleary turned to him in an agitated state. "I believe I see what you were after, Detective."

"I am taller than Mr. Wright, and yet, standing on that chair, even I could not manage to place my head in the belt once it was looped around the beam."

"So that means—"

"Henry Wright did not hang himself," Ian said, crouching to examine the floor beneath the beam.

"What are you looking for?" McCleary said, hovering over him anxiously.

Sweeping his hand over the polished wood surface, Ian felt coarse bits of fiber remnants. Scooping them up, he held them in his palm so McCleary could see. "This," he said. "I was looking for this."

The manager peered at them. "Dear me, I shall have to speak to the maid about her carelessness."

"The careless person was not the maid but whoever killed Henry Wright," Ian said with a grim smile. "And his carelessness may put a noose around his own neck."

"Where did it come from?"

"From a rope."

"What rope?"

"The one used to hoist a murdered man up in order to make his death appear as a suicide. Even for a very fit man, it would be a daunting task to lift an inert body that high, but quite easily done if you used a rope over the beam as a hoist. You could tie it off and place his neck in the belt loop and then just remove the rope."

"Goodness, that requires quite a lot of planning," McCreary said, wringing his hands.

"The man we're looking for is quite adept at planning."

"Dear me," the manager said, eyes wide, "who on earth would do such a thing?"

"That, Mr. McCleary, is an excellent question."

CHAPTER
SIXTY-THREE

As it was a bright moonlit night, Ian decided to walk back through the sleeping city. No one on the staff had seen anyone enter or leave Henry Wright's room—but getting in and out of buildings unobserved was no doubt easy for a conjurer. There was no certainty the hypnotist had been murdered by the Holyrood Strangler—the absence of a playing card was indeed puzzling. But every fiber of Ian's being told him he was closing in on the perpetrator. The night manager could not recall Henry Wright receiving visitors during his stay, nor could any of the other staff members. Ian longed to interview the chambermaid who had found the body, but it was past midnight, and he supposed the poor girl would be calmer in the morning.

He turned south onto George IV Bridge, which arched over the streets below like the back of a whale. As he swung onto Victoria Street from the bridge, Ian saw the tower of Greyfriars Kirk poking through the cloud cover, its gray stone steeple somber in the moonlight. He rarely visited his parents' graves in the kirkyard. The fire had left little more than charred ashes and a few scattered bones—the caskets they lowered into the ground were so light, it seemed a pity to waste the space burying a pile of bones. Afterward he had the wild notion that the charred remains found in the house were not his parents'—that they had somehow escaped the conflagration, and someone else was buried in that churchyard.

When Donald disappeared shortly after the fire, not even staying for the funeral, Ian was left adrift, with no one to share memories of his childhood. His response was to bury them as deeply as the caskets in Greyfriars Kirkyard. Something grew in him, fierce and hard and cold, a sticking place where neither light nor joy could enter, forged on that night when he felt the utter indifference of the universe. Surrounded by his aunt's affection, embraced by the dark city that was now his home, he felt like an outlier, doomed to roam the earth, calling men to account for their evil deeds.

Lost in thought as he rounded the corner of Fleshmarket Close, he was unaware of his attackers until they were upon him. Only moments after that, he realized the hard object that had come in contact with his face was a fist.

Hit so hard that he spun clear around, Ian found himself face-to-face with the second assailant, who landed a blow to his stomach, sending him to his knees. His kneecaps had no sooner hit the cobblestones than he felt a kick to the ribs, and fell heavily on his side beneath a shower of blows. Blood spurted from his nose and trickled from his forehead into his right eye. The first ruffian lifted him to his feet and whispered in his ear with horrible, cheap whisky breath.

"Rodney sends his regards."

The first thought in his fuzzy brain was that he knew no one by that name. But as the thug released his grip and Ian sank to the ground, he recalled the two toffs who had insulted Derek the day before. The second one had called his friend Rodney. Ian braced himself for more blows, but to his surprise they didn't come. He raised his head, dimly aware of the presence of a third person.

He heard an exclamation of pain coming from the first assailant. Wiping the blood from his eyes, Ian could just make out the third individual—an enormous hulk of a man. He remembered the fight behind the Hound and Hare, Rat Face, and his companion.

"Jimmy," he gasped, "is that you?"

The giant lifted the second man by the collar as if he were made of straw and flung him against the side of the nearest building. He landed with a thud, sinking to the ground with a groan, and then was silent. The first assailant, seeing what short work Jimmy had made of his companion, took to his heels, scampering away down Fleshmarket Close.

"Never could stand an unfair fight," said Jimmy, and before Ian could thank him, he vanished into the night.

Getting painfully to his feet, Ian hobbled the last few blocks to his flat. When sleep came to him that night, crawling into his bed like a reluctant lover, he sank gratefully into blessed oblivion. Just prior to losing consciousness, he was aware of something kneading his legs as if they were dough, and realized it was the cat. He tried to lift his hand to pet it, but before he could summon the will, unconsciousness overtook him.

CHAPTER
SIXTY-FOUR

DCI Crawford looked up from his steaming cup of tea when Ian presented himself at the station house around noon.

"Sorry I'm late, sir. I had a rather eventful night."

"Something tells me I'll regret asking, but what the devil happened to you?"

"My face had the discourtesy to interrupt the forward motion of a fist."

"Do I want to know any other details?"

"Probably not."

"You may have a broken nose."

"Quite possibly."

"Well, it can only improve your appearance. What else? You clearly have something on your mind."

"You have heard of the hypnotist found hung in his room at the Waterloo Hotel yesterday afternoon?"

"I have."

"I went round there last night to have a look, and—"

"Wait—don't tell me," he said, holding up a plump hand. "It wasn't suicide—it was murder."

"If you say so, sir."

The chief ran his fingers through his thinning ginger hair. "I assume you have a theory for this one as well."

"I think Henry Wright was killed by the Holyrood Strangler."

Crawford stirred his tea and licked the spoon before placing it carefully on the desk. "Go on."

Ian described his findings at the scene.

"Do you think the killer was looking for something in the desk?" asked Crawford when he described the open desk drawer.

"I believe Henry Wright was looking for something to defend himself with."

"The letter opener?"

"Aye, which means he didn't expect the attack."

"And yet no sign of forced entry indicates—"

"He knew his killer," Ian said.

"But the front desk clerk saw no one go to Mr. Wright's room?"

"So he claims."

"Could he be lying?"

"More likely asleep. He looked pretty drowsy when I saw him."

Crawford hauled his bulk out of the chair and lumbered over to the filing cabinet. "An open desk drawer, a dropped letter opener, and a few bits of rope fiber are precious little evidence."

"But apart from that, Henry Wright was a fastidious man."

"We all have our little corners of untidiness. My wife is an excellent housekeeper, but her sewing basket is appallingly disorganized. It's full of stray needles likely to stab you if you're not careful—"

"What about the length of the belt?"

"Couldn't he have pulled himself up by his hands and placed his neck in it?"

"Possibly. But why not use something longer—say, a bedsheet?"

"I'll grant you it's a more logical choice, but can we suppose someone in that state of mind is thinking clearly?"

"I just think it bears consideration, and given all the other clues—"

"Very well," Crawford grunted. "Let's move on, shall we?" He plucked a sheet of paper from atop the filing cabinet. "Your little Nancy-boy showed up early this morning and gave a credible description of the young rake who went off with Kerry O'Donohue Friday night. Oh, and your aunt is a damn decent sketch artist."

Ian snatched the sketch from Crawford and studied it eagerly. The resemblance to Henry Wright was remarkable. The face looking back at him was handsome, with the same firm chin and broad forehead as the dead hypnotist. He was struck by the deep-set eyes, intense and brooding.

"Judging from this," he said, "I believe this victim may be related to his killer. Brothers, perhaps."

"That puts a new twist on the case," Crawford said, stroking his lush whiskers. "Your aunt did a good job on the sketch, assuming it's a decent likeness. She was very patient with the little pervert."

Ian winced at the word. "I'm glad he was able to be useful."

"So?" Crawford asked. "Does the likeness call anyone to mind?"

"There's a resemblance between this man and Henry Wright— they could be brothers," Ian said, threads of excitement spiraling in his stomach.

"Mind you don't fiddle the facts to fit your theory," Crawford warned.

"I'm going to interview the chambermaid who found the body at the Waterloo Hotel. May I take this along just in case?"

"Right," said Crawford. "Off you go, then."

Before Ian could move, the door to the office swung open, and a disheveled Sergeant Dickerson lurched into the room. His uniform was unbrushed, his boots in need of polish, and one of the brass buttons on his jacket had come undone. "Sorry, sirs," he panted. "I meant to be here earlier."

"Good Lord, Sergeant," Crawford began, but Ian stepped between them.

Dickerson stared at his bruised face. "Are you all right, sir?"

"Quite all right, thank you. What did Constable McKee have to say about the Waverley Station incident?"

"Nowt useful, I'm afraid, sir. No one saw anythin'—no one were even lookin' at the poor bloke when it happened, and there were too much smoke fer those what were around."

Crawford shook his head. "I feared as much. Poor fellow."

"If it were our man," said Dickerson, "why d'you s'pose he killed Inspector Gerard?"

"Perhaps he thought there was incriminating evidence in Paris that Gerard hadn't yet discovered," said Ian.

"Well, we'll never know now." Crawford sighed.

"What now, sir?" asked Dickerson.

Crawford scowled at him. "First of all, you can explain why you were late. And your appearance—"

"You're just in time to help interview a chambermaid," Ian interrupted.

"Sir?"

"I'll explain on the way," Ian said, hustling him out of the room before DI Crawford could vent his spleen on the sergeant.

"Thank you, sir," Dickerson said as they stepped out onto the Parliament Square side of the building.

"What on earth were you up to last night?" Ian asked, taking in his unshaven face.

"Nowt so much as you, by the look of it, sir."

"Never mind about me—what about you?"

"I, er, saw a young lady, sir."

"Anyone I know?"

"I—I'd rather not say."

"I never would have taken you for a Lothario."

"It's a question a' her privacy, y'see."

"Everyone has secrets, Sergeant."

"Even you, sir?"

"Especially me," Ian said as they passed beneath the shadow of North Bridge, turning south on Niddry Street.

"If ye say so, sir," Dickerson replied, sidestepping a coach-and-four careening around the corner onto High Street. "I ought t'write bloody bugger up," he muttered as mud thrown up from the rear wheels splattered his uniform. "If that's not 'riding recklessly and furiously,' I dunno wha' is."

"Never mind," Ian said. "We have more important business—we must pay a call on Miss Abigail Farley, chambermaid at the Waterloo Hotel."

Miss Farley lived in a dilapidated tenement in the Cowgate known as Happy Land—a fine example of Scottish irony, in its utter failure to live up to its name. Happy Land was filthy, unsafe, and unsanitary; it stank of sin, sorrow, and surrender. Behind its crumbling walls lived a collection of thieves, rogues, and whores, as well as a few murderers. Sprinkled in among them were unlucky, impoverished souls doing their best to make a living on the right side of the law.

Abigail Farley was one of those unfortunates. A plump, round-faced young woman with curly black hair, she answered the door immediately, beckoning them inside after glancing left and right, as if expecting brigands to dart out and attack at any moment.

She took in Ian's battered face without comment, leading them into a small parlor, which was clean and swept, the well-worn furniture free of dust. She obviously had made an effort to create an atmosphere of what comfort she could; the rickety tea table was covered with a hand-crocheted antimacassar, and a threadbare woven rug covered the rough-hewn wood floors.

"Won't you sit down?" she said nervously, gesturing to the room's only chair, which had seen better days. Her accent suggested her Irish roots, light and lilting.

Sergeant Dickerson began to lower himself into the tattered armchair, but Ian glared at him and he leapt back to his feet.

"Perhaps you would like to sit instead," Ian suggested to their hostess. "This must a very trying time for you."

"I won't call you a liar," she said, sinking into the armchair with a sigh. "I've had better days, so I have."

"Did the hotel give you the day off, Miss Farley?" Ian said.

"Everyone calls me Abbie. Mr. McCleary—he's the night manager, y'see—told me I was on no account to come in today, nor tomorrow if I didn't feel up to it. He's payin' me wages an' all, bless 'im."

Ian's opinion of Mr. McCleary took an upward swing. So he was not an unfeeling man, perhaps just one given to hysteria.

"So you discovered the body?"

She nodded and looked down at her nails, torn and ragged—scrubbing floors with harsh chemicals was hardly conducive to having nice hands.

"I was to turn the bed down, like—that's one of me jobs, y'see."

"Every evening?"

"Yes, and t'see if they would be wantin' fresh linen or anything. In a fancy hotel, you're wantin' to keep the customers happy, y'see?"

"Indeed," said Ian. "Please continue."

"Well, I didn't receive an answer when I knocked, so I finally just opened the door, figuring Mr. Wright weren't in . . . and that's when I found the poor man as I did. So help me, sweet Jesus, I dropped me arm of linens and let out a scream to raise the dead."

"So you didn't touch anything?"

"Good Lord, no! I backed out of there as fast as me legs could carry me, and it weren't but a moment afore Mr. McCleary showed up."

"Did you chance to pass by the room at all earlier?"

"An hour or so before I was a few doors away, near the staircase, when I thought I heard voices comin' from that room. I can't be sure, though—it might 'a been another room."

"What sort of voices?"

"Two men it was—they weren't exactly shoutin', but you could tell there was tension atween 'em, y'know?"

"Did you hear what they were saying?"

"No, but a few minutes later, I heard a crash, like something fallin' to th'floor."

"Coming from that room?"

"I can't say for sure. There's ten rooms in that hallway alone."

"Anything else?"

"No. I went on about my business—Mr. McCleary says it's not right to spy upon the guests."

"And you saw no one coming or going from Mr. Wright's suite?"

"No, but I went upstairs shortly after that, so if someone did leave, I wouldn't have seen nothin'. Was he murdered, then?" she asked, her frank green eyes wide.

"Have you ever seen this man before?" Ian said, showing her the police sketch.

"Lord if he don't bear a resemblance to poor Mr. Wright," she said. "Could be 'is brother, so he could."

"But you've never seen him?"

"I can't say as I have, no—never saw no one comin' or goin' in Mr. Wright's rooms. Never knew a man who liked 'is privacy more—"

She was interrupted by the sound of the front door opening and slamming, followed by the sound of stamping boots in the hallway, accompanied by a fit of consumptive coughing.

"It's me brother, Seamus," Abbie said, "back from the docks early."

A young man entered the room. Clad in mud-encrusted boots, and a well-worn vest and jacket over a green flannel shirt, he was the very image of Edinburgh's working class. In his right hand he clutched a handkerchief spattered with fresh droplets of blood. Upon seeing Ian and Dickerson, he pulled the tweed cap from his head, staring at them while hovering on the edge of the hooked rug. He had the same features and coloring as his sister, but his skin was bronzed from the sun, and he had the lean build and sunken chest of a consumptive.

"Take those boots off," Abbie commanded. "I just swept in here."

He obeyed without taking his eyes off the two policemen. "What are they doin' here?"

"Asking 'bout the death of poor Mr. Wright."

"Oiy—what happened to you?" he asked Ian.

"My face had a disagreement with a fist about occupying the same space. The fist had the upper hand."

"That's good, sir," Dickerson murmured. "The upper *hand.*"

Seamus frowned as he pulled off his heavy-soled boots, setting them on the metal rack by the door. "There's not much ta tell. Abbie found the poor bugger hangin' in his hotel bedroom. End o' story."

"I'm afraid there's a bit more to it than that," Dickerson declared officiously.

Seamus gave a harsh laugh, which set off another fit of coughing, a deep hacking that sounded as if his lungs would explode.

"That's a nasty cough ye got there," Sergeant Dickerson remarked. "Ye should see someone about it."

"Good idea," Seamus Farley shot back. "I'll just pop 'round an' drop a month's wages on one o' those fancy Princes Street surgeons, shall I?"

"Seamus!" Abbie scolded. "There's no reason to be rude. It just shows your bad breeding, so it does."

"God forbid these fine gentlemen should think we're ill-bred, Abbie," he responded with a bitter laugh, which set off another coughing fit.

Ian knew the type: working class, resentful of the system that kept him on the edge of poverty, a chip on his shoulder the size of a caber. The Scottish Enlightenment had barely touched people like Seamus

Farley, who could just see over the edge of their own misery onto what they didn't have.

"Is there anything at all you observed about Mr. Wright that may help us find his killer?" Ian asked Abbie.

"He was *murdered*?" her brother said, his face slack with amazement.

Abbie rolled her eyes. "Why d'you think they're *here*, Seamus?"

"Your sister is not a suspect," Ian assured him. "We merely want to find out—"

"Who'd want to murder a fellow like him?" Seamus said, shaking his head. "Maybe a jealous husband, d'ya think?"

"Let the policemen do their job," Abbie said. "Then I'll be about gettin' you a mustard plaster for your chest."

"I'll get me own plaster, so I will," he said, stomping off in the direction of the kitchen. The sound of muffled coughing came from behind the closed door.

"How long has your brother been sick?" Ian asked.

"Since last winter," Abbie said. "The cold and wet makes it worse. I told him I'd take in sewing so's we can live off what I make, but he won't hear of it."

"Right he is, too," Dickerson remarked. "No self-respecting man would let a woman support him."

"Thank you for your enlightened social views, Sergeant," Ian said. "Now then, Miss Farley, if there's nothing else—"

"Hang on a minute," she said. "There was one thing."

"What's that?"

"It's just a detail, so maybe it weren't nothin'."

"The solution of a crime often turns on the smallest detail, Miss Farley. What is it you saw?"

"It's more what I *didn't* see."

Dickerson cocked his head to one side, like a confused spaniel. "I don' take your meaning, miss."

"It was a vase, sir. Or rather, it wasn't a vase—that is, it was gone."

"Can you be more specific?" said Ian.

"That room had a pair o' Chinese vases—big ones, like ye find in rich people's houses. Only these are only reproductions, o' course."

"Go on."

"Well, sir, whilst I was waitin' for Mr. McCleary to come up, I happened to notice one of 'em was missing."

"Are you certain?" asked Ian.

"Hadn't I dusted them both earlier in the day?"

"Did you mention it to Mr. McCleary?"

"There was so much rumpus an' all, I didn't think to mention it till now. A missing vase didn't seem very important at the time."

"Miss Farley," said Ian, "that is where you are mistaken. A great deal could ride upon that detail. Your missing vase could prove to be very important indeed."

CHAPTER
SIXTY-FIVE

"What's significant about the vase, sir, if you don' mind my askin'?" Sergeant Dickerson asked Ian as they trudged up the High Street toward police headquarters.

"It could be proof that Henry Wright was murdered."

"How's that, sir?"

"I believe it was broken in the attack, and the killer removed the broken bits to cover the fact that there was a struggle."

"I see—very clever, sir."

"I'd like you to pay another visit to the Waterloo Hotel and have a look round the room for any broken pieces left behind. Then ask the manager—Mr. McCleary—if he had the vase removed from the room for any reason."

"Now, sir?" asked Dickerson as they stepped aside to make room for a blacksmith leading a pair of chestnut geldings down the hill toward the foundry section of town. The man's face was smeared with grease and soot, shiny as the glistening coats of the horses.

"No time like the present," said Ian. "Off you go."

"Yes, sir," Dickerson replied, scurrying away in the direction of the New Town.

Ian continued toward the station house, passing a group of school-children playing pitch-and-toss underneath George IV Bridge, their halfpennies clattering hollowly against the gray sandstones. The sun was just coming to rest from its daily labors when he entered the building, mounting the stairs to the main room on the second floor.

He found DCI Crawford in his office, staring out the window, slumped in his chair.

"Sir, I believe I have definitive proof that Henry Wright was murdered."

"Good for you," Crawford replied listlessly, without turning around.

"Sir? Are you quite all right?"

Crawford sighed heavily. "It's strange, isn't it? We live in the city with one of the greatest medical colleges in the world, and yet . . . I don't know, Hamilton. Sometimes I don't know why I get out of bed in the morning."

"Sir?"

"Never mind—what were you saying?"

"The death of Henry Wright. I have evidence indicating it was murder."

Crawford gave a little chuckle. "You don't let up, do you? Good on ye, mate." He took a deep breath, but instead of a laugh, what came out was a ragged sob. It was followed by another, and another. Ian stood uncomfortably, hands at his sides, staring at the ground, while his boss wept. After a couple of minutes, Crawford pulled out a blue-striped handkerchief, blew his nose loudly, and stuffed it back into his pocket.

"Sorry you had to see that, Hamilton."

"It's all right, sir."

"It's damn unprofessional, and I apologize."

"I understand, sir."

"Do you indeed?"

"Your wife is not well, sir, and you're worried about her."

"Humph." The chief inspector gazed out the window at the darkening city, then turned back to Ian. "Have you ever been in love, Hamilton?"

"When I was young, perhaps."

Crawford gave a disgusted snort. "You're still young, man."

"When I was younger, then."

"I have been in love only once, with the woman I married."

"Quite commendable, sir."

"Watching her suffer is unbearable, and thinking about losing her is even worse."

"Have you consulted any doctors at the medical school?"

"My physician is going to try to get a referral to a specialist, but they're so busy, I'm afraid they won't have time for her."

"Then we shall simply have to see that they *make* time."

Crawford swung his head around to gaze up at Ian. "I'm beginning to think I was wrong about you, Hamilton."

"Maybe my brother can help find you someone."

"Your brother is back in town? Last I heard he was—"

"He's back," Ian interrupted, "and he's thinking of applying to the medical school."

DCI Crawford rose from his chair and stretched his long, ungainly body. "Hamilton, why the blazes don't you have a woman?"

"Perhaps I don't like fat little wives, sir."

Crawford frowned. "What?"

"You once told me to find a fat little wife."

"Oh, yes—I remember," he said, pulling a bottle of Glenlivet from his desk drawer. He poured some into a couple of empty teacups and handed one to Ian. "I was just trying to snap you out of your damn earnestness about this wretched job. You look terrible, by the way."

"Thank you, sir."

"Not sleeping?"

"Perhaps no more than you."

"See here, Hamilton, the world is full of evil wretches who seek nothing but their own self-gratification, and they don't give a damn whom they hurt in the process. We'll never catch every single one of them."

Ian took a sip of scotch, sharp and peaty and tasting of the earth. "Sir, I—"

"You believe such a person is responsible for your parents' death. While you may never bring that criminal to justice, you can still seek justice for others. Very noble, I'm sure, but mind it doesn't crush you in the process."

"Is that what happened to my father?"

"Your father was a gifted policeman."

"You worked with him. What happened?"

"There was an allegation of accepting bribes."

"Was it true?"

"It was never proven. You seem very drawn to questions that have no answer, Hamilton."

"I'm afraid it comes with being a Highlander, sir."

Crawford took a long swallow of scotch. "So you believe Henry Wright was murdered by his brother, whom you also believe to be the Holyrood Strangler? How the blazes are we going to find him?"

"Remember the word poor Freddie Cubbins was trying to utter when Daft Lucy found him?"

"Magi—"

"Magician."

"Yes, so you thought." Crawford squinted and rubbed his forehead. "Which means we're looking for a murderer who's also a bloody magician?"

"The cards he left on the victims—it shows someone with a flair for the dramatic. Henry Wright was a stage performer—a hypnotist. I have reason to believe his brother is a magician."

Constable Bowers appeared at the office door, a telegram in his hand. "This just came for you, sir," he said, handing it to Crawford, who read it over quickly.

"Have a look at this," he said, giving it to Ian.

RE: INSP GERARD INQUIRY. SKELETON PLAYING CARDS PURCHASED BY M. EDWARD WRIGHT IN NOV. LAST YEAR AT LE MAGASIN DE MAGIE. REGARDS, INSP. LAROUE, SURETE NATIONALE

"He must have sent an inquiry to his colleagues in Paris before the killer got to him," said Crawford. "Good man."

"Now we have a name," said Ian.

He handed the telegram back to Crawford, who tossed it onto his desk. "This Edward Wright has to be staying somewhere," he said. "Find out where. Take as many men as you need."

"Then what?"

"Then, by God, we will smoke him out of his hiding place. We'll show him no magician is a match for the Edinburgh City Police."

CHAPTER
SIXTY-SIX

As Ian left the station house, he saw Sergeant Dickerson staggering up the High Street toward him.

"Hang on a minute, sir—I've got sommit you'll want t'see!"

"Yes, Sergeant?"

"Look!" Dickerson said proudly, digging a folded handkerchief from his pocket. Tucked inside were small shards of blue pottery. "Found it in th'room, just like you said!" he panted, sweat prickling on his ruddy face.

"Well done! That confirms Miss Farley's story. We'll have a noose around his neck yet."

"Why d'you 'spose he killed his brother, sir? D'you think they were workin' together or somethin'? Maybe bloke was about t'rat him out, so 'e kills 'im?"

"Or perhaps his brother just knew too much." Ian pulled his aunt's sketch of the suspect from his vest pocket. "We'll knock on every door in Edinburgh until we find him."

"Wouldn't it help t'have copies?"

"It would indeed. Perhaps Aunt Lillian can make copies."

"Shall I take it round to her?"

"If you would. I have to stop by my flat and—er, feed the cat."

Dickerson smiled. "So you kep' it, then, sir?"

"He's a good mouser."

"Yes, sir."

"And the dog? Did you overcome your allergies or give it away?"

Dickerson coughed delicately. "Me, uh, lady friend is lookin' after Prince."

"You're being very mysterious about her, Sergeant."

Dickerson's face turned scarlet. "I'll jus' get this over to yer aunt's house, then, shall I, sir?"

"Off you go," said Ian. He watched as Dickerson fled, scurrying toward the university as fast as his stubby legs could carry him.

Ian continued on to his flat, weariness trailing him like an unwanted companion. His legs felt so heavy, he could barely lift them, and his bones ached. The ribs on his right side where he had been kicked twinged with every step. Edward Wright's face swam in his vision, his intense, pale eyes burrowing into Ian's soul.

When he reached his flat, he was surprised to find the door unlocked. At first he thought he had left it open—exhaustion seemed to have softened his brain—but the next instant he was on his guard. Someone was inside. Leaving the door ajar, he crept down the front hall. As he neared the parlor, he heard snoring.

Rounding the corner, he saw Donald's bulky figure splayed upon the sofa. Snoring loudly, he looked as if he had dropped unconscious onto the couch. One arm was flung over the arm of the sofa, the other dangling off the side. His clothing was in disarray, his face bore scratch marks, and the skin on his knuckles was raw and bleeding. Dried blood was caked on his upper lip. The stench of alcohol was overwhelming.

Ian had half a mind to leave him where he was, but as he gazed at his brother, love and loathing warred in his heart. Memories of their boyhood together vied with revulsion at what his brother had become.

Why did he have to enter Ian's life now, when there was so much else at stake? Turning to leave, Ian tripped over the fireplace poker, which clattered to the floor. Donald stirred and opened his eyes.

"Hello," he said groggily, his voice slurred from drink. "I suppose you're wondering what I'm doing here."

"Should I be surprised to find you pissed and out stone-cold on my couch?"

"Steady on, now!" Donald said, heaving himself into a sitting position. "Good Lord, what happened to you?"

"I was in a fight."

"Then let's not have any pots calling the kettle black."

"Where have you been?" said Ian.

"What does it matter?"

"You look like something the cat dragged in."

"Speaking of which, I fed him, and he went out through that cunning little door in your kitchen. Did you make that?"

"Who gave you that bloody nose?"

"What about yours?" Donald said, burping loudly.

"You're drunk," Ian said with disgust.

"Perhaps a wee bit," Donald replied with his bad-boy smile.

"You're shot tae fuck," Ian shot back in his aunt's Glaswegian slang. "Your charm doesn't work on me. It worked on our poor mother, God rest her soul, but—"

"Really? You're bringing her into this?"

"She pampered you, which is one reason you're such a wastrel."

"She was *kind* to me, which is more than our father was."

"So he favored me—that's a poor excuse for your debauchery!"

"*Favored* you—that's an understatement!"

"Is it my fault he preferred me to you?"

"You fancy yourself a great detective," Donald replied, hauling himself unsteadily to his feet, "but when it comes to our family, you're blind as a bat."

"You're crazy, piss drunk—"

Donald laughed bitterly. "Not drunk enough, unfortunately, to forget what he did to me."

Something in his voice made a chill run down Ian's spine. "What are you talking about?"

"He thought he could 'change' me—make me more of a 'man' by hardening me up."

"What do you mean?"

"Some things can't be changed, but he didn't realize that."

"What are you talking about?"

"For Christ's sake, Ian, wake up! Don't you remember anything about him—what he could be like?"

"Well, he was stern, but—"

"*Stern?* He was a bloody tyrant!"

"You're exaggerating."

"Is this an exaggeration?" Donald said, rolling up his sleeve to show a round indentation in his skin. A scar had formed, brown around the edges, the skin in the center sunken.

Ian's heart froze. "What is that?"

"It's a cigarette burn."

Ian stared at his brother. "Are you saying—did he—"

"Yes. And it wasn't the only time."

"Good Lord." Ian sat heavily on the end of the couch. His head suddenly felt twice its size, and his ears rang.

"They both hid it from you, what he did to me. She colluded in hiding it as much as he did, to protect the family image."

"But why? Why on earth would he do something like that to you?"

Donald gave a bitter laugh. "He actually told me it was for my own good, that it would help teach me how to be a 'proper man.' Obviously I didn't fit his image of what a son should be. I was 'different.'" Donald fixed him with earnest gray eyes. "This must be very distressing for you, Brother. You do so like everything to be *tidy*, don't you? Well, people aren't like that—*life* isn't like that. It's messy and unpredictable and frightening. You want to control everything, but you can't, Ian. Just when you think you have it all sorted out, along comes something you hadn't planned on—"

"How did you get bloody? What happened to you?"

"Nothing."

"'Nothing will come of nothing.'"

"Good Lord, Ian, don't you ever tire of quoting Shakespeare?"

"Then tell me what happened."

Donald rubbed his neck and plopped back down onto the sofa. "I haven't been out strangling young boys, if that's what worries you."

Without replying, Ian went to the spare bedroom and pulled the deck of cards from the rucksack. He brought them back into the parlor and held them in front of Donald's face.

"Where did you get these?"

Donald looked away. "I won them in a card game."

"I thought you'd given up gambling."

"I had a relapse."

"Did you really win them in a card game?"

"I bloody well did—got them off a strange little fellow called Rat Face."

"Did you say Rat Face?"

"You know the chap?"

"Who else was playing?"

"How am I supposed to remember?"

"You have a photographic memory."

"Not when I've been drinking."

"Maybe you *are* the strangler after all," Ian said, so giddy with exhaustion, he hardly knew what he was saying. "Here I am trying to catch a criminal, and he's been right under my nose the whole time!"

"Don't, Ian—it's been a bad week for us both," Donald said wearily.

"What if you really *are* a killer? Wouldn't that just be too rich? The detective and the murderer! What a story that would make!" Ian said bitterly, confusion and exhaustion conspiring to strangle his control over the rage bubbling up inside him.

"Ian—please."

Donald's expression was pleading, but Ian felt driven by a sharp, savage need to hurt not only his brother but himself as well.

"I wish you *were* the strangler, so help me—then I could solve the crime and get you out of my hair once and for all!"

The minute the words escaped his mouth, Ian wished he could take them back, but one look at Donald's face and he knew it was too late. Something had broken between them.

"The worst thing you can do to anyone is give up on him," Donald said in a voice all the more terrifying because it was so quiet. Springing from the couch, he seized his coat and stalked out of the room.

Ian stood frozen in a state of shock before throwing on his cloak and following his brother out into the night.

CHAPTER
SIXTY-SEVEN

The man standing on George IV Bridge Monday night gazed at the city slumbering around him and smiled. His fingers closed around the scarf in his pocket, the cloth cool and smooth against his skin. With his two strong hands, it was the only weapon he needed. He liked the purity of it, being so near to his victims as he watched the light fade from their eyes. He had followed the case closely in the papers, and instinct told him his pursuers were closing in. If caught, he did not intend to go quietly. Life in prison held no allure—he was determined to fight his way to the bitter end.

The easiest thing would be to fade into the night—with the right disguise, he stood a good chance of getting away. But he wasn't ready to leave—he had one more task to accomplish first. It was risky, he knew, but that was part of the appeal. The threat he posed to his victims was only part of the thrill; the danger he placed himself in during the commission of his crimes was exhilarating. Twice he had nearly been spotted; only the cover of night had allowed him to slip around the corner and escape detection.

He licked his lips, salty sweat mixing with the light rain that had begun to fall. He pulled his sou'wester tightly around his neck as he scanned the streets below. From where he stood, he had a good view of this section of Old Town; sooner or later his prey was bound to pass by. This time he had his victim picked out in advance—and a tasty morsel he was. It wouldn't be easy, but it would be his crowning achievement, a fitting end to his career in Edinburgh. Then he would move on to fresh territory before the net closed in around him.

He caressed the scarf, savoring the familiar tingling in his groin. Sweet anticipation flooded his limbs as he thought about what he was planning. This one wouldn't go down easy. He pulled his oilskin cap over his eyes and leaned against the railing to wait. He was patient— unlike his victim, he had all the time in the world.

In the glint of a streetlamp, he caught sight of a figure leaving the building he was watching. His heart thumped in his chest—could it be? No, it was someone altogether bulkier and more solidly built. The man stopped beneath the lamp to light a cigarette, and in the flair of the match, the face was plainly visible to his observer. In an instant, the killer's plan changed. This was not the one he sought, but he would do nicely—very nicely indeed. Deep inside the bowels of the city, a rabbit screamed as an owl's talons pierced its neck.

CHAPTER
SIXTY-EIGHT

"I say, Sergeant Dickerson—wait up!"

Dickerson turned to see a plump man in an expensive frock coat running toward him. He looked familiar, but the sergeant wasn't good with faces and couldn't remember where he had seen him. Having left Lillian's flat, Dickerson was nearly at the intersection of Cowgate and Grassmarket.

"It's me—George Pearson!" he said, pulling up next to Dickerson, beads of sweat prickling his broad forehead. He looked even less accustomed to physical exertion than the sergeant. "We met at the Hound and Hare, remember?"

"Right—the same night we met up wi' those two shady characters. Rat Face and his pal, the big fellow . . . wha's 'is name?"

"Snead," Pearson replied. "Jimmy Snead."

"Yeah, 'at's it. What can I do for ye?"

"Actually, it's more what I can do for you."

"I don' follow."

"I'm helping Detective Hamilton on the case—acting as a sort of adviser ex-officio—"

"Hold on a sec," Dickerson said, eyeing him suspiciously. "Why 'aven't I been told about this?"

"I'm surprised he didn't mention it. I've been giving him all sorts of advice, you see—"

"Wha' is it you want wi' me, then?"

"I've just been 'round to his flat and he's not there, so I thought you might know where he is."

"Me 'an him parted company half an hour ago. He could be any-wheres." Dickerson was concerned as well as put out by this informa-tion. He had been expecting to find Hamilton at his flat; after dropping the sketch off with Hamilton's aunt, he intended to meet the detective at Victoria Terrace. He wasn't about to tell Pearson, though—something about the librarian irritated Dickerson. Maybe it was his posh English accent, air of self-importance, or soft white hands—whatever the rea-son, the sergeant felt antipathy toward him.

"Are you meeting up with him in the near future?" Pearson asked, wiping the sweat from his face with a monogrammed handkerchief.

Dickerson shrugged and resumed walking north. "I don' see as I can avoid it, since we're workin' case together." The monogram was the last straw—really over-the-top, he thought disdainfully.

"Mind if I join you?" the librarian asked, falling in step beside him.

"Well, it's not really . . . ," he began, stopping to watch a stout man lurch past them. The man's demeanor was preoccupied, his eyes focused straight ahead; he barely seemed to notice Dickerson and Pearson as he passed. His gait was unsteady but determined. There was something familiar about his face—the odd thought occurred to Dickerson that he resembled a much heavier version of Detective Hamilton. Not for the first time, the sergeant cursed his bad memory for faces. Curious, Dickerson decided to follow him.

"Where are we going?" Pearson bleated as the sergeant started off after the man, who was headed east, in the direction of Holyrood Castle.

"Jus' shut up!" Dickerson hissed as the librarian scurried after him. "I didn't ask f'your company."

"Surely a man in this town may walk where he likes," Pearson replied moodily.

"Then keep quiet, will ye?"

"Very well," he answered as the two of them passed beneath George IV Bridge. Neither of them noticed another man trailing them at a distance, hugging the shadows of the buildings. They continued on, pressing deeper into the heart of the Old Town, to be swallowed up by the night.

CHAPTER
SIXTY-NINE

Donald Hamilton wasn't so drunk that he didn't see the two men following him along Cowgate Street. Thinking they were thieves planning to roll him, he resolved to give them the slip. He saw his chance in a band of carousing footballers stumbling toward him, singing loudly. As they neared, he abruptly changed direction and joined up with them. Clapping his arm around the shoulder of the brawniest lad, he joined the singing, belting out the words lustily.

> If Nell were a lady, she'd be just fine
> But since she's no lady, she's a gal o'mine

The footballers seemed quite content to embrace him as part of their drunken band, as they continued their merry way west toward Edinburgh Castle. Donald concluded his pursuers weren't very experienced—when he peeled off, slipping into a narrow wynd just past Old Fishmarket Close, they failed to spot him. He leaned against the wall of the building, breathing in the heavy night air, the sandstones damp against his back.

When the last strains of the footballers' singing had disappeared into the distance, he stepped back out into the street. It was late, but a few pubs were still open. He shoved his hands into his coat pockets and pushed on in the direction of his favorite, the Lion and the Lamb.

He failed to notice the figure following him at a distance—a man far more experienced in the art of tracking than the two clumsy fellows now engaged in a desultory wild-goose chase trailing a harmless band of footballers.

Monday night at the Lion and the Lamb was much like any other—loud, smoke-filled, and crowded. Donald shouldered his way to the bar, ordered a pint, and headed for a corner booth. As he did, his elbow caught another man's sleeve, and his beer splashed all over the stranger's jacket.

"So sorry," Donald said. "I do beg your pardon."

"My fault entirely," the man replied in an educated English accent. "Let me buy you another."

"But it wasn't—"

"Please—I insist."

A glance at the quality of his London tweed jacket and Italian leather shoes told Donald the man was well-heeled.

"Jolly decent of you," he said, unconsciously sliding into his companion's British inflections. There was something compelling about the man's commanding personality, though Donald felt oddly repulsed at the same time.

His companion handed him a pint and held up his own mug. "That's better—cheers."

The two men touched glasses, and the stranger gave him a smile. Donald was struck by the power of his gaze, concentrated in the deep-set, powder-blue eyes. The smile, though intended to be friendly, was intense and strangely cold. He felt the man was sizing him up, and yet there was an energy about him that made resistance difficult. Though the room was warm, Donald gave an involuntary shiver.

"Do you like card tricks?"

"I suppose so." Donald wanted to walk away, but he couldn't seem to summon the will. "I've never thought much about it."

With a flourish, the man produced a deck of cards. "Pick one."

Feeling the heat of his gaze, Donald hesitated.

"Go ahead—any card."

Donald reached for a card.

Outside the pub, deep in the night, an owl hooted as the pale moon slid behind a dark cloud.

CHAPTER SEVENTY

"Shall we call it a night?" Sergeant Dickerson said to George Pearson as the two stumbled down Cowgate Street in the company of the gang of footballers.

The footballer nearest to him put a hairy arm around his neck. "Oiy—ye can't go yet, lads! The fun's only just beginnin'!"

Pearson shot Dickerson a desperate look. The footballers had appropriated George and the sergeant, annexing them to their merry little band when they'd pressed forward in search of the man they'd thought they were following. Sandwiched between two swarthy fellows with calves like hitching posts, the librarian was sweating miserably, the beery fumes coming from his companions making him nauseated. He squirmed uncomfortably in their embrace, but the larger one gave him an affectionate squeeze.

"Oiy, Georgie boy, what position d'ye play?"

"Uh—forward?" Pearson replied hopefully, trying to catch Dickerson's eye. But the sergeant was trying to fend off the flask of whisky another of the players was pressing upon him.

"Forward, is it?" the giant roared. "Hey, lads, Georgie 'ere plays forward!"

The hulk on George's other side bellowed with laughter. "Fer which team, then—George Heriot's School fer boys?"

The others howled and slapped one another on the back. A flat palm between George's own shoulder blades knocked the air out of him, and he gasped as he stumbled forward.

Two strong pairs of hands reached to steady him, but Pearson saw his chance and wriggled away, twisting off to stand on the side of the road. With a final frantic pull, Dickerson wrenched himself from the clutches of his companions and staggered after the librarian.

The two men took to their heels, scurrying away as fast as their lack of fitness would allow, followed by the disappointed cries of their newfound friends.

"Don' go, Georgie boy!"

"Oiy—where ye off tae?"

"The night's still young!"

The two kept running until they reached Tron Square, where they stood panting, their breath forming white puffs in the chill air.

"I thought we'd never git away," Dickerson said finally.

"We were lucky to escape with our lives," Pearson remarked, wiping the sweat from his brow.

The sergeant barked out a laugh. "I were tryin' t'imagine you as a footballer—not bloody likely!"

"I might say the same of you."

Dickerson laughed again, out of relief. "Yer not 'alf bad, mate."

"Very kind of you, I'm sure," Pearson replied. "But I think I'll be getting along home before we are apprehended by another gang of sports-minded ruffians."

"Me, too," said the sergeant. "I've 'ad enough for one night."

"Good night, then," said the librarian, heading off toward New Town.

"'Night," Dickerson replied, watching him for a moment before turning in the other direction.

CHAPTER
SEVENTY-ONE

It was well after midnight when Ian staggered back to his flat. He had searched every pub and gambling den nearby, but exhaustion tore so fiercely at his body that after two hours he was forced to give up the search. With the beating he had sustained two days earlier, combined with lack of sleep, he felt as if he had been drugged. He had no sooner crawled into bed than he succumbed to the pull of sweet oblivion.

A pounding at the front door jolted him into consciousness. He sat bolt upright in bed, aware of morning sounds coming from the street below, the clatter of carriage wheels and horses' hooves vying with the cries of street vendors and tradesmen. The angle of the sun suggested it was midmorning. The knocking sounded again, and he sprang from the bed. Seized by a wave of dizziness, he grasped the bedpost to steady himself before hurrying to answer the door.

Sergeant Dickerson stood alone on the stoop, a grave expression on his pale face. The implication was clear: another victim. Without a word, Ian let the sergeant in, closing the door behind him. He headed back to the bedroom to get dressed, but Dickerson's voice stopped him.

"Sir."

Something in his tone made Ian's blood freeze. He turned slowly and regarded Dickerson, dread seeping into his limbs.

"What is it?"

Dickerson opened his mouth to speak, but no words came. Unable to hold Ian's gaze, he averted his eyes, which were rimmed with red.

"Who is it this time?" said Ian. "For God's sake, *who*?"

Staring at his shoes, the sergeant muttered in a strained monotone. "He was found this morning, sir, outside the Lion and the Lamb. Just like the others."

"*Who*, Sergeant?"

"It's . . . Pearson, sir."

"What?" Ian said. "George Pearson?"

"We haven't moved him yet, sir. If you could just come with me—"

Relief crested over him like a wave. What he had feared, more than anything, was to hear his brother's name, but . . . His knees buckled, and he grasped the wall to steady himself.

Dickerson stepped forward. "Y'all right, sir?"

Ian's vision blurred as relief was replaced by boiling rage that the killer had claimed poor, harmless Pearson. The librarian's only desire was to help Ian—instead, he became another victim. Even though he had tried to keep Pearson at a distance from the investigation, Ian felt responsible for his death, and his guilt was replaced by a cold, hard thirst for vengeance. Without a word, he went to his bedroom and put on his clothes. When he reappeared in the foyer, the face he turned upon Sergeant Dickerson was the stony mask of a basilisk.

"Take me there."

The sergeant peered at him like a frightened rabbit before scurrying out the door.

DCI Crawford was not prepared for the man who appeared in his office at 192 High Street later that morning. He *looked* like DI Hamilton, and *sounded* like him, yet there was something unsettling about the frosty, faraway look in those gray eyes. He showed no traces of human emotion as he stood, stiff as a rod, in front of the chief inspector's desk.

"Rotten news about your friend, Hamilton," Crawford began, but the look on the detective's face silenced him. It was chilling, the gaze of an automaton, not a human being.

"Here are the copies of the sketch my aunt drew last night," Hamilton said, thrusting a handful of papers onto the desk.

"I'll see that these are distributed," Crawford said. "And one for the bulletin board, of course."

"I would like you to see that an article appears in the evening edition of the *Scotsman*," Hamilton said, "announcing we have a suspect in custody in the case of the Holyrood Strangler."

"But we have no such—"

"Furthermore, it should state that we feel the case will soon be closed, and will soon be revealing the name of the suspect."

"But why—"

"If you do as I say, it will become clear."

"You could at least explain what you have in mind," Crawford said. Damn it, Hamilton was making him uneasy with that bloody stare.

"He knows we're closing in—he may be planning to leave town. It's imperative he believe he is safe for the moment so he relaxes his guard."

"And then . . . ?"

Hamilton gave a grim smile that sent chills up Crawford's back.

"He will find that there is no safe hiding place in the city of Edinburgh."

CHAPTER
SEVENTY-TWO

Wednesday was Edinburgh's midweek market day. Local farmers herded their livestock into town and along the Cowgate to the Grassmarket, transforming it into a pulsating mass of bleating and lowing. The smell of the animals was ungodly, especially the cattle, which emanated a noxious odor. People walked by with handkerchiefs pressed to their faces—all except the herdsmen in their rubber boots and flat-brimmed hats, who seemed unperturbed by the stench. Black-and-white border collies paced restlessly beside their masters, sharp eyes fixed on their hooved charges.

Observing the gathering crowd, Derek McNair stood at the top of the same staircase he and Freddie Cubbins had scurried down less than a week ago. Street buskers had set up shop, each claiming their corner. A trio of jugglers wearing motley tossed brightly colored balls into the air while a pair of acrobats did cartwheels; across the wide square, a hurdy-gurdy man cranked the handle of his case, sending out strains of familiar Scottish ballads and folk songs. Derek recognized the tune to "Annie Laurie":

Maxwelton's braes are bonnie,
Where early fa's the dew,
'Twas there that Annie Laurie
Gi'ed me her promise true.

He scanned the crowd, looking for potential marks. He preferred pick-pocketing men—for one thing, they were less attentive than women, but he also felt fewer pangs of conscience about stealing from a man. A good-looking toff in an elegant frock coat and gold brocade vest caught his eye. The man was on the young side, with perfectly coiffed hair beneath a well-brushed top hat. Derek licked his lips and rubbed his fingertips lightly across his moistened mouth, to sensitize them and make them stickier. It was his ritual before performing a "lift," to put himself in the mood and focus his concentration.

He loped casually down the stone steps, taking care not to stare at the man. When he reached the bottom, he was surprised to see his intended victim remove his top hat and release a live dove; with a flutter of wings, the bird flew into the air. Disappointment flared in the boy's breast—the blasted fellow was just another busker! *Bloody magician,* Derek thought bitterly as he watched the man pull a row of colorful silk scarves from his sleeve. Several women in the crowd turned, attracted by the flash of color. Their keen expressions softened into something altogether different as they took in the handsome face and graceful figure in the fashionable frock coat.

Caught in the magician's spell, Derek loitered at the foot of the stairs. All hope of stealing from him had vanished—his lightning hands were quicker even than Derek's—but the boy lingered to watch. The magician offered a silk scarf to each of the ladies who had formed a semicircle around him. Their tittering and lowered eyes did nothing to relieve the impatience on their husbands' faces. Attempts to disengage their wives from the spectacle met firm resistance.

The boy couldn't help admiring the man's aplomb as he winked and smiled at the delicate flowers of womanhood gathered round him. Hoping to learn a few tricks of the amorous arts, Derek stood at the edge of the crowd as the magician produced an egg from behind a small girl's ear—which immediately hatched, revealing a snowy white chick. The girl clapped her hands in delight, while her blushing young mother laughed as he presented her with the chirping hatchling. He took out a pack of cards, deftly tossing them into the air. His quicksilver fingers flicked the cards out in a way that made them return to him as faithfully as homing pigeons.

Derek was astonished. Entranced, he watched the magician's hands slide gracefully through the air. Edinburgh had its share of street performers, but nothing like this. He would have expected such skill only in fancy theaters, at shows you had to pay good money to see. He stood, arms crossed, his mouth open in amazement as the man cut the deck again and again with one hand—then, fanning it out, offered it to the prettiest young woman in the front row.

"Pick a card—any card."

She blushed and giggled, turning to her exasperated husband, who rolled his eyes. Ignoring him, she plucked a card from the middle of the deck with delicate gloved hands.

"Look at it—don't show it to anyone—and put it back in the deck."

The lady obeyed, and the magician began shuffling the cards. As he did, a man on the other side of the crowd caught Derek's eye. The boy barely recognized DI Hamilton—he looked terrible. His face was drawn and haggard, and there were dark circles under his eyes. His right cheekbone glistened with a bright purple bruise, and his face bore other cuts and gashes. Next to him stood Sergeant Dickerson, blue eyes as bright as ever, his ginger hair vivid even under the bleak Edinburgh sky.

Both men were attentively watching the performer, but Hamilton's gaze wandered long enough to notice Derek. The boy frowned, as if to say, "What are you doing here?" but the detective just shook his head.

Puzzled, Derek looked back at the magician, who had turned the deck he was handling upside down, so the face of the top card was visible. A chill shot through Derek as he saw the dancing skeletons on the face of the card. His jaw dropped open as the magician's eyes met his. The smile slid from the man's handsome face, replaced by the most murderous look Derek had ever seen. Without warning, he slipped the cards back into his pocket, and, to the astonishment of the crowd, abruptly bolted.

Derek heard Detective Hamilton's voice above the clamor of the market-day crowd. "Stay where you are—Edinburgh Police!" That was followed by a shrill blast from Sergeant Dickerson's police whistle. Two constables at the far end of the Grassmarket heard the call and gave chase.

But the magician had already taken to his heels, running toward the center of the square just as a drover was leading his flock of black-faced sheep into it. Skirting the front of the herd, the fleeing man managed to clear it and get to the other side of the Grassmarket. Following in hot pursuit, Ian and the constables were not so lucky, finding their path blocked by a bundle of bleating white bodies.

Derek took in the situation and headed straight toward the herd. Falling to his hands and knees, he scrambled beneath the animals, through their legs. The fit was tight and the smell was horrid, and he wasn't entirely successful in dodging either the kicks of the skittish sheep or the piles of manure, but he managed to reach the other side, emerging just in time to see the magician head toward the maze of tenements on the other side of George IV Bridge. Gulping a lungful of air, Derek took chase, weaving nimbly past shoppers and tradesmen. As he cleared the shadows thrown by the overhanging bridge, Derek heard a low whistle coming from behind one of the stone arches. He spun around just in time to register a sharp blow to the back of his head. He fell to his knees, stunned, as a pair of strong hands grasped him around the throat. He struggled for breath, but blackness descended upon him like a thick fog.

CHAPTER
SEVENTY-THREE

Ian Hamilton watched helplessly as the magician disappeared into the tumbledown neighborhood known as Little Ireland. He had no choice but to weave through the dense congregation of sheep, grabbing their thick, oily coats in an attempt to shove them out of the way. But sheep like to huddle against one another, and it took all his strength to push through them.

He reached the other side and looked around for Sergeant Dickerson, who was still floundering through the thick herd of fluffy white bodies, followed by the two uniformed officers, both of them madly blowing their whistles. Unfortunately, the sound panicked the animals, and they pressed together even more tightly. The newspaper ruse had worked—Wright was arrogant enough to think he had given them the slip—but Ian was astonished at the magician's audacity to perform in public.

He ran east on the Cowgate, beneath George IV Bridge, and into the gloom of the streets below. In front of him stood a blacksmith shop, its sign reading "Wm. Dyers & Sons." A grime-encrusted smith in a leather apron with the shoulders of an ox pounded iron into submission with his hammer, sparks flying. The embers in his forge glowed red as the flames of hell.

"Did you see a well-dressed man run past here?" Ian shouted, keeping a safe distance from the shooting sparks.

The man looked up from his anvil, eyes shining fiercely blue through his blackened face. Lifting his hammer, he pointed it toward the center of the huddle of tenements. Ian took a deep breath and plunged into the maze of buildings, where families were stuffed in cheek by jowl, and right angles were rare as hen's teeth. It was as different from the stately esplanades and lavish mansions of Princes Street as it was from the rolling hills and vales of the Highlands.

The rain of the past weeks had lifted; clothes fluttered on laundry lines strung between the buildings as housewives beat their rugs from open windows, dust flying, borne away on the greedy west wind. Children and dogs darted in and out of alleys, staring up at Ian curiously as he searched the streets frantically. Venturing deeper into the web of wynds and alleys, he reached a dead end between two moldering buildings. There was no sign of life—no skittering children or pets, only shuttered windows and the slow drip of water from overhanging eaves.

He had turned to leave when he heard a sound—not a loud noise, just the shuffling of leather soles on cobblestone. But there was something furtive about the way it ceased abruptly when he stopped to listen. He looked at the sign nailed to the crumbling mortar of the building nearest him: "Skinner's Close." He crept around the corner, stepping over a dead rat next to a rain barrel before creeping cautiously down the darkened alley. The feeble February sun had dipped behind a cloud, and the narrow passage lay entirely in shadow, sandwiched between two tenement buildings.

Stealing down the alleyway, he came to the end, disappointed to find it empty. Inhaling the musty odor of damp mortar and sandstone, he had begun to retrace his steps when he noticed a double set of wooden storm doors at his feet. The padlock joining them together lay open, which seemed odd. His next thought was how easy it would be for a magician to pick a simple padlock. Removing it, he lifted one of the doors, revealing uneven stone steps leading to a basement. Leaving the door open, Ian crept down the stairs into a large underground room lit only by a narrow slit of windows, covered by iron bars. It was dank and moldy, the damp chill immediately invading his bones. A shiver rippled through his body as he tiptoed across the cement floor, past chicken crates, flowerpots, and an old hay wagon missing a wheel.

As he passed one of the thick wooden posts near the center of the room, he thought he heard breathing. But before he could peer around the side of the pillar, a pair of hands shot out from behind, grasping him by the neck. He spun around but found himself in a headlock, one arm around his neck, the other twisting his left arm behind him and digging into the small of his back, where the ruffians had recently delivered a swift kick to the kidneys. The pressure on his injured muscles was agony, and he let out a groan as he attempted to wriggle free.

"At last we meet, Detective."

The voice in his ear was soft, a bizarre contrast to the pain being inflicted upon his body. Unable to speak, Ian continued to struggle, but his opponent held him tight, Ian's neck caught in the crook of his arm.

"Shall I kill you like all the others? It would be such a pleasure." The accent was English, cultivated, but with a coarse undertone. "How sweet to watch you die, DI Hamilton."

"Edward Wright?" Ian managed to gasp out.

"Do I get a prize if I say yes?" he said, tightening his grip.

Ian tried to speak again, but his strength was ebbing; he cursed himself for handing Wright the advantage of surprise. Desperately summoning his remaining will, Ian wrenched his left hand from his opponent's grasp. Grabbing Wright's forearm with both hands, Ian threw his own body forward, lifting his adversary off his feet. With a roar, he yanked hard on Wright's arm, flipping him over his own shoulder. It was a classic wrestling move, one he had used dozens of times, but never when fighting for his life.

Wright landed hard on the concrete floor. Ian lunged forward to seize the advantage, but his opponent gave him a vicious kick before rolling out of the way. Winded, Ian staggered to his feet and faced his adversary, who was also breathing heavily. The two men stared at each other, catching their breath. They were equally matched: roughly the same height and weight, though Ian was perhaps a stone leaner. Wright had unusually powerful shoulders, visible even in his frock coat, which he peeled off and tossed aside. Ian did the same.

"If this were ancient Greece, we'd be wrestling naked," Wright panted, wiping away sweat on his upper lip. "Wouldn't that be delightful?" His cold blue eyes shone with the fervor of insanity.

"Why?" Ian said, gulping air into his lungs. "What made you do it?"

"Stalling for time to catch your breath, Detective?"

"I need to know," Ian panted.

Wright smiled, but it was more like a grimace of pain than a smile. "Oh, there is so much evil in a man, one hardly knows where to begin."

"But—*why*?" Ian insisted.

Wright threw his hands in the air. "You might as well ask a river why it flows, or a rooster why it crows. It's my nature."

"Is that all you can say? It's your *nature*?" Ian replied, casting his eyes about the room for a weapon. There wasn't much—in addition to other discarded items like the broken wagon and chicken crates, the basements contained little else besides a few bales of hay. The only promising thing was a wooden handle protruding from behind the hay—perhaps a farm tool of some kind—but before he could move, Wright leapt over the pile of flowerpots and seized it. Ian's heart sank when he saw it was a rusty scythe—even caked with mud and corrosion, it was a lethal weapon.

"An appropriate tool, don't you think?" Wright said, advancing on him. "If I'm going to dispatch you to the next world, I might as well *look* the part, eh?"

"You don't want to kill me," Ian said, backing away.

"That's where you're wrong," Wright replied. "I'd prefer to strangle you, but you're too skillful an opponent, so I'll have to settle for this. It should decapitate you nicely."

"You'll hang for it."

"I'll hang anyway—if they catch me. But I don't intend to let that happen."

He lunged at Ian, swinging the scythe viciously. Ian sidestepped the blow, but the edge of the blade caught him in the ribs, ripping through his shirt and tearing a gash in his side.

"Oops," Wright said with a grin. "If at first you don't succeed—" He raised the weapon to strike again—but it was heavy, and difficult to wield with accuracy.

Ian picked up a flowerpot and threw it at him. Wright ducked, but its edge caught his shoulder.

"Bloody hell!" he yelped. "That wasn't nice—perhaps I shall have to kill you more slowly."

Ian threw another pot at his head. He ducked, and it smashed against the wall behind him.

"You're only prolonging the inevitable, you know," said Wright. "Why don't you take it like a man?"

"Is that how your victims took it?"

"They were boys—especially that young fellow, the blond one. I've got his mate here, you know," he said, glancing at the dark corner behind the bales of hay. "I'll take my time with him later, after I'm done with you."

Alarmed, Ian strained to see into the hidden corner, but the bales were stacked too high. "Derek!" he called. "Are you all right?" In response, he heard a faint moaning emanating from behind the hay.

"Foolish boy," Wright said. "He actually came after me! He'll be my swan song before I depart for greener pastures."

Ian calculated the distance between him and the nook protected by the stacks of hay. His fingers closed around the stone Derek had given him, still in his pocket. He flicked it toward the back window, where it clattered to the floor. Wright spun around in the direction of the sound, and Ian took his chance. With two running steps and a leap, he dove behind the bales of hay. Brandishing the scythe, Wright lunged at him, but Ian scrambled on his hands and knees underneath the wagon. Wresting the broken wheel from its axle, he emerged from beneath the vehicle, holding it in front of him as a shield.

With a roar, Wright swept the scythe at him, making a great arc in the air. Ian managed to catch the blade in the wagon wheel, and with a mighty yank, pulled it from his opponent's grasp. It clattered to the floor, and both men flung themselves upon it. Wright reached it first, but Ian managed to get him in a half nelson. His opponent twisted around and tried to bite him, but Ian used the momentum to flip him onto his side. Releasing Wright, he reached for the scythe. As his hands closed over the handle, he staggered to his feet, swinging it over his shoulder, the blade pointed at his opponent.

"Come along quietly, now, and no one will get hurt," he said.

"It's far too late for that," Wright said, crouched amidst the bales of hay. Seizing his discarded coat, he plunged a hand into the breast pocket. With the lightning dexterity of a master magician, he whipped out a box of matches, lighting the entire box in an instant, and flicked the lit matches around the room, igniting each bale of hay. The dry straw leapt into flames instantly, filling the air with smoke.

"Here's a dilemma for you," Wright said. "Unless you let me pass, we'll both die here."

Ian knew it was only moments before the entire room was aflame. His body was flooded with fear and panic, and he fought to think clearly.

"There are only two options: let me escape or kill us both. What's it to be?" Wright said, coughing from the fumes.

Ian looked around desperately—and saw the open door at the top of the stone steps.

"You're wrong," he said. "There's a third option." He delivered a vicious kick to Wright's knees; the magician went down hard on the concrete floor. Seizing the moment, Ian leapt over the stacked hay to where Derek lay crumpled on the ground, half-conscious. He scooped the boy up in his arms and headed for the steps, but a hand clutched at his ankle and he stumbled, falling to his hands and knees. Derek slid from his arms, groaning.

"Run, Derek—get out!" Ian said as the smoke curled around them. The boy staggered to his feet and obeyed, climbing the stairs on his hands and knees as Ian fought to throw off his opponent's desperate grip on his leg.

"Not . . . so . . . fast," Wright hissed between clenched teeth. "You die with me!"

Ian pried his hand from his ankle and lunged for the exit as Wright scrambled frantically toward him, his fingers clawing at the ground in search of the scythe. But the smoke had thickened, covering everything in its gray haze. Coughing as it filled his lungs, Ian slithered on his belly to the stairway. Springing up the steps, he closed the door behind him, throwing the padlock through the metal loops, and flung himself down next to Derek, who sat leaning against the wall of the building, a dazed expression on his soot-blackened face.

Wright had roared with rage as the heavy doors clanged shut, sealing him inside. Now his screams had turned to terror. Ian fell to his knees on the cobblestones, soaked with sweat, and tried to block out the sound, but he could not bear the pure animal terror in the man's voice.

"Help me—please! For God's sake—help!"

It brought back still-fresh memories of his parents' unheeded pleas on that dreadful night. Half-delusional with exhaustion and pain, Ian thought he could hear his parents' cries once again.

"Ian, darling—help! Please, help me!"

Staggering to his feet, he pulled off the lock with trembling fingers, yanked open the door, and stumbled back down the stairs, to be swallowed up in the fiery pit of smoke and flames.

CHAPTER
SEVENTY-FOUR

When Sergeant Dickerson finally made it through to the other side of the bleating mass of sheep, there was no sign of Detective Hamilton or the man they pursued. Looking around frantically, he saw a small boy, whom he recognized as Derek McNair, stumbling toward him. His face was covered in soot, his clothing was torn, and he looked half-dead.

"Come quick!" the boy called.

"Which way'd they go?" Dickerson panted.

"This way!" Derek called over his shoulder, loping down the street on his thin legs.

"Oiy, this way, lads!" the sergeant called to the two constables, who had just extricated themselves from the flock of sheep. They staggered after him, truncheons flapping on their thighs. The boy led the little band of policemen through dim and dusty streets, into the unsavory neighborhoods beyond George IV Bridge.

As they entered the tenements of Little Ireland, they were followed by a few raggedy children and their scraggly dogs, barking with excitement. The odd cavalcade rounded the corner, looking like something out of *The Pied Piper of Hamelin*.

"How . . . much . . . farther?" Dickerson panted.

"Down there!" Derek shouted, pointing to a narrow alley, Skinner's Close.

He headed into the alley, the two policemen galloping after him.

"Quick—down 'ere!" Derek called, and Dickerson broke into a dead run.

Smoke billowed from an open cellar. Holding his hand over his nose and mouth, Dickerson peered into the flames and could just make out two prostrate forms at the bottom of the steps.

"Call the fire squad!" he barked at Derek. The boy blinked once and took off back down the alley. "You!" he said to the constables. "Help me get these men out of 'ere!"

The policemen obeyed, coughing as they followed the sergeant down the stone stairs. Just as Dickerson feared, one of the unconscious men was Detective Hamilton. The other was the magician they had chased from the Grassmarket.

"Don' jes stand there!" he barked at the constables. "Give us a hand, then!"

They carried both men up the stairs to the street just as the clang of the bell on the fire truck sounded a few streets away.

"Are they dead?" one of the constables asked, staring down at the unconscious men, their faces black with soot.

"I hope not," Dickerson replied, but hope felt like a faint and feeble creature indeed.

CHAPTER
SEVENTY-FIVE

Ian awoke to the smell of rubbing alcohol and disinfectant. The first thing he noticed was that he was not in pain. The thought crossed his mind that he was in heaven, even though he didn't believe in it. Opening his eyes, he half hoped to see his brother, but instead the worried face of Aunt Lillian came into focus. Her expression instantly changed to disapproval, and she shook her head.

"You behaved like a proper idiot. You know that, of course."

He rubbed his eyes and looked around the room. The white walls and sharp smell of antiseptic told him he was in hospital. A young nurse in a crisp white uniform was fussing with his covers at the foot of the bed. She had a soft, round-cheeked face and pale blond eyelashes.

"How did I get here?" he said.

"I brought ye." The voice belonged to Sergeant Dickerson, standing on the other side of Ian's bed, his face and hands blackened with soot.

"Sergeant Dickerson saved your life," his aunt said. "He pulled you from the flames."

"Me an' another bloke," Dickerson clarified.

"What about Wright?"

Dickerson looked away. "He didn' make it, sir."

"Damn," Ian said. He felt like crying—not because Wright was dead, but because he had failed to save him—and because it was over. Relief and disappointment vied for mastery in his breast; the events of the past few days felt like a hollow dream.

"What's all this about you almost dying, Hamilton?" a voice bellowed from the doorway.

"Bosh and bunkum, sir," said Ian as DCI Crawford approached his bed. His skin was pasty, his small eyes rounded with red.

"You look like bloody hell," he observed.

"You don't look so good yourself, sir."

The nurse who had been hovering at the foot of his bed stepped forward. "I must caution you against too much commotion—Mr. Hamilton needs his rest."

"It's *Detective Inspector* Hamilton, miss," Crawford declared, scowling from beneath bushy eyebrows.

"Be that as it may," the nurse said firmly, "he's my patient, and—"

"It's all right—I'll go," Dickerson said, glancing nervously at the door. "I, uh, got somewhere t'go anyway."

Ian was amazed to see the beautiful Caroline Tierney lingering just beyond the entrance.

Crawford looked at the sergeant with newfound respect. "Is she—you've been seeing *her*?"

"Yeah, sorta, like," Dickerson said, blushing furiously.

The chief inspector shook his head. "I'll be a monkey's uncle."

"If ye don' mind, sir."

"You're an inspiration to us all. Off you go, then."

"Yes, sir—thank you, sir."

"Thank *you*, Sergeant," Ian said, "for saving my life."

"T'weren't nowt, sir—anyone woulda done it."

"But you're the one who did."

"Right—I'll just be off, then." Tipping his hat to Lillian, he walked quickly to where Caroline waited for him. He took her arm, and the two strolled off together down the hall.

"Cheeky devil," Crawford remarked, watching them.

"I never would have taken Dickerson for a ladies' man," Lillian said.

"'There are more things in heaven and earth than are dreamed of in your philosophy,'" said Ian.

"For Christ's sake, Hamilton, why can't you quote a proper Scottish writer like Robbie Burns?" Crawford said.

"I shall endeavor to do so from now on, sir."

Crawford stroked his whiskers. "Wonder what she sees in him?"

"What any sensible woman sees in a worthwhile man—kindness," Lillian remarked.

"Is he a good fellow, Hamilton?" Crawford asked.

"It's not every day a man saves your life, sir."

"I'm afraid I must ask you all to leave now," the nurse said, fluttering about the bed like a restless white bird. "Mr.—er, Detective Hamilton needs his rest. And who might *you* be?" she asked sharply, looking in the direction of the entrance.

Standing in the doorway was Derek McNair, hat in hand. Beside him stood Donald Hamilton. He did not look well, but he looked sober.

"We're here to see DI Hamilton, miss," Derek said, stepping forward.

"Well, you shall have to wait awhile," she replied tartly.

"Donald," Ian said, reaching out a hand toward him. "I was afraid you—"

His brother frowned. "Afraid I was the killer?"

"No . . . afraid you were dead," Ian said. His mouth was having trouble forming words.

"That's enough," the nurse said sternly. "Out you go—the lot of you."

"Come along—we'll get you some tea in the canteen," Lillian said, bustling them out. "I know the way. Would you care to join us, Chief Inspector?"

"Thank you, ma'am, but I must be getting home," Crawford replied, putting on his hat. "Oh, and on behalf of the Edinburgh City Police, I'd like to add you to our roster of sketch artists, if you don't mind."

"I should be honored," said Lillian. "On one condition."

"Yes, ma'am?"

"That you stop calling me 'ma'am.' I'm not that much older than you are."

"Of course—sorry," Crawford replied, nonplussed.

"You'll get used to my aunt," Donald remarked. "In time."

Ian smiled. It wasn't often he saw the detective chief inspector put in his place, much less by a woman.

"Mind you take care of this one," Crawford told the nurse, with a glance at Ian. "We need him."

"I'll do my best," she said. "Now off you go."

"'Good night, sweet prince,'" Donald said to Ian before following the others out of the room.

Within moments of their departure Ian's eyes had grown unreasonably heavy, and by the time the nurse returned from the linen supply closet with fresh towels, he was asleep. He dreamed of roaming Highland meadows, thick with purple heather in the spring, his brother at his side. When the nurse came back to check on him, she thought she saw a little smile on his face. When she pulled the covers up to his chin, he murmured something she couldn't quite make out—it sounded like "Sorry."

"Don't know what ye have to be sorry about," she murmured, gazing longingly at his face, "but I hope you have a lass waiting for you somewhere."

CHAPTER
SEVENTY-SIX

"I still maintain you acted like a fool," Lillian remarked to Ian a week later as he and Donald shared a glass in front of her fireplace. Ian and Lillian drank sherry while Donald sipped from a bottle of ginger beer.

"That's a rather harsh assessment," his brother commented.

She frowned at him. "He nearly *died*, Donald."

"I had good reason," Ian said.

Lillian drained the last of her sherry and set the glass down. "There are only two kinds of people who may behave idiotically with impunity—the very young and the very old. You, unfortunately, are neither."

"And you, Auntie?" said Donald. "Surely you are not old enough to qualify, either."

Lillian drew herself up. "Flattery is the province of fools—those who give it and those who believe it."

"Is it flattery to suggest that your eternally youthful quality belies your age?" Ian asked.

"Ach, enough of this," his aunt said, rising from her chair with as much grace as she could manage. Ian suppressed an impulse to help— she still believed she was hiding the discomfort of her arthritic joints.

She poked at the fire and turned to Donald. "When will you find out about your application to the university?"

"By the end of the month. Hopefully I will find my own place to live by then."

"I don't see why you should do that," said Ian.

Donald avoided his gaze. "I've gotten on your nerves long enough."

"Isn't that rather for me to say?"

"Surely you don't want me to stay."

"I have no objection to it, so long as you—"

"I very much plan on remaining sober."

"Then I see no problem with it."

Lillian refilled her sherry and sat down again. "Did you really think Donald could be the strangler?"

"By then I didn't know what to think . . . not really, I suppose."

"You jolly well did," Donald said. "Those blasted cards put you in a proper funk."

"I even suspected Rat Face for a while," said Ian, "with his skill at cards."

"I should hardly think he was capable of such feats," said Lillian.

"One thing you learn as a policeman is that anyone may be capable of anything."

Lillian turned to Donald. "Is it true you met the killer—did he really try his trick on you?"

Donald nodded. "When I saw the cards, I made an excuse to leave and went to fetch a policeman, but he ducked out into the night straightaway."

Lillian shivered. "To think that could have been you . . ."

"Poor Pearson wasn't so lucky," Donald added. "But I thought you said he knew about the cards?" he said to Ian.

"He did. Derek told him when they had breakfast together. I imagine he was ambushed—he wasn't very fit, probably not much of a fighter."

"I still can hardly believe that story Sergeant Dickerson told about the gang of football hooligans," said Lillian.

The sergeant had told of his adventure repeatedly. Each time, it acquired a new layer of absurdity, until one would think he had been kidnapped by marauding Vikings.

"And that young urchin—what has become of him?" asked Donald.

"I persuaded him to take up residence at the Dean Orphanage," Lillian said with a satisfied smile.

"We'll see how long that lasts," Ian said. "He has an aversion to nuns."

"If the good sisters can put up with him, he should consider himself lucky," Lillian replied.

A silence fell between them, the only sounds in the room the ticking of the grandfather clock in its walnut case and the crackle of kindling in the fireplace.

"I am sorry about your librarian friend," Donald said. "I regret I never had a chance to meet him."

"Thank you for coming to George's funeral."

"It was so touching," said Lillian. "So many students and professors showing up like that."

Donald looked out the window at the salty gray day and cleared his throat. "I must be getting back to my medical textbooks. I have a lot of catching up to do. By the way," he told Ian, "I've persuaded Richie McPherson, an old school chum of mine who's a surgeon now, to look in on Crawford's wife."

"Thank you."

"Richie and I were thick as thieves back in our school days. Now I suppose all the other medical students will think I'm an old codger—if I manage to get in, of course."

"You will," said Ian. "You're bloody brilliant. A total ass, but bloody brilliant."

"I'll see you out," said Lillian, rising from her chair.

"Please don't disturb yourself. Thank you for the ginger beer. I'll see you back at the flat," he said to Ian.

"I won't be late."

Donald smiled. "I won't wait up."

He leaned down to kiss Lillian, put on his hat and coat, and stepped out into the night.

Lillian leaned back in her chair and regarded Ian, who was staring into the flickering fire as if it held the answers he craved. "You must snap out of it sooner or later, you know."

"I will."

"You've rid the world of a terrible scourge."

"Not soon enough to save the life of a young boy—or poor George Pearson."

His aunt waved a dismissive hand. "If you're determined to castigate yourself, I shan't discourage you."

"When I look at myself, I don't entirely like what I see."

"Ach, if you were perfect, this world would have no use for you."

"Aunt Lillian," Ian said suddenly, "what was my father really like?"

She looked startled by the question. "Why do you ask?"

He rose from his chair and leaned against the fireplace mantel. "That night Donald stormed off, he told me things about our father . . ."

"Well, he could be a bit—zealous, perhaps."

"About what, exactly?"

"Everything, I suppose. Catching criminals, going to church, even housekeeping—he was a stickler for order. You're a bit like him."

"That's what I'm afraid of."

"You inherited his stern Presbyterianism, but without the faith."

"Did he really—"

"What?"

Ian clenched his fists, staring into the flames. "Inflict violence on Donald?"

Lillian paused before answering, and in that pause the answer was clear.

"He showed me a cigarette burn. He said there were others."

"I didn't know the specifics, but I did know there were things about your brother that didn't sit well with him."

"And my mother helped cover up what he'd done."

"Emily always had a secretive streak—like your brother, I suppose. He takes after her in that way."

"So my father . . . was a monster?"

"Is that what Donald said?"

"Not in so many words."

Lillian stared into the fire, which had burned down to embers. "Carmichael Hamilton was many things to many people. I don't believe any of them thought he was a monster."

"But he—"

"He was a complicated person, Ian. As you are—as we all are, in one way or another."

"He was good to me."

"He was proud of you. Donald was another story."

"But why? We were both his sons—"

"Life isn't fair, Ian. Parents have favorites, and families are . . . complicated."

"Is Donald a—a 'pervert,' Auntie?" he said, feeling his face redden at the harsh word. "Is that what my father couldn't stand about him?"

"That's not my place to say. I suggest you bring it up with your brother."

"As you wish, Auntie," Ian said, fetching his cloak from the hallway. The thought of talking to Donald about something so private made his head ache.

"It looks as good on you as it did on dear Alfie," she said as he fastened it around his neck. "Dear me—in like a lion," she remarked as a gust of wind nearly took the doorknob from her hand.

So it was March already. When he wasn't looking, February had slipped quietly away, giving way to the promise of spring and rebirth. Ian kissed his aunt and stepped forth into the darkened streets. Even when the city was quiet, the silence itself seemed to buzz with kinetic energy. He gazed at the buildings surrounding him. What secrets they held within their ancient walls he might never know, but he would have to learn to live with the not knowing. Their gray stone was cold and hard, yet they possessed a reassuring solidity, dependable as the sunrise. There would be time enough for family secrets to reveal themselves, he supposed as he drew his cloak closer, and time to explore what kind of relationship was possible with his prodigal brother. For now, though, Ian wanted to leave all such questions aside. As he swung out onto George IV Bridge, the sight of Edinburgh spread out beneath him took his breath away. He stopped to admire the glistening of a thousand lamps, touched by the Promethean hand of the city's leeries, bringers of light amidst the northern Scottish darkness.

No matter where his journey might take him, Ian knew he would spend the rest of his life coming to know this city of saints and sinners, with all its dark corners and contradictions. There was some comfort in that—as well as the promise of adventure, he thought as he trudged up the hill toward Victoria Terrace, and home.

ACKNOWLEDGMENTS

Thanks first and foremost to my awesome agent, Paige Wheeler, for her belief in this book, her endless energy and patience, and fierce commitment to her authors. Deepest gratitude to the amazing David Downing and Jessica Tribble for their superb editorial advice, unfailing good cheer, and unwavering support.

Thanks to my faithful travel companion, Anthony Moore, for prowling the streets of Edinburgh with me, always sharing my passion and sense of adventure—and for dragging me out to the Scottish countryside to go castle hopping on off days. Deepest thanks to Liza Dawson for her friendship, advice, and help, and to Alan Macquarie, scholar, musician, and historian, for vetting the manuscript from a uniquely Scottish perspective—thanks to both him and Anne Clackson for being such gracious hosts at his splendid Glasgow flat.

Thanks to Hawthornden Castle for awarding me a fellowship—my time there was unforgettable—and to Byrdcliffe Colony in Woodstock, where I enjoyed many happy years of residency, as well as Lacawac Sanctuary, a magical place I hope to return to often.

Thanks to my friend and colleague Marvin Kaye for instilling in me a fascination for Edinburgh, and for his continued support in all my literary endeavors. Thanks to my assistant, Amanda Beatty, for her patience, intelligence, and support. Thanks, too, to my good friend

Ahmad Ali, whose support and good energy have always lifted my spirits. Special thanks to Robert ("Beaubear") Murphy and the folks at the Long Eddy Hotel, Sullivan County's best-kept secret. Thanks to my mother, Margaret Simmons, for her continued support and editorial advice, and to all the brave men and women who risk their lives every day to catch the bad guys. I just write about this stuff—you are the real thing.